Praise for beloved romance author Betty Neels

"Neels is especially good at painting her scenes with choice words, and this adds to the charm of the story."
—USATODAY.com's *Happy Ever After* blog on *Tulips for Augusta*

"Betty Neels surpasses herself with an excellent storyline, a hearty conflict and pleasing characters."
—*RT Book Reviews* on *The Right Kind of Girl*

"Once again Betty Neels delights readers with a sweet tale in which love conquers all."
—*RT Book Reviews* on *Fate Takes a Hand*

"One of the first Harlequin authors I remember reading. I was completely enthralled by the exotic locales…. Her books will always be some of my favorites to re-read."
—*Goodreads* reviewer on *A Valentine for Daisy*

"I just love Betty Neels!… If you like a good old-fashioned romance…you can't go wrong with this author."
—*Goodreads* reviewer on *Caroline's Waterloo*

Romance readers around the world were sad to note the passing of **Betty Neels** in June 2001. Her career spanned thirty years, and she continued to write into her ninetieth year. To her millions of fans, Betty epitomized the romance writer, and yet she began writing almost by accident. She had retired from nursing, but her inquiring mind still sought stimulation. Her new career was born when she heard a lady in her local library bemoaning the lack of good romance novels. Betty's first book, *Sister Peters in Amsterdam*, was published in 1969, and she eventually completed 134 books. Her novels offer a reassuring warmth that was very much a part of her own personality. She was a wonderful writer, and she is greatly missed. Her spirit and genuine talent live on in all her stories.

BETTY NEELS

A Girl in a Million
& Saturday's Child

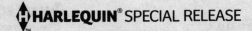

HARLEQUIN® SPECIAL RELEASE

ISBN-13: 978-1-335-04504-1

A Girl in a Million & Saturday's Child

Copyright © 2018 by Harlequin Books S.A.

The publisher acknowledges the copyright holder of the individual works as follows:

A Girl in a Million
Copyright © 1993 by Betty Neels

Saturday's Child
Copyright © 1972 by Betty Neels

Recycling programs for this product may not exist in your area.

Printed in U.S.A.

www.Harlequin.com

CONTENTS

A GIRL IN A MILLION

Chapter 1

The thin spring sunshine had little warmth and the pale blue sky looked cold, but together they turned the row of old gabled houses into a charming picture. They faced a narrow canal, tree-lined, the water dark, the arched bridge at its end leading to a street busy with traffic.

The girl walking along the narrow pavement paused to look about her and then, studying the street plan she was carrying, hitched the small package she held under one arm and crossed the narrow street to stand under the budding trees and study the houses opposite.

They were impressive, two and three storeys high with small windows in their various gables, heavy front doors with fanlights above them and with a double flight of steps leading to the door. Some of them had numbers on their walls; one or two had a coat-of-arms carved in stone above the fanlight.

Satisfied, she crossed the street again and mounted the steps of a tall house with high wide windows on each side of its door and an impressive gable, and thumped at the heavy knocker.

The man who opened the door was old, very thin and very upright with a fringe of white hair and pale blue eyes. He was dressed neatly in a black alpaca jacket and striped trousers and he addressed her in civil tones but, unfortunately, in Dutch.

She held out the packet she had been carrying. 'I'm sorry, I don't understand Dutch. This is for Mr van Houben, from Corinna.'

The elderly face slowly wrinkled into a smile. 'I will see that he receives it, miss. Do you wish to give your name?'

'No—no, thank you. Corinna asked me to deliver it here since I was coming to Amsterdam.' She smiled nicely. 'How very well you speak English.'

He gave a grave inclination of the head. 'Thank you, miss.'

'Well, goodbye.' She smiled again and went down the steps. She ran down on to the bottom one as a dark blue Bentley drew up. She turned her head to look at it, took a step which wasn't there, and fell in an untidy heap on to the pavement.

She wasn't hurt, she assured herself, and then said so to the enormous man crouching beside her. 'So silly of me,' she added politely.

He took no notice of that. 'Arms and legs all right?' he asked, and it seemed perfectly natural that his English should be as good as her own. 'You have a graze on your arm—any pains anywhere?'

When she said no, he heaved her gently to her feet, dusted her down and urged her back up the steps.

'I've just been there,' she told him. 'There's no need to bother anyone—I'm quite all right…!'

He had bright blue eyes in a handsome face dominated by a powerful nose. He studied her now, standing on the step by the door. 'You need a wash and your hair could do with a comb.' His voice was impersonal but kind.

The colour came into her face, made pale by the shock of falling. A pretty girl, she reflected bitterly, could get away with that, but she couldn't, she hadn't the looks—a small tip-tilted nose, a wide, generous mouth and a great deal of light brown hair didn't amount to much, although her eyes were beautiful; grey, thickly fringed. She held her tongue and allowed herself to be ushered back up the steps and into the house.

The hall was impressive and so typical of the Dutch Interior paintings she had been at pains to study at the Rijksmuseum that for a moment she wondered if this house was a museum too. Apparently not. She listened without understanding while there was an exchange of Dutch over her head and the elderly man went away, to return in a moment with a middle-aged woman with a formidable bosom and a kind face who clucked over her in a kindly fashion and led her away to the back of the hall and into a cloakroom secreted behind the dark panelling, the very antithesis of the hall: comfort—no, luxury with its elegant fittings, thickly carpeted floor and mirrored walls and a shelf full of just about everything needed to improve one's appearance. The girl washed her face and hands and the quite nasty graze on her arm and, since there was no help for it, took the pins out of her hair and combed it with one of the ivory combs on the shelf, and pinned it neatly again. A little lipstick and powder would have been nice, but she didn't like to use any of these, arranged so beguilingly on the shelf.

She looked awful, she decided, and went back into the hall, to the stout woman who led her into a room on the other side of the splendid staircase.

There was another unintelligible exchange of Dutch before she was asked to sit down.

'I'll take a look at that graze,' said her host, and, having done so, went and rummaged in a black bag on the enormous desk under the window, to return with gauze and strapping and a tube of something.

'A soothing ointment,' he explained, and added, 'Keep it covered for a couple of days.' When he had finished he asked, 'You know Corinna? Fram tells me that the parcel you were kind enough to bring is from her.'

The graze felt much better but she was aware of several sore spots on other parts of her person. 'Yes, I know her...'

'You are a nurse too?'

'I'm not trained yet. Corinna has almost finished, but we've been working on the same ward.'

'Will you tell her that I'm delighted to have the book?' He had gone to sit behind his desk. 'I had better introduce myself—Marius van Houben.'

She said gravely, 'How do you do? I'm Caroline Frisby. Thank you for your kindness and you saw to my graze quite expertly; lots of people have no idea what to do even for the simplest cut.'

'One does one's best,' murmured her host. 'May I offer you a cup of coffee?'

She got to her feet. 'No, thank you, I must get back: there's a tour of the city this afternoon and I should like to go on it.'

He went to open the door and Fram was waiting in the hall. She shook hands, thanked the butler for opening the door, and went carefully down the steps and walked briskly away, very aware of the tender spots on her small, too thin person.

It was quite a long way back to the hotel, but she had plenty of time. Aunt Meg had intended to do some shopping and had arranged to meet her at noon, when the hotel would provide them with coffee and sandwiches. It was a small hotel squashed into a narrow street near the Amstel River, very clean, the bedrooms small but the beds comfortable, serving a breakfast of rolls and cheese and jam and coffee each morning, coffee and sandwiches again if needed at midday and a substantial meal at night to its guests, who were for the most part quiet middle-aged couples with not much money to spend, content to roam the streets of the city, explore the museums and churches and gaze into shop windows. Caroline had come with her aunt because that lady hadn't liked the idea of going alone although she was determined to explore Amsterdam, a city she had always wished to visit. Caroline, with two weeks' holiday due, had willingly agreed to go with her; Aunt Meg had given her a home when her parents had died within a few weeks of each other of a particularly virulent flu. Not only had she done that, she had made her welcome, treated her as a daughter, strained her resources to have her educated and, when Caroline had decided that she would like to be a nurse, had encouraged her to leave the small house at Basing, a small village to the east of

Basingstoke, and enrol at one of the London teaching hospitals. She had been there almost eighteen months now, and although she still missed the quiet life of the village it wasn't too far for her to go back there twice a month.

Her aunt was waiting for her, a comfortable matronly figure, sensibly clad in various shades of brown.

'Well?' she wanted to know. 'Did you find the house?'

'Yes, Aunt. It was one of those patrician town houses beside one of the small canals branching off from the Herengracht.'

'Who answered the door?'

'I suppose he was a butler. He was very polite and he spoke English.' She paused. 'I fell down the steps as I left. The cousin of Corinna's who was to have the package picked me up and put something on a graze...'

'Did you like him?' Aunt Meg never beat about the bush.

'Well, he seemed very nice—kind, you know, and lovely manners. I felt a fool.'

'One always does. Never mind, dear, you're not likely to meet him again. Let us go and eat our sandwiches; I'm looking forward to this tour.'

The coach, with its guide, took them around the city: the Oude Kerk, the Nieuwe Kerk, the Koninklijk Paleis, a bewildering succession of museums, Anne Frankhuis and, finally, the Rijksmuseum. Caroline, a sensible girl, aware that she might never get the chance to see Amsterdam again, listened and looked and stored away a multitude of odd sights and sounds to think about later, and in between whiles she thought about Corinna's cousin. He had looked like a man of leisure and he lived in a splendid house; probably he did nothing much—sat on a few committees perhaps, lent his name to boards of directors. She didn't know Corinna well enough to ask. It was only by chance that Corinna had got to hear that she was going to Amsterdam and had asked her to take the package and deliver it. 'It's only books,' she had said, 'but they cost the earth to post and they might get lost...'

There was a trip to Alkmaar on the following day but her Aunt Meg hadn't had her fill of Amsterdam yet. She spent the day wandering up and down the narrow lanes and streets and Caroline, nothing loath, went with her. They got lost several times but that, as her aunt pointed out, was half the fun. It was a pity that their wanderings took them nowhere near the Herengracht; Caroline, keeping her eyes open for a dark blue Bentley, saw no sign of it.

It was a good thing, she told herself firmly, that they would be going back home on the following day.

Their return home was made on a drab and chilly day, a remnant of winter. From the coach windows Holland looked flat and dull and very wet, but England looked dull too, even if not as flat, as they sped Londonwards from the ferry. Caroline had two more days' holiday before she had to return to hospital, so once they reached Victoria and wished their fellow passengers goodbye she and Aunt Meg were able to take themselves off to catch the next train to Basingstoke and from there get a taxi for the two miles to Basing.

Aunt Meg had shopped prudently in Amsterdam, with forethought, and while Caroline lit the fire in the sitting-room and carried their cases upstairs to the two small bedrooms her aunt opened a Dutch can of soup, warmed rolls in the oven and made a pot of tea.

Tea made, they ate at the kitchen table since it was already evening and the journey had been tiring. 'Not that the coach wasn't comfortable,' observed Aunt Meg, 'and everyone in it very pleasant, but it's not the same as going on your own, is it?' She smiled across the table at Caroline. 'We could have done with that Bentley car you were telling me about—now that's the way to travel.'

Caroline, spooning the thick Dutch soup, agreed. The memory of Marius van Houben was still vivid; it was also a waste of time. 'We'll unpack in the morning,' she told her aunt. 'There'll be time to get the washing and ironing done before I go back.'

She was up early to make tea, load the washing machine and then go into the garden to take a look around her. Another week or so and it would be April; her aunt's flower-beds were bursting with green shoots and the rhubarb was coming along nicely under its bucket. It was a bit early to go across the street and collect Theobald, Aunt Meg's cat who had been boarded out while they were abroad, so she contented herself with poking around the seedlings in the tiny greenhouse before going back indoors and setting the table for their breakfast.

The meal over, she filled the washing-line at the end of the garden and went across to Mrs Parkin's for Theobald. The sun had come out now, and the village, so peaceful and quiet despite its nearness to Basingstoke, looked delightful. She paused to admire the small houses and cottages around her before thumping on Mrs Parkin's door knocker.

Theobald, an elderly tabby with a torn ear and handsome whiskers, was pleased to see her. 'Good as gold,' avowed Mrs Parkin. 'Got 'is wits about 'im, 'e 'as. 'As you 'ad a nice time in foreign parts?'

'Lovely, thank you, Mrs Parkin. Aunt Meg will be over to see you presently and she will tell you all about it.'

Caroline bore the cat back to his own home, pegged out the rest of the washing and, with her aunt having a chat over the coffee-cups with Mrs Parkin, took herself off to the village stores. There were several customers there, all of whom she knew, and all of whom wanted to know if the holiday had been a success.

'Historically a most interesting city,' observed the vicar's wife, who prided herself on being cultured. 'Of course you visited all the museums and art galleries?'

'Well, as many as we could cram in,' said Caroline, 'and we walked around, just looking, you know—some of the houses are very beautiful…'

'Now, you can't beat an Italian villa,' chimed in Miss Coates, who lived alone in a large house at the end of the village and went to Italy each spring, and enlarged upon the subject until she had been served with half a pound of butter, a tin of sardines, and half a dozen stamps from the Post Office end of the shop.

When she had gone Mrs Reece, who owned the shop said, 'Now she's gone, do tell us, Caroline, did you meet anyone nice?'

Everyone there knew that she meant a young man. 'Well, no, the other people on the trip were middle-aged couples, and two schoolteachers…'

'You must have met a lot of people—in the street, I mean,' persisted Mrs Reece, who had a fondness for Caroline and would have liked to see her married.

'I did meet one person—I had to deliver a parcel…'

Caroline related her visit to the magnificent house by the canal and her tumble. 'I felt a fool,' she ended, 'and I ruined a pair of tights.'

'Was he very handsome?' asked Mrs Reece.

'Oh, yes, very—and tall and big.'

'"Ships that pass in the night",' the vicar's wife quoted, 'One so often meets a person one would wish to know better if one had the opportunity.' She handed Mrs Reece a list of groceries, 'I remember when we were in Vienna…'

Caroline was the last customer. 'Well, dearie, I'm glad you enjoyed yourself, though it's a shame that there weren't any young folk around.'

Never mind the young folk, reflected Caroline, inspecting the cheeses, Mr Marius van Houben would do very nicely.

That day and the next went all too quickly. She took a late afternoon bus to Basingstoke and got on the train, hanging out of the window until the last minute, waving to Aunt Meg. She would be back again in two weeks' time for her days off but at the moment she derived little comfort from that. She hated going back and yet once she was there, in the hospital, busy on the ward, she was happy.

The nurses' home, a grim appendage to the hospital, looked bleak from the outside, but inside it was cheerful enough, and although the rooms were decidedly small they were nicely furnished and there were three sitting-rooms, one for the sisters, one for trained staff and one for the student nurses. Caroline poked her nose round the door of the last mentioned and was greeted by several girls lounging around reading and drinking tea.

They begged her to put her case down and tell them

all about her holiday while she drank a mug of tea, unpacked the cake her aunt had made for her and handed
it round.

'Meet any nice men?' asked one of the girls, Janey,
a pretty fair-haired girl.

'No—at least, I did meet one, I'm not sure if he was
nice…'

She had everyone's attention. 'Do tell…'

She told and when she had finished Janey exclaimed.
'You could have fainted or burst into tears, you know—
captured his attention.' She sighed. 'Really, Caro—for
a woman of twenty-four you're hopeless at catching
the male eye!'

'I didn't feel faint, and you know how hideous I look
if I cry.'

There was a protesting chorus telling her that she
hadn't needed to feel faint; just to look pale and helpless would have done very well.

Caroline said meekly that she would know what to
do next time, with the secret thought that being pale
and helpless would cut no ice with a man like Mr van
Houben. His eyes, compellingly blue though they were,
were razor-sharp.

She went on duty the next morning, back to Women's
Surgical, chock-a-block since it was take-in week, with
beds down the centre of the ward and several disgrun-
tled ladies forced to sleep in Women's Medical where
they had beds empty.

'It's a funny state of affairs,' observed Staff Nurse
James, deftly shortening a tube and putting on a fresh
dressing while Caroline handed things and made cheerful remarks to the nervous patient. 'Here's us bursting at the seams, and two whole wards closed because

there's no money to keep them open. There, that's done, Mrs Crisp, and I'm sure you'll feel more comfortable now. Clear away, will you, Nurse, and then go and get your coffee?'

Corinna was in the canteen and as Caroline went in she called her over to the table where she was sitting. 'Did you find the house?' she wanted to know. 'I hope it wasn't too much of a nuisance for you? I'm very grateful—the book was far too precious to send by post—a first edition. Thanks awfully. Did you have a good time?'

'Yes, delightful, thank you.' Corinna, she thought, was very like her cousin; her eyes were bright blue too, although her nose was a delicate beak, which rather added to her good looks. If she had known Corinna better she might have told her that she had met her cousin; as it was, she went and got her coffee and sat down at another table with several of her friends.

She was tired by the time she went off duty at six o'clock; there had been two emergency admissions who had gone to Theatre during the day and one of the student nurses had gone off sick during the afternoon, which meant that two of them were doing the work of three.

Caroline kicked off her shoes, made a cheerful telephone call to Aunt Meg and curled up with a book in the sitting-room. Exercise in the fresh air was essential to a nurse's well being, Sister Tutor had been telling decades of students that, but Caroline decided that her day had provided enough exercise, and anyway the air, laden with fumes from the never-ending traffic of the East End of London, wasn't fresh. The book, she de-

cided after ten minutes' reading, was dull, so she closed
it and allowed her thoughts to wander.

The holiday in Amsterdam had been a success; Aunt
Meg had had a long-cherished dream fulfilled and they
had seen as much as possible of the city. It would have
been nice to go inside some of the magnificent houses
they had inspected so avidly from the streets. It was a
pity she hadn't had the wit to do as Janey suggested; if
she had fainted, or appeared to faint, she would have
had to spend much more time inside Mr van Houben's
house and had a chance to look around. As it was she
had barely glimpsed the hall before the brief session
in his study while he dealt with the grazes. She would
know better next time—only there wouldn't be a next
time. She and her aunt had saved for some time for their
holiday; there wouldn't be one next year, and if there
was enough money for the year following that Aunt
Meg would want to go somewhere else. When holidays
were few and far between one couldn't afford to go to
the same place twice, not if one wanted to see as much
of foreign parts as possible.

Impatient with herself for feeling discontented, she
went away to wash her hair and by the time it was
dry and fastened neatly once more it was time for supper. Afterwards, everyone lucky enough to be off duty
crowded into the sitting-room to drink tea, talk shop
and compare notes about their boyfriends. There was
the usual hospital gossip too: who was going out with
which house doctor, Mr Wilkins' nasty fit of temper in
Theatre that afternoon, Casualty Sister's unjust treatment of one of their number who had had the misfortune to drop a pile full of sterile dishes... By the time
she got to bed she had forgotten her discontent. Life,

she thought sleepily, was really quite fun, and somewhere, some time, she would meet the man she would
marry. He had until now been a nebulous figure, vague
as to feature and voice, but now he bore a striking re-
semblance to Mr van Houben. 'Which really won't do
at all,' muttered Caroline as she closed her eyes.

Life was by no means fun the next day. Mr Wilkins'
morning round was far from smooth; he had come on to
the ward in a bad temper to start with, which rendered
the already nervous students even more nervous so that
they were either struck dumb or gave all the wrong answers; moreover, several of the ladies lying in their beds
dozing peacefully deeply resented being wakened so
that he might examine them. Sister Cowie, who prided
herself upon the perfection of her ward, pursed her lips
and said very little; later several people would get the
sharp edge of her tongue. Certainly her nurses would
be held to blame for allowing the patients to drop off
when Mr Wilkins' round was imminent. Those who
could kept prudently out of sight, but Staff Nurse and
Corinna, following in Sister's footsteps bearing charts,
X-ray forms and all the impedimenta needed to keep
Mr Wilkins happy, were very aware of her displeasure.
Staff would get the blame, of course, which she would
pass on to everyone else.

Two more patients and the round would be finished
and Mr Wilkins and his registrar would drink coffee
with Sister. He was approaching the last bed when he
was nudged aside, his foot trodden on and urged to wait
a moment. Caroline, bearing a bowl, reached the patient
in the nick of time. An arm around the heaving shoulders, the bowl nicely in position, and sitting on the bed
because it was easier, Caroline turned a cheerful face

to Mr Wilkins. 'So sorry if I hurt your foot, sir, but Mrs Clarke is always sick without warning—so awkward and horrid for her.'

Mr Wilkins gobbled wordlessly; he was a pompous man, short and stout and middle-aged. He was a splendid surgeon and the students held him in awe, something he rather enjoyed, and here was a dab of a girl actually pushing him aside, telling him to wait. The fact that if he hadn't waited the consequences would have been unpleasant to himself cut no ice. He opened his mouth to administer a dignified rebuke, but Caroline spoke first. 'There—Mrs Clarke is better now.' She mopped the lady's pallid brow and picked up the bowl. 'I do hope,' she added in a motherly voice, 'that your foot isn't painful, sir.'

She slipped away and Sister, Staff and Corinna, who had been holding their breath, let it out with a sigh of relief. Mr Wilkins looked around him but the various faces looking back at him seemed solemn. 'We will now examine Mrs Clarke,' he told them and embarked on a rather lengthy dissertation concerning that lady's insides, very much to her discomfort.

Drinking his coffee presently, Mr Wilkins voiced his disapproval of Caroline's conduct. 'I have neither the time nor the inclination to speak to this nurse,' he observed, 'I rely upon you, Sister, to deal with her as you think fit. I intend to speak to the senior nursing officer, of course. I cannot have my authority undermined.'

Sister, a strict disciplinarian but always fair, spoke up. 'Nurse acted with foresight, sir. If she hadn't reached Mrs Clarke with the bowl you would have been—er...' She paused delicately.

'She pushed me,' said Mr Wilkins crossly, 'and trod

on my foot, and then had the impudence to hope that she hadn't hurt me.'

His registrar said quite quietly, 'It was either that or vomit all over your suit, sir. I agree with Sister—Nurse acted promptly in the best interests of both you and your patient.' He added, 'It would be most unjust to blame her for what she obviously saw as her duty.'

Mr Wilkins had gone red. 'Since I am to be outnumbered I shall overlook the matter, but rest assured that I shall make it my business to keep a strict eye on the girl. What is her name?'

'Nurse Frisby. She has just entered her second year. She is a promising student.'

Mr Wilkins said, 'Pish,' and went away, his registrar, poker-faced, with him. He didn't like his chief overmuch, and he was glad that Caroline had escaped his bad temper. He grinned at the thought of the medical students recounting the episode to their fellows. Most of them had suffered at some time from Mr Wilkins' ill humour and would relish a good laugh at his expense.

All the same, something would have to be done about it, Sister decided, and took herself off to the office to see her superior.

Two days later, before Mr Wilkins' next ward round, Caroline was transferred to the children's ward.

It was a happy choice made by her two superiors. The paediatric unit was housed at the back of the hospital, a modern wing built on to the ponderous Victorian main hospital. It was presided over by an elderly woman, Sister Crump, reputedly as mad as a hatter but none the less a miracle-worker when it came to getting her little patients well again and, what was more important, keeping them happy in the process.

After the strict regime of Women's Surgical, Caroline found it very much to her liking. Here there were no orderly rows of cots; they were wheeled here, there and everywhere according to Sister Crump's mood, and down the centre of the long ward there were low tables cluttered up with toys, teddy bears and picture books and the children who were well enough were allowed to scamper around within reason. On first sight it appeared to be a madhouse, but there was order too, and if a nurse couldn't fit into Sister Crump's way of working she was moved to another ward, for she demanded meticulous care of the children in her charge. Dressings were done, little patients got ready for Theatre, temperatures taken, medicines given to the strains of cheerful music. Since the children, unless they were very ill, shouted and screamed a good deal, the nurses had to lift their voices above the din. There was discipline too: the children addressed all the nurses as Nurse—Christian names, according to Sister Crump, carried no authority with them, and authority, gentle though it might be, was needed at all times.

Sister Crump had liked Caroline at once; nothing to look at, as she observed to Staff Nurse Neville later, but from all accounts she had acted with commendable promptness on the surgical ward even if she had upset Mr Wilkins' sense of importance. 'A fuss about nothing,' she declared, and sailed into the ward, to clap her hands and tell the children to shout more softly. At the same time she observed that Caroline was sitting on the edge of a small bed, holding a little wriggling girl on her lap while a senior nurse dressed the wound, beautifully stitched, on the small arm.

There were side-wards leading from the main wards

where the very ill children lay. It was quiet here, the rooms with glass walls, equipped with all the paraphernalia necessary for urgent treatment and nurses constantly going from one child to the other. In a few days, Staff Nurse had told Caroline, when she had got to know the ward thoroughly, she would take her turn too with the other nurses, looking after one or two children, giving them the specialised treatment they had been ordered. Caroline looked at the array of monitoring screens, tubes and drips and hoped that she would know what to do. Of course, Sister Tutor had explained it all, but applying theory to practice demanded the keeping of one's wits about one.

She got on well with the other nurses—they were all her senior but she was a little older than most student nurses and made no effort to call attention to herself; besides, she was willing to help out on occasion and made no demands about having days off to suit herself and not the ward. By the end of the week she had been accepted by both nurses and children alike; moreover, Sister Crump had taken care to introduce her to the various housemen who visited the ward, cheerful young men who were quite willing to waste ten minutes playing with the children, eyeing the nurses and coaxing mugs of coffee out of Sister Crump. And when the consultant paediatrician came to do his round she wasn't exactly introduced, although she was pointed out to him as being the new nurse on the ward. He stared at her, gave her a nod and took no more notice of her; indeed, it would have surprised her very much if he had. He was a youngish man with a long, thin face which lit up when he was with the children. One of the other student nurses, standing discreetly in the background while he went from one small patient to the other, whispered that he had three small children of his own and had married a nurse from the hospital. 'The children love him,' she added, 'and he and old Crumpie get on like a house on fire.'

Certainly the round had none of the formality of a grown-ups' ward. Mr Spence sat on the cots and small beds, carrying, from time to time, a grizzling infant over a shoulder while he discussed something with his registrar and the housemen. Caroline went home for her next days off happier than she had been for some time, although she had to admit to herself that if only she could banish Mr van Houben from her mind she would be completely happy; he was taking up too much of her thoughts, which was absurd; she had exchanged only a few words with him and none of those exciting enough to engage his attention, and besides, she had made a fool of herself falling down his steps. If he ever thought of her at all, which she doubted, it would be with an amused laugh.

When she went back on duty after her days off it was to be told by Sister Crump that they were short-handed, what with days off and one of the third-year students off sick and a badly injured child brought in late the evening before. 'Ran away from his nanny, climbed a wall and fell on to a concrete path. Head injuries and in a coma. Mr Spence doesn't want to operate until he improves; unfortunately he has broken ribs and a punctured lung, makes giving an anaesthetic very tricky. He's being specialled, Nurse, which means that for long periods you may be alone in the main ward. Can you manage that?'

'I'll do my best, Sister. There's no one very ill there,

is there? It's a question of keeping them happy and potting them and feeding them...'

'Just so. You'll have another nurse with you whenever it's possible and I don't believe that you're a girl to panic. Now, we will go through the charts—there are one or two children you must keep an eye on...'

It wasn't until the afternoon that Caroline was left alone, and it would only be for an hour or so while the other nurse took two children down to the X-ray department. The children had had their after-dinner nap and she had got those who were allowed out of their cots and beds and organised them into manageable groups around the little tables. They were for the most part good; only Bertie, four years old, was a handful. He had been admitted ten days previously, having fallen off a swing in the play-pit below the high-rise flats where his mother lived, twelve storeys high. He hadn't been found for some time and had been taken, concussed and bruised, to the hospital. Sister Crump had spoken severely to his mother about the risk of letting a very small boy play so far out of her sight and she had promised to go to the social worker and get him taken to a pre-school playgroup. In the meanwhile he was enjoying himself enormously, doing everything he shouldn't.

He hadn't settled down with the other children who were up. Caroline, distributing sheets of paper and coloured pencils, saw him making for the ward doors at the other end and darted after him, to catch him into her arms—just as the doors opened and Mr van Houben walked in.

Caroline, clasping a struggling Bertie to her person, stared up at him, her face alight with surprise and delight. Quite forgetful of where she was, and for that matter who she was, she said happily, 'Oh, hello!'

Chapter 2

Caroline saw at once that he wasn't going to remember her. She hoped that he hadn't heard her little burst of speech and asked in her most professional voice, 'Can I help you? Are you looking for someone?'

He looked at her then, but it was impossible to tell if he had recognised her. His handsome face was bland and unsmiling. 'I'm looking for Mr Spence.'

'He's in one of the side-rooms. I think he may be busy. I'm afraid I can't leave the children to tell him that you want to see him.'

She had wasted her breath for he was striding away down the ward and through the archway to the side-rooms. 'Oh, my goodness, I shall get eaten alive,' observed Caroline, a remark which sent Bertie off into a fit of the giggles.

The other nurse had come back presently and they

were busy getting the children washed and potted and back into their cots and beds. Caroline was urging the recalcitrant Bertie into his bed when Mr Spence and Mr van Houben came through the ward, walking slowly, deep in talk and followed by Sister and the registrar and two of the housemen. Bertie's loud, 'Hey, Doc,' brought them to a momentary pause, but only long enough to give them time to reply, and that in a rather absent-minded manner. Obviously they had grave matters on their learned minds.

It was Staff Nurse who told her later that the child in the side-room was to be operated on that evening. 'That's why Mr van Houben came—he's a wizard with anaesthetics.' Caroline, all ears, would have liked to have known more, but Staff was busy and presently she went off duty, to change into outdoor clothes and go with various friends to the local cinema.

The ward was its usual bustling, noisy self when she went on duty in the morning; she helped with the breakfasts and then with the rest of the day staff who could be spared, went to Sister's office for the report.

It had been a good night in the main ward; duties were meted out in Sister Crump's fashion, apparently haphazard but adding up to a sensible whole. 'Little Marc in the side-room—he'll be specialled of course—usual observations and I'm to be told at once if there's anything you aren't too happy about. Nurse Frisby, you will stay with him until you are relieved at noon. Either Staff Nurse or myself will be checking at regular intervals. The operation was successful—a craniotomy and decompression of the vault—but there is some diffuse neuronal damage and the added complication of a punctured lung. The child is gravely ill but we'll pull him through. There is oedema and some haemorrhaging so be especially on the look out for coning.' She added briskly, 'Back to work, Nurses.'

Staff Nurse went with Caroline, who was relieved to see that there wasn't anything complicated she couldn't understand. The various scans, machines, tubes and charts she had already worked with on Women's Surgical. It was a sharp eye and common sense that was needed, said Staff encouragingly. The child was in a deep coma; all Caroline had to do was to check pulse, breathing and temperature at the time stated on the chart, note any change and let her or Sister know at once. 'Just keep your hand on the panic bell,' she was advised, 'and keep your head.' She looked at her watch. 'It's time for observations, so I'll leave you to get on with it.' She cast an eye over the small boy in the bed, his head swathed in bandages, his person attached to various tubes. 'Someone will bring you some coffee,' she added kindly as she went.

Caroline did everything that was necessary, examined the little white face anxiously and took the chair by the bed. The nurse she had relieved had written 'No change' on the chart and with one eye on the child she read the notes on his board. Mr Spence had written a great deal and it took her some time to decipher his writing. Mr van Houben had written a whole lot too. It took her even longer to read, since his writing was so illegible that it could have been in Greek or Sanskrit.

She had just finished her second round of observations when Mr Spence and Mr van Houben came in. They both wished her good morning as she got to her feet and handed over the chart. As she did so, she realised something which she had known subconsciously when she had first studied the chart. Marc's surname was van Houben. Mr van Houben's son? If it were so, where was his mother? She had her answer quicker than she had expected.

'Marc's mother will be here shortly,' said Mr van Houben. 'She will stay only briefly—remain with Marc while she is here. She is likely to be upset.' He smiled briefly from a grim face and turned to Mr Spence. 'Would it be a good idea if...?' He launched into technicalities and Caroline sat down again to keep watch. They thanked her as they went away. It invariably surprised her that the senior men were always civil—with the exception of Mr Wilkins—whereas some of the housemen tended to throw their weight around, wanting this and that and the other thing on the wards, leaving messes to be cleared up.

She was relieved at noon and there was no sign of Marc's mother. She was sent to first dinner and over the cottage pie and spring cabbage she regaled her friends at the table with her morning's work.

'At least it gave your feet a rest,' said someone.

'Yes, but I was so afraid something awful might happen—he's been unconscious ever since he hurt himself and the operation took hours.'

She bolted rhubarb and custard, drank a cup of tea far too hot and went back on the ward. It was time for the children to have their afternoon rest. Sister had gone to lunch, taking all but the nurse specialling Marc with her, leaving Staff and Caroline to the task of seeing to the children who were up and enticing them into their beds and then going around making comfortable those who were bedridden.

'Marc's mother came,' said Staff. 'Mr van Houben came with her, of course.'

Caroline said, 'She must be terribly upset.'

'She was—she's expecting a baby in a week's time. She came over from Holland. She's beautiful—you know—fair hair and blue eyes and the most gorgeous clothes.'

Caroline didn't want to hear about her—of course she would be beautiful, Mr van Houben wouldn't have married a girl less than perfection. 'Is Marc the only one? Other than the baby?'

She lifted out a small sleepy toddler while Staff put in a clean sheet.

'Yes. Mr Spence seems to think that Marc will live but the thing is if he's going to come out of this coma. He may have to operate again.'

'Oh, the poor little boy.' She kissed the top of the baby's head; he had a cleft palate and a hare lip but Mr Spence would see to those in a day or two. She put him gently back into his cot and tucked him in.

Staff said, 'You like kids, don't you?'

Caroline was at the next cot, changing a nappy. 'Yes.'

Staff was feeling chatty. 'Sister says you're a natural—I dare say you'll end up with a ward full of children and make it your life's work.'

'Yes,' said Caroline again. She did like children, but she would prefer to have her own; vague thoughts of a charming house in the country with dogs and cats and a donkey and, of course, children filled her mind. She would need a husband, of course. Mr van Houben's rather frosty features swam before her eyes and she said, 'Oh, dear, that won't do at all,' so that Staff looked at her and observed kindly,

'Well, there's always the chance that you'll marry.'

She was to special little Marc each morning for the foreseeable future. Sister rambled on rather about his subconscious getting used to the same person by his bedside, so that the three of them shared the twenty-four hours between them. It was towards the end of her eight-hour stint that Mr van Houben came again, and this time with Marc's mother.

Staff hadn't exaggerated. Marc's mother was lovely despite the fact that she was desperately worried and pale with anxiety. She stood by the little bed, staring down at the small face, and Mr van Houben put an arm round her shoulders.

Mr Spence came in then and the two men conferred quietly and Caroline said, 'Sit down for a minute and hold his hand...'

His mother lifted unhappy blue eyes to hers. 'He does not know?'

'Well, we don't know, do we? I hold it all the time unless I'm doing things for him.'

His mother smiled then. 'You're very nice,' she said, and they sat silently until the men had finished their talk, checked the charts and the three of them had gone away. Caroline sat down again and picked up the limp little paw and held it firmly. It was a way of communication—that was, if communication was possible.

Several days went by and each morning Mr van Houben and Marc's mother came to see him until one morning Mr van Houben arrived early by himself. His, 'Good morning, Nurse,' was curt and he looked as if he had been up all night. If she had known him better she would have told him to go home to bed.

'Well, Marc has a little sister.' He stared down at the

inert little figure in the bed and Caroline said, 'Oh, you must be delighted. Congratulations, sir.'

He turned his head to look at her. He looked as though he was going to speak but he only smiled slightly, made sure that Marc's condition was unchanged and went away. He came back with Mr Spence just as she had handed over to her relief, but since there was no reason for her to remain she went away to eat a late lunch in the empty canteen. The boiled cod and white sauce, boiled potatoes and carrots, edible in company and when freshly cooked, had rather lost their appeal. She ate the apple crumble which followed, coaxed a pot of tea from the impatient girl behind the counter and then went to her room and changed into outdoor things—she was off duty until five o'clock and a brisk walk would do her good. She took a bus to Victoria Park and marched along its paths, in no mood to admire the first of the spring flowers braving the chilly day. She had no idea why she was feeling so edgy; perhaps she was hungry or just a little homesick for Aunt Meg's cosy little house—or was she just anxious about Marc, who was making no progress at all. Walking back presently to catch her bus back to the hospital, she admitted to herself that it wasn't any of these things—it was Mr van Houben's smile when she had congratulated him. It had been faintly mocking, slightly amused, as though she had made a bad joke. Sitting squashed between two stout women with bulging shopping bags, Caroline told herself to stop thinking about him, that there was no point in doing so, and when presently, as she was crossing the forecourt to the hospital entrance, he went past her, on his way to the consultant's car park, she glared at him so ferociously that he paused and turned to look at her small person; even from the back she looked cross.

When she went back on duty it was to be told that it was intended to operate on Marc again. 'Seven o'clock, Nurse,' said Sister Crump. 'You'll probably have to stay on duty; Mr Spence wants two of you specialling for the first twelve hours. You'll stay until a second nurse can come on around midnight. That'll be Staff or myself.'

She nodded, her cap slightly askew. 'You and Nurse Foster get Marc ready for Theatre—she's off duty at six o'clock, and you'll take him to Theatre. Understood?' She smiled at Caroline. 'Run along. We'll have to fit in your supper somewhere, but at the moment I don't know when.'

Marc would be wheeled to Theatre on his little bed; they did everything needed, checked the equipment, did their observations, and when Nurse Foster went off duty Caroline sat down to wait, holding Marc's small hand in hers. She liked Theatre work, although she didn't know much about it; she had done a short stint during her first year but it hadn't been enough for her to learn much beyond the care of instruments, the filling of bowls and the conveying of nameless objects in kidney dishes to and from the path lab. She hoped now that she wouldn't have to go into Theatre; she had grown attached to the silent small boy, away in some remote world of his own, and the thought of Mr Spence standing with scalpel at the ready made her feel a little sick.

Mr van Houben was in the anaesthetic room, somehow managing to look distinguished in his Theatre kit—a loose pale blue smock and trousers topped by a cap which would have done very nicely to have covered a steamed pudding. He was joined by Mr Spence

and then by his registrar and all three men held a muttered conversation while Caroline stood patiently by
the bed, admiring the back of Mr van Houben's head,
never mind the cap.

It was a disappointment to her that presently one of
the staff nurses from Theatre took her place and she was
dismissed with a laconic, 'Thanks, Nurse.'

She went back to the ward and made up the bed and
checked the equipment and was then sent to her supper. 'They'll send down one of the ITC nurses,' Sister
Crump told her, 'but you'd better be there to fetch and
carry.'

The day staff were going off duty when Caroline
went back; the children were sleeping as Sister Crump
did a round with the night nurses, and paused to speak
to Caroline as she went. 'I'll be back presently,' she
told her.

It was after ten o'clock when Marc came back to
his little room. Once he was again in his own bed, it
was just a question of his being linked up with the ap-
paratus around him and a careful check made as to his
condition. Sister Crump had appeared silently to see
things for herself and presently Mr Spence and Mr van
Houben came in. The little room was full of people, and
Caroline, feeling unnecessary, tucked herself away in a
corner. Sister Crump caught her eye presently. 'Go off
duty, Nurse,' she said briskly. 'Come on at ten o'clock
tomorrow.'

Caroline went, feeling anxious about little Marc and
rather put out since her off duty had been changed—
and she had agreed to go to the pictures on the following evening with Janey and several other of her friends.

She yawned her way into a bath and, despite her concern for the little boy, went to sleep at once.

Marc was still there when she went on duty in the morning; she had been half afraid that he wouldn't have survived the night but there he lay, looking just as before, with Mr van Houben checking the tangle of tubes around the bed, calculating the drip and then taking a sample of blood from the small hand lying so still on the very white coverlet. He turned to look at Caroline as she went in. 'Ask Sister Crump to come here, will you, Nurse? You're taking over here?'

'Yes, sir.' She sped away to fetch Sister Crump and then con the charts with the nurse she was to relieve. He had looked at her, she thought sadly, as though he had never seen her before.

It was two days later, halfway through the morning, that Marc's hand, lying in Caroline's, curled gently over. For a moment she couldn't believe it and then she wanted to shout for someone to come, press the panic bell, do a dance for joy… Her training took over; she sat quietly and waited and sure enough within a minute or so his hand turned again, a graceful languid movement as though it were returning to life. Which of course it was.

She did press the panic bell then. Sister Crump got there first.

'He moved his hand in mine—twice,' said Caroline.

'The good Lord be thanked,' said Sister Crump. The two other nurses had arrived. 'One of you ring Mr Spence or his registrar—one or other is to come at once. The other nurse to go back to the ward.'

The nurses went and Caroline said softly, 'Look, Sister.'

The small hand was moving again, curling round her thumb.

Mr Spence had just finished his list in Theatre and he still wore his Theatre kit as he came soft-footed to stand by the bed, followed by his registrar.

'Give your report, Nurse,' said Sister Crump.

Which Caroline did, trying to keep the quiver of excitement out of her voice. Put into a few sparse words it didn't sound much, but as she spoke Marc lifted his arm very slightly as though he wanted to make himself more comfortable. 'Eureka,' said Mr Spence softly. 'Someone get hold of Mr van Houben.'

He wasn't in the hospital, although he had left a phone number where he could be reached. It was two or three hours later by the time he entered the room, looking calm and unflustered, giving no indication that he had been driving hell-for-leather down the M1 from Birmingham where he had gone to give his opinion concerning the anaesthetising of a patient with a collapsed lung and a tracheotomy into the bargain.

It was at that moment that Marc opened his eyes, blinked and closed them again.

'Too soon to carry out any tests,' said Mr Spence. 'Another three or four hours—do you agree?' When Mr van Houben nodded, he added, 'We'll be back around four o'clock, Sister.' His eye lighted on Caroline, sitting like a small statue, not moving. 'You are to stay with Marc, Nurse.'

Which made sense; she had seen the very first movements, and she was in a better position to gauge his progress or deterioration than anyone else coming fresh to the scene. All the same, she hoped that someone would bring her a cup of coffee before Mr Spence returned.

They did better than that. A tray of tea and sandwiches was brought and arranged where she could get at it without disturbing the child, and, besides, Sister Crump was in and out every hour or so. Marc hadn't moved again; Caroline had charted his movements carefully, noting with delight that his temperature had come down a little. Certainly his pulse was steady.

She was stiff and cramped by the time the men came back. Mr Spence said, 'Good—take over, Sister, will you?' And watched while Caroline withdrew her hand, only to have it clutched again.

'You'd better stay; we don't want him disturbed in any way.'

A silly remark, thought Caroline, watching the gentle poking and prodding, the tickling of the small feet with a pin, the meticulous examination for pupil reaction, for Marc was disturbed, making small fretful movements and wriggling at the touch of a pin. But of course that was what they had hoped for: all the signs of a return to consciousness. The three men and Sister Crump bent over the bed and Caroline sat on a hard chair out of their way. She was happy about little Marc; it was the nicest thing which had happened to her for a long time. Mr van Houben must be over the moon, she reflected, although it was too early to tell if there would be lasting damage to little Marc; he had a long way to go still… Feeling selfish and uncaring, she longed for a cup of tea. At such dramatic moments cups of tea and feeling tired were not to be considered.

Little Marc had fallen asleep again—natural sleep now, not a coma—and the men were still discussing

further treatment. It was Sister Crump, her eyes lighting upon Caroline's small person in a corner, who exclaimed, 'Go off duty, Nurse, I'm sorry you're late.
You've missed your tea—go to the canteen and see if
they'll boil you an egg or let you have your supper early.
You missed your lunch?'

Caroline nodded and stood up. The men were writing
now, absorbed in their problems. She whispered, 'Good
evening, Sister,' and slipped out of the room and down
the ward and out on to the landing beyond before anyone had a chance to say anything to her. Presumably the
nurse to relieve her was already waiting; Sister Crump
would be there to brief her. She made her way down to
the canteen and found no one there, something she had
half expected, for tea had been finished hours ago and
first supper wasn't until seven o'clock. All the same
she went up to the counter in case there was someone
beyond it in the serving-room.

'No good your coming in here, Nurse. You know
as well as I do that there's nothing to be had between
meals. Supper's at the usual time; you'll just have to
wait.'

So calmly Caroline went away again, back up the
stairs to the ground floor; she would make a pot of tea
and take off her shoes and sit and drink it and then, tired
though she was, get into a coat and go for a brisk walk.
The streets round the hospital were shabby and houses
down at heel, but it had been a grey April day and dusk
cast a kindly mantle over them. She didn't much care for
a walk in such surroundings, but fresh air and exercise
seemed more important than any other consideration.

She started along the corridor which ran at the back

of the entrance hall and then stopped with a small gasp when she was tapped on the shoulder.

Mr van Houben, unhurried and as always, immaculate, was at her side. 'When did you go on duty, Nurse?'

'Ten o'clock, sir.'

'You have had no off duty?'

'I'm off now,' she told him and added, 'sir' as she started off again.

'Not so fast. Did I hear Sister Crump say that you have had no proper meal today?'

'I have had sandwiches and coffee...' She stopped to think—it seemed a long time ago.

'Yes, yes—I said a meal.'

'I shall go to supper presently.'

'You deserve better than that. I'm hungry too; we'll go and find somewhere to eat.'

'We'll what?' She goggled at the sight of him, her mouth open like a surprised child. 'But you can't do that...'

'Why not?' he asked coolly. 'I am not aware that I am restricted in my actions by anyone or anything.'

'Well, no, of course you're not. I mean, you don't have to bother, do you? But it really wouldn't do, you know. Important people like you don't take junior nurses out to dinner.'

'You are mistaken, we aren't going to dinner. Go and put on a coat and some powder on your nose and we will go to the Bristling Dog down the street and eat sausages out of a basket.'

He didn't wait for her reply. 'And comb your hair,' he advised her kindly as he gave her a gentle shove in the direction of the door to the nurses' home. He added,

'If you aren't back here within ten minutes I shall come and find you.'

'You can't…' He must be light-headed with hunger, she decided, or in a state of euphoria because Marc had shown the first tentative signs of recovery.

He said coldly, 'Can I not?' and gave her a steely look which sent her through the door and up the stairs to her room.

He had said ten minutes and he had undoubtedly meant what he had said. Caroline had never changed so fast in her life before. She raced out of her room and almost fell over Janey.

'Hey—where are you off to?' Janey made a grasp at her arm.

'I can't stop,' said Caroline breathlessly, 'he said in ten minutes…'

She raced down the stairs and Janey, five minutes later, told those of her friends who were in the sitting-room that Caroline had gone out with a man.

'Good for her,' said someone. 'It's time she had some fun.'

If Caroline had heard that remark she would have felt doubtful about the fun. Mr van Houben was waiting for her, looking remote, almost forbidding, and she very nearly turned tail and went back through the door. The prospect of a good supper was a powerful incentive, however, and she went to where he was standing and said quietly, 'Well, here I am, Mr van Houben.'

He stood for a moment looking down at her. She had got into the first thing which had come to hand, a short jacket over a thin sweater and a pleated skirt, and, because ten minutes hadn't been nearly long enough, her hair, though tidy, had been pinned back ruthlessly into a bun instead of its usual French pleat, and there had been even less time to spend on her face.

Mr van Houben laughed inwardly at his sudden decision to take this small unassuming person out for a meal. It had been triggered off by the sight of her sitting by little Marc; she had been the one who had first seen his faint stirrings and acted promptly, but no one had so much as spared her a smile and she had been sent off duty without so much as a thank-you. She must have longed to share their triumph and relief. He was a kind man; at least he could make up for that by giving her a meal.

He said with impersonal friendliness, 'You hadn't anything planned for this evening?' As he ushered her through the doors and out into the forecourt.

She answered him in her sensible way, 'No, nothing at all.'

He took her arm as they crossed the busy street. 'No boyfriend to disappoint?' He was sorry he had said that for, looking down at her in the light of a street lamp, he saw the look on her face and to make amends he added, 'I should imagine that there is little time for serious friendships while you are training. Plenty of time for that once that's done with! You might like to travel— there are quite a number of English nurses in our bigger hospitals in Holland.'

He eased the conversation into impersonal channels until they reached the Bristling Dog, where he urged her into the saloon bar, half filled already, mostly by elderly couples and a sprinkling of younger people, most of them eating as well as drinking, and several, Caroline noticed, from the hospital.

Mr van Houben sat her down at a small corner table

and fetched the well-thumbed menu card from the bar. It held a surprising variety of food, but Mr van Houben had suggested sausages... 'Sausages and chips, please,' she told him, anxious to fall in with his own wishes.

'Splendid,' he said, and with unerring instinct, 'and a pot of tea?'

He was rewarded with her smile. 'That would be nice.'

The food came, hot and tasty, and with it a pot of tea and thick cups and saucers. Caroline poured out and handed him his cup. It was strong, and even with milk and sugar he found it unpalatable. All the same, he drank a second cup because it was obvious that Caroline expected him to. He was rewarded by her sweet smile and the observation given in matter-of-fact tones that a cup of tea was a splendid pick-me-up when tired.

Over the last of the chips he asked her what she thought of London. 'You live here?' he asked casually.

'No, I live with my aunt at Basing—that's near Basingstoke. I go home twice a month.'

'The English countryside is very charming,' he observed, and from then until they returned to the hospital they talked about it, and the weather, of course, a conversation which gave him no insight as to her likes and dislikes. She was a sensible girl with nice manners and a gentle way with her, and he was surprised to discover that he had rather enjoyed his evening with her. He bade her goodnight in the entrance hall and listened to her nicely put thanks and didn't tell her that he would be returning to Holland in the morning. Marc's father, recalled from a remote region of South America where he was building a bridge, would be installed with his wife and baby daughter by now, and Mr van Houben could return to his own work with a moderately easy mind.

He watched her go through the door at the back of the hall and made his way to the children's wing where he found Mr Spence, his brother Bartus and Sister Crump, who quite often stayed on duty if she saw fit.

'Very satisfactory,' said Mr Spence. 'We're not out of the wood but there's plenty of movement. You'll be over again?'

Marius van Houben nodded. 'In a few days, just a flying visit.' He put a large hand on his brother's shoulder. 'You'll stay with Emmie until we know how things are? As soon as he's fit, perhaps we could get him back home with a nurse but that's early days yet...'

'A good idea all the same,' agreed Mr Spence. 'Familiar surroundings may be the answer.'

'I'm going along to Theatre to collect up my equipment, I'll give you a lift back, Bartus—see you at the car presently.' He bade Mr Spence goodnight with the remark that he would see him before he left the next day, and with a last look at his small nephew he went away. Sister Crump caught up with him as he reached the end of the ward. It was very quiet, the children slept and the night nurses were sitting in the middle of the ward at the night table, shadowy figures under the dark red lampshade.

'I'm sorry you're going,' said Sister Crump in a whisper. 'Marc wouldn't have pulled through without your expertise.'

She wasn't praising him, just stating a fact. 'I don't like to lose a patient.'

'He has had splendid nursing care.'

'Yes—they're good girls.' She frowned. 'I hope that

child had a meal—I should have made sure. She went off duty very late too.'

Mr van Houben smiled down at her worried face. 'She had sausages and chips and a pot of the strongest tea I have ever been forced to drink.'

'You? You were with her?'

'We met in the entrance hall and I happened to be hungry too.' He opened the door, 'Goodnight, Sister.'

Sister Crump went back to Mr Spence. She was smiling widely but she rearranged her features into suitable severity as she joined him.

Caroline was pounced upon by Janey on her way to the bath. 'Where have you been?' demanded her friend. 'And who with? And why were you in such a hurry?'

She had been joined by various of Caroline's friends and one of them added, 'Have you been out to dinner?'

'No—just the Bristling Dog.'

There was a concerted gasp. 'But nurses don't go there. Whoever took you there and why didn't you tell him?'

'Well, I didn't like to—I suppose he can go where he likes and if I was with him it wouldn't matter.'

'Who?' They hissed at her from all sides.

'Mr van Houben.'

One of her listeners was doing her six weeks in Theatre. 'Him? That marvellous man who came specially to give the anaesthetic for Marc? Caroline, how did you do it? We've all had a go at him...'

'He asked me if I was hungry and when I said yes, he said he was too.'

'Oh, love,' said Janey, 'you were wearing that jacket you've had for ages, the one that doesn't fit very well across the shoulders.'

'He told me to be ready in ten minutes or he'd come and fetch me. I hadn't time...'

Her friends groaned. 'What did you eat?'

She told them. 'And a pot of tea.' She thought for a bit. 'And we talked about little Marc and the weather and how flat Holland is...'

'He won't even remember you,' groaned Janey. 'Why didn't you tell him that you would like to go out to a splendid meal at the Savoy or something? He might have taken the hint.'

'I didn't think of anything like that. I mean, I don't really think that anyone would want to take me to the Savoy.' Caroline was quite matter-of-fact about it. 'Least of all someone like him.' She hitched up her dressing-gown. 'I'm on early.'

When she got back to her room there was a note waiting for her telling her to report for duty at ten o'clock instead of half-past seven. A nice surprise, and she switched off her alarm clock and went quite contentedly to sleep.

By the time she arrived on the ward in the morning, Mr van Houben had been to see Marc, bidden goodbye to Sister Crump and left the hospital. He had, for the moment, quite forgotten Caroline.

Chapter 3

Little Marc was restless; Caroline watched with some anxiety as Mr Spence examined him soon after she had taken over from the other nurse. 'A good sign,' he pronounced at length. 'Keep an eye open, Nurse, and try and keep him with us—talk to him…' He glanced at her. 'You always held his hand, didn't you? Quite right too…'

He went away and she was left alone with the little boy and her charts. Presently he began to fidget again, although he quietened when she began to talk to him and then sing. She chose, 'Sing a song of sixpence' and sang it in a rather small clear voice. She went through all the verses several times and was rewarded by his sudden reluctant smile and, even better, a fleeting look from his eyes. She had embarked on the song again when Sister Crump came in and he opened his eyes again.

Mr Spence, called by a delighted Sister Crump, rumbled his satisfaction. 'Sing, did you?' he asked Caroline. 'Be good enough to sing again and let us see what happens.'

She went through the first verse of the rhyme again and Marc opened his eyes once more and this time said something which sounded very much like sixpence before dropping off into a refreshing sleep.

'Well, well,' said Mr Spence, 'bar accidents, I do believe we're out of the wood.'

She was preparing to hand over to the relieving nurse when Marc's mother arrived, accompanied by a thickset man with a good-looking, rugged face and Sister Crump. She was quite beautiful, only a little pale. She gave Caroline a quick smile and went to the bedside. 'He is better?' she asked softly.

'Coming along nicely,' said Sister Crump gruffly. 'Responded to Nurse singing to him, spoke—only one word, but he spoke.'

The man had his arm round Marc's mother and they stood together looking down at the sleeping boy. Then she asked, 'You are the nurse who has been so watchful and kind; my brother-in-law tells me this.'

She had come to stand by Caroline, smiling a little.

'Your brother-in-law?' Caroline shot a look at the man still by the bed.

'That is my husband—my brother-in-law—the anaesthetist, Marc's uncle…'

'Oh—oh, I see. I thought he was Marc's father.'

'No, no. My husband was in South America, so far away he could not come at once, you understand, and I also… Marius came at once. So lucky he is devoted to Marc. Now my husband is here with me, Marius was able to go back to Holland where he is much occupied in many hospitals.'

She turned to Sister Crump. 'We may stay?' she asked. 'If we are very quiet and do not speak.'

'Of course you may stay,' Sister Crump was brisk, 'and talk to him, take a chair by the bed and hold his hand and talk—sing too, if you like. His father can sit on the other side of the bed. He is going up and down through layers of consciousness and it is very likely that when he is only lightly unconscious he will know you are here.' She frowned. 'Do you understand me? It's difficult to explain.'

'I understand you well, Sister, and we will do as you say.' She turned to Caroline. 'And we shall see you again, yes?'

'No, I'm going off duty now, but Nurse Foster is here in my place—we take it in turns. I hope he opens his eyes while you are here.' She smiled widely. 'You could tell him about his baby sister...'

'Yes, yes, we will. She is so beautiful—he will love her.'

Caroline handed over to Nurse Foster, bade everyone there a good afternoon and went off duty.

She loitered along the corridors, thinking about Mr van Houben. She was filled with a pleasure she didn't quite understand because he wasn't married after all, but this was rather damped down by the knowledge that he could have told her that but hadn't chosen to do so. There was no reason why he should, she told herself reasonably as she climbed the stairs to her room, and since she would certainly not see him again, or, if she did, briefly if he came to visit his nephew, there was no point in pursuing the matter further. She had a shower, changed into her outdoor things and caught a bus to Oxford Street to look at the shops. She was to go on duty at seven o'clock the next morning and then, that same evening, go on night duty to special Marc. She quite looked forward to night duty but it did mean that a brisk walk before bed was the only excitement she would have. Of course there would be nights off and she would go home to Basing for three days. It was a cheering thought.

She was off duty again by midday next day, and went to have her dinner and retire to her room to doze until the early evening, when it was presumed that she would get up, dress and present herself at night nurses' breakfast, served at half-past six in the evening. Officially this was what everyone did, although in reality the afternoon rest was cut short and tea was drunk with whoever happened to be off duty too.

Caroline filled in the afternoon with writing a few letters, phoning her aunt and washing her hair before joining such of her friends as were off duty for tea, and then getting back into her uniform and going to the canteen.

Marc was asleep when she took the report from the nurse she was relieving. He had had a good day; his moments of wakefulness were getting more frequent and he had opened his blue eyes and looked at his mother. In the early hours of the morning he woke, and started to talk, normal childish chatter as far as she could judge, and, since there was nothing else to do about it, she answered him in English, and presently, apparently altogether satisfied with what she had said, he went back to sleep.

'Very hopeful,' observed Mr Spence, coming to see

how he was a short time before she went off duty. 'A pity you don't speak Dutch. Let us hope that he is wakeful when his mother comes later on today.'

Caroline, by now tired and sleepy, gave him an owlish look. She longed for her bed and the very idea of speaking any other language than basic English at the moment filled her with unease. She gathered her wits together, gave a succinct report to Sister Crump and the nurse taking over and went down to her supper. Topsyturvy meals took a day or two to get used to; she drank a great many cups of tea, dozed peacefully in the bath and climbed into bed, to sleep all day.

Marc improved by the day, and at the end of her fourth night of duty, with welcome nights off within her grasp, she surveyed his small sleeping person with deep satisfaction. He was sleeping naturally now and having quite long periods of consciousness. She still sang to him, for he seemed to like that, and when he had something to say she answered him in a soothing voice, and when he smiled she smiled too. They had established a rapport which took no heed of the language barrier.

Mr van Houben came just after six o'clock in the morning, faultlessly turned out, his linen spotless, looking as though he had risen from a long, refreshing sleep.

Caroline's heart gave a pleased lurch at the sight of him and instantly it was overshadowed by the knowledge that her own face needed urgent attention and that her hair had escaped the smooth coils she had pinned back so ruthlessly. It was all very well for him, she thought, suddenly peevish, he'd had a splendid night in bed...

Mr van Houben, who had caught a late-night ferry and driven himself to London during the very early hours of the morning, read her thoughts accurately and smiled. His 'good morning' was brisk and he went at once to look at his small nephew.

'Marc,' he said softly, and the little boy opened his eyes and chuckled. His uncle sat down on the edge of the bed and she listened to his quiet voice and after a moment to Marc's hesitant answers. They were interrupted by Night Sister who, Caroline saw with envy, had found time to put on more lipstick and powder her nose. She was a handsome young woman and she gave him an intelligent report using, Caroline noted even more peevishly, Caroline's own carefully written account of the night.

Mr van Houben listened with courteous attention, his eyes on Sister's face and at the same time aware of Caroline's feelings. Very prickly, he reflected; probably tired. He still felt vaguely guilty about her, although he had no reason to be so. He would ask to see Corinna before he left the hospital and see if there was something to be done to show Marc's parents' appreciation. Tickets for the theatre, he thought vaguely and thanked Sister nicely for her excellent report.

He went away with her, nodding to Caroline and giving her a smile. 'I wish he hadn't come,' she whispered to Marc, who smiled widely and went back to sleep.

Corinna, called from her breakfast to speak to her cousin, flung herself at him. 'Darling Marius, how nice to see you. Are you here for days or just a quick visit? Isn't it wonderful about Marc? I spent my days off with Emmie and Bartus and the baby—she's gorgeous. Do hurry up and get married so that I can be an aunt. Are you going there now?'

'Yes. Tell me, Corinna, that girl who delivered the book—Caroline? She's been looking after Marc?'

'She's one of three—they do eight-hour shifts round the clock. But she gets marvellous reactions from him; I think he likes her very much—well, she's a nice person, you know.' She glanced at him. 'Have you seen her? She's been on night duty—got nights off this morning, though. I saw her yesterday when I went to see Marc; she's going home.' She glanced at him enquiringly. 'Did you want to see her?'

His 'no' was casual. 'I'm only over for a couple of days; I've a consultation in the morning. If you're free this evening I'll take you out to dinner?'

'Lovely, I can be ready by half-past seven, but don't you want to see Emmie?'

'I'll go there for lunch.'

She leaned up and kissed his cheek. 'You're really rather a nice cousin,' she told him, 'Now I must fly— I'm late.'

She blew him a kiss and raced away and he went through the hospital, had a word with the head porter and went out to his car. The street beyond the forecourt was teeming with traffic and the pavements jammed with people hurrying to work. He carefully eased the car into the westbound traffic and waited patiently behind a bus stop while the queue slowly dwindled. The last person in it was Caroline, a small holdall clutched in one hand. He opened the car door and leaned across. 'Caroline, get in,' and even while he was saying it he wondered what had possessed him to do it.

She hesitated and the bus conductor growled, 'Make up yer mind, lady,' pinged the bell and the bus drew away from the curb.

'Get in, do,' said Mr van Houben urgently, impervious to the car behind him, whose driver was leaning on the horn. 'And look sharp about it.'

Caroline, who had no intention of doing any such thing, felt that circumstances were beyond her control. She got in and was barely seated before he drove on. 'I've missed my bus,' she told him tartly. 'Be good enough to put me down at the next bus stop or I shall miss my train.'

'I'm going your way; I'll give you a lift, since I'm the cause of your missing your train.' He spoke carelessly, without a word of truth. He was on the way to his house in the quiet corner of Chiswick where his sister-in-law was staying, and he wished that he hadn't given way to a sudden impulse to give Caroline a lift: heaven knew his day was full enough without the added chore of driving to some small village he had never heard of, yet he had said that he was going her way. He searched his excellent memory for the name of the place and remembered it. 'You'll have to direct me when we get near Basingstoke,' he told her. 'It's close by, I believe.'

He glanced at her; she was looking straight ahead; her profile looked disapproving, her tip-tilted nose in the air, her chin lifted. He couldn't see her eyes, only the curling sweep of their lashes.

'You need to turn off at the roundabout, on to the A30, then there's a small road to Basing.'

He drove out of London and on to the motorway, driving fast and making desultory conversation from time to time. At least they had something in common—the recovery of little Marc. He found that he was enjoying talking about the child, for she was an intelligent listener, but presently they lapsed into silence until they reached the roundabout and turned off the motorway.

'The turning is on the right,' said Caroline once they were on the A30, 'a few miles still. I hope this hasn't taken you out of your way.' She spoke stiffly and then, because she was tired and cross, added, 'It's your own fault if it has; you insisted on giving me a lift.'

Mr van Houben's eyebrows rose a fraction. He was being taken to task for a charitable act which was costing him ill-spared leisure time with his sister.

He sighed and said silkily, 'I see that I have unwittingly annoyed you. How mortifying it is to have what one hoped was a kindly act thrown in one's face. I must bear it in mind in the future.'

An urgent hand came down on his coat sleeve. 'Oh, I'm sorry, I'm sorry, I definitely didn't mean that, truly I didn't. I'm tired and cross but that's no excuse—do please forgive me.'

He glanced down at the small hand in its rather shabby glove and slowed the car to a halt in a lay-by. 'Nothing to forgive,' he told her soothingly. 'I have it on the best authority that you are good tempered, patient and a young woman of sound common sense, all of which virtues have been put severely to the test during the last week or so. Let fly at me if you feel you would like to; it won't bother me in the least.'

She looked away from him out of the window; he was being kind, but what girl would wish to be known for the attributes he had just mentioned? What was the use of any of them if one had a face which Aunt Meg's neighbour had once described as homely? She said quietly. 'It's very kind of you not to mind. I expect I need a day or two away from the hospital.'

Mr van Houben said cheerfully, 'We all need that from time to time, don't we? What do you do when you're at home?'

'Oh, potter in the garden and go out with my aunt.' She searched her mind for something more exciting without success. 'It's just nice being free.'

'The bright lights don't appeal to you?' he asked idly.

A difficult question to answer if by bright lights he meant dinners and dancing and being taken to the theatre. True, she had been to see various shows with such of her friends who, as she had done, had saved up to join the queues for the cheaper seats. Of course there was the annual Hospital Ball, when the consultants danced with each other's wives and the sisters and the housemen picked the prettiest nurses. She had never lacked for partners, for she was much liked, but being liked was quite different from being fallen in love with, and that never happened. She said carefully, 'I don't get a great deal of time to go out and about.'

Mr van Houben thought of his cousin Corinna, who as far as he could make out was burning the candle at both ends and thriving on it. He said kindly, 'No, I don't suppose you do. Is this the turning to Basing?'

The village was red-brick, the small houses each with a garden, and nice little green patches here and there well shaded by trees. There was no one about, no car to be seen or heard, and he stopped the car before Aunt Meg's door...

'Will you come in and have a cup of coffee?' Caroline spoke diffidently.

He had got out to open her door. 'That would be delightful. What a charming village this is. I'm not surprised that you enjoy coming back to it.'

Theobald was sitting in the centre of the little porch, sunning himself, and since it was clear he had no intention of moving they stepped carefully around him and through the half-open door into the narrow little hall. The door at its end led directly onto the back garden and they could see Aunt Meg bending over a flower-bed. She looked up and saw them, dusted her hands off on her apron and came to meet them.

'Nice and early, love,' she told Caroline, kissing her briskly. 'And who is this?'

She held out a hand and smiled up at Mr van Houben's face. 'Whoever you are, you'll have a cup of coffee, won't you?'

'This is Mr van Houben, Aunt Meg; he kindly gave me a lift as he was coming this way.' She glanced at his impassive face. 'My aunt, Miss Frisby.'

They shook hands and her aunt said cosily, 'Now, isn't that nice? Come in, do—coffee is ready, I was just going to have mine.'

It was a small house, a cottage really, low-ceilinged with a small sitting-room and a larger kitchen leading from it. Mr van Houben, urged to sit down, chose a chair which he hoped would sustain his not inconsiderable weight and looked around him. The room was nicely furnished with some nice pieces, too good for the cottage. Possibly they had been salvaged from a larger house. There were one or two pieces of good silver on the small mahogany side-table too… Caroline had joined him, sitting uneasily on a small Victorian balloon chair, and he began a casual conversation, trying to put her at her ease, sensing that she was shy, although why she should be in her own home was something that he found strange, and nowadays a shy girl was almost unknown.

Aunt Meg came in and he stood up and took the tray from her and put it down on the pedestal table in the centre of the room, taking care not to bang his head on the ceiling beams.

The coffee was hot and delicious and there was a plate of homemade biscuits with it. He sat for twenty minutes or so, talking about nothing much and then listening to Aunt Meg's enthusiastic account of their holiday in Amsterdam, putting in a word here and there, surprised to find someone so knowledgeable about the city and enjoying her views of it.

Presently he turned to Caroline, 'You enjoyed your stay too?' he asked her.

'Oh, yes, very much, only two weeks isn't long enough, is it? But I'm glad we went, and we saw as much as we could, although we missed places—we walked a lot, just looking at all the streets and houses.'

'The best way to see a place,' he said. He put his cup down. 'I must get on—thank you for the coffee and a delightful talk—I hope you will visit Holland again some time.'

He shook hands with Aunt Meg, but he only smiled at Caroline. 'I expect I shall see you at the hospital—I like to keep an eye on young Marcus.'

She went with him to the gate. 'Thank you for bringing me home. I hope it hasn't interfered with your plans.'

He assured her that it hadn't. He sounded impatient, so she didn't believe him. He got into the car and with a casual wave drove away, and she went back indoors, puzzled as to why he had given her a lift—there had been no need, and she was more and more sure by the minute that it hadn't been in his plans for the day.

Which of course it hadn't. He drove himself back to London telling himself that he had repaid Caroline, although it escaped him for the moment why he had to repay her. He dismissed her from his mind and drove to Chiswick to have lunch with his sister-in-law.

The house was in a quiet street, one of a terrace of Georgian villas, all immaculately kept, their front doors with handsome transoms above and splendidly polished brass knockers. Steps led to their doors from the pavement and the street was divided by a narrow strip of tree-shaded grass, iron railings guarding it. Mr van Houben got out of his car and mounted the steps of the end house, inserted the key in the lock and let himself in.

He was met in the hall by a dignified middle-aged man who gave him a faintly disapproving good morning. 'Or should I say good afternoon, sir?'

Mr van Houben shrugged off his coat. 'Yes, well, Breeze, I got held up. Is Mevrouw van Houben here?'

'In the drawing room, sir; Mrs Breeze held back lunch.'

'Splendid—ask her to hold it back about five minutes more while I have a drink, will you?'

He crossed the hall and went into the room at the front of the house and found his sister-in-law sitting by a brisk fire.

'There you are, Marius. Bartus had an appointment with someone or other and he hopes to be back this afternoon. You're very late.'

'I got held up. How's my niece?'

'Gorgeous.' She took the glass of sherry he had

poured for her and smiled a little tremulously. 'Marius, Marc will be all right, won't he? He talks to me now, but every now and then he—he goes away...'

'As he improves he will go away less and less, my dear. You must have patience—a day at a time, and never let him see that you worry about him.'

'I do try—I wish I could be like that funny little nurse with the enormous eyes—she's—I think the word is serene. I have the feeling that when she is with him he feels safe—do you know what I mean?'

'He will need a nurse when you go back to Holland— it will be too much for the nanny you've engaged to cope with the baby and him, and however much you want to be with him you will have to have help.'

They went into the dining-room across the hall, a small room furnished with great good taste in mahogany; lovely old pieces beautifully carved and cared for. Facing him across the oval table, with its lace mats and shining silver and glass, Emmie said, 'But he'll hate having to be looked after by a stranger.'

Mr van Houben picked up this spoon and surveyed the watercress soup Breeze had set before him. 'Yes, I think he will.'

'Then you'll have to do something about it.' She sounded quite fierce.

'Very well,' said Mr van Houben, allowing a vague plan to take shape at the back of his powerful brain. 'I'll see what can be done.'

He wouldn't say any more. They ate their duckling with orange sauce, straw potatoes and baby carrots, followed by feather-light castle puddings, and then sat over their coffee.

'I must say that you live very comfortably,' said

Emmie, reverting to Dutch. 'I mean, you've got the house in Amsterdam and Fram and Anna to look after you, and when you come here you've got the Breezes— I must say she's a splendid cook.' She glanced at her brother-in-law across the table. 'Don't you ever want to marry and spend your money on a wife and children?' She saw his quick frown. 'Oh, I know you almost married, but that was years ago. Do you ever think about her?'

He said rather curtly, 'No,' but Emmie persisted.

'I don't suppose you remember what she looks like any more…?'

He gave a reluctant laugh then. 'No, I don't.'

'So there you are. Come and stay with us when you have a few days to spare, Marius, and I'll line up some girls for you to meet.'

'The very idea terrifies me. Shall we go back to the drawing-room? Bartus should be back soon. I'm taking Corinna out to dinner, by the way.'

He had closed the door in her face; they were fond of each other but he had never permitted her to know too much of his private life. They spent the next half-hour talking about nothing in particular, although Emmie returned over and over again to Marc.

'Try not to worry,' her brother-in-law advised her gently. 'I think it's very likely that Marc senses your fears and that isn't going to help him.'

He was sitting opposite her in one of the comfortable armchairs scattered about the room, unshakeably calm. He smiled at her very kindly and she smiled shakily back. 'You're really a very nice man,' she told him. 'I'm going to feed the baby. When Bartus comes, will you both come up and see her?'

Bartus came in very shortly afterwards and the two men sat talking until the maternity nurse who was to stay until Emmie and Bartus went back to Holland came to tell them that *Mevrouw* was waiting for them.

Mr van Houben took Corinna to the Savoy, a cousinly gesture which delighted that young lady. 'You have no idea how dull it is in the hospital,' she confided. 'Oh, I like the work, I really do, and when I've trained I shall come home and specialise in something or other.'

'No, you won't—you'll get married.'

'Well, yes, I intend to do that as well, but I'm not going to sit idle waiting for someone to come along and fall in love with me. You wouldn't if you were me, would you?'

'Certainly not. How much longer do you have to do?'

'Four months.'

He watched her spoon her raspberry sorbet and added, 'You can't leave before then?'

'Of course I can. Trained staff have contracts, or if they don't they have to give quite a long notice.'

'But students may not return and resume their training if they change their minds?'

'I'm not sure, but I shouldn't think so; if they did they'd have to lose training-time—make up whatever time they'd been away for. I didn't know you were interested in nurses?'

He shrugged. 'Idle curiosity.' He sat back while she studied the sweet trolley. Just for a moment he wondered if Caroline would enjoy dinner at the Savoy. No, not the Savoy, somewhere quiet and small...

'I shall have the trifle,' said Corinna. 'It's loaded with calories but it's mince tomorrow and I never eat that, so it won't matter.'

She gave him a wide smile across the table. 'You really are a dear, Marius. I got out quite a bit with some of the housemen, but they don't run to the Savoy.'

He took her back to the hospital and drove thoughtfully back to his house.

The next morning he went in search of Sister Crump. He found her with little Marc, checking his charts, and since he was asleep she went with him to her office.

'I shall be glad when Nurse Frisby gets back from nights off. I suppose it's a dull job, sitting with the child for hours on end, but they don't seem to have the good sense to stimulate him when he wakes. He's getting on well though. Have you come to see Mr Spence? He'll be here directly—it's his round.'

'Yes, I have, Sister, but I wanted to talk to you too.'

She sat down behind her desk and he took the only other chair in her office, a small wooden one which creaked alarmingly under his giant person.

'This may not be possible,' he began, 'but regarding little Marc's future treatment...' He talked for some time and Sister Crump listened without interrupting.

Only when she saw that he had finished speaking did she say, 'Well, it would be an ideal arrangement. Marc has always responded to her, you know, and she is—how shall I put it?—steadfast. It is possible for a nurse not to give up meticulous treatment upon an apparently moribund patient while in her mind she has convinced herself that it is useless. Nurse Frisby is like a bulldog; once she gets her teeth into something, she doesn't let go. We have her to thank for his recovery, I consider. Just sitting there day after day, enticing him back, if you see what I mean.'

For Sister Crump, who never spoke more than half a dozen words at a time, this was an unusual speech.

'You will do all you can to further my idea?'

'Yes, most certainly. I pride myself on getting my patients well, by whatever means. It remains for Mr Spence to agree…'

'Oh, he'll agree. What about the nursing hierarchy?'

Sister Crump chuckled. 'There will be three of us… but of course, Nurse Frisby has to agree without any coercion.'

'Of course. I shall leave that to you and Mr Spence.'

She shot him a thoughtful glance. 'Very well.' She looked at the clock. 'He should be here at any moment.'

Mr Spence came into the office as she spoke.

He wished her good morning and turned to Mr van Houben. 'Marius—the very man I wanted to talk to. You will be going back to Holland in a day or two? I think we should come to some decision about Marc, don't you? I'm taking him off everything in easy stages; we shall have to keep an eye on that lung for a while but I'd like to get him back to normal life in moderation. You agree? That means his return to his own home, and to be on the safe side I'd like a nurse with him for a period of time, depending on how he gets on. Could you find a suitable nurse and drill her before we send him back?'

'We were talking about that when you came in. What's wrong with sending Nurse Frisby home with him for a while? He responds to her more so than to any other person, other than his parents, of course. It might cause a bit of a set-back if we change his nurses midstream?'

Mr Spence nodded. 'I like the idea. What about Nurse Frisby?'

'She doesn't know anything about it,' Mr van Houben said blandly. 'She might possibly refuse—she would have every reason to do so; she is still training and I'm not sure how a period away from the hospital would affect that.'

'A special case?' Mr Spence looked at Sister Crump. 'What do you think, Sister?'

'I should have thought the two of you could bend the rules a bit. You'll need to get the SNO on your side. I think it's a good idea and I'm sure that if Nurse Frisby is approached in the right way she will agree. Whoever sees her had better be ready with all the answers—she's a quiet little thing, but no fool.' She glanced at the clock. 'No time like the present,' she said briskly. 'The SNO will be in her office for the next half-hour.'

Mr van Houben leaned over the desk and kissed her cheek. 'You're a jewel of a woman,' he told her. 'When I marry we shall have you for godmother for our eldest.'

'That's as likely as a pig flying,' she said, but all the same she smiled widely. 'And remember to let me know what is to happen.'

Mr Spence was at the door. 'I'll be back,' he promised her.

Caroline had four nights off and the weather was kind, so that she could spend her days in the garden, planting seeds and bedding out the various things her aunt had nurtured in her tiny greenhouse; and when she wasn't doing that they shopped in a leisurely fashion in the village stores, and she and Aunt Meg went into Basingstoke and had a good prowl round Marks and Spencer, planning her spring wardrobe. Each morning, as soon as they had had breakfast and she had helped with the chores around the house, she took herself off on her bike and wandered round the ruins of Basing House. There wasn't much left of it, it had been looted and destroyed by fire during the Civil War, but there was a beautiful dovecote, quite undamaged, and the surrounding grounds were a pleasant place in which to wander. They had been excavated and yielded a rich harvest of Iron Age pottery, Roman coins and bits and pieces left over from the Civil War, and Caroline was always hopeful of finding something herself. Not that she looked very hard, but mooned around, enjoying the quiet and the splendid views, her thoughts vague and dreamy until she looked at her watch and remembered that she had promised to do the shopping and plant the wallflowers... Her aunt never reproached her if she had been away too long, only Theobald, sitting as usual in the porch, cast a reproachful eye upon her.

Three days didn't last forever, and the cumbersome pile of the hospital looked unwelcoming as she crossed the forecourt, thankful that she was on the morning shift for a week...

She went on duty at half-past seven the following morning, delighted to find that Marc had shed most of the paraphernalia to which he had been attached for so long. She took the report from the night nurse and was delighted when he woke up and smiled at her.

'Well, well, and what have you been doing since I saw you last?' she wanted to know.

He told her in his own language, of course, and she nodded and smiled and said, 'Well, well I never...' and tickled him gently so that he gurgled with delight.

Mr van Houben apprised of her arrival and approaching quietly, congratulated himself on the brilliance of his scheme. It merely remained for him to convince the girl that she would be rendering a vital service by going to Holland with Marc.

His good morning was casual but pleasant. Caroline, who hadn't expected to see him, murmured something as she sat down and he sat on the edge of the bed.

'I think we might have a talk,' he said, and smiled charmingly.

Chapter 4

'What about?' asked Caroline, refusing to be charmed.

'Mr Spence considers that Marc is almost well enough to go back to his home in Holland—another week or ten days; he has suggested to me,' said Mr van Houben, lying with a calm face, 'that a suitable nurse should go with him—a new face might bother the little chap. It seems to be a good idea, do you not agree?'

'Well, yes, but it's nothing to do with me...'

'No, no, of course not. I expect you will be glad to get back to your usual ward duties.' He stayed a little longer but didn't mention the matter again and presently he went away, well satisfied. Unless he was mistaken, Caroline Frisby, seeds of the idea planted in her head, would be all the more willing to listen to Mr Spence, if only to take him down a peg for assuming that the thought of sending her with Marc had never entered his head. He

strolled into Sister Crump's office and over coffee told
her that he would be in touch with Mr Spence. 'I have
to go back to Holland this evening,' he added, 'but I'll
get him to talk to my sister—if Nurse Frisby agrees...'
He smiled slowly. 'But she will, of course.'

Caroline, reciting 'Hickory, Dickory Dock' over and
over again, because Marc found the bit about the mouse
running up the clock irresistibly funny, allowed her
thoughts to dwell on Mr van Houben. He hadn't said
so, but it seemed to her that he didn't consider her suitable to go back with Marc to his home; indeed, he had
implied that she was longing to go back to the ward.
Of course, it was for Mr Spence to decide, but the pair
of them seemed on very good terms and from what she
had seen of Mr van Houben he possessed great powers of persuasion coupled with an ability to keep things
to himself if he wished. Perhaps it was Nurse Foster
he had in mind. Caroline left the mouse and the clock
for the moment and started on 'Goosey Goosey Gan-
der' for a change. Madge Foster was all right, she supposed—very clever theoretically, and quite unable to
make a patient comfortable in bed. However, she was
also a pretty girl; not only that, she had heard with her
own ears Madge telling Marc's mother that she loved
foreign languages; seemed to have an ear for them and
had no difficulty in picking up the basics... 'The sly
creature,' declared Caroline loudly, with the result that
Marc laughed and brought her to her senses.

There was absolutely no point in getting annoyed;
she wasn't even trained yet and Madge would be taking her finals in a few months.

Three days went by, and there was of course no sign
of Mr van Houben. It wasn't until Marc's mother men-

tioned casually that he was in Holland that Caroline knew that. A good thing too, she reflected, always poking his nose in… That she missed him was something she had no intention of admitting even to herself.

Mr Spence came twice a day, but beyond routine questions and a polite hello and goodbye he had nothing to say to her, and Madge was looking very smug.

'Never mind how I know,' she whispered to Caroline before she went off duty, 'but a nurse is to go back with Marc to Holland—' she smiled in a pleased manner '—and I think it's going to be me. After all, I'm almost trained and I speak fluent French and German…'

'I thought they spoke Dutch in Holland,' said Caroline matter-of-factly, and Madge gave her a sharp look to see if she was being got at.

'Well, of course they do, but I'm very quick at languages; besides I've been top of my set for all the tests.' She paused to think. 'I wonder what kind of social life there is there?' She closed her lovely blue eyes for a moment and sighed happily. 'They're loaded, you know.'

Caroline chose to be dim. 'Who? The Dutch?'

'Don't be so stupid—Marc's people, of course.'

'Did you ask them?'

Madge turned to go. 'You're hopeless; no wonder none of the men will even look at you—your brain's as dull as your face.'

Caroline watched her go; if you were pretty enough you could get away with any amount of rudeness. All the same, remarks like that had a nasty habit at least of hovering at the back of one's mind.

She turned her attention to Marc and was sitting on his bed giving him his morning milk when Sister Crump and Mr Spence came in together.

It was after an unusually lengthy examination of the little boy that Mr Spence asked, 'Could a nurse be found to relieve Nurse Frisby for a little while? I should like to have a talk. You too, Sister.'

Caroline, following them out into the ward and into Sister Crump's office, wondered what she had done, and was still going over her various duties as Mr Spence politely stood aside to let her enter Sister Crump's office on the heels of that lady.

Inside she was offered the chair while he leant against the wall, his hands in his pockets. He stared at her in a rather intimidating way so she looked at Sister Crump, her hands quiet in her lap while her insides churned.

'Marc will be going home in a week's time,' said Mr Spence. 'I should like you to accompany him and stay for a couple of weeks while he adjusts to home life again. He likes you and his parents approve of you. They live in Alpen-aan-de-Rijn, which is near Leiden and is surrounded by very pretty country. Mevrouw van Houben would of course wish to talk to you should you agree to go with them to settle all the details and so on...'

'I wouldn't be allowed to go,' sighed Caroline. 'I'm not trained, sir, I'm only in my second year, and I'm not sure if I would be able to break my training.'

'That is a matter which I think can be dealt with satisfactorily if you agree to go with Marc. You would perhaps like a little time in which to think it over?'

Caroline knitted her mousy brows. 'No, I don't think so, thank you, sir. If you think it is a good idea for me to go back with Marc, then I'll go. As long as it doesn't interfere with my training.'

'Spoken like a sensible woman. I will see that you are kept informed, Nurse.'

At a nod from Sister Crump she went back to Marc, nettled at being called a sensible woman, although she was fair enough to assume that he had meant it as a compliment. Her feelings were soothed by Marc's pleasure at seeing her again. He was a dear little boy, still given to lapses of silence alternating with restlessness, but there was every chance that within a few weeks now he would be leading the normal life of a small boy of his age.

She telephoned to Aunt Meg when she got off duty and that lady expressed her satisfaction. 'Never mind if you have to make up the weeks you're away,' she said cheerfully. 'Obviously they think you're right for the job, so take it, love, it's an opportunity to see more of foreign parts. I envy you.'

The following day Mevrouw van Houben arrived just as Caroline had finished getting Marc ready for his day. She sat down in the comfortable chair by the bed and Caroline lifted Marc on to her lap with the advice that presently he could be taken for a brief walk around the ward.

'He gets a little giddy, but Mr Spence is quite satisfied. He can't go by himself, of course. Shall I get you a cup of coffee, *Mevrouw*?'

'No—no, thank you. Mr Spence has spoken to me of you, yes? So I have come to talk...'

Caroline was to have the care of Marc and no other duties, and after a week or so she was gradually to integrate him back into family life, always allowing for their doctor's approval. 'You will have him all day— you will not mind that? But each afternoon when he rests—does he not?—you will be free for an hour or so, and in the evenings if you wish to go out when he is in bed, someone will stay nearby him.' Emmie van Houben looked anxious. 'You will not mind this? Here in the hospital you have free days, but when you are with us I think that is not possible for a week or two and you will always be—how do you say?—on call.'

Caroline said in a reasonable voice, 'Well, I shan't know anyone in Holland, shall I? I mean, I won't want to go out socially. I think I shall be quite content with your arrangements, *Mevrouw.*'

All the same, despite her quiet reply, under her neat uniform her heart was pounding with excitement. Life until now had been uneventful, although happy. For some years she had had no illusions about her future; she had friends, but the young men she met had felt no urge to fall in love with her, and she could quite understand why. She had no clever conversation, she hadn't enough money to dress in the latest fashion and, over and above these drawbacks, she had no looks to speak of. Each by itself would have been overcome, but the three together...

Mevrouw van Houben heaved a sigh of relief. 'That's splendid. Mr Spence tells me that we may go home in five days' time. My husband will drive Nanny and the baby back, but we shall fly. An ambulance will take us to Heathrow and he has chartered a plane for us. We shall fly to Valkenburg airfield and be met by an ambulance and driven home. It is not far.'

Sister Crump gave her four days off; it was inconvenient, but she was fair enough to realise that Caroline would need to pack her things and go to her home. Caroline was very glad to go, since Madge, on hearing the news, had taken it as a personal insult and probably Caroline's fault that she had been passed over for the job. 'Heaven knows why they chose you,' she said bitingly. 'You won't understand a word anyone is saying and I dare say the upper classes speak French among themselves and, as you know, I'm rather good at languages.'

Caroline didn't say a word; she very much doubted that the Dutch would speak any other language than their own unless they needed to. The fact that she spoke passable French herself and even had a smattering of German wasn't worth mentioning. She made soothing replies and went to Basing to collect what she would need in the way of clothing.

She wasn't to wear uniform, Mevrouw van Houben had been adamant about that. Under Aunt Meg's kindly eye, she packed her blue denim skirt and several cotton blouses, a silvery grey cotton shirtwaister she had had for years, still elegant even if not in the forefront of fashion. Just in case the spring weather turned really warm, she added a flowered skirt and a cotton dress. A handful of woollies, the inevitable cardigan, a plastic mac and a second pair of shoes and she considered that then she was well equipped.

'Enough undies?' asked Aunt Meg. 'You never know…and what about something a bit dressy for the evening?'

'I won't need that—I'm sure I shan't have my meals with them.'

'How do you know that? A fine thing it would be if you turned up at the dinner table in a blouse and skirt and everyone else in silk crêpe and diamond earrings!'

'I don't think—' began Caroline.

'Well, good. We'll go into Basingstoke tomorrow morning and buy a dress.'

Aunt Meg was what one would call a sensible dresser, and Caroline, however much she drooled over the mini-skirts and vivid tops much in fashion, was aware that they hardly suited the occasion. After a good deal of to-ing and fro-ing, she settled on a pale green voile two-piece with a darker green pattern of leaves. A sensible buy, for she could wear the top as a blouse if she wished, and the skirt with one of her white blouses. It was as they did a final prowl round Marks and Spencer that she saw the cream silky top, loose and short-sleeved—just right with the skirt in the unlikely event of needing a change of outfits.

Very satisfied with her purchases, the two of them went back home, had their tea, fed Theobald and, since Caroline was going back to the hospital that evening, sat down to check that she had everything she would need. She prudently arranged to change some money into *gulden*, and it only remained to decide what to wear for the journey. Finally she unpacked the jersey dress; it wouldn't crush, and if it got messed up during travelling she could wash it, and since they were going by ambulance she wouldn't need to take a jacket or mac with her. She packed her shoulder-bag with everything she might need for the next twenty-four hours, locked her case and got into the local taxi, waved away by several of the neighbours as well as Aunt Meg and Theobald.

Caroline was on the ward, getting Marc ready for the journey soon after seven o'clock the next day. They weren't to leave until nine o'clock, but he became excited and unhappy if there was too much commotion around him. She gave him his breakfast, and, when

Mevrouw van Houben arrived presently, went away to have her own meal in the company of various of her friends who had contrived to leave their wards on some errand or other.

'You'll have a heavenly time,' said Janey enviously. 'You'll meet a dashing Dutchman and come back engaged.'

There was a good-humoured laugh at that, and Caroline joined in, not in the least put out.

They left promptly, made an uneventful journey across London and out to the airport and were tenderly put aboard the plane. To Caroline, used to queues for tickets, Customs and baggage, it was a matter of surprise that travel should be so carefree. It was a relief, too, for Marc needed a good deal of attention; away from familiar surroundings he was inclined to be fretful, and it was only as they circled to land that he dropped off into a light doze. He stayed sleeping as they drove in the ambulance away from the airport, through Leiden and along the road running beside the Oude Rijn, then going through the town, to turn off on to a country road running between water meadows with here and there prosperous-looking farms lying well back from the road. They passed through two villages before Mevrouw van Houben said, 'We are nearly home. You see the lake? The village is close by.'

The village, when they reached it, was very small, a group of small houses, one or two fair-sized villas, a very large church and a tiny shop. The ambulance turned off into a narrow lane leading from the village square and turned into an open gateway between high walls and stopped before a square solid house set in a garden ablaze with spring flowers. Its door was flung

open as the ambulance came to a halt and Mijnheer van
Houben, followed by a stout elderly woman, came hurrying out. He embraced his wife and peered anxiously
at his small son, still asleep, his head on Caroline's lap.

'He is well? Not sick? Is there any need for a doctor?'

'He seems perfectly well. I think if we could get him
straight up to his bed—I'll get him undressed the moment he wakes...'

'Yes, that is best. I will carry him to his nursery and
you will stay with him.'

Caroline following hard on the heels of the master
of the house, had no time to look around; she had a
fleeting impression of sombre panelled walls, a massive side-table with a clock, and two hideous matching vases, probably very valuable, upon it before she
nipped smartly up the wide staircase leading to the gal-
lery above, along a short passage and into a large sunny
room at the back of the house. Bartus van Houben laid
his son gently on to the bed.

'You will stay just for a short time? My wife will
wish to see the baby, but then she will come and our
housekeeper will show you your room and you will have
time to unpack if you wish. There will be lunch shortly.'

It was half an hour before Mevrouw van Houben
came, and in the meantime Marc had woken up, been
undressed and put into his bed, where he lay holding
Caroline's hand while she talked. He didn't understand,
of course, but that didn't seem to matter; her soft voice
was something with which he was familiar.

'He must eat,' said his mother. 'There is food ready
for him, but you must eat also, Caroline. I have had
lunch, so I will give him his meal while you have yours.
Bep—the housekeeper—will take you to your room and

show you where the dining-room is. It is a muddle for today; tomorrow we will be normal again.' Bep was the elderly woman who had come to the door with Bartus van Houben. She nodded and smiled at Caroline and led her across the passage to a pleasant room overlooking the side of the house, nicely furnished with a small bathroom leading from it. Caroline's case had been brought up and stood ready to be unpacked but that, she decided, could wait. Breakfast had been a long time ago; she hoped that lunch would be a satisfying meal...

It came up to expectations; an omelette, a basket of bread and rolls, butter, cheese and a dish of ham and cold meat, and a pot of coffee. She fell to and was buttering a final roll when the door opened and Marius van Houben sauntered in.

Caroline, her mouth full, uttered a surprised hello in a thickened voice and wished that she didn't blush so easily. At the same time she had to admit that she was pleased to see him.

Mr van Houben swept a casual glance over her. 'No problems with Marc?' he wanted to know, and waited with polite impatience while she swallowed her mouthful.

Rude man, she reflected, he can't even say good day. Out loud she said in a businesslike voice, 'None, thank you, sir,' and poured herself another cup of coffee.

'Don't let me hurry you,' observed Mr van Houben very evenly. 'When you have finished your meal I should like to take a look at him.'

Caroline took a sip of coffee. She was, upon reflection, not in the least pleased to see him. Hopefully he would go away presently and leave the family doctor, whoever he was, to take over the care of Marc.

She took another sip and he sat himself down on the edge of the handsome table at which she was sitting. Rightfully she should have swallowed her coffee and leapt to her feet, but she had no intention of being treated like a doormat. Too bad if he was a busy man...

She finished her coffee without haste and pushed back her chair.

'I'm ready when you are, sir,' she said politely.

He held the door open for her. As she went past him he said softly, 'Do not cross swords with me, young lady—you might come to grief.'

She judged it prudent not to answer that.

Marc had eaten his dinner and was lying quietly listening to his mother reading from a story-book, but she stopped as they went in, smiling at the sight of Mr van Houben, getting up to kiss him and talk at some length. Caroline, standing by, not understanding a word, waited quietly until he said, 'Well, shall we take a look, Nurse?'

Marc had no objections to being examined by his uncle, and Caroline had to admire the way he made a game of it, allowing the child to play with his stethoscope, teasing him gently so that he chuckled. He glanced at her. 'Everything seems in good shape.' He glanced at her. 'Continue the treatment he has been having, Nurse, but try letting him walk around for longer periods. An hour or so in the garden might be a good idea, but don't let him get tired.'

He turned away to speak to his sister-in-law and presently he went away, giving her a brief nod as he went, and when Mevrouw van Houben came back Caroline asked, 'Is Mr van Houben to look after Marc, or do you have a family doctor?'

'Dr Berrevoet—he will come, he lives in the village, but Marius has always looked after Marc—he was born prematurely and for weeks he was never well—his chest was weak, but Marius made him better; he is so very good with children and has—how do you say it?—a technique with anaesthetics especially for children and for those who need special treatment with an anaesthetic. He is a very clever man.'

Caroline had already been told that several times; she wondered what he was like as a person. She would try and discover that while she was in Holland. Just out of curiosity, she hastened to remind herself.

Marc was restless and peevish for a few days; he still wasn't quite himself and Caroline had to acknowledge the good sense in sending her home with him; she was someone he knew, even if his surroundings were different. His mother and father spent as much time as possible with him, but the baby took up a good deal of Mevrouw van Houben's time and his father went early and frequently came back late, after Marc was asleep. All the same, he was making progress, talking more, happy to sit in the garden with Caroline carrying on the peculiar conversations which they held, each in their own language, playing simple childish games and walking to and fro on the lawn at the back of the house.

Caroline established some sort of routine within the first few days; it was obvious that Marc would need plenty of rest and she was firm about that, tucking him up in his bed after his midday dinner and then joining Mevrouw van Houben for lunch. She didn't dare leave the house or the gardens, not until he had settled down; she took a book into the garden and sat under the nursery window, ready to fly upstairs if he should need her. Actually, she didn't mind her lack of freedom.

She wrote long letters to Aunt Meg and read several books about the local countryside which Mijnheer van Houben lent her, and in between whiles she just sat, day-dreaming. Vague dreams, in which she lived in a lovely house in the country, wore beautiful clothes and was surrounded by handsome children, cats, dogs and the odd donkey and pony. There would be a car for her use, naturally, and she would speak fluent Dutch. There was a husband, of course; a dim figure in the background with nebulous features and an unlimited income. He tended to be very large, blue-eyed and handsome...

She would be roused from these fantasies by the family dog, Bruno, or the gardener, clipping the already neat hedges, or by Bep, with whom she had struck up a rather guarded acquaintance, and laugh at herself and admit silently that, although she was happy with the van Houbens, the sooner she got back to her hard working life the better.

She saw Mr van Houben rather more often than was good for her peace of mind, for despite her stern resolution not to let him intrude into her life she found it hard to do that. She did her best, though, greeting him with cool civility, giving him succinct reports as to Marc's progress; she even managed not to blush...

He came frequently, arriving unexpectedly and at any time of the day which suited him. On his third visit—at eight o'clock in the morning, while Caroline was bathing Marc—he sat on the damp edge of the bath while she dried the little boy, listening while she gave him details of Marc's progress during the last couple of days.

'Good.' He sauntered to the door. 'It is likely that you think that I am either distrustful of you or uncertain as to your ability to look after Marc. Neither—these visits have to be very carefully fitted in around my day's work.'

He nodded casually and went away, leaving the door open.

'I have never met such a man,' declared Caroline crossly to Marc, who giggled and then shouted with glee as his uncle put his head round the door.

'I choose to take that as a flattering remark, Caroline,' he told her silkily, and this time he shut the door after him.

She had been there just over a week when Mr Spence came. Mr van Houben arrived shortly after and the two men spent some time examining Marc while Caroline did as she was told, as professional as if she were in hospital, but presently she was left to dress him again while they went away to talk to his parents.

It was a pleasantly warm day; she carried Marc downstairs and into the garden, aware of voices coming from the drawing-room as she crossed the hall. Perhaps, she thought, they were deciding to tell her that she was no longer needed. Marc was making splendid progress now, and now that the new nanny had settled in Mevrouw van Houben had much more leisure to be with her small son.

She set Marc on his feet and walked him slowly across the lawn to the little summer-house at the end of the garden; it was a pretty, rustic affair which could be turned to face the sun or away from the wind. She swivelled it round so that they would be facing away from the house and sat down with Marc beside her and then, with an arm around his small person, opened the picture-book she had brought with her. It seemed to be a favourite of his and they recited the names of the various animals drawn on its pages, Marc's small voice sometimes a little slurred, and Caroline making heavy weather with the Dutch words.

'*Paard,*' recited Marc.

'Horse,' said Caroline, which made the little boy laugh.

'Never tell me that you jib at a few Dutch words,' remarked Mr van Houben, appearing silently and sitting down beside Marc.

She cast him a cold look. 'Certainly not, but since there is no need for me to learn your extremely difficult language I see no reason why I shouldn't speak my own tongue when no one is listening.'

'Marc is listening and so am I.' He smiled suddenly, 'It is a difficult language to learn, you're quite right. I've come to fetch you back to the house. Mr Spence wants to talk to you.'

He stood up and hoisted his nephew on to a shoulder, and she perforce got up too and walked beside him across the lawn and in through the French windows of the drawing-room, where the van Houbens and Mr Spence were sitting drinking coffee.

'Come and sit,' invited Mevrouw van Houben, and beckoned her to go to the sofa beside her, 'and you will have a cup of coffee with us while we talk.'

So Caroline sat, aware that she showed up badly beside her companion, whose golden hair framed a charmingly made-up face and whose blue two-piece, unless Caroline was much mistaken, was cashmere. If I had known, she thought peevishly, I would have put on the jersey dress...

She accepted the coffee and glanced briefly at Mr van Houben, sitting opposite her with Marc on his knee.

It was Mr Spence who spoke. 'I am delighted with the progress Marc has made; he has still a long way to go but time is on his side, his lung seems to be healed and he eats and sleeps well. We think, Mr van Houben and I, that he should go into the children's hospital in Amsterdam for a brief period while we run a few tests. In order to see that he is disturbed as little as possible, we would like you to go with him. He knows you well now and you will be able to carry out all the usual chores which in the hands of a strange nurse might upset him. Mr van Houben can arrange for a bed in two days' time and his parents will drive you both to Amsterdam. You can appreciate that it is impossible for Mevrouw van Houben to stay with him; there is his little sister to consider.'

Mrs van Houben turned to Caroline and took her hand. 'You will do this, won't you, Caroline? I would like to be with Marc, but you can see that it is difficult while the baby is so very small.'

'Of course I'll go.' Caroline gave the hand a reassuring squeeze. 'And I'm so glad that he's making such good progress. You must all be so pleased and relieved...'

Mr van Houben offered Marc a biscuit. 'There is an EMI scanner at the hospital which means that most of the diagnostic techniques are unnecessary. He should be there a few days only. I suggest that nothing is said to him until a few hours before you leave.'

He looked at her as he spoke but it sounded as though he was doing a ward round and giving polite instructions to Sister. A cold fish, reflected Caroline, at the same time aware that he wasn't anything of the sort.

She went back to the garden presently with Marc, and at lunch, although both Mr Spence and Mr van Houben were careful to include her in the conversation, she sensed that they would have been just as happy without her. A pity, she thought, spooning soup, that she hadn't thought to suggest that she should have stayed with Marc after she had given him his dinner, and had something on a tray. Mevrouw van Houben was so kind that she would never have suggested it herself. She excused herself when the meal was over, refusing coffee on the grounds of making sure that Marc was asleep. 'Because if he isn't I will read to him for a while,' she explained.

Mr van Houben went to open the door for her; his manners, she had to admit, were faultless. 'Dutch or English?' he asked as she went past him.

'When there is no one to listen, Dutch. Marc is a very tolerant listener.'

His crack of laughter sounded annoyingly in her ears as she went upstairs.

Leaving the baby with her nanny, they were driven to Amsterdam two days later. It was a fine spring day, the country looked charming, and the gardens before the houses they passed were bright with flowers. Caroline, sitting at the back of the car with a cheerful Marc on her lap, wondered if she would have the chance to do some shopping; she had been paid before she left the hospital and so far she had spent nothing save for a *gulden* or two on stamps. She was wearing the jersey dress with a bright scarf knotted at the neck, and in her bag she had packed the green voile as well as the

Marks and Spencer top to go with the denim skirt. She had prudently added the plastic mac, although she knew that it did nothing for her, but she had the good sense to know that it rained very frequently and the weather, if she was lucky enough to get some time to go sightseeing, wasn't going to keep her indoors.

They drove through a part of the city she had never seen before, but after a little while she recognised some of the buildings as those she had seen with Aunt Meg and then got lost again as Bartus van Houben drove away from the heart of the city towards the Rhine, saying over his shoulder, 'The hospital is close by. There is a frequent tram service to the shopping centre.'

The hospital was right on the main road, its white walls with its many windows rising rather bleakly from the pavement, but once through the doors and the gates at its side it looked more welcoming, with a wide forecourt and a good-sized entrance. Bartus stopped in front of it and got out with his wife, and Caroline got out with Marc, carrying him, because he had taken fright and buried his face against her shoulder.

She kept up a flow of gentle talk as they all went inside and were taken upstairs at once in one of the lifts. Clearly they were expected, for no time was lost in asking where to go or whom to see: they were ushered into a small room on the second floor and a moment later a ward sister joined them. It was only then that Caroline wondered how she was going to manage about the language. Her Dutch, after so short a time, was about as basic as it could be, and presumably she would have to be told what was going on from time to time… A needless worry; Zuster Tregma introduced herself to the van Houbens and then she turned to Caroline.

A Girl in a Million

'Miss Frisby, I am pleased to meet you. Do not worry about being understood. I speak English and the nurse who will relieve you while you are here also speaks good English.'

She looked at the back of Marc's head, still buried against Caroline. 'I think if we put him to bed, I will talk to Mijnheer and Mevrouw van Houben and presently Mr Spence and others will come. That will give him time to recover from his fears, will it not?'

So Caroline detached a reluctant Marc from her person and, with a good many pauses, singing and the odd five minutes here and there looking at one of his picture-books, she got him ready for bed. His mother came then and sat with him while Caroline saw where she was to sleep. A small room next door to Marc; someone had already put her bag there and she went to look out of the window. It overlooked the busy street below and she wondered where the nearest park was.

It only took a few minutes to unpack, tidy herself and go back to Marc. Mr Spence was there and so was Marius van Houben, sitting one each side of the bed, rumpling the covers and the little boy, quite recovered from his uneasiness, was laughing and shouting at their gentle teasing.

They got up as she went in. 'We'll have him up tomorrow afternoon, Nurse,' said Mr Spence. 'Arrange your off duty so that you will be with him, and I shall want to have you with him afterwards—he may be a little unsettled.'

Mr van Houben had nothing to say and presently they went away, but at the door he turned back. 'There is a small park close to the hospital,' he told her. 'Go left when you get to the main street and take the first

turning on the left; it's five minutes' walk, no more.
You will be glad of a breath of fresh air.'

Before she could thank him, he had gone.

Chapter 5

There was no chance of going to any park for the rest of that day: Marc's mother and father went away presently, leaving Caroline to look after Marc. He had become fretful at the sight of so many strange faces and clung to her like a limpet, so that she had spent the rest of the day with him, and not until he had finally fallen asleep in the early evening was she able to go down to the canteen with one of the Dutch nurses and eat her supper. When she went back to the ward the *hoofdzuster* came to talk to her. 'It will be difficult for you tomorrow,' she observed. 'Marc is restless without you or his mother. Do you wake early?'

Caroline said that yes, she did.

'Then it is a good idea, yes? If you are roused at six o'clock and go for half an hour to walk in the park—it is close by. Does Marc wake early?'

'About seven o'clock, but then he's usually asleep by half-past six. He's so unsettled now—' She glanced at her watch. 'It was well after seven o'clock before he slept this evening.'

'That is good. So you can walk before he wakes and if he is quieter tomorrow you will be able to have some free time during the day.' She nodded her severely coiffed head. 'A night nurse will be here within the next half-hour. Her English is good; tell her all that she should know. Someone will call you in the morning.' She went away to her office and Caroline went back to the sleeping Marc and presently, when she went off duty, she went to telephone to Mevrouw van Houben and assure her that her small son was asleep.

She went to bed early, for there was nothing else to do, so that she was quite ready to get up when she was called in the morning by a friendly night nurse bringing a mug of coffee. She was dressed and out of the hospital in fifteen minutes, intent on finding the park. It was a lovely morning, already light and getting warmer every minute under the sun beaming from the wide blue sky. She found the park without difficulty, less than five minutes' walk away from the hospital. It wasn't large, but there were trees and grass and beds of bright flowers on either side of its narrow paths, and here and there an inviting seat. There was a small fountain in the centre surrounded by a little pool. Sitting on its stone rim was Mr van Houben, and she stopped short at the sight of him, so very much at his ease. He, on the other hand, showed no surprise at seeing her, but got to his feet and came over to meet her.

'Good morning, Caroline.' He sounded friendly.

'Having a breath of air before the day's round? A delightful morning, isn't it?'

'Good morning,' said Caroline, pleased to see him but anxious now to show it. 'Yes, I am to go back in ten minutes or so, before Marc wakens. He's had a good night, the night nurse told me.'

'Come and sit down for a minute.' He pulled off the sweater he was wearing and arranged it on the rails. 'You'll come with him, of course. He is bound to get upset during the tests, but they must be done.'

'Do you think that he will make a complete recovery?'

'Yes, I do. It will be slow but that's to be expected, and it's possible that he may have the odd relapse—by that I mean a slight impairment of speech if he should get over-excited or very angry, and that isn't very likely. The main thing now is to get him used to being home again and back into his normal way of living. Emmie has a splendid woman engaged to be his governess for the next year or two; she will be introduced gradually of course, taking over from you in easy stages.' He glanced at her. 'You're quite happy here?'

'Yes, thank you.'

'A good thing, since you will be needed for another week or two at least. Juffrouw Grote is coming at the end of this week, provided the results of the EMI scanner are good.' He got to his feet and pulled her to hers, then picked up his sweater. 'Time you were going back.'

They walked together out of the little park and she paused there.

'I do hope all will go well, Mr van Houben.'

'It will, it will.' He didn't say goodbye but walked

beside her back to the hospital. 'My car is parked round the back—I'll see you later.'

Marc was still asleep; Caroline had time for another cup of coffee and a slice of bread and butter thickly spread with cheese before he roused himself.

The tests went well; all the same Caroline was glad when it was at last the end of the day, for she hadn't been able to leave the little boy for more than brief periods. He was to spend one more day in hospital while final checks were made. Fortunately it *was* only one day, she thought as she tucked him up for the night, for he was fretful and wanting his mother and his own home. She bent to kiss him goodnight and he put his thin arms around her neck and gave her a throttling hug.

'Now be a darling boy and go to sleep and I'll sing "Sing a Song of Sixpence" to you and you shall sing it with me.'

He had picked up the words with the ease of a small child, although he had no idea what they meant, only the last line when a blackbird came along and pecked off her nose he sang with tremendous glee, sensing it was the high point of the rhyme. They sang the last line with gusto and Mr van Houben, watching from the doorway, smiled a little. Caroline, he reflected, was a funny little thing; no looks worth mentioning, a sharp tongue at times and, while not entirely careless of the way she looked, certainly not fashion-conscious. She was, however, a good nurse; his small nephew would make a complete recovery, largely thanks to her care and wholehearted efforts.

He went into the room then, bade Marc goodnight while casting a keen eye over him and then looked at

Caroline. 'Off duty?' he wanted to know. 'We might have dinner together...'

He hadn't meant to say that, indeed he had no idea what had made him utter the words, so it was all the more puzzling that when she told him politely that she was going out with some of the nurses he should feel disappointment.

As for Caroline, she had uttered the lie with complete conviction. She would have liked above all things to have spent the evening in his company, but several good reasons had prompted her to refuse without hesitation; nothing to wear; the certainty in her own mind that he had asked her on the spur of the moment and was even now regretting it; a strange reluctance to be in his company and the even stranger wish to get to know him a lot better.

She watched him go away with mingled regret and relief and presently, having handed Marc over, took herself off to the canteen for supper. It was a lovely evening, chilly but still light; she fetched her jacket and, after cautiously checking that there was no sign of Mr van Houben or his car, left the hospital.

The car was parked round the back, out of her sight, and Mr van Houben was standing at the window of the consultant's room, looking out, when he saw her. He watched her pause on the pavement outside the hospital and peruse the street map she had prudently taken with her before setting out towards the centre of the city. There was no sign of anyone with her; she looked small and lonely as she started to walk. She hadn't gone more than a few yards when two men stopped to speak to her; he watched her shake her head and then walk on briskly, leaving the two men laughing.

Mr van Houben sighed and went out of the room, out of the hospital and into the street beyond. Caroline was walking faster now, pausing at each crossing to make sure that she was going in the right direction. They would probably be gone tomorrow, she had decided, and this was her only chance of seeing something of Amsterdam again. Aunt Meg would want to know where she had been and it was a chance to see what the city was like after dark. She remembered that their guide-book had said that the Rembrandtsplein was ringed around with cafés—she would go there, have a cup of coffee and then walk back or even take a tram…

There were plenty of people about and the streets were well lit, and she had no intention of leaving the main road. She walked on, pausing now and again to look at a picturesque house or a stretch of canal. Once or twice people spoke to her, but when she took no notice they melted away into the crowds. She wasn't a nervous girl, she had little money with her and there was nothing about her unassuming person to attract attention, but as the crowds grew thicker she wondered if she should have come so far alone. She stopped again to look at the map under a street lamp. Rembrandtsplein was close; it would be a great pity to have come this far and not seen it so that she could describe it to Aunt Meg. She walked on and found her way barred by a young man. He was ill-kempt, with a dirty face and long greasy hair, and naturally enough when he spoke to her she had no idea what he was saying.

She removed his grubby hand from her sleeve. 'So sorry, I don't speak Dutch,' she told him, and made to pass him. His hand took a firmer grip and she didn't care for his smile. 'Let go, please,' she said in what she hoped was a firm voice, which didn't help at all, for he gripped her other arm as well. She had no wish to make a scene and for all she knew she thought he might be asking her for money. Unfortunately she couldn't get at the purse in her jacket pocket. 'Take your hands away, please,' she told him in a voice which shook just a little, 'or I shall be forced to call for help.'

It seemed most unlikely that anyone would hear or take any notice; there were a good many young people darting about making a lot of noise, arms entwined or arm-in-arm singing; all the same it was worth a try. She opened her mouth and drew a breath just as Mr van Houben said gently in her ear, 'No need to scream, Caroline,' and addressed himself to the man, who muttered uncertainly and then disappeared into the crowd.

Relief flooded her person but so did indignation. 'I had no intention of screaming,' she said with a snap. 'I was merely going to call for help.'

He tucked a hand under her arm. 'You're a long way from the hospital—we might as well have a cup of coffee before we go back. Were you making for the Rembrandtsplein?' When she nodded, he went on easily, 'Quite a tourist attraction. Did you go there with your aunt at all?'

She quelled an absurd wish to burst into tears. 'Only during the day; I—I thought I would like to see it lit up, then I can tell her about it.'

'Good idea.' They had reached the square now, its cafés and restaurants spilling out on to the pavements and thronged with people. He passed these and ushered her into the foyer of the Canansa Crest Hotel, which, while bustling and brilliantly lit, was entirely respectable, something which Caroline noticed at once and for

which she gave him a shy grateful smile. 'It's rather—
that is, I didn't know that it was so popular—the Rembrandtsplein, I mean.'

He ordered coffee and sat back at his ease, and she
waited uneasily for him to ask her what she thought she
was doing roaming around a strange city in the evening.
Probably he would read her a lecture into the bargain...

He didn't mention it, but while they drank their coffee he talked of this and that in an offhand fashion
which was somehow reassuring. She wasn't going to
admit it, even to herself, but she had had a bad fright
when that man had caught her by the arm; she would
thank Mr van Houben when they got back to the hospital, and apologise.

They walked back presently, this time through small
quiet streets, and when they reached the hospital she
bade him a quiet goodnight and added, 'Thank you for
sending that man away; it was very silly of me to go
off on my own...'

'Why? I suspect that you are perfectly capable of
looking after yourself, Caroline. But it was very silly
of you to lie to me—don't ever do it again. Goodnight.'

He pushed open the door for her and she went past
him, her cheeks red and angry tears in her eyes. He was
quite right, of course, but he need not have sounded so
coldly angry.

They went back to Alpen-aan-de-Rijn the next day,
fetched by Mijnheer van Houben and seen off by several of her new acquaintances among the nursing staff.

'You must come to Amsterdam again,' said Mijnheer van Houben kindly. 'You have made friends and
you can perhaps spend a day sightseeing with them.
You will have some free time now that Juffrouw Grote

is engaged as governess. She will come each afternoon at first, when Marc wakes from his nap, and stay with him until teatime, and then after a few days she will come in the morning until his lunchtime, and then, if all is well, she will come all day. We hope that you will stay with us for the next ten days or so, Caroline, so that he will be quite used to her by then. He is fond of you, so it would not do for you to leave suddenly, Marius agrees with me about that, and so does Mr Spence. You do not mind?'

She said that of course she didn't mind; there was nothing else she could have said, after all; it was a sensible solution and little Marc was also almost ready for a normal life again.

Juffrouw Grote arrived the next day, a generously built girl with a pleasant, kind face, not much older than Caroline. Caroline liked her at once and, invited to help her unpack, sat on the bed, giving Juffrouw Grote a succinct résumé of Marc's accident and its consequences, and, since her successor's English was more than adequate, she was able to add a good many ideas and tips of her own.

'I can't go on calling you Juffrouw Grote,' said Caroline. 'My name is Caroline…'

'Tine—Te-ne. I shall ask the little Marc to address me as that also. I am told that he is very fond of you.'

'Only because I've been with him for some time. He's a very loveable little boy; I'm sure he'll take to you.'

'Take to me? I do not understand.'

Caroline explained. 'I expect you will see Mr Spence before he goes back to England.'

Tine nodded. 'Yes, I am to see him tomorrow and

also Mijnheer van Houben, but today I am to stay with Marc for the afternoon—you know this already.'

Caroline, who had been a bit doubtful about handing over to someone she didn't know, heaved a sigh of relief—she and Tine liked each other and she couldn't leave little Marc in better hands. Tine had lunch with them presently and Marc, wary at first, decided that he liked her too and went off happily enough with Caroline for his nap knowing that when he woke up it would be Tine who would see to his small wants. Caroline, said Tine cheerfully, was going to have a walk that afternoon, but she would be back in plenty of time to give him his tea.

The new regime worked well; each day Caroline saw a little less of Marc and Tine saw more, and by the end of a week she was getting him up each morning and giving him breakfast with Tine and herself and then handing him over until the afternoon with no ill effects. He had grizzled a bit to start with but he liked Tine and slowly he was becoming accustomed to seeing more of her than of Caroline.

Another week, reflected Caroline, walking down to the village to buy postcards and stamps, and she would leave; Mr Spence was coming that afternoon and she expected to be told that she was no longer needed. Indeed, she was beginning to feel that she was quite surplus in the household, although the van Houbens treated her with great kindness and made no mention of her leaving. But that afternoon Mr Spence put an end to her speculations. She might return to the hospital at the end of the next week; Juffrouw Grote was coping admirably with Marc, the van Houbens were quite satisfied that she was a kind and caring girl and observant of any unlikely set-backs he might have. 'No doubt they will arrange your return to London,' he told her, 'and I have had a talk with the hospital committee and they are inclined to be lenient about your absence. Possibly you may need to work for an extra month; they will deal with that when the time comes.'

Not very satisfactory from her point of view, but one didn't argue with consultants; she would go and see the SNO when she got back and find out exactly where she stood. She was bidding Mr Spence a polite if rather cold goodbye when Mr van Houben joined them.

'Still here?' he wanted to know cheerfully and, not waiting for her reply, 'Everything as it should be?' he enquired of Mr Spence. 'I hear from Emmie that Juffrouw Grote is ideal for the job.' He glanced at Caroline. 'Get on well together, do you?'

'Yes, thank you.'

'Splendid. Well, we won't keep you—I dare say I shall see you from time to time at the hospital.'

She eyed him thoughtfully. 'I think it unlikely that you see—actually see—any of the junior nurses, sir. Good afternoon, Mr Spence—Mr van Houben.'

She made a dignified exit, her back very straight. The two men stared after her for a moment and then fell to discussing the patient's condition. Neither of them gave her another thought, only as Mr van Houben got into his car he reflected that she had been quite right, he rarely actually looked at any of the nurses—ward sisters occasionally, and staff nurses, since he had to discuss cases with them. He smiled a little; he must remember next time he was in London to make a point of singling her out and speaking to her.

He drove himself home to Amsterdam, changed for

the evening and took a charming widow of his acquaintance out to dinner. She was an amusing companion and very pretty, but rather to his surprise he found himself wishing that it were Caroline sitting opposite him. He dismissed the thought with a hidden smile; small, energetic young women with a fund of common sense and a complete disregard for making the most of themselves were hardly to his taste.

He drove his companion home presently, refusing in the nicest possible way to go in and have a cup of coffee. He wasn't a conceited man but he was aware that women liked him, and not only him: his wealth, his background, his important work in the medical field... work which, however, filled his days and his powerful mind. It would have to be a girl in a million to make him change his mind and marry.

He let himself into his lovely old house by the canal and went along to his study, followed by Fram and a small untidy-looking dog. Mr van Houben glanced down at the beast and bent to pat him. 'He's no trouble, Fram?'

'None, *mijnheer*. A grateful animal too, and so he should be.'

Mr van Houben sat down at his desk and the little dog settled by him, looking up adoringly into his face. 'He'll soon have a name?'

'Something watery,' suggested Fram, 'Anna thought, seeing that you fished him out of a canal. Shall I bring you a nice cup of coffee, *mijnheer*?'

'Yes, please. We'll call him Neptune—he came out of the deep, didn't he?'

Fram allowed himself a dignified smile. 'Oh, very good, *mijnheer*.' He then went away to tell Anna and fetch a tray of coffee. He had been with the family a very long time and he had a strong affection for Marius; he said now as Anna added wafer-thin biscuits to the tray, 'A pity he can't find a good wife, but he'll be hard to please.'

'He'll meet his match one day,' said Anna comfortably, and for no reason at all remembered the English girl who had fallen down outside the house. It would have surprised her very much to know that Mr van Houben was remembering her too, sitting in his chair, doing nothing. He had a heavy schedule ahead of him for the next week or two but at the moment he wasn't concerned with it, he was in fact making plans, with his usual meticulous attention to detail, to take Caroline out for the day before she returned to England.

He addressed the little dog. 'You see, Nep, she had very little fun while she's been here and it isn't possible for Emmie and Bartus to spend a day away from home.'

Nep thumped a straggly tail. 'You agree with me? She isn't quite whom I would choose to spend the day with, but one must do what one considers is one's duty.' He added, 'There is, of course, the possibility that she will refuse to come; I'm not sure that she likes me.'

Neptune licked the large elegant shoe he was leaning against as if to say that he for one could find no fault with the shoe's wearer.

Caroline had time to herself now as Tine took over more and more of her day's work, but beyond going into Alpen-aan-de-Rijn to look at the shops and buy a modest present for Aunt Meg she hadn't gone far away. For one thing she hadn't a great deal of money left. She was to fly back; Mr van Houben had given her her ticket, assured her that he would drive her to Schiphol himself, and written down the time of the flight so that she could make her own arrangements when she reached Heathrow, but there would still be some small expenses and she would have to get back to the hospital from the airport. She didn't allow it to worry her; it was nice to have a few hours each day in which to explore and Bep actually lent her an old bicycle and she tooled around the bicycle paths, safe from the traffic, admiring the very pleasant countryside.

There was still plenty for her to do; Marc, now that he was almost well again, was frequently peevish and when that happened she and Tine took it in turns to amuse him, take him for short walks or read to him, but he slept through the night now so that the two of them, after dining with the van Houbens, were able to sit together and talk.

Mr van Houben came twice, the first time with Mr Spence, before the surgeon returned to London, the second time alone. Both times Caroline was out on the bike. When Tine mentioned it she felt regret mixed with relief that she hadn't seen him again. They had, after all, said goodbye, and, as she had pointed out so sensibly to him, even if they saw each other in the hospital, there would be no reason for them to speak to each other.

However, he came a third time, two days before she was due to go home, and this time she was with Marc when he came into the nursery with his sister.

She was on the floor, teaching the little boy to play marbles, and the pair of them scrambled to their feet, he to run to his mother and uncle, she to stand composedly, her dress rumpled and her hair anyhow. Not that it mattered, she reflected, watching Mr van Houben with his nephew. Presumably he was either coming or going to hospital—or possibly he had a private practice as well—for he was wearing a sober grey suit and a silk tie which probably had cost more than the dress she was wearing. He looked very handsome, self-assured and a little remote; indeed his, 'Good morning, Caroline,' had been uttered in a polite impersonal tone.

Her own reply had been suitably colourless.

He came to stand by her presently, his nephew clinging to one long trouser-leg. 'You return home on the day after tomorrow?'

He knew that already—hadn't he bidden her goodbye only a few days ago?

'Yes.'

'If you are free tomorrow I should be delighted to show you more of Amsterdam and anywhere else you would like to see.'

He watched the utter astonishment on her face followed by a slightly mulish expression—she was going to refuse. Indeed she had her mouth open to frame a polite reply when Mevrouw van Houben exclaimed happily, 'Is that not a splendid idea, Caroline? There must be a good deal that you have not yet seen, and Marius is a splendid guide. Such a nice end to your stay with us. What time will you come, Marius?'

'Half-past nine? If that suits you, Caroline?' said Mr van Houben blandly.

She had thought up several good reasons for not going while at the same time at the back of her head was the nagging thought that she wanted to go very much. 'I've one or two presents still to buy,' she began—not true, of course, but she hoped she sounded convincing. 'And my packing to finish.'

'Marius will take you to the shops,' declared his sis-

ter-in-law, 'and I'm sure your packing won't take more
than half an hour—you're not going until after lunch.
You will so enjoy yourself, Caroline.'

Caroline doubted that, and, as for Mr van Houben,
she very much doubted if he would find enjoyment in
her company—and for how long? And what would they
talk about?

Mr van Houben, in his most persuasive voice but
with a note of steel in it, said casually, 'Well, that's settled. I'll be here and see you at half-past nine.'

They stayed a little longer, and when they had gone,
taking Marc with them for a stroll in the garden, Caroline went in search of Tine, who was washing her smalls
in the bathroom they shared. She listened to Caroline's
news with smiling pleasure. 'So nice for you, you will
have a good day with Mr van Houben and fine memories of Holland when you leave. I shall be sorry that you
go but we must write to each other. You will be glad to
finish your training and then you will be free to do as
you wish, yes? Come back to Holland and visit—you
know us all—we shall all welcome you.'

Caroline wondered if Mr van Houben would welcome her—well, he'd do that because he had nice
manners, but she thought it would only be a frosty welcome...

She said, 'What shall I wear? Tomorrow...'

'You will be in the car? Then wear the silk top and
that pretty green skirt and, since you are an English
lady, you will take a cardigan with you.'

'Well, yes, I suppose that would do—I've got that
cream wool one.' She sighed—he wouldn't notice anyway.

She was mistaken, Mr van Houben standing in his

sister-in-law's hall, watched Caroline coming down the staircase and found to his surprise that he approved of what he saw; probably Marks and Spencer, he judged, but chosen with an eye to the general effect. Clever, too; the outfit would pass muster anywhere.

She had done her face with extra care but it didn't need much; she had a lovely creamy skin and she had borrowed one of Tine's lipsticks for her too wide, gentle mouth. The eyes needed nothing, framed in curling lashes—looking at them, he reflected, one forgot the unassuming face...

Farewells said, he stowed her into the car, got in beside her and drove back to Amsterdam. It was a glorious spring morning, although there was a cool breeze and the country was serene and flat and somehow soothing.

Her companion glanced at her, sitting very composed beside him. 'Is there anything you missed when you were here with your aunt?' he asked. 'I thought a stroll round Amsterdam, perhaps? You won't mind if we go to my house first? I must pick up Neptune.'

She turned to look at him. 'Oh—a dog?'

'Yes—well, a puppy still.'

'That's a strange name...'

'We call him Nep.'

Who is we? wondered Caroline, and made one of her sensible remarks about the weather.

The house was just as lovely as she had remembered it, and the old man who opened the door to them was just as dignified. They were barely inside before there was a scrabbling from behind the baize door at the end of the hall and Nep rushed to meet them.

Caroline sank to the floor and hugged the little beast.

'He's beautiful,' she cried, 'and he's laughing. Have you had him long?'

'A few weeks.' He stood watching her; she was quite unselfconscious, absorbed in the little dog. He turned to Fram and asked for coffee in a quiet voice. Fram went away to the kitchen to state in his dignified way that the English miss who had fallen down outside the house earlier that year was in the house, a guest of the good doctor. 'And a very nice young lady she is,' said Fram, 'though she is not pretty.'

'Come and have coffee,' invited Mr van Houben at his most urbane. 'Would you object to Nep in the car? I thought that after lunch we might drive around here and there.'

'Where?' asked Caroline, getting up and going into a large lofty room with Nep prancing between them.

'You haven't seen the Keukenhof, have you?' and when she nodded he went on, 'but not the Linnaeushof? Shrubs and trees as well as flowers in season? I prefer it to the Keukenhof although it isn't as colourful. And Haarlem—did you go there? No? Then we will go and look at the market square; there is some fine architecture there.'

As he talked, he ushered her to a chair by the open window at the back of the house overlooking a surprisingly large garden, long and narrow.

'Not all the houses have gardens,' he explained, sitting down opposite her while Nep arranged himself across his shoes. 'My ancestor was one of the lucky ones.'

She allowed her eyes to roam around the room; it was very beautiful, with a vast stone hood over the fireplace, panelled walls hung with a great many paintings and two bow-fronted display cabinets filled with china and silver. Very grand, she decided, and gave a surprised look at the basket in a corner of the room in which a cat lay curled around three sleeping kittens. Somehow it made the room a friendly place despite its magnificence.

'That's Jane—nothing to look at but a charming character and a splendid mother. Ah, here is the coffee—will you pour?'

While they drank it he suggested a number of places she might like to see. 'All within walking distance; we will come back here for lunch and then take the car. Unless there is anything you would prefer?'

She shook her head and was presently borne away by Fram's wife to tidy herself before setting out from the house, leaving a doleful little dog in the hall. Mr van Houben saw her backward glance. 'He will come with us this afternoon,' he promised.

He took her first to the Willet Holthuysen Museum on the Herengracht, only a short distance away—a seventeenth-century merchant's house where she could have lingered for hours but, urged on by fresh delights in store, they walked the short distance to Waterlooplein and spent half an hour at the flea market, where Caroline bought a small Delft plate. When she admired a painted papier mâché box, he bought that too. 'A small memento of Holland,' he told her casually. He took her to the antiques shops next, strolling through narrow little streets lined with even narrower shops, their windows filled with a miscellany of treasures.

Caroline, her small nose quivering with a wish to see everything at once, went from shop to shop while he patiently translated prices and the names of the window's contents, amused at her absorption and to his surprise enjoying himself.

Lunch was waiting when they got back: cucumber soup, grilled sole stuffed with shrimps, and strawberries and cream. At her look of pleased surprise Mr van Houben murmured, 'I know someone with glass houses.'

He had learnt, years ago, how to put people at their ease, and he was succeeding very nicely with Caroline. She had lost her shyness and the rather stilted conversations she had offered became normal, so that he was able to draw her out and presently listen to her answering the questions he asked until she said abruptly, 'I'm talking too much about me, I'm sorry.'

He had smiled at her then, a kind smile which set her at ease again.

Linneaushof was delightful, its flower-beds laid out informally, the trees and shrubs newly green. It had turned quite warm and they wandered along its paths with Nep trotting on the end of his lead until Mr van Houben suggested that since they were so near they might as well take a look at the sea.

He drove her to a very small village behind the dunes, left the car and, with Nep running free, walked her along the smooth sands, stretching north and south as far as her eyes could see. It was almost chilly in the wind coming off the sea but the air had given her a lovely colour and her severely pinned hair had become a little loose. She was happy, happier than she had been for a long time, and she wasn't sure why, but suddenly life was wonderful and exciting. They didn't talk much but the silence was a friendly one and she no longer felt that she had to say something, no matter what. She

could have stayed there for hours but presently they re-
traced their steps and got back into the car.

'Tea?' asked Mr van Houben, and drove to Haarlem.

He took her to Le Chat Noir and gave her an elegant
tea with a selection of cakes to satisfy the fussiest of
appetites, and when they had finished he took her to
Market Square to show her the lovely old houses lining
it and then he drove her back to Alpen-aan-de-Rijn in
time for dinner. There she thanked him for her lovely
day. 'You have been very kind and I enjoyed it,' she told
him in her quiet voice, while the unbidden thought that
probably he was glad to be rid of her went through her
head. As though she had voiced the thought out loud he
said, 'I should have liked to take you out to dinner but
I have several appointments this evening.'

'You have given me more than enough of your time.'
Her grey eyes, with their incredible lashes, stared up
into his face. 'I'm most grateful. Don't let me keep
you—you mustn't be late.'

He thought of the two meetings he had to attend
that evening before going to a reception at the Burger-
meester's house and found himself wishing that he was
spending it with her. He said casually, 'Will you tell
Emmie that I'll phone her in the morning? Goodnight,
Caroline.'

'Goodbye, Mr van Houben.'

It really was goodbye this time. He drove away without a backward glance and she went into the house. Everyone was in the drawing-room but just for a moment
she wanted to be alone. She had discovered something,
and she was trembling with the discovery. She had just
said goodbye to the man she loved; she had only just
discovered that too. It left her shaken and suddenly un-

happy, all the lovely euphoria of the day swept away, for was there anything more hopeless than loving a man who didn't look at one except to smile kindly and rather vaguely? As though I were one of his patients, thought poor Caroline.

She took a deep breath and opened the drawing-room door. Life had to go on.

Chapter 6

Parting from little Marc wasn't easy, Caroline had grown fond of him over the weeks and he of her. Although they had been careful to tell him that she would be leaving him, when the actual moment of parting came he burst into tears and became so upset that nothing else would do but to promise him that she would come and see him again soon—a promise made by his father and which, on their way to Schiphol, he reiterated to Caroline. 'You would not mind?' he asked, 'if we were to send you your ticket to fly over and spend a few days with us? There was no chance to ask you, but you could see for yourself that Marc was upset and that was all that I could think of.'

'Of course I'll come, but please give me plenty of warning, for I would have to ask for leave—just for a few days...'

In those few days, she thought, she might see Mr van Houben or at least hear of him. The future, which had looked bleakly empty, held a tiny glimmer of light now.

Bartus van Houben went as far as he could at the airport, leaving her finally with an armful of magazines and an envelope tucked into her handbag. She opened it once they were airborne and found a cheque inside— a generous one—accompanied by a charming letter of thanks. She hadn't expected that; they had been more than kind to her while she had been with them and her duties had been light, even if the hours were sometimes long and irregular. She spent the short flight planning how she would spend the money, much hindered by thoughts of Mr van Houben.

The hospital, after the extremely comfortable surroundings in which she had been living, looked awful; Caroline wanted to turn and run as she got out of the taxi and looked up at its gloomy pile, but once she was inside and in the nurses' home, being greeted by such of her friends as were off duty, it didn't seem so bad after all. Then she reminded herself sensibly that she had been lucky enough to enjoy several weeks of gracious living and she must be thankful for that, never mind that her heart was breaking because she would never see Mr van Houben again—well, she would see him, of course, but it wouldn't be the same; he would forget her soon enough. Indeed, she wondered if she had made sufficient impression upon him for him to have anything to forget.

Mindful of Home Sister's injunction that she was to report to the office as soon as she got in, she made her way downstairs to the main block where the SNO had her office, flanked by her two deputies and a formidable secretary. It was after six o'clock by now and all the ladies looked as though they needed a rest from their various tasks but the Senior Nursing Officer received her kindly enough, observed that it was a feather in the hospital's cap that little Marc should have made a recovery, and said that, since Caroline had fulfilled the task she had been given by Mr Spence in a satisfactory manner, the hospital committee were pleased to allow her to take her final assessment provided she made up the time she had been away afterwards.

She offered this news with the air of one conferring a genuine favour, and Caroline supposed that it was and did her best to look suitably grateful. The SNO's next piece of news, that she was to return to the children's ward, under Sister Crump, did cheer her up, however, and so did the advice that she might take four days off at the end of the week.

She phoned Aunt Meg with the news before she went to bed and then, fortified by several cups of tea and a good gossip catching up with the hospital news, she slept, and just before she did so she thought of Mr van Houben and wondered what he was doing.

He was sitting at his desk correcting examination papers submitted by the first-year medical students at Leiden Medical School; he was wholly engrossed, frowning and tut-tutting and writing terse remarks in the margins, and he hadn't spared her a thought.

Sister Crump was pleased to see her in the morning. 'A nice little job of work, Nurse Frisby—only what I would have expected from one of my nurses, mind you, but all the same I'm pleased with you. We're busy and I want some of the cots moved and it's Mr Spence's round so don't dawdle.'

It fell to her lot to make beds with Madge Foster, who was still smarting at the injustice of being overlooked by Mr Spence. 'I dare say you wouldn't have any fun,' she said spitefully. 'I mean, if you haven't any idea what people are talking about, it must have been pretty dull.'

'Not a bit of it,' said Caroline cheerfully, 'everyone spoke English, even the butler…'

'Butler? Was there a butler? But you didn't actually *meet* people?'

'Any number—the nurses at the children's hospital in Amsterdam were very friendly and I had the chance to look around the city too.' She paused, not wishing to say any more about that and then went on, 'The van Houbens had a lovely house just outside a charming little town—they had lots of friends too…'

'You didn't speak to them, though…'

'Well, of course I did; there were guests to dinner most evenings.' Which was a slight exaggeration, but Madge deserved that. 'And I had lunch and dinner with the family. Marc had a lovely nursery and before I left his new governess took over—we got on awfully well.'

'Did you see Mr Spence?'

'Oh, yes—he came over twice.'

'I suppose he talked to you too,' sneered Madge.

'Well, of course he did—about Marc.' She mitred her corner of the sheet carefully and, the last cot seen to, went to help with the mid-morning feeds.

She was sitting patiently with a six-week-old baby who had neither the inclination or the energy to feed, so that every drop needed to be coaxed into his small mouth, when Mr Spence paused by her chair.

'Back at work, I see, Nurse—er—Frisby. You had a good journey back?'

'Yes, thank you, sir.'

'Did you leave Marc in good spirits?'

'Oh, yes—a bit put out that I was leaving, but he loves Tine, his new governess.'

'Good, good, splendid.' Mr Spence looked as if he wanted to say more but wasn't sure what. He nodded at her and gave her a wintry smile and moved away to the next patient and Caroline continued tickling the baby under its tiny chin, encouraging it to swallow while she thought about Mr van Houben. How would she feel if he were to come through the ward door at that very moment? Delighted to see him, of course, but what would be the point? What, indeed, was the point of being in love with a man with whom one had nothing in common?

The baby opened its eyes and stared up at her and she kissed the top of its bald head; he wasn't a pretty baby and he had that pugnacious look and a nasty temper; he would probably turn into a tiresome little boy. 'And good luck to you, poppet,' said Caroline, urging down the last of his feed. 'You're putting up a good fight...'

She lifted him over her shoulder to burp and went on talking to him, since there was no one there to listen. 'And if you can put up a fight I don't see why I can't— I can but try.' Her lovely eyes narrowed. 'I could have something done to my hair and buy some make-up and some clothes—there's that cheque, even if I do give Aunt Meg some of it.'

The baby blew a very small raspberry into her ear and she laughed then and took him away to change him and put him back into his cot.

The prospect of four days off made the rest of the week go quickly enough. She packed her weekend bag, wrapped the plate she had bought in the flea market and caught an evening train from Waterloo, and, since she had been paid, she took a taxi to Basing in time for a late supper with Aunt Meg.

They sat at the kitchen table with Theobald between them, eating one of Aunt Meg's steak and kidney pies while Caroline gave a detailed account of her stay in Holland. When she had finished, having skimmed lightly over any mention of Mr van Houben, Aunt Meg observed, 'Well, isn't that most satisfactory, love? Getting the little boy well again and you having such a nice time too. You said you saw Mr Spence there, and Mr van Houben too I dare say—I expect he was anxious about the little lad.'

'He came from time to time, sometimes with Mr Spence.'

Her aunt gave her a thoughtful look. 'And how kind of the little boy's father to give you a present. You must go shopping, love—some dresses and shoes, and Marks and Spencer have some lovely undies.'

'You're going to have a new dress too,' said Caroline, 'There's plenty of money for both of us. We'll go tomorrow, shall we?' She paused. 'I thought I'd go to the hairdresser's too.'

'What a good idea—there's that new salon—you know the one I mean? You could ring up and make an appointment before we go in the morning.'

They got home the next evening with not a penny left of the cheque. Aunt Meg had her dress and for once had consented to choose a colour other than her usual useful beige. Blue, a soft blue, and the material was soft too, and made up in a style suited to her sturdy frame. As for Caroline, she had remembered her resolution and cast good sense to the winds. She had made a beeline for Laura Ashley and returned to Basing laden with a most satisfying collection of garments: a pale pink dress with a wide lace collar, a navy and white dress with a little navy jacket to go on top of it, an assortment of well-cut T-shirts, a flowered skirt in raspberry-pink and a white cotton blouse of fine lawn, lavishly embroidered, and there had been money enough to buy a pair of low-heeled sandals. She had been to the hairdresser too and had her hair cut and washed and dressed most becomingly in a French pleat. Trying everything on that evening, she wished that Mr van Houben could see her now.

She hadn't intended to take any of her new finery back to the hospital, but it was Aunt Meg who persuaded her. 'Take the lot,' she advised in her sensible way. 'Why leave them hanging in the cupboard here? Wear them just for the pleasure of it, love, and you can leave those dresses from I don't know how many years back and I'll take them along to Oxfam or one of the charity shops. If you haven't got them you can't wear them,' she added triumphantly.

So Caroline took her new wardrobe back to London and hung it in her bedroom cupboard and wondered when she would wear it; the T-shirts and the flowered skirt would do very nicely for off duty, but the pink dress was something special, so was the navy and white outfit, and special occasions only rarely came her way.

She had been back several days when she met Corinna as she went off duty.

'You're back,' said that young lady unnecessarily. 'How are Marc and Emmie and the baby, and did you do anything exciting while you were there?'

'They're all very well. Marc is almost fit again—he has a governess, an awfully nice girl—Tine.'

Corinna, who knew all about Marc, and Tine for that matter, since she had a habit of ringing up her cousin whenever she felt like it, said chattily, 'You're off duty? Good. I'll meet you at the front entrance in twenty minutes and you can tell me all about it. We'll go to Chiswick and get Breeze to give us supper.'

She saw the look on Caroline's face and added kindly, 'It's all right, Marius lets me use his house when I'm off duty.' She patted Caroline's shoulder. 'Don't keep me waiting.'

She sailed away and Caroline, watching her go, reflected that it was easy to see that she was Mr van Houben's cousin; they both had the same air of expecting people to do what they wished and no questions asked. All the same, she went to her room and showered and changed into the navy and white dress and the little jacket, crammed her tired feet into the new sandals and went back to the front entrance. Corinna was already there, talking to one of the housemen, but she bade him a cursory goodbye when she saw Caroline.

'Are we going by bus or tube?' asked Caroline.

Corinna had lifted an imperative finger to a passing taxi. 'I never go on either. If there's no one with a car I have taxis.'

'How nice,' said Caroline rather feebly as they were whisked away from their dreary surroundings across the city to Chiswick, which seemed like another world.

Breeze opened the door to them and admitted them with unsurprised benevolence.

'We're dying from hunger,' declared Corinna the

moment they were inside. 'Do you suppose that Mrs Breeze could find us a sandwich or something?'

Breeze allowed himself a small smile. 'Allow her half an hour, Miss Corinna; I'm sure she will find you something.'

He led them across the hall to the drawing-room and Caroline, gazing raptly at the charming surroundings, said in surprise, 'But Mr van Houben has a house in Amsterdam...'

'Well, of course he has—he has to live somewhere, doesn't he? Besides, that's his family home; this place suits him very well when he comes over here, and he comes very often. He has a nice little cottage in Friesland too.'

Corinna went over to the table by the window and examined the bottles and decanters on it. 'Pale sherry?' she enquired, and didn't wait for an answer. 'I dare say,' she went on carelessly, 'if Marius marries he'll get a small place in the country as well—it would be nice for the children.' She motioned Caroline to a small velvet armchair and gave her a glass. 'I wouldn't mind marrying an Englishman and living over here; on the other hand I know some very nice young men in Holland.'

Caroline sipped her sherry and murmured politely while she looked around her. It was a much smaller house than the one in Amsterdam but it was just as charmingly furnished. She asked, 'Will you go back to Holland as soon as you've finished?'

'I expect so—my family live in The Hague; I've four brothers but they all live away from home, they're older than I am. Have you brothers and sisters?'

'No, I live with an aunt.'

'I dare say you have a lot of friends.'

'Well,' said Caroline cautiously, 'I do know just about everyone in the village. I've lived there since I was twelve.'

'London must seem a bit grim...'

'Most of the time we're in the hospital, aren't we?'

Corinna, who spent most of her free time as far away from the hospital as possible, agreed. She was a good nurse, liked by everyone, and she never failed to pass the various tests with the highest possible marks, but once she was finished she had every intention of going back to The Hague and enjoying herself and then getting married. She was a pretty girl, the somewhat spoilt daughter of wealthy parents, and there were young suitable men enough for her to choose from; her future was pleasant and secure. She was a nice girl and warm-hearted too, and she said now, 'I daresay Emmie will invite you back to see Marc—they are undyingly grateful to you.' She added carelessly, 'Did you see anything of Marius?'

'Your cousin? Yes, he came several times to see Marc and he was at the hospital when he went in for his tests.' Caroline had gone rather pink, although she spoke in her usual quiet way, and Corinna gave her a thoughtful look. A pity if this nice quiet little thing had lost her heart to him; Marius, as far as she knew, was immune from romantic encounters of a lasting nature. A pity; he would make a splendid husband...

Breeze appeared in the doorway to say that Mrs Breeze had prepared a supper for them and would they be good enough to go to the dining-room?

'Thank heaven, I'm famished,' declared Corinna, and urged Caroline across the hall and into the dining-room.

Breeze hadn't done things by halves; the table was

laid with a crisp linen cloth, sparkling silver and glass, and there was a bowl of early roses at its centre, and Mrs Breeze had conjured up a splendid supper: chicken soup and cheese soufflé with a salad and ice cream to round their meal off.

'Won't Mr van Houben mind?' asked Caroline, drinking coffee in the drawing-room afterwards.

'Of course not—I'm his cousin, I can come and go as I please—I come here for my days off and when he comes over to England he takes me out.' She said suddenly, 'Do you like him, Caroline?'

A question that Caroline didn't want to answer. 'He's very clever, isn't he? I don't—I don't really know him; I mean, you know how it is at the hospital, the consultants and registrars and those sort of people don't have anything to do with the junior nurses.'

Corinna poured more coffee. 'Now tell me all about Marc when you got him home and don't miss a thing—he is such a darling, isn't he? So is the baby...'

Caroline answered as best she could, recounting in great detail the day to day activities at the van Houbens'. It was almost ten o'clock when Corinna said, 'Well, I suppose we must go back—I'll ask Breeze to get us a taxi.'

Parting company in the nurses' home, Caroline said, 'Thank you for asking me to supper, I enjoyed it very much.'

Corinna smiled. 'Good, so did I, and it was nice to catch up on the news. Goodnight, Caroline.'

Caroline had a bath and went to bed but Corinna went back to the hall of the nurses' home where there was a telephone. No one was supposed to use it after ten o'clock, but that had never bothered her. She made herself comfortable on a stool taken from Sister's office and dialled a number, and when she said who she was, 'You should be in bed,' replied her cousin Marius. 'I suppose you're short of money or worse—fallen in love again.'

'Don't be horrid.' They were speaking Dutch and she made no attempt to lower her voice for fear of waking anyone and them coming to see what she was doing. 'Guess who spent the evening in Chiswick with me…'

'My dear girl, I've had a hard day and I'm beyond guessing anything.'

'Caroline! Remember her—she looked after Marc.'

'Of course I remember her, she's only been gone a week.' He paused. 'She isn't ill?'

'Of course not—she was off duty at the same time as I was and it was an opportunity to hear about Marc. She's a dear creature, isn't she, Marius?'

'Marc was fond of her. It was largely due to her that he has made such a good recovery. Whether she is a dear creature or not I do not know.'

'Don't you like her?'

'My dear Corinna, I am quite indifferent to her, and now shall we say goodnight? I've a heavy day again tomorrow.'

'Poor Marius—so have I—up with the lark and run off my feet. *Wel te rusten.*'

She went back to her room, smiling angelically at one of the older sisters who had opened her door and was looking suspicious. 'Make a little less noise,' snapped that lady, and closed the door again.

Corinna took her time getting ready for bed while she went over the evening. Caroline had blushed when she had mentioned Marius and she hadn't said whether she liked him or not—and Marius had been equally evasive. She was fond of her cousin and had long ago decided that he should find himself a wife; she knew all about his earlier love-affair but that was years ago, and she had and so had his family, produced suitable young women from time to time in the hope that he would fall in love with one of them. He enjoyed their company, took them out—theatres and dinners and dancing—but he was still heart-whole. Could it possibly be, thought Corinna as she at last settled herself into bed, that they liked each other? A most unlikely pair, but Caroline was the kind of girl who would make a good wife, loving and serene and sensible and on occasion not afraid to speak her mind. Marius needed someone like that to go home to each evening. And soon, she thought sleepily, before he becomes a confirmed bachelor.

She and Caroline saw little of each other for almost a week; they were on different wards and Corinna was senior, with her own circle of friends and fully occupied leisure time. When Marius telephoned to say that he would be coming over to England in a couple of days, she had no chance to tell Caroline, and even if she had she wouldn't have said anything. If Marius wanted to see Caroline he could do so easily enough, but if he was as uninterested as he said he was then it would be kinder to Caroline if she knew nothing about his coming.

So when he walked on to the children's ward with Sister Crump two mornings later Caroline was taken by surprise. She had just come out of the sluice-room and turned round and went straight back in again, hoping that she hadn't been seen. She didn't think he would be in the ward long; it wasn't as though he did a round like Mr Spence. He had come to check on the small girl with the terrible cleft palate and double hare lip who would need careful anaesthetising; she should have thought of that.

She began to clean the already clean sink and a student nurse, only just on the ward put her head around the door.

'Sister Crump wants you,' she hissed. 'She's in the ward.'

With the greatest reluctance Caroline followed her, shut the sluice-room door carefully behind her and went to where Sister Crump and Mr van Houben were standing in the middle of the ward.

He looked her over carefully. 'Good morning, Nurse. You expressed the doubt that I would remember you. You see that I have. Sister Crump tells me that you have settled down again. I have just been telling her how very grateful my sister-in-law is for the care you gave little Marc.' He turned to Sister Crump. 'Perhaps we might have Nurse to special this little girl I've come to see—Shirley, isn't it? A difficult case which will need all our care and attention.'

'Mr Spence suggested that too; as far as I'm concerned, sir, it seems a good idea. Shirley will need all the patience there is for a week or so.'

Mr van Houben allowed his eyes to rest on Caroline, standing there outwardly meek and inwardly, he felt sure, boiling over because they were deciding everything without so much as a token request for her services.

'Good, good,' he said in an absent-minded manner. 'Then that's settled.' It had been settled between Mr Spence and himself previously—indeed it was he who had suggested it in the first place. Finally he added, 'We shall be obliged to Nurse—it may mean awkward duty hours and so on. You have a reliable night nurse, Sister?'

Sister Crump gave him a look implying that all her nurses were reliable.

'The child's going to Theatre at four o'clock. If you want Nurse Frisby to go with her, she had better go off duty…when are you off today, Nurse?'

'Five o'clock, Sister.' And she had planned a trip to a West End cinema with several of her friends.

'Change with Nurse Foster and go off duty at midday. We'll worry about tomorrow when we get to it.'

'Nothing planned for this evening?' asked Mr van Houben casually.

'Yes.' She was aware of Sister Crump's annoyance. 'Yes, sir, but it doesn't matter in the least.'

It didn't. They had met again—he was standing in front of her and he'd remembered her. The day was suddenly splendid; she would, if necessary, stay all night and all day with Shirley if he asked her to. Her grey eyes shone at the thought so that Mr van Houben, seeing their sparkle, decided that he had been mistaken in thinking of her as a plain girl.

'Shall we take a look at Shirley?' he asked, and Sister Crump sent Caroline back to see to the ten o'clock feeds. Which meant that she could think about him while she bottle-fed the three babies one after the other.

She went off duty punctually, leaving a cross Madge Foster to do her work, and during the somewhat lengthy walk through the hospital to the nurses' home had time to lose some of her euphoria. Just because Mr van Houben had turned up, she had no reason to get excited. He hadn't come to see her, and in a way it was a pity that they had met again, for she had been doing her best for ages to forget him. Not very successfully, but with practice it would probably be easier. She suited the action to the thought and started to plan her few hours of freedom. Never mind her dinner, she would get a sandwich and a cup of coffee somewhere, but first she would take a bus away from the hospital. Victoria Park was the nearest green space she could think of. She ran down the last of the stairs and almost overbalanced against Mr van Houben's waistcoat.

He set her back on her feet. 'Ten minutes,' he told her. 'I'll be outside with the car, don't keep me waiting.'

She gaped at him, her gentle mouth open. 'Ten minutes—what do you mean? Outside—why?'

'Don't argue, there's a good girl. Just do as I say. I have so many messages for you from Emmie and Marc and Tine, and neither of us has much time.'

Rather to her own surprise she heard herself say, 'Very well, I'll be as quick as I can,' and she sped away, racing through the nurses' home to her room and almost upsetting Sister on the way.

'Late for a date?' asked that kindly lady, dusting herself down while Caroline apologised.

'Yes—no, not yet, but I shall be. So sorry, Sister.'

It would have to be the navy and white dress and the little jacket, she decided as she tore out of her uniform, found stockings and sandals, made up her face in a sketchy fashion and pinned her hair into the French pleat. Nothing startling, she decided, peering into the small looking-glass, but it would have to do. Only a man would expect a girl to get ready to go out in ten minutes.

It had taken her a little longer than that but when she went outside into the forecourt he opened the car door and stuffed her in without a word. 'We can talk over lunch,' he told her, getting in beside her and driving away without fuss, into the stream of midday traffic, leaving the small houses standing in red-brick rows and the rather shabby little shops, crossing the city until they reached Chiswick.

As he stopped Caroline said, 'Oh—I came here with your cousin Corinna the other evening—she wanted to know about Marc and we happened to meet as we were going off duty.'

'It's her second home while she's over here.' He had got out and paused to open her door and Breeze was standing by the open front door ready to admit them.

'We're both hungry, Breeze,' said Mr van Houben, 'but give us ten minutes for a drink, will you?'

He sat her down in the drawing-room by the open window. The garden behind the house was small but full of colour and there were birds singing in the birch trees at its end. It seemed a thousand miles away from the hospital.

'Sherry?' he asked. 'Or white wine?'

She chose the sherry, and when he sat down in a large wing chair near her a ginger cat came in from the garden and sat down between them, washing himself.

'Blossom,' said Mr van Houben. 'Mrs Breeze's devoted companion, but he prefers the drawing-room if he can get in there.' He glanced at her with a smile. 'Your aunt has a cat—Theobald? A handsome beast.'

Blossom got up and jumped on to Caroline's lap and she said, 'Blossom is handsome too,' and was racking her brains as to what to say next when Breeze came to tell them that lunch was served.

Mr van Houben so far hadn't mentioned Marc or anyone else she had met in Holland, and it seemed that he didn't intend to for the moment, for he kept up a flow of small talk while they ate potted shrimps, lamb cutlets with creamed potatoes and tiny peas and carrots and then a glazed apple tart with whipped cream. Caroline, who had been very hungry, enjoyed every morsel.

'I think your Mrs Breeze must be a marvellous cook.'

'Oh, indeed she is.'

'Well, I do hope you tell her so from time to time, though I expect you do. It's nice to be appreciated.' She blushed then because it sounded as though she was asking to be appreciated too, for nursing Marc, and he watched the colour creep into her cheeks with amusement tinged with concern because she was upset.

'Don't we all?' he observed lightly. 'And you would be surprised at the number of patients I have had who take one's skills for granted and don't say thank you.'

'You find that?' She was astonished. 'I should have thought they would have been so thankful—I mean, quite a lot of them might have died because there was no one to give them a complicated anaesthetic.'

'I only hope that we can deal with little Shirley—has she good parents?'

'No. They left her with her granny—no one knows where they are now.'

'All the more reason to turn her into as pretty a girl as possible! Mr Spence is a wizard with a scalpel, you know.'

They were having their coffee in the drawing-room before he told her about Marc. The little boy was doing well and Tine was a great success, although he still had brief bouts of childish rage. 'Emmie sends her love and hopes they will all see you again some time.'

'That would be nice.' Caroline wished she could

think of something interesting to say. Actually it surprised her that she could talk at all, for just being with him was enough to render her speechless, which wouldn't do at all. She must at all costs preserve a placid front, just as though she hadn't the least interest in him. All the same, while they sat there and he kept a flow of undemanding talk going, she wondered about him. She knew all about his love-affair, but that had been years ago, Corinna had told her that, and from remarks Mevrouw van Houben had passed she rather gathered that he knew a great many people and any one of them must be the kind of woman he would marry—tall and graceful and always suitably dressed. She hadn't a chance, even if she were silly enough to try and interest him... She was sure he hadn't noticed her new clothes or the way she had done her hair.

Mr van Houben, rambling on about the pleasures of gardening, watched her from under his lids and felt a faint stirring of interest. She was quite different from any other girl he knew, and she was making no effort to engage his attention; indeed she was only half listening to what he was saying. He wondered what was going on inside that mousy head—there was more to the girl than one would suppose. He found himself thinking that it might be very interesting to find out.

He finally drove her back to the hospital and went in with her.

She stopped just outside the entrance to thank him. 'It was a lovely lunch,' she told him, 'and I did enjoy the afternoon. Thank you very much, Mr van Houben.'

He smiled down at her earnest face. 'The pleasure was mine, Caroline,' he told her, and he meant it.

Chapter 7

Caroline saw Mr van Houben an hour later, only this time he took no notice of her except to request this or that as he began the delicate job of anaesthetising Shirley, a procedure which took all his attention, and when presently a theatre nurse came to relieve Caroline he dismissed her with a nod and a, 'Thank you, Nurse,' uttered in a cool, detached voice.

It would be late in the evening before Shirley would be back on the ward; Caroline made up the bed in one of the side-rooms, made sure that the equipment was in order and went to have her tea. The night nurse was to come on duty at ten o'clock that evening, and since Shirley would spend the first hour or so in the recovery-room Caroline helped around the ward and went to her supper at seven o'clock. The day staff had gone off duty and the two nurses who would look after the ward during the night were already busy tucking the children up for the night. Sister Crump was in her office, where Caroline knew she would stay until Shirley was safely back in her bed.

The child was brought back just after nine o'clock and by the time Sister Crump and Caroline had settled the unconscious little form and connected up the drip, attached her to the monitoring system and seen that all was as it should be, the night nurse had come on duty. Shirley wouldn't wake for some time, but when she did, Mr Spence warned, she would need very careful nursing. The nasal feeding tube was already in position and great care must be taken to see that it didn't become dislodged. The operation had been a success and later he would need to do some plastic surgery on the lip. He added irritably, 'A pity she wasn't referred to me sooner.'

Mr van Houben came next, pronounced himself satisfied with Shirley's condition, gave Sister Crump a telephone number where he might be reached should he be needed, and with a quiet goodnight went away again, leaving Caroline to hand over to the night nurse and take herself off to bed.

She was tired, but not too tired to think about Mr van Houben before she slept.

She had little time to think about him during the next few days. Shirley was a difficult patient and, unlike a very small baby, aware that there was something wrong, yet not old enough to have things explained to her.

She was small and undernourished and looked far younger than her eighteen months. Caroline found it sad that the small creature had had very little love in her short life and easily forgave her for her tantrums and grizzling, but she made tiring work all the same.

Mr Spence came each day, but of Mr van Houben there was no sign. She thought that he might have gone back to Holland but there was no one she could ask; Sister Crump would tell her it was none of her business in her gruff way and the night nurse was a girl senior to her whom she didn't know well. It was a week before she met Corinna going on duty one morning.

'No time to talk,' said that young lady. 'I'm late again. Did you see Marius?'

'Yes—yes, I did, when he was here for Shirley's operation.'

'Pity he didn't stay longer; he had to get back for some meeting or other then he was off to the States… must fly.'

She sped away, and Caroline, her head full of what little news Corinna had given her, went on duty too.

She went to Basing for her days off and found Aunt Meg and Theobald very soothing to her troubled thoughts; it was easier to forget about Mr van Houben now that she was away from the hospital and the chance of seeing him again, and Aunt Meg's sensible observation that it was a good thing that she hadn't stayed in Holland too long, for it might have unsettled her, warned her that she was unsettled already and likely to stay that way unless she became her sensible self once more. She went back to the hospital full of good intentions, but since there was no sign of Mr van Houben she was unable to try them out, though she did fill her off-duty hours with activity: playing tennis on the hard court at the back of the nurses' home, going window-shopping with whoever of her friends were off duty, studying hard instead of dreaming; but even with all this she still thought of him before she slept at night, wondering what he was doing.

It was several days later that Mr Spence brought a new houseman on his round. A thin, tall young man who looked vaguely unhappy. He had nice eyes behind spectacles but his ears stuck out and his hair was unruly above a face which held no good looks at all, except that when he caught Caroline's eye and smiled tentatively she saw that he was really quite nice.

He came along the next morning, to take a sample of blood from one of the children, and she was sent to hold the child while he did it.

'You've just come?' said Caroline, stating the obvious for lack of anything interesting to say and wanting to put him at his ease.

'Two days ago. It's all a bit strange. I don't know London at all—I'm from Birmingham, doing a six-month course in paediatrics. Do you live here?'

'No, in a village in the country—not far away, though.' She had the small boy on her lap, his head tucked into her shoulder, his small hands firmly held, his jacket already rolled up. 'He'll scream,' she warned, 'but don't let it worry you, he'll be all right. I've a sweetie in my pocket for him.'

He looked as though he would be nervous and clumsy but he wasn't; true, the child screamed, but Caroline was quick with the sweetie and a cuddle and the screams dwindled into gulping breaths and then, when she blew into his small neck, chuckles.

'What's your name?' He was tidying up after himself very neatly.

'Caroline Frisby.'

'Robert Brewster.' He smiled; he had a very nice smile. 'I say, would you come out with me one evening? Just for a sandwich or something…' His eyes behind the glasses looked anxious. 'I don't know anyone…'

She wasn't sure if that was a compliment. 'Yes, I'd like that. I'm off duty on Friday evening and on Sunday, I'll call at the lodge on my way off duty—you can leave a message there.'

'I say, will you really—you won't forget?'

'No.'

There was a note for her on Sunday evening—would she be at the entrance at half-past six? There were no details; she got into the green-patterned two-piece, caught up a cardigan and went punctually to the entrance.

He was waiting for her and met her with a broad smile. 'I've an old car—I thought we might go to Regent's Park. Do you know the way?'

She said that she did as she got into the battered Mini. 'There won't be much traffic,' she told him. 'Sunday is a good time to see London.'

He drove well, parked the car at a meter and suggested that they might have something to eat.

'That would be nice—I'm not very hungry,' said Caroline, thinking of his pocket. 'There's a café on the next corner outside the Park; I dare say it's open.'

It was. They ate beefburgers and drank several cups of coffee while Robert talked. He was lonely; he hadn't been in the hospital long enough to get to know any of the other housemen and he had no friends in London. 'The nurses are all so…' He paused and she wondered if he had been going to say pretty and decided not to, but he went on, 'I'm engaged to a girl in Birmingham.'

He added ingenuously, 'She wouldn't mind me being friendly with *you*.'

She supposed that a left-handed compliment was as good as any. 'You must miss her very much. Once you're settled in and can arrange a free day you must go and see her, or perhaps she could come here?'

'Yes, I'll do that. You don't mind my telling you about her?'

'No. What is she like?' asked Caroline obligingly.

Robert had been waiting for that; he launched into a glowing account of his Miriam which lasted through coffee and Bath buns.

Back at the hospital he thanked her warmly for her company. 'Could we do it again some time?' he asked.

'That would be nice. Do bring a photo of your Miriam.' She gave him a motherly smile—perhaps it was the unfortunate ears or the spectacles, but he looked as though he needed someone to look after him. 'Six months isn't long,' she added in a comforting voice. 'Do you plan to go on working in a hospital?'

'There's a first-class children's hospital in Birmingham, I shall try for a job there.' He beamed at the thought. 'We could get married...'

'A very sensible idea,' said Caroline, and wished him goodnight.

Over the next few weeks she went out with him several times; they had slipped into a kind of brother-sister relationship although the hospital grapevine would have it otherwise. She was on her way to the path lab with some specimens when she met Corinna who put out a hand and stopped her.

'I've been wanting to see you—messages from the family and news of Marc. What's all this romantic chat about you and our Dr Brewster? Out every night in that car of his—are we listening for wedding bells?'

Caroline laughed. 'What rubbish—of course not— he's engaged to a nice girl called Miriam—but he doesn't feel at home here so I go out with him and we talk—or rather he talks about her. That's all.'

'Out of sight, out of mind—you say that, don't you?'

'Yes, but he loves her. He's a friend—nothing more.'

'It's time you fell in love,' said Corinna, and blinked at the tide of warm colour which flooded Caroline's cheeks and added quickly, 'I fall in love every few weeks, you know; it's great fun.' She smiled widely. 'I'm late, as always, and so will you be. We must have another evening together soon.'

She was gone, running along the corridor, ignoring hospital rules.

Marius telephoned his cousin that evening to tell her that he would be coming over to London in two days' time. 'I'll take you out to dinner if you can bear with a middle-aged cousin,' he told her. 'It will be the last time, I dare say; you leave again soon now, don't you?'

'Yes, I'm so excited about it, I'm going to have a lovely holiday—out every night dancing...'

'You haven't done so badly in London,' said Marius drily. 'Is Caroline still on the children's ward? She wrote to Emmie but didn't say where she was working.'

'Oh, yes, she's still there,' said Corinna airily. 'She's due for a move soon, though.' She began to talk about something else; it had been on the tip of her tongue to tell him about Caroline and Robert Brewster but something had made her change her mind. Marius might have asked after her out of politeness; on the other hand, if he was interested, it might shake him up a bit to discover for himself that plain little Caroline was by no means on the shelf yet.

He arranged to call for her in two days' time, gave her the latest family news and then rang off. Presently he picked up the phone again. Emmie answered. They chatted for a while about Marc's progress. 'He's doing splendidly, but I was wondering if a visit from Caroline might be a good idea.'

'She writes almost every week and sends little drawings for him, and of course I tell her how he's getting on; so does Tine. We'd love to have her if she could get a holiday. Have you asked her?'

'No. It merely crossed my mind. I'm going over to England in a day or so; I'll see Corinna and probably I'll see Caroline too and see what she says.'

He put the phone down and applied himself to the notes on the desk before him but presently he pushed them away and Nep, watchful at his feet, wriggled nearer and uttered a hopeful bark.

Mr van Houben bent to scratch Nep's ear. 'Not just yet, old fellow. Do you suppose it would be a good idea to see Caroline again? It is a great pity that I am unable to forget her, for I have no reason to remember her except as a good nurse…'

Nep muttered gently and Mr van Houben went on thoughtfully, 'If I compare her with the other ladies of my acquaintance she is completely outshone; she is, after all, a student nurse, one of hundreds with whom I come in contact almost daily. Granted, she played a large part in getting Marc back on to his feet, but any good nurse could have done that.' He frowned. 'No, that is not true, she held on when others might have let him

slip through their fingers. But I must not allow gratitude to colour my thoughts about her.'

Nep laid his chin on his master's shoe and muttered
again and Mr van Houben said, 'I'm glad that you agree
with me.'

He called for Corinna two evenings later and had
just settled her in the Bentley and was preparing to
drive away when Caroline and Robert came out of the
hospital entrance. It was the tail-end of a lovely day
and Caroline had put on her flowered skirt and the silk
top and done her face and hair with extra care because
she had been invited to have a meal with Robert and
his Miriam, who had come to London on a short visit.
She hadn't been too keen on going, remembering the
old adage about three being a crowd and not fancying
playing gooseberry, but Miriam had written her a letter
saying how much she wanted to meet her, so Caroline
had agreed reluctantly.

Mr van Houben took his hands off the wheel and
sat back watching. He said casually, 'Caroline has a
boyfriend?'

'Oh, Robert Brewster—he's doing a six-month paediatric course. From Birmingham. He's rather a dear.'
Corinna took a quick glance at her companion; his face
held no expression but she knew him well enough to
know that that indicated that he was hiding strong feelings of some sort. She went on cheerfully, 'He's got a
frightful old Mini. I hear he's pretty good at his job;
even the great Mr Spence thinks well of him.'

They watched the Mini leave the forecourt before
Marius drove away in his turn. He didn't mention Caroline again during the evening, and when they returned

to the hospital the Mini was back, parked with the other staff cars.

'Shall I see you tomorrow?' said Corinna.

'I shall be here some time in the morning. There is that burns case they will need me to look at to see if it will be possible to give an anaesthetic.'

'She's in our ward—her mouth and throat are badly damaged but I expect that you know all about it.'

'Yes. I've talked with Mr Spence. We must see what can be done. Goodnight, my dear.'

He walked her to the entrance to the nurses' home and got back into his car and drove himself back to Chiswick. Breeze, silently seeing to the locking up and going to wish his master goodnight, observed to his wife later that Mr Marius seemed quite put out about something. 'Miss Corinna after him for some more spending money, I dare say,' he chuckled. 'We shall miss her when she leaves us.'

Caroline, happily unaware of Mr van Houben's arrival, got ready for bed, had tea with several of her friends and recounted the pleasures of her evening. 'A very nice girl,' she observed, 'just right for Robert. I like her. He's managed to get a week off at the end of the month so he can go to Birmingham and be with her. They're devoted.'

'What did you eat?'

'We went to a small restaurant behind Oxford Street. We had soup and steak and kidney pie and ices after— oh, and coffee, of course. I wasn't too keen to go but it was all right, they treated me like a sister, if you see what I mean.'

Her audience nodded, Caroline was a dear girl, they all liked her, but there was no denying the fact that her lot in life seemed to be that of faithful friend. They went off to bed presently and she put her head on the pillow and slept, first of all allowing herself a few loving thoughts about Mr van Houben.

He had spent a good deal of the morning with the burns case, conferred with the surgeon who wanted to operate and then made his way to the children's ward. Shirley, he had been told, was still there, ready to leave, but since her granny didn't feel she could cope with her efforts were being made to get her into a children's home.

Sister Crump was in her office, and so was Robert Brewster, writing up notes. He got up as Mr van Houben went in and Sister Crump said, 'Good morning, sir— nice to see you—you'll be wanting to look at Shirley? This is Dr Brewster, he's on a six-month course…'

The two men shook hands and Mr van Houben leant his vast frame against a wall and observed in his calm unhurried way that yes, he would be glad to see the child, and he added, 'And don't disturb yourself Sister, I'm sure Dr Brewster will go with me.'

Shirley's cot was at the far end of the ward, and since she had just wet her bed Caroline was changing the sheets with one arm round the toddler propped against the cot sides. An awkward business, but the other nurse on duty was in the sluice-room and Shirley was grizzling.

She looked over her shoulder at the sound of feet and at the sight of Mr van Houben went first very red and then pale; he was a glorious surprise, but the unexpectedness of it had taken her breath away, so that for a moment she was perfectly still.

'Hello, Caroline,' said Mr van Houben at his bland-est. 'I've come to take a look at Shirley.'

He leaned over and lifted the small creature out of her cot and Caroline said belatedly, 'Good morning, sir,' and finished off the cot, not looking at him or Robert.

Mr van Houben was very much at his ease; he went and sat on one of the low tables where the children played, and sat Shirley on his knee, and Robert went with him. Not a perceptive young man, he yet had the feeling that neither of the two persons with him was re-ally aware of his presence, and Caroline was looking flustered. He coughed, and Mr van Houben turned his handsome head to speak to him.

'Mr Spence did a splendid job of work here,' he ob-served, 'and of course the nursing of such a case is all-important—no easy task as you can imagine, with the child's arms splinted to prevent interference with the wound and the great difficulty in feeding and pre-venting crying.' He had opened the small mouth with a gentle hand and was peering inside. 'Of course, Sis-ter Crump is one of the finest ward sisters there is, and trains her nurses to her own high standard.'

Caroline had finished making up the cot and wished that she had something to occupy her. It wouldn't do to walk away and leave the men there; one didn't leave consultants on their own; on the other hand she felt a fool standing there doing nothing.

She looked at Robert but he was listening to Mr van Houben and presently invited to give his opinion as to the best method of feeding a child with a cleft palate; he ventured a few of his own ideas, during which Shirley was handed back to her with one of Mr van Houben's bland smiles.

She put the child back into her cot, arranged suitable toys and locked the cot sides, taking as long as possible until he said, 'Don't let us keep you, Nurse,' and dismissed her with a kindly smile.

It was fortunate that there was an outburst of tears from a small boy on the other side of the ward; it gave her something to do but unfortunately prevented her from hearing what the men were talking about. Presently they strolled away with a 'Thank you, Nurse,' uttered in her direction by Mr van Houben and a sidelong glance from Robert.

'What plans do you have for the future?' asked Mr van Houben pleasantly of Robert.

'I want to go back to Birmingham—to the children's hospital there, sir. They've more or less agreed to consider me and I could work my way up to registrar in time.'

'You wish to remain there?'

'Well, yes. We plan to marry as soon as I'm appointed.'

'Your wife will work too?' asked Mr van Houben smoothly.

Robert nodded. 'But only until I've got started; she's keen on paediatrics too.'

Mr van Houben's face was impassive. 'Then I must wish you every success—the work is very rewarding.'

They had reached Sister's office and Robert didn't go in. 'It's been a privilege meeting you, sir,' he declared. 'I hope we shall meet again at some time.'

'Bound to—I come here from time to time, although my main work is in Holland.' He nodded an amiable goodbye and opened the office door.

Inside he sat down on the edge of the desk. 'Shirley's

doing well. How is Nurse Frisby placed as regards holidays? My sister-in-law wants her to go over and spend a couple of days with Marc.'

'Well, she is due for a move in a couple of weeks; she could have four days off at the beginning of next week and go straight to Casualty. I shall miss her; she's a good nurse. I retire in four years; she might very well get my job provided she stays on here. She might marry, of course.'

Mr van Houben withdrew his gaze from the view of the chimney pots and shabby roof-tops outside the window. 'It seems likely,' he observed. He got up. 'I'll get Emmie to phone Caroline. Does she know that she is to be transferred?'

'No—but I'll tell her.'

She watched him go. There was nothing in his manner to indicate it, but she had the feeling that he was in a towering rage.

Caroline, going off duty in the afternoon, looked to see if his car was in the forecourt. It had already gone; indeed, he was on his way back to the ferry and Holland.

Emmie van Houben phoned her that evening. 'Marc does want to see you again,' she begged. 'Could you come just for a day or two, so that he knows that you haven't forgotten him? Please, Caroline—we will send your ticket and meet you at Schiphol. Could you not explain to Sister Crump? She is so kind and understanding?'

'I saw Mr van Houben this morning...he didn't say anything about Marc.'

Emmie's surprise sounded very real. 'Did you? Well, I don't suppose he would—he's going to Brussels and then on to Rome.' Quite true, only he wouldn't be going for several weeks.

There would be no fear of meeting him, thought Caroline, something she longed to do but which common sense told her would be useless and upsetting. 'I'll ask Sister Crump in the morning,' she promised, and put the phone down. But Emmie didn't; she went back to the switchboard and asked to speak to Sister Crump.

Caroline was a little surprised at Sister Crump's willingness to let her have four days off at the weekend. 'You are going to Casualty next Wednesday,' she was told gruffly, 'so it will fit in very well.'

'Casualty? Must I? Couldn't I stay here for another few weeks, Sister Crump?'

'Good heavens, girl, you want to finish your training, don't you? You've done well here and we shall miss you, but you mustn't get in a rut.' She waved dismissal. 'Take Friday evening off—you'll need to pack and so on.'

Aunt Meg, when telephoned, thought it was a splendid idea. 'And take a pretty dress with you, love, I dare say they'll take you out.'

The weather was splendid, Caroline wore the navy and white and the little jacket and, mindful of Aunt Meg's advice, packed the green voile two-piece and, after careful thought, the pink cotton and lace Laura Ashley dress she had bought in a fit of extravagance. Her ticket had arrived by special delivery and she left quite early in the morning for the eleven o'clock flight. Mevrouw van Houben had said that she would be met, and she had almost all her month's pay in her handbag; she had nothing to worry her. She had been sent a first-class ticket and had every intention of enjoying the flight. Which she would have done, if only she could have stopped herself thinking about Mr van Houben.

By the time she arrived at Schiphol she was wishing—contrary to all her good intentions—that he would be there waiting for her. Of course he wasn't. Bartus van Houben, beaming with pleasure, was there with the car, full of questions as to the comfort of her journey. 'We are all so pleased that you can come,' he assured her.

'I am delighted to see you all again—I only hope that Marc remembers me. He is well?'

It took almost the rest of the drive to Alpen-aan-de-Rijn for Marc's doting father to enlarge upon his progress, and when they arrived at the house she saw that he hadn't exaggerated. The little boy was walking steadily and he had gained weight; what was more, after the first few seconds he recognised her and rushed to be hugged and kissed and made much of.

'You see,' cried Mevrouw van Houben delightedly, 'he remembers you. Come in, Caroline, come in. You will wish to go to your room, but please come down soon and we will have a drink before lunch. Tine is even now there arranging the flowers.'

So Caroline followed Bep up the stairs and into the room she had had previously, and found Tine there, filling a bowl with roses.

'So nice to see you again,' said Tine, and flung her arms round her. 'I talk of you each day to Marc and he does not forget you, and we do not forget you either. He is now a well boy; Mr van Houben was here and he is most satisfied.' She had sat down on the bed while Caroline tidied herself and took off her jacket. 'Such a pity that he is not here to see you, but you meet in London?'

'Well, I see him on the ward...' Caroline poked at her hair in a dissatisfied fashion. 'I'm going to go to Casualty when I go back.'

'You will like that? And he goes there also?'

'Most unlikely,' said Caroline.

They went down to the drawing-room together and found everyone there—the baby and her nanny, Marc and his parents, and since it was an occasion to celebrate they drank champagne.

They sat down to lunch presently, with Marc between Caroline and Tine. He was excited but not boisterous, and he ate his lunch very nicely, chattering to Caroline as though she had never been away, and she answering him, as she always had done in her own language, neither quite understanding what the other one was talking about but perfectly happy to let matters rest as they were. He was taken away for his rest presently and Tine came back to join them in the drawing-room again. Mevrouw van Houben was full of questions. 'Corinna will be home very soon now; it is fortunate that she has not fallen in love seriously with any of the young men with whom she goes out. She will settle down perhaps and choose a good Dutchman. She is a dear girl but spoilt by her parents. And you, Caroline— do you have a serious young man? Corinna told me that you were friendly with a new doctor. Is he nice?'

Mevrouw van Houben had bent her head over her tapestry work and didn't see Caroline's face. 'He's just a friend...'

And Tine laughed and said, 'That is what everyone says when they are asked such a question. We have to wait and see, perhaps?'

'Perhaps,' said Caroline, unable to think of a better reply.

It was delightful to be back in the comfortable and pleasant life which the van Houbens led; Caroline went to bed that evening happily aware that they were really pleased to see her again and that they liked her. Marius van Houben had a nice family, she reflected sleepily; she supposed that he was in Brussels or even Rome by now, unaware that she was in Holland. Not that he would mind; he had treated her like a stranger—well, almost a stranger—on the ward, and he certainly wouldn't put himself out to see her while she was here. She tried to think indignant thoughts about him but it was too difficult, she loved him too much.

The van Houbens went to church in the morning, and since Caroline offered to look after the children Tine went with them. It was delightful in the garden; the baby slept and little Marc sat on a rug while she sprawled beside him, showing him his picture-book and struggling to read the simple sentences in it, and when everyone came back from church they sat around drinking coffee, carrying on a rambling conversation about nothing in particular. Caroline found it very restful; there was a lot to be said for the lack of Sunday papers in Holland; it made for idle hours spent in idle talk instead of silence and the rustle of the supplements.

Mr van Houben arrived silently, not coming out of the house through the French windows, but taking one of the narrow paths at one side. Caroline was kneeling on the grass, tossing a ball to Marc, her back to the house, so that his quiet, 'Hello, Caroline,' took her by surprise. She scrambled to her feet and lifted a pale face to his.

'Oh, I thought you were in Rome or Brussels.'

'Otherwise you wouldn't have come?' he said. His smile was gently mocking. 'We must contrive to be civil for an hour or so. I'm only here for lunch.' He picked up Marc and tossed him gently in the air. 'And how is the hospital? and your friend, young Brewster?'

'Busy, and Dr Brewster gets on very well with everyone.'

The blue eyes scanned her face. 'He should go far.' He turned away from her then to speak to his sister-in-law and presently sat down by his brother and became immersed in a discussion which kept them occupied until they went indoors for lunch. Over that meal, although the conversation was general, he barely spoke to Caroline.

It seemed that he was leaving for Brussels in the morning, staying there for several days before going on to Rome and not returning to Holland for the best part of two weeks, and Caroline, peeping at him discreetly whenever she had the chance, was suddenly filled with a recklessness quite alien to her calm nature. Before he went, she decided, she would ask him why he disliked her—no, that wouldn't do—'ignored' was a better way to describe his pleasantly casual manner towards her. They had known each other for several weeks now, never mind that she was a student nurse and he a well-known consultant: Never mind too, that she was head-over-heels in love with him; he would never fall in love with her, but at least they could clear the air and perhaps even be friends in a limited way.

They sat around talking after lunch and Mr van Houben showed no signs of leaving, so that when Tine came down from the nursery to say that Marc was grizzling for a woolly toy he had left in the little summer-house Caroline offered at once to go and get it. She didn't hurry, for she was mulling over what she intended to say to him presently; there was bound to be a moment when she could speak to him. She found the toy and started back to the house. The drawing-room was empty and she hurried through to the hall, just in time to see the Bentley driving away from the open front door.

Mevrouw van Houben turned to smile at her. 'Marius had to get back—he leaves early in the morning. He asked me to say goodbye to you and also to wish you every happiness in the future.'

Caroline clutched the woolly toy to her as though it were a lifebelt and she were drowning. 'I hope he has a pleasant journey,' she said in a voice which didn't sound like hers at all. 'I'll take this up to Marc...'

Tine took one look at her face. 'You have had bad news?'

'No, no, I ate too much lunch...'

She gave Marc his woolly animal and stayed for a minute or two talking to them both, reflecting that perhaps it was best this way: no awkward goodbyes when her tongue might have run away with her and she might have said things that she would have regretted. He thought so little of her that he hadn't even wished to say goodbye or given her the chance to do the same.

She went back downstairs, and no one seeing her sitting there listening to the van Houbens' friendly talk would have known that her heart was breaking.

'So silly,' she muttered to herself, lying awake in her bed later, 'for he never gave me any reason to suppose he was even the slightest bit interested in me.' To prove it she got out of bed and turned on the light by the dressing-table and examined herself in its looking glass. 'You're a fool,' she told her reflection.

Chapter 8

Mr van Houben drove himself back to Amsterdam with controlled ferocity and Fram, going to open the door as the car drew up, sighed at the sight of his inscrutable face. The master was in a nasty temper, no less nasty for being under control; he wasn't going to be best pleased to hear that Mevrouw van der Holle, recently widowed, attractive and making the most of the brief meetings she had had with him at other people's houses, was sitting in the drawing-room, intent on inviting herself out for the evening. She would be out of luck, thought Fram, closing the door soundlessly and informing Mr van Houben in a toneless voice that he had a visitor.

Mr van Houben bent to scratch Nep behind the ear and didn't say a word beyond a brief, 'Thank you, Fram. I'll ring when I want you,' before opening his drawing-room door.

Mevrouw van der Holle was a handsome woman in her late thirties; she had no children and spent a good part of each day keeping middle age at bay. She was skilfully made up and slim to the point of thinness; she dressed very well too. She came to meet him as he opened the door, smiling charmingly as she offered a hand. 'Dear Marius—I have taken you quite by surprise? I was driving past and I thought how pleasant it would be if we were to have a drink together and perhaps spend the evening. You were always so good to Jan when he was alive—' she looked suitably sorrowful '—and you are a person to whom I can talk seriously.'

'How kind of you to say so, Mevrouw van der Holle, and to suggest an evening together. It is my misfortune that I am on my way to the hospital and shall be there for the rest of the evening and probably half the night. I just called in to let Fram know. I do hope he has taken good care of you.'

She pouted very prettily. 'Oh, yes, but is there no one else who can take over from you? On a Sunday evening, too; it is too bad that an important man like you has to work.'

'Unfortunately accidents and illness take no account of the time of day.'

He had remained standing and after a few minutes of general talk she had no choice but to leave as gracefully as possible, escorted to her car very civilly by Mr van Houben but without the hoped-for invitation to dinner.

He went back into his house deep in thought. He had, of course, no need to go to the hospital that evening; it had been an excuse made in order to refuse his visitor's invitation. There was no reason why he shouldn't have invited her to dinner, which was plainly what she had expected; he knew her only slightly, but she was an amusing companion and it would have passed the evening. He sat down in his chair and Nep, who had retired under a table and growled softly at Mevrouw van der Holle, came and sat beside him.

Mr van Houben bent to stroke him. 'It is a ridiculous thing, but I find that I prefer to sit here with you and think about Caroline. An absurd situation—we hardly know each other and yet I feel I have known her all my life, and what is unfortunate is the fact that she appears to be perfectly happy with the idea of a future with that young Brewster.' He sighed. 'Nevertheless, when I next go to England I shall see her.' He glanced down at the little dog. 'Do you consider that I am too old for her, Nep?'

Nep's short brisk bark was reassuring.

The last two days of Caroline's visit passed pleasantly enough; the van Houbens had many friends; there were people to lunch, a picnic on the Monday and a drive along the River Vecht so that she could view its scenery and the old houses along its banks, and in the evening more people came over for drinks, and ample time to play with little Marc. She was glad that she had seen him again, for he had made a splendid recovery and he was happy with Tine. When it was time to say goodbye she went with real regret; she was unlikely to see the van Houbens again, and indeed it seemed to her that Marc should be allowed to forget her—she belonged to a period in his short life which he would remember only vaguely. She would write from time to time, she assured Mevrouw van Houben, and would never forget him or them. She went back to England laden with flowers and parting gifts without anyone once mentioning Marius van Houben, and she hadn't summoned up enough courage to ask. What would have been the point in doing so anyway? she asked herself.

Casualty was so different from the wards that it took her a few days to adjust to its ways. It was almost always full; old ladies who had tripped up and broken wrists or legs, babies who had been scalded by a carelessly placed teapot or kettle, toddlers who had poked beads up their small noses or into their ears, the victims of street fights when the pubs closed, neglected cuts, boils, poisoned fingers and drunks, and over and above these the street accidents. The nurses were frequently run off their feet, driven remorselessly by the senior sister, middle-aged, and domineering and never at a loss, however awkward the situation. There was a junior sister too, just as efficient but a good deal more pleasant to her staff. As for the nurses, there were several part-time staff nurses as well as two full-time ones and three student nurses, of whom Caroline was the most junior. She knew none of them well; seldom did Sister speak to her; she was sent hither and thither from one patient on to the next, for most of the time not sure what she was doing and, since the other three nurses weren't disposed to be helpful, muddling along as best she could and going off duty thankfully and wishing heartily that she didn't need to go back. Airing her grievances with her friends off duty, she was given a good deal of sympathy.

'We all know how beastly Old Moss can be.' Old Moss was the Senior Sister. 'She's been there for twenty years and can't imagine life outside Casualty—Sister Taylor's scared of her and anyway there's always a rush on down there—no time to be friendly.' Janey spoke cheerfully. 'Rush around with everyone else, love, and think about the good time you had in Holland.'

Caroline had been doing that already; not so much thinking about Holland as about Mr van Houben. He would be away from home and she wondered what he was doing. Working in a hospital? Being consulted? Giving lectures to eager students? What exactly would he be doing when he wasn't doing any of these things? The world, she reflected gloomily, was full of attractive young women, any one of whom would make a splendid wife for an eminent medical man.

'I wish I'd never met him,' she muttered as she cleared a dressing trolley, aware that she wished no such thing.

She had been back for a week when she had days off and went to Basing.

Aunt Meg's solid form looked safe and comforting as she got out of the train at Basingstoke and Caroline almost ran across the platform to hug her.

'Well, well,' said that lady bracingly, 'it's nice to see you again, love—it seems a long while since you were home, but that's because you've been in Holland.'

She led the way out of the station. 'There's a bus in ten minutes; we can just get it, I fancy. Only two days, I suppose? Well, that's better than nothing, and they say it will be fine and warm for the rest of the week.' She glanced at Caroline's rather pale face. 'You look as though you could do with some fresh air.'

The bus was half empty; the early evening bus had taken the workers home already and those who were staying in Basingstoke for a meal or a film would take the late evening one. Caroline and her aunt sat side by side, not saying much but pleased to be in each other's company. Something wasn't quite right, reflected Aunt Meg, and she hoped that Caroline would tell her what it was before she went back to the hospital. She was far too wise to ask.

It was the following evening before Caroline talked about her trip to Holland. It had been a lovely day and now, in the early evening, they were sitting in the garden at the back of the house with Theobald on Aunt Meg's lap.

'It was nice to see Marc so well,' observed Caroline, apropos of nothing much. 'He seems to have made a complete recovery, and Tine is just right for him.'

'He remembered you?'

'Yes—it was just as if I hadn't been away. I hope he'll forget me now, though—after all, he's still only a little boy; in a year or two he will have forgotten his illness, and that will be a good thing.'

'What about you? Will you forget him, love?'

'Oh, no. It was an experience, but it has nothing to do with my way of life although I enjoyed it.'

'The van Houbens will be eternally grateful to you,' said Aunt Meg in her sensible way. 'Besides, you will meet Mr van Houben at the hospital from time to time and get news from him, I dare say.'

Caroline said, too quickly, 'Oh, I am most unlikely to see him again; he wouldn't come to Casualty, and besides, we—that is…he…' she sighed '… I think he doesn't like me—he's always polite and kind but that's all.' She added rather wildly, 'We haven't anything in common.'

What has that to do with falling in love? reflected Aunt Meg, and made a soothing reply. For that was undoubtedly what was the matter with Caroline; she was

of course unable to speak for Mr van Houben, but he
had, as far as she knew, remained heart-whole until now
and he must have had the opportunity to fall in love a
dozen times with the kind of young woman Caroline
was not, and apparently he hadn't. She was an optimistic soul; she gathered up her knitting, begged Theobald
to get off her lap and suggested that they went indoors
for their supper.

Two days' peace and quiet in Aunt Meg's company
did a lot to restore Caroline's good sense; she didn't like
Casualty but she wouldn't be there forever, and once
she had found her feet and didn't have to keep asking
where things were kept she might even enjoy it, and indeed, after another week she was beginning to find that
the work was to her liking. There was rarely a leisurely
moment while she was on duty and there was no question of finding the work monotonous; she marvelled at
the variety of people she encountered during the day's
work and, since she was willing and good-tempered,
even Sister Moss forbore from criticising her more than
once or twice a day. And once the other nurses realised
that she had no interest in the casualty officer they were
disposed to be quite friendly.

It was a Sunday evening, half an hour short of going
off duty, when a woman came in with three small children. Sister was in her office, Staff Nurse had the weekend off and the two nurses on duty with Caroline had
gone to their suppers, for it had been an unusually quiet
period and they could be brought back quickly enough
in an emergency.

The woman came in slowly, youngish, dressed in
bright cheap clothes, her hair badly in need of washing,
and heavily made-up. The children were too thin, and

ill dressed, and Caroline longed to pop them into a bath and then into bed with nice clean nighties.

She crossed to where the woman was standing. 'Can I help?'

The woman said belligerently, 'You're a nurse, aren't you? It's Tracey 'ere. 'Asn't been too well for a bit; now she's got a cough and don't eat—keeps me awake at night, she does—perfect little nuisance.'

None of the children looked particularly healthy but Tracey was easy to spot; she stood between the other two children, holding their hands, her pale face even paler by reason of her red-rimmed eyes, her small nose running.

'Come into this cubicle,' suggested Caroline, 'and I'll fetch Sister.' She put Tracey on the couch.

Sister Moss was writing the report and was annoyed at being disturbed, but she put her pen down and went to look at the child.

'Get her undressed and into a gown,' she told Caroline, 'I'll get the CO down to have a look at her.'

She went away and Caroline began peeling off the few clothes Tracey was wearing. They were very dirty, and she put them into a plastic bag and wrapped the skinny little body in a clean gown. The child would be admitted, she felt sure; her temperature was high and her breathing was far too rapid. Besides that, she had noticed faint brown marks on the child's body.

The CO, called from his supper, came within five minutes with Sister Moss. Caroline could see that he was tired and on the verge of ill temper and Sister Moss made things worse by stating firmly that Caroline would see to him as she had her report to finish.

The CO gave Caroline an impatient look, although he sounded civil enough. 'Well, what is it all about?'

Caroline didn't waste words: temperature, breathing, cough, brown marks and dirt were described in less than a minute as he bent to look at Tracey.

He stood up presently. 'Broncho-pneumonia and from the look of that ear she's got a nasty infection there.' He gave Caroline a quite friendly look. 'Smart of you to spot the brown marks—we'll have to admit her. Neglected measles with its complications.' He turned to the woman, 'Now, Mrs White—I want to know when Tracey was first ill. Did you call a doctor? And the other children...?' He glanced at Caroline. 'Get Sister to admit the child, Nurse. I'd better take a look at these two while they are here. Now, Mrs White...'

Sister Moss was snappy after a long day. She was crosser still when Sister Crump said they couldn't have the child until they had a side-ward emptied. 'You'd better clean the child up,' she told Caroline, 'and then wait with her until they are ready for her. The night staff nurse will be on duty shortly. Her junior can take over from you.'

So Caroline went back and started to clean up Tracey; it would take several good warm baths to get the child clean but at least she removed the grime from the small face and gently washed as much of her as possible. The child was too ill to cry and Caroline was relieved when the porters came for her. Her mother didn't go with her; the CO had persuaded her to wait with the other two children until the social worker could come and take them to a hostel. From all accounts the woman was incapable of looking after the children, both of whom were probably harbouring measles too; to let them return to what was almost certainly an unsuitable home was quite out of the question. Caroline thankfully left the social worker dealing with the problem and went off duty at last. She hadn't been relieved; there had been a road accident in and both nurses were fully occupied.

She had her days off the next weekend and went home thankfully. It had turned warm and Casualty had been busier than ever, so that most of her off duty had been after a day's work, too late to go to Victoria Park and get a breath of air. She told herself that she would make up for that over the weekend.

Aunt Meg gave her a critical look. 'You look washed out, love. I don't think that Casualty does you any good. Can't you get moved?'

'Only when they say so. It's been a bit hot indoors all day; I'll be fine after a couple of days here.'

However, by Sunday evening she didn't feel fine despite the hours spent out of doors. All the same, she declared that she felt much better and went back to the hospital, lay wide awake for most of the night with a headache and in the middle of an exceptionally busy morning fell down in an untidy heap, fainting for the first time in her life.

Several of the patients waiting to be seen screamed, Staff Nurse came running and the CO, emerging from one of the cubicles, scooped her up and put her on one of the couches.

She didn't say, Where am I? when she opened her eyes. 'So sorry,' sighed Caroline. 'So silly. I'm quite all right now.'

She was prevented from saying anything else because Staff Nurse had thrust a thermometer under her tongue. The CO read it. 'Any headache?'

'Well, yes.'

'Sore throat?'

'Yes.' She nodded, and, being told to do so, opened her mouth for him to peer inside.

'Koplik's spots—you've got measles. That child just over a week ago.' He turned to Staff Nurse. 'Nurse will have to be warded.' He looked down at Caroline. 'Had them as a child?'

'Yes. But not badly—I was about six years old, I think.'

'Well, Dr Wright will look after you.' Dr Wright was the senior medical consultant. 'I'll see Sister. You'll be as right as rain in a couple of days.'

She didn't feel well; she was taken to a side-ward on Women's Medical, helped to undress, and slid thankfully between the sheets to fall into an uneasy sleep at once, only to be roused to take antibiotic pills and be examined by Dr Wright, who was a nice old thing and called her 'little lady' despite the fact that she looked like a hag. She went to sleep again and didn't wake when the SNO came to look at her and, after her, at intervals and without permission, such of her friends as were able to gain access to the ward on some excuse or other.

Corinna heard of it during dinner and, being Corinna went to Women's Medical, walked boldly into the ward while Sister was in her office and went to look at Caroline. She was asleep still, her long hair loose from its plait, her face shiny with sweat, a blotchy red rash making her pale face seem even paler. Corinna stood looking at her for a minute or so and then, since Sister had just come on to the ward at the far end, went down the fire escape to the ward below where she was working, went to Sister's office and asked if she might go to her room and change her apron, as a patient had been sick all over it: Sister viewing her apronless person, agreed absent-mindedly, busy writing up patients' notes.

The nearest phone was in the porter's lodge and she had always been on good terms with the head porter. Besides, he knew that Mr van Houben was her cousin and was an important man, even if he wasn't a regular consultant on the hospital staff. Corinna dialed a number and waited until she heard Fram's voice, when she asked him to fetch Marius.

'He's having his lunch,' objected Fram.

'It's urgent, Fram…'

'Now what?' asked Marius a moment later. 'It must be something very urgent to phone me at this time of day.' He sounded amused. 'What have you done, Corinna?'

'It's not me—it's Caroline. She's ill. I've just been to see her—she caught measles from some child in Casualty—she looks awful. I thought you would want to know.'

Mr van Houben was no longer amused. 'Very perceptive of you, my dear. How long has she been ill?'

'She fainted on duty this morning; she's warded. Dr Wright's seen her.'

Marius sounded very calm. 'Good. Now let me see, there's a theatre case this afternoon and an appointment in Rotterdam tomorrow at three o'clock. I'll be over sometime tomorrow morning, probably early.'

'You'll never get there and back…'

'Easily—I'll charter a plane.'

Corinna was serious for once. 'You didn't mind me phoning you? I thought, well, you have seen quite a lot of each other while she looked after Marc.' She tried again, 'What I mean is, if it were Fram or Breeze you'd want to know about them, wouldn't you?'

'You did quite right, Corinna, one should look after one's own.' He added in a kind voice, 'Don't worry, dear, she's in the best possible hands.'

They said goodbye and he went back to his lunch but after a moment pushed back his chair and declared that he was no longer hungry. 'I'd like coffee in the study, Fram. Miss Frisby is ill and I must make arrangements to go to England and see her.'

Sitting at his desk with the faithful Nep's chin on his shoes, Mr van Houben suppressed a natural desire to leap on to the first fast-moving vehicle there was and get to Caroline without delay and studied his schedule. If he flew over in the early hours of the morning he could be back in good time to get to Rotterdam by three o'clock.

'You see, Nep,' he explained to the little dog, 'I must go to her. I know she will have young Brewster to hold her hand but I must be sure that she gets the very best treatment.' He sighed. 'Is it not unfortunate that I should find myself in love with a girl in a million who already has the admirable young Brewster waiting to scoop her up and rush her off to Birmingham?'

He picked up the phone and set in train everything necessary to get him to the hospital by the next morning.

Caroline felt very ill and she really didn't care if she lived or died, slipping in and out of fitful sleep, aware of being made to drink and swallow pills and of feeling far too hot. Her throat was filled with barbed wire too, and the various voices telling her that she should feel better soon did nothing to convince her that would be the case. She was aware of Dr Wright standing by the bed but she couldn't be bothered to speak to him, only dozed off again.

It was barely seven o'clock in the morning after an endless night that she opened her swollen eyelids and saw Mr van Houben standing there looking down at her.

'So there you are—and about time too,' she said, and closed her eyes again and was instantly asleep, suddenly convinced in her feverish head that everything would be all right now.

He had gone, of course, when she woke up again, and since she was convinced that she had dreamt the whole thing she didn't ask if it had been a dream or not.

Aunt Meg, neat in beige and not a hair out of place, was no dream, however. Caroline saw her sitting there when she woke again and this time her throat was bearable and she felt quite clear in the head.

'I thought it was Mr van Houben,' she whispered.

'So it was, love. But that was this morning, very early; he's gone back to Holland.'

'Oh—why?'

Her aunt chose to misunderstand her. 'He has his work like everyone else.'

'I feel better,' said Caroline and went back to sleep again.

Mr van Houben, back at his home again after his appointments in Rotterdam, went to his study and shut the door. He had, with a terrific effort, erased Caroline from his mind while he dealt with a particularly difficult case to be anaesthetised, but now he allowed himself to reflect upon his visit. The sight of her pale face blotchy with the measles rash, eyes puffed up and hair tied back, lank and terribly lustreless, had wrung his heart. He had wanted to pick her up and carry her off to his home until she was better and then marry her out of hand. The strength of his feelings for her left him speechless, so that Sister, standing beside him, had begun a résumé of Caroline's treatment, under the impression that something had annoyed him.

He eased a foot carefully from under Nep's whiskery chin. 'How could I have been so blind?' he asked the little dog, 'and now she has the worthy Brewster to care for her. In due course he will carry her off to Birmingham and he will be a good husband and father to their children, and because I shall encounter him from time to time—for undoubtedly in the years to come he will make his mark—I shall be reminded of her, even meet her again. I have only myself to blame, have I not?' He gave Nep a pat at his answering bark.

Then he added, 'The least we can do is to send her some flowers.'

He picked up the phone and ordered roses, lilies, freesia and sweet-smelling carnations and then he dialled again this time to Dr Wright.

His flowers were the first thing she saw when she woke the next morning and the sight of them made her feel better at once. Then Corinna, coming to see her despite the strict rule that no one was to go near her for fear of infection, poked her head round the door, declaring that she looked better. 'Who are the lovely flowers from? Surely not Dr Brewster?'

'They were here when I woke up...'

Corinna nipped into the room and picked up the card by the bouquet.

'They're from Marius. "Best wishes for a speedy recovery".'

'How did he know that I had the measles?'

Corinna turned innocent blue eyes upon her. 'No idea— Oh, probably he and Dr Wright rang each other about something or other.'

'How kind of him.' Caroline closed her eyes and went to sleep again. She slept a great deal, waking only to drink what was offered to her and to try and eat the minced chicken and junket and yoghurt presented to her at intervals. She wasn't hungry and she wanted to be left alone, but pills and potions were proffered every few hours and Dr Wright came far too often, accompanied by the SNO, and once, after a day or so, by Mr van Houben.

Caroline was still feverish, but awake after a refreshing nap, stared up at him and said, 'I don't need an anaesthetic…'

He looked down at her, unsmiling, and it was Dr Wright who answered with a fatherly smile, 'Mr van Houben is over here to give a lecture; naturally he wished to see you so that he could reassure Marc's parents.'

Of course that was his only reason for coming to see her. She felt the tears pricking her eyes and swallowed them back so that she was able to say politely, 'It was very kind of you to send the flowers. I'm really very much better.'

Mr van Houben studied her thoughtfully. Perhaps she didn't look quite as wrung-out as previously, but she still looked what in hospital parlance was described as poorly. The rash was fading to an unattractive pale brown and a high temperature had caused her eyes to sink into their sockets. They were as beautiful as ever and nothing could destroy the beauty of the curling lashes or the gentle curves of her mouth. Her hair was deplorable, though, and the tip of her nose was pink. Nothing in his impassive face allowed her to see that he found her enchantingly beautiful and that he was head-over-heels in love with her.

He said in his calm way, 'I'm glad to hear that; Emmie will be delighted to know that too. They all sent their love.'

He smiled kindly and went away with Dr Wright, and presently Sister came to see how she was and found her in tears.

'Tired you out, did they?' she wanted to know. 'Nurse shall bring you a nice drink and you just have another nap.'

She didn't sleep but lay with her eyes shut, thinking about Mr van Houben, and when she opened them again there was another great bouquet of flowers. Its accompanying card was lying on the coverlet under her hand and she picked it up and read it. It was from Bartus and Emmie, and to her annoyance she felt the tears welling into her eyes again; she had hoped that the flowers were from Mr van Houben. 'So silly,' she muttered. 'He's already sent some.'

The staff nurse, finding her in tears, scolded her gently, changed her nightie and sat her up in bed. 'Not to worry, now, measles often leaves you weepy. Your aunt's coming this evening for half an hour. Even though you feel rotten, you're over the worst.'

Caroline agreed meekly; she was over the worst of the measles, she reflected tiredly, but how long would it take to get over Mr van Houben?

Aunt Meg, coming presently, brought a brisk common sense with her which made Caroline ashamed of her self-pity. 'Another week,' declared that good lady, 'and you will be allowed home—a week of good fresh air will put you back on your feet in no time.'

Caroline assured her aunt that she was very much better. 'You're a dear to come all this way—you will take a taxi to the station, won't you? It can be a bit rough around here in the evenings...'

'No need. Marius came for me; he has to see someone or other here and he will drive me back presently.'

'Is he coming up here to fetch you?' Caroline tried not to sound eager.

'He said he'd send a message when he was ready.'

'Oh, yes—of course. How is Theobald?'

He was discussed at length and then Caroline said, 'I'm to get out of bed for an hour tomorrow; I'm sure I'll be able to come home in about a week's time. I'll get Robert to drive me down.'

Aunt Meg let this pass; she had listened to Marius van Houben while they had driven up to the hospital and had drawn her own conclusions. She began a soothing chat about the garden.

Mr van Houben hadn't purposely avoided young Brewster, although he had no wish to meet him, but coming from the consultant's room he came face to face with him.

The young man wished him a polite good evening and Mr van Houben, well mannered even when not feeling like it, agreed and paused to ask how he was settling in.

'Oh, getting the hang of things, sir, in fact I'm liking it very much.'

'Good. You will return to Birmingham when you have finished here?'

'Yes—I hope to apply for a post there—a flat goes with it, which means that we can marry—we've waited almost two years…'

Mr van Houben, on the point of bidding him goodbye, paused. 'Two years?'

Robert Brewster looked sheepish. 'Well, we got engaged although I'd only just qualified—Miriam said that being engaged would give us a good solid reason for planning for the future. I must say that I miss her very much; in fact I wanted to give the whole thing up and go back to her when I first came here, but Caroline—Nurse Frisby, sir—made me stick to it. Miriam and I are everlastingly grateful to her for her friendship—the two of them get on like a house on fire—she's to be a bridesmaid…'

Mr van Houben registered a strong resolve to make Caroline a bride before that could happen, but beyond lending a sympathetic ear to his youthful companion's enthusiastic talk he said nothing, but presently parted with young Brewster, who went on his way reflecting that old van Houben wasn't such a bad stick, even if he hadn't much to say for himself.

As for Mr van Houben, he took himself off to Women's Medical where he spent five minutes charming Sister before going to the side-ward where Caroline lay, listening dreamily to Aunt Meg's soothing account of the garden's prolific crop of salad vegetables.

His, 'Hello, Caroline,' was uttered in a casual manner, but the sight of him sent the colour into her white face and he was pleased to see that. 'On the mend?' he asked cheerfully, and eyed her deliberately. 'I must say you do look more yourself.'

'I look a fright, so you need not pretend,' said Caroline peevishly. 'Aunt Meg said you weren't coming...'

'Otherwise you would have combed your hair and powdered your nose. Never mind.' He smiled at her in a kindly fashion and noted with hidden delight that her spirit was returning. 'Has the rash all gone?'

'Yes, and my temperature is down and I'm going home very soon.' She spoke snappily; he could at least appear sympathetic instead of being horrid. She wasn't sure that he wasn't secretly laughing about something too. What had possessed her to fall in love with such a tiresome man?

She wouldn't look at him, so she didn't see his slow smile, but Aunt Meg, an interested spectator, did.

'You'll be wanting to go home,' she said, and got to her feet. 'I'm so glad you're better, love. I'll come again in two days; perhaps you'll know when you're coming home by then.' She bent and kissed her niece and Mr van Houben watched her, debating whether he might do the same, but, much though he wanted to, he resisted the temptation. It wouldn't be fair; Caroline wasn't well enough to know her own mind for the moment. He could wait.

Chapter 9

Caroline continued to improve; despite her small size she was healthy and strong and once she was pronounced fit enough to get out of bed she quickly found her feet, ate everything offered to her and slept soundly at night. Indeed, her progress was so rapid that Dr Wright saw no reason why she shouldn't go home and complete the good work there.

'Two weeks,' Caroline told Aunt Meg when she came to see her during the week. 'Sick leave, not holidays. I can hardly wait.'

Which wasn't quite true; the sensible part of her couldn't wait to get away from the hospital, the quicker the better, and perhaps by the time she got back Mr van Houben would have gone to Holland, for he was still in London, her various friends had told her that, but he had made no effort to come and see her and why should he? she asked herself unhappily while at the same time wishing to remain as long as possible on the ward in case he might visit her. Of course, he didn't. Aunt Meg came for her quite early in the morning, helped her pack a case after suitably thanking Sister and the nurses and offering the usual box of chocolates, and followed the porter carrying her case to the entrance.

When Caroline had asked what time their train was her aunt had been evasive. 'Oh, plenty of time for that,' she had declared, and went on to the business of stating her opinions on the hospital's surroundings.

'Well, yes, I know,' said Caroline, 'but there are masses of buses all day and the Underground isn't far...'

'No need of that,' observed her aunt as they went through the doors. Breeze was there, standing by an immaculate Rover. He bade her good morning, expressed the hope that she was well again, smiled at Aunt Meg, took the case from the porter and held the door open for them to get in.

Caroline hesitated for so long that her aunt was constrained to give her a gentle shove from behind. 'So kind of Marius,' she observed comfortably, 'lending us Breeze and his car. He kindly fetched me this morning.'

'Is Mr van Houben in London?' asked Caroline.

'Oh, yes, dear. Several engagements, I believe. What a busy man he is. Did he come and see you?'

'No,' said Caroline. She would have liked to add something to that but she wasn't sure what to say, and anyway she was saved from doing so by Breeze getting into the driving seat and asking if they were quite comfortable, and, if she was rather silent as they drove to Basing, her aunt made no comment.

The village looked charming, and, after the drab

streets around the hospital, doubly so. The cottage gardens were full of flowers and the trees were in full leaf. Breeze pulled up sedately in front of the garden gate and Theobald came to meet them. Caroline scooped him up and he sat purring against her shoulder as they all went into the cottage.

'You will have a cup of coffee?' asked Aunt Meg of Breeze. 'And I baked an apple cake… I'm sure I can't compete with Mrs Breeze's cooking; I hear from Mr van Houben that she is quite splendid.' She ushered Breeze into a chair. 'And you sit down too, love, you mustn't overdo things for a few days. You have had measles, no doubt?' she addressed Breeze.

'Indeed yes, Miss Frisby, when I was a nipper, as you might say. A very nasty thing it is too. It is a great relief to us all that Miss Caroline has made such a speedy recovery.'

He didn't stay long and he didn't mention Mr van Houben's name once.

She had been home for four days and was already looking more like herself, with colour in her cheeks, and her hair, shining from frequent washing and brushing, tied back in a long pony-tail, and since the weather was warm and sunny she had spent her days out of doors and acquired a faint tan. Aunt Meg cooked wholesome food and made sure that she ate it, so that her person, rendered skinny by high fever, began to fill out nicely in all the right places, and although when she thought no one was looking her face was sad, she was bright and cheerful enough in her aunt's company. Now that she felt almost well again she began pottering in the garden, going to the village to shop for her aunt and even riding around on her bike.

'I feel marvellous,' she assured Aunt Meg. 'I'm sure I could cope with anything.'

'Or anyone?' asked her aunt in an offhand way, making it sound like a joke.

'Or anyone,' said Caroline, full of good resolutions. Now that she was away from any chance of seeing Mr van Houben, she told herself that forgetting him would be much easier; she reminded herself of this each day in the vain hope that if she did so Mr van Houben would gradually fade away. Of course he didn't.

He came on a Saturday morning, quite early, bringing with him Robert Brewster. Caroline, picking strawberries in the back garden, looked round to see who it was coming round the side of the house and jumped to her feet, upsetting the bowl of fruit.

She said the wrong thing, witless with delight and desperate to hide it. 'Now look what you've made me do,' she snapped.

Mr van Houben ignored the berries but Robert got down on his knees and began to gather them up. 'A pleasant surprise, I hope,' he said blandly. 'Good morning, Caroline; I have brought young Brewster to see you—such a pleasant day.' He was smiling a little with an air of reproof.

'Oh, yes, well…how nice. Hello, Robert.'

If Mr van Houben had any lingering doubts about Caroline's entertaining more than a liking for Robert, they were put at rest. Nothing could have been more sisterly than her manner towards the young man.

She took the bowl from Robert and said with belated hospitality, 'Do come in, I'm sure you would like a cup of coffee.'

She started across the small lawn between the two

men and her aunt, looking out of a bedroom window smiled. If she had been a betting woman she would have risked her pension backing Mr van Houben. She withdrew from the window and went downstairs to greet her visitors.

'Well, this is a pleasant surprise,' she declared warmly, 'and just in time for coffee too. You don't have to rush back, I hope? There's a farm chicken roasting in the oven and strawberries and cream—you'll stay to lunch?'

Mr van Houben, watching his Caroline's face, replied for both of them. 'That would be delightful. We both happen to be free this morning and young Brewster looked in need of country air.'

'Now isn't that nice?' declared Aunt Meg to no one in particular. 'Marius, would you get the chairs out of the garden shed? And perhaps Mr Brewster—Robert, is it?—would put the table under the apple tree? Caroline, get the cake that you made yesterday, will you?'

Sitting under the apple tree presently with the coffee-pot on the table and the cake—pronounced delicious—nothing but crumbs on the plate, Mr van Houben took stock of Caroline. If he had found her beautiful when she lay on her bed hot and cross and covered in blotches, he found her quite bewitchingly beautiful now. Her hair was tied back, glossy and thick, she had no make-up on, but she really didn't need any; the faint tan and her pink cheeks—rather pinker than usual since he was there—had given her face just what was needed to turn its ordinariness into near prettiness; her eyes sparkled and her person was nicely rounded. She was wearing a cotton dress, a simple well-washed one suitable for pottering in the garden, and her bare feet were thrust into sandals. He wanted to whisk her away and tell her how much he loved her, but he could see that she was still cross; it wasn't the time or the place. Perhaps he shouldn't have taken her by surprise like that.

He was partly right—of course she was cross; if she had known that he was coming she would have pinned her hair into its tidy French pleat, done her face and put on one of her new summer dresses. As it was she looked a fright. She could have wept with rage and love and longing.

She went to replenish the coffee-pot presently and Mr van Houben continued to make easy conversation with his companions, his face pleasantly attentive to what was being said, looking as though he hadn't a care in the world, and when after a while Aunt Meg suggested that Caroline should stroll round the village with their visitors while she kept an eye on the chicken he voiced his willingness to do so in just the right casual voice. Robert echoed him, so there was nothing for it but to walk down to the church. 'Norman,' explained Caroline, 'and there's a sixteenth-century tithe barn a little further on.' When they had admired the barn, she said, 'There's a splendid ruin too, a Saxon castle—it's in the Domesday Book and then it was Norman and after that a Tudor mansion—Cromwell beseiged it for years.' She paused. 'It's a bit far, I think we'd better go back, it's almost lunchtime.'

She had avoided saying anything much to Mr van Houben; now she asked Robert about his Miriam and what his prospects were, and that took them back to the cottage just in time to sit under the apple tree again and drink the sherry Aunt Meg kept for visitors.

Young Brewster had forgotten to be shy; the talk was

light-hearted and over their meal it continued, largely due to Aunt Meg's and Mr van Houben's efforts, for Caroline had very little to say for herself.

Aunt Meg, watching him looking at Caroline from under heavy lids, drew her own conclusions. It was quite obvious that young Brewster treated Caroline like a sister—they were good friends and nothing more—but she felt sure that her niece and this quiet, self-possessed Dutchman shared deeper feelings. Caroline, for some reason known only to herself, was treating him with decided coolness, and he—he was secretly amused by it. Why? thought Aunt Meg, offering coffee. He looked almost smug...

It appeared that they had no need to return until the early evening, and since the pair of them offered to wash the dishes Aunt Meg was constrained to invite them to stay for an early tea.

Sitting comfortably in a basket chair under the apple tree, listening to the subdued sounds of washing-up, she remarked casually to Caroline, 'How pleasant to have such nice visitors—I was afraid you would find it dull here after hospital life. Robert is a pleasant lad—a slave to Marius, of course. Such a good man—Marius, I mean—not young any more...'

'He's nowhere near forty,' said Caroline quickly, not looking at her aunt.

'Good heavens, no—he's in his prime—it is a pity you don't like him, dear.' She sounded gently guileless.

'But I do, I do.' She gave her aunt a beseeching look. 'Please, Aunt Meg, don't let's talk about him.'

'Well, of course we won't if you don't want to, although personally I should like to get to know him better. Such a pity that he lives in Holland, and anyway, he told me that he has been asked to lecture in one of those South American countries—quite a long tour. Chile, was it? Or perhaps it was Colombia. Anyway it's a long way away. A good thing he isn't married.' She looked up to watch the two men coming to join them. 'How very nice to have the washing-up done for us—you didn't find it too tiresome?'

Mr van Houben, who had never washed up in his life before, assured her that it had been no trouble at all. 'Although I dare say we've put everything away in the wrong cupboards and drawers.'

'Never mind that, it will make laying the table all the more interesting. The grass is quite dry if you want to lie on it and take a nap.'

He took her at her word and stretched his vast person in the shade and closed his eyes, and presently Robert said quietly, 'He was up for most of the night; he was called in to anaesthetise a girl who had had her throat cut—very difficult.'

'So I should imagine. What time do you have to be back?'

'I'm on call from six o'clock. Mr van Houben is going out to dinner...' A remark which sent Caroline's imagination into overdrive. Naturally he would know any number of people in London—and by people she really meant women; she had him partnered with a glamorous blonde in no time at all, eating a delicious meal at a fashionable restaurant and going on elsewhere to dance and then driving the beauty back in his Bentley...

'Are you asleep, love?' asked Aunt Meg, 'If you're not, could you make some scones for tea? And there's that fruit loaf...'

Caroline was quite glad to go into the kitchen and

gather together what she would need. The oven turned on to warm up, she made her dough and rolled it out before cutting it into neat rounds with the pastry cutter. While they were baking she could cut the loaf and butter it and lay a tray—it was too nice to come indoors, and as she worked she allowed her thoughts to wander, as usual, to Marius van Houben. Chile, or wherever it was, was a long way away and he would be gone for a long time, she supposed. At least while he was in Holland he could come over to England easily and there would always be the chance that she would see him now and then. Not that that was of much use, she reflected sadly, what with his indifference and glamorous blondes all over the place.

She arranged her scones in neat rows on the baking tray, put it in the oven, started to wash up—and became aware that he was standing in the doorway.

He didn't say anything, so she carried on, casting around in her head for a suitable remark to make.

'Why were you cross?' he asked mildly.

It didn't enter her head to pretend that she didn't know what he meant.

'I hadn't done my face or my hair and I'm wearing an old dress… I wasn't expecting you—anyone…'

'My dear girl, I hardly noticed.'

She was scrubbing the rolling-pin with enormous vigour. 'Oh, I know that.' She wrung out the dishcloth quite viciously and emptied the sink.

'So why should you be vexed?' he wanted to know.

She wasn't going to answer that, instead she said in a stony voice, 'Aunt Meg told me that you are going to Chile. How very interesting.'

'Colombia, actually.'

'I expect you will meet some interesting people.'

'We may not see each other for some time.'

He was leaning against the door, his eyes on her face, so that she turned away to busy herself with seeing if the scones were ready. He had put into words what she already knew; it made it very final.

'Well, yes, I suppose so.' She turned round to face him. 'But that's not important, is it? I mean…' She stopped. It was quite impossible to tell him what she meant.

'You mean?' he prompted.

'Oh, nothing.' She started to slice the fruit loaf. He took the knife from her. 'I'll do that. How delicious these scones smell. It really is most kind of your aunt to let us spend the day. Young Brewster is enjoying every minute.'

She buttered the slices as he cut them. 'Why did you bring Robert?'

'Oh, I wanted to be sure about something.'

She gave him a puzzled look. 'About his work? He's very keen. I do hope he gets that job in Birmingham so that he can get married to his Miriam.'

'I can't see why he shouldn't. He's proving very satisfactory, I hear. You'll miss him?'

'Me? Well, it was nice to have a friend.' She added awkwardly, 'I—I don't go out very much.'

He cut the last of the loaf, took the butter knife from her and took her hands in his, bent his head and kissed her on her astonished mouth.

'Oh,' said Caroline, 'why did you do that? Is it because you're going away—a kind of goodbye?' She was pleased to hear that her voice sounded normal, although she felt as if she had had an electric shock.

She would never know; Robert, anxious to give a helping hand had come into the kitchen intent on carrying trays. Mr van Houben handed him the bread and butter plate and then picked up the tea-tray. 'I'll be back to fetch the scones,' he said.

She had made the tea and taken the scones out of the oven, and was on her way to the apple tree with a dish of jam and a pot of cream for the scones before he returned, and during tea, although she joined in the talk with rather more liveliness than usual, she didn't actually speak to him.

They went directly they had had their tea, their offer to wash up again firmly refused by Aunt Meg. Robert had given Caroline a brotherly pat on her shoulder and reminded her that he would look out for her when she got back to the hospital, but Mr van Houben had bidden her goodbye in a vague and casual manner completely at variance with the kiss he had given her. Watching the car slide away from the gate, she reflected that he was probably an expert at kissing. She had from time to time been kissed, mostly medical students who had just passed their exams or had good news of some sort and were prepared to kiss anyone who happened to be there, but none of them had prepared her for Mr van Houben's expert performance. For that was what it had been, she was sure about that.

She filled the rest of the two weeks with hours of activity, gardening and biking, taking her aunt to Basingstoke to shop, walking old Mrs Tremble's pug dog while she spent a day or two in hospital, shopping and helping with the church jumble sale. Aunt Meg said nothing, only made cheerful conversation about the possibility of future holidays and enlarged upon the pleasures in store once Caroline had taken her final exams. Caroline went back to the hospital determined to let common sense take over from daydreams.

A good thing too, for she found herself back in Casualty once more, run off her feet, for the tourist season was in full swing and although the hospital wasn't in an area frequented by visitors to London there was a lot more traffic in the city and more careless driving, causing an unending stream of street accidents. There was a sprinkling of more adventurous tourists who wished to explore the East End and rather unwisely had chosen the evenings in which to do so, when they were a splendid target for muggers and youths out to make mischief.

After the peaceful orderliness of Basing, Caroline found it tiring and sometimes a little frightening. Casualty, thought of by a great many people as dramatic and exciting, was in reality gruelling hard work and sometimes sad. She did all her work as well as she was able and, with her being a kind girl, the patients liked her, and since she did her fair share the other nurses liked her too. Even Sister Moss, never known to praise, forbore from grumbling at her, although this didn't prevent her from telling Caroline that since she had returned to work on a Tuesday she need not expect her days off until the end of the following week. The off duty, she pointed out was already made out and there was no point in altering it. Caroline had just had two weeks' holiday anyway.

Caroline would have liked to remind Sister Moss that it hadn't been a holiday but sick leave, but she decided prudently to keep her tongue.

She had to admit after the first few days that there was something to be said for Casualty after all; it kept her mind off Mr van Houben, at least while she was at work. Off duty it was another matter; even at the cinema on an evening out with some of her friends his face loomed large before her eyes, so that the film became meaningless.

Two days after her return she met Corinna. 'Better?' enquired the Dutch girl. 'I must say you gave everyone a fright. Emmie phoned last night and she wanted to know if you were back at work. I must tell her that you are, although you still look a little off colour.'

'I'm fine.' Caroline cast discretion to the winds. 'Has Mr van Houben gone to Colombia yet?' She regretted the words the minute she uttered them. 'My aunt mentioned it.'

'Marius? He does get around, doesn't he? Time he settled down and took an interest in a wife and children—I'm always telling him that. He had better be around for the party I'm having when I get back home—only a few weeks now. I bought the most divine dress last week—there's a lovely boutique behind Harrods—I shall look quite beautiful in it.'

She beamed at Caroline, stating an established fact without a trace of conceit. Caroline said that she was sure she would look lovely and if she stayed talking any longer Sister Moss would kill her.

'You don't like it on Casualty?'

'It keeps me busy. Please thank Mevrouw van Houben for her good wishes when you hear from her again.'

'And love to Marc, of course.'

'Oh, of course. I'll never forget him.'

'I don't suppose you'll forget Marius either, will

you?' asked Corinna, so unexpectedly that Caroline went red. 'He's not easily forgettable, is he?'

'I must go,' gasped Caroline. 'Sister Moss…'

She fled, ignoring the rule that no nurse ever ran except for fire and haemorrhage, and she found Sister Moss waiting for her.

'Why have you taken so long to fetch the films from X-Ray?' she demanded. 'Mr Stone is getting very impatient. Take them to him at once and then go along to the end cubicle—there's a carbuncle waiting to be dressed.'

Caroline, going in search of the owner of the carbuncle, reflected that life must be strange to Sister Moss if she saw everyone as an accident or a surgical condition. The carbuncle's unwilling owner was an elderly man with a patient face and a shocking smoker's cough.

'I dare say you smoke a great deal,' observed Caroline in her friendly way.

'Be the death of me, Nurse,' said the man cheerfully.

She changed his dressing, gave him some mild advice about his cough, aware that he would take no notice, and he went on his way.

'I 'opes I gets you next time,' he observed as he went. 'Yer don't nag.'

Caroline was to have the following Saturday and Sunday off and she began to think that they would never come; she was quite sure that once she was away from the hospital she would find it easier to forget Mr van Houben, something she was finding it extremely difficult to do. With all the goodwill in the world she was unable to stop herself from wondering what he was doing, and since this was before she slept, naturally enough she pictured him with a variety of young ladies, handsome creatures, splendidly dressed, with a witty flow of conversation to keep him amused.

'Oh, well, who cares?' said Caroline on Thursday evening, climbing into bed. 'Tomorrow evening I'll be going home.' She curled up in bed. 'I wonder what he's doing?'

Mr van Houben, a man who believed in getting things done once he had made up his mind to something, was giving his registrar lengthy instructions before booking himself and his car on to a midday hovercraft from Calais. He had discovered from Corinna that Caroline would be free at the weekend and would be going home on the Friday evening and he planned to get to the hospital during the late afternoon. That done to his satisfaction, he picked up the receiver and dialled the hospital, had a lengthy conversation with the SNO and then dialled in turn the various hospital governors. Finally he put the phone down and sat back in his chair.

'I hope and expect that the future, both yours and mine, Nep, will be an exceedingly happy one. I do not dare to contemplate otherwise.'

Nep gave a small, encouraging bark.

On Friday afternoon there was still an hour to go before Caroline could go off duty. Sister Moss was in her office and two nurses on duty with her were at the other end of Casualty strapping a sprained ankle. Caroline tidied the cubicles, collected the used linen and began to arrange the clean paper sheets on the couches. She was busy with the last one when she stopped to listen. Someone was coming through Casualty towards her, unhurriedly, and she knew who it was.

She turned round in time to see Mr van Houben draw

aside the curtain and then lean negligently against a wall. His, 'Hello, Caroline,' was uttered with breezy friendliness.

'Hello,' said Caroline and, since she was finding it difficult to speak, she stood staring at him.

Mr van Houben rattled the loose change in his pocket. 'Ready to go off duty?' he enquired pleasantly.

She nodded again. Then, as the silence lengthened asked, 'Shall I fetch Sister?'

'No,' he smiled then, a smile of such gentleness and love that she actually took a step towards him and then paused to ask,

'What do you want?'

'You,' said Mr van Houben.

She went a little pale. 'Oh, no—I mean, I expect I'm just a passing fancy...'

'My dear, darling girl, most certainly I fancy you, I have indeed fancied you for some time and have no doubt of it, I shall continue to do so for the rest of my life. Moreover I'm in love with you, and life without you does not bear contemplation.'

For such a big man he moved very swiftly, and she found herself crushed against his waistcoat and told to look up.

She would have to anyway, for she could hardly breathe, her nose buried in clerical grey cloth. 'That's better,' observed Mr van Houben, and after a moment studying her face kissed her gentle mouth. He took his time, pausing just long enough to ask, 'Will you marry me, my little love?' before kissing her again.

Presently Caroline said, 'Yes, Marius, I will, for I love you too. Only I've thirteen months' training to finish.'

He took off her cap and kissed the top of her head. 'I've dealt with that,' he told her. 'You can leave as from now, with the blessing of the board of governors and the SNO. We must mention it to Sister Moss as we go.'

'She'll never allow me to leave,' began Caroline.

'Don't be a goose, my darling. Put on your cap for the last time and come with me.'

She did as she was told, for there seemed no point in not doing so. She gave a final pat to the paper sheet on the couch and went with him through Casualty to Sister's office.

Mr van Houben had her by the hand and he made no effort to relinquish it. He met Sister Moss's astonished face with a bland smile.

'Nurse Frisby and I are to be married,' he observed in a voice as bland as his smile. 'She is leaving as from today, with the full permission of the board of governors.'

Sister Moss rose from her chair, her complexion dangerously puce.

'I never heard of such a thing...'

'Well, no, I grant you that it is rather unusual, but the board of governors...'

'*You're* on the board, sir,' observed Sister Moss awfully.

'Indeed yes, Sister. You will wish us happy?'

'I don't know what the world is coming to. In my day...' She suddenly looked so forlorn that Caroline leant forward and kissed her cheek. 'I hope you will come to our wedding,' she said.

Walking along the gloomy passage which connected Casualty with the rest of the hospital, Caroline said, 'I hope you don't mind—my asking Sister Moss to our wedding, I mean.'

He stopped to take her in his arms again. 'Ask the entire hospital staff if you wish, my love, only don't waste too much time over it. A week or two…'

'I've nothing to wear—Aunt Meg—and where will we live?'

He brushed away a few untidy wisps of hair and tucked them under her cap. 'Why, in Amsterdam, of course. I promised Nep I would bring you back as soon as possible. Shall we go and see Aunt Meg and then come back to Chiswick? I've an appointment with a rather worthy bishop in the morning—I thought a special licence?'

He smiled down at her. 'Think of poor Nep waiting so patiently.'

'You had it all arranged…?'

'Oh, yes.'

'Supposing I had said no?'

'I would have thought of something else.'

She reached up and kissed him. 'There's no need for that. I said yes.'

* * * * *

SATURDAY'S CHILD

Chapter 1

The room was chilly and severe, as was the woman sitting behind the desk in one of its corners. The desk lamp, which only partly held at bay the fog of the darkened January sky outside, also served to illuminate her features, and the girl who had taken the chair on the opposite side of the desk in answer to the woman's brisk nod occupied herself in giving her interviewer a softer hair-style, appropriate make-up and a more becoming dress. These alterations, mused Miss Abigail Trent, as she admitted to that name, would take away at least ten years from the age of her unconscious interviewer, who looked up and repeated, 'Your age, Miss Trent?'

'Twenty-four.'

'Your education?'

Abigail murmured the name of a well-known girls'

boarding school. When her father had been alive there had been money enough…

'You are State Registered?'

Abigail nodded and when asked to give the name of her training school mentioned a famous teaching hospital in London.

'Have you family ties?'

She thought of the two cousins in Canada; they sent her Christmas cards each year, but they could hardly be described as ties, nor, for that matter, could Uncle Sedgeley, her mother's brother, married to a peer's sister and landed gentry, and totally disapproving of her father, her mother's marriage to him and to Abigail herself. She said quietly in her pleasant voice: 'No,' and when she was asked what branch of nursing she had most recently been in, said: 'Surgery—the operating theatre too.'

'You're willing to travel?'

It sounded like the beginnings of an advertisement in the Personal Column of *The Times*. She said, 'Certainly,' and smiled at the woman, who didn't smile back but looked at her watch as though time was rationed for her interviews and she had used it all up on Abigail. She got up briskly and went across to the filing cabinet against one wall and started pulling out its drawers. Presently she came back with a small folder and sat down again. 'I think we could offer you a post immediately if you are prepared to take a medical case. A patient in Amsterdam—an American woman staying with friends there, in their flat. She has been in hospital with severe gastric symptoms and is now back with them—still in bed, of course, pending the doctor's decision. She didn't care for the hospital, for she speaks no Dutch and found the regulations a little trying. She is, I gather, rather...' She wisely left the sentence unfinished and went on: 'You will be paid twenty pounds a week and receive your board and lodging, and she is prepared to pay your fare at the end of a fortnight. The flat is, I believe, in one of the best parts of the city. You will have two and a half hours free every afternoon, and such other times as you can arrange for yourself. Should you take the post, you will pay this agency twelve and a half per cent of your salary until such time as you leave.'

She finished speaking and sat, tapping her ballpoint on the blotting pad in front of her. After perhaps half a minute she enquired, 'Well, Miss Trent, do you care to take the case?'

It wasn't quite what Abigail wanted, although she hardly knew what she did want—only to get away from London—from England, for a while, so that she could adjust herself to a future which no longer held her mother. And she needed the money. She got to her feet. 'Yes, I'll take it,' she said. 'When do you want me to go?'

'Please sit down again.' The woman looked more severe than ever. 'I'll give you the patient's name and address and advise you on the easiest way of getting to the case. I suggest that you fly over early tomorrow, so that you will arrive in Amsterdam by lunch time—that should give you time to unpack, see your patient and begin your duties without delay.'

Abigail blinked the fine silky lashes of eyes which were her sole claim to beauty in an otherwise ordinary face. They were brown and large and the brows above them were silky too. But her nose was too short, her mouth too wide and her hair too mousy to give her even a modicum of good looks. She wasn't sure at this moment if the change would be for the better; probably not, but she could always go back to hospital again. She held out a hand in its slightly shabby glove and took the papers which the woman was holding out to her.

Two minutes later she was outside in the street, standing rather uncertainly on the pavement while the passersby pushed and jostled her first one way, then the other; not meaning to treat her roughly, but intent on getting to wherever they were going as quickly as possible. Presently she crossed the road, drawn by the cheerful lights of a Golden Egg restaurant, and went inside. It was almost twelve o'clock on this damp and foggy day in the first week of January; lunch in a pleasant warmth seemed a good idea. She chose egg and chips and coffee and while she was waiting for them got out her little notebook and started doing sums. Twenty pounds a week would be a godsend; she hadn't earned any money at all for three months now. When her mother had fallen ill, she had given up her job at the hospital and stayed at home to nurse her, because the doctor had told her that her mother had only a few months to live anyway, and Abigail couldn't bear the thought of her living out those last few weeks in some strange hospital bed. She had gone home for almost three months, and her mother had had every small comfort and luxury she wished for or needed, and Abigail had spent what money she had saved, which wasn't much, to pay for them. Her mother's pension had paid the rent of their small flat and the household expenses, but when she had died there had been nothing left at all. The furniture went with the flat, her mother's jewellery, never very valuable, had been sold over the last five years, and Bollinger, who had served her father faithfully until his death and had refused to leave them after it, was owed almost a year of his low wages. The funeral had taken almost all the money she had, and now today, barely a week later, she had gone out to get a job, and it had had to be private nursing—that way she would get her board and lodging free and would get paid sooner.

The egg and chips arrived and she ate them, still doing sums in her head. She would just about be able to get to Amsterdam and have a pound or two in her purse until she was paid. Two weeks wasn't long to wait, and anyway it didn't look as though she was going to get much free time in which to spend her money. Even when the twelve and a half per cent had been deducted, she would still be able to send Bollinger some money. He would retire now, she supposed, but he would only have his old age pension, and that wouldn't go far in London. She began to worry about where he would live; after that night they would have to leave the flat and she wasn't going to leave him to struggle on his own after the years of service he had given them, and he had been so kind and helpful to her and her mother. The food on her plate became dimmed by the tears in her eyes, but she fought them back and doggedly went on eating the chips on her plate and drinking the coffee she didn't want any more.

She took a bus back to the flat, the small top flat just off the Cromwell Road where they had lived since her father died and Abigail had started her hospital training. As she put her key in the front door at the top of the long flights of stairs, she could hear Bollinger in the kitchen; he came to its door as she went inside and said comfortably:

'There you are, Miss Abby, the kettle's on and I

treated us to some crumpets. Nothing like a nice hot crumpet.' He went back to the gas stove. 'How did it go?'

'I've got a job, Bolly—twenty pounds a week, in Amsterdam, nursing an American woman. I'm to go tomorrow, and isn't it lucky I've still got my passport from that trip we had to Ostend? So everything's going to be OK.' She cast her coat and hat over the back of one of the wooden chairs at the table and went to get the teapot from the dresser. 'Now, about you—did you manage to find anything?'

'I did—the woman at the paper shop, remember her? She's got a daughter with a house just round the corner from here. I can have a room and me meals with her and her husband. Four pounds and fifty pence a week—leaves me plenty, so don't you worry your pretty head about me.'

She looked at him with deep affection, loving him for the cheerful lie. He was almost seventy, she knew, and he had worked very hard around the flat since they had moved into it, shopping and cooking and repairing fuses and waiting on her mother hand and foot. It was impossible to repay him, but at least she would see that he got the money which they owed him and then a small weekly pension after that so that he could find a proper home and not some small back room where he would be lonely. Years ago he had been her father's gardener and odd job man, and when her father had died he had somehow stayed on with them, smoothing her mother's path, offering practical advice when it was discovered that there was no money at all, and Abigail had never quite discovered how it was that he had persuaded her mother to keep him on at such a ridiculous wage.

She made the tea and they sat down together with the plate of crumpets between them. 'I'm glad you've got somewhere to go for the present,' began Abigail. She opened her handbag. 'They gave me five pounds in advance on my salary,' she went on mendaciously. 'I've got more than enough and this'll help you to get started, then each week, once I get my pay, I shall send you some money,' and when he began to protest, 'No, Bolly dear, you're my friend and you were Mother's and Father's friend too—I can well afford to pay you back the wages we owe you and then pay you a little each week. It won't take me long, you see, for I get my room and my food for free, don't I? And in a little while I'll get a hospital job again and perhaps we can find a small place and you can come and run it for me while I work.'

She smiled at him, trying not to see that he was getting quite elderly now and wouldn't be fit to do much for many more years—something she would worry about when the time came, she told herself vigorously. She poured more tea and said cheerfully: 'How funny Uncle Sedgeley was yesterday. I wonder what he and Aunt Miriam would have done if I'd accepted their invitation to go to Gore Park and stay with them? They hated Father, didn't they, because he was a Methodist parson and hadn't any worldly ideas and they hadn't been near…' She paused, unable to bear talking of her mother. 'Aunt Miriam told me how fortunate I was that I had a vocation, for all the world as though I'd taken a vow not to marry.'

'Of course you'll marry, Miss Abby,' said Bollinger, quite shocked.

'That's nice of you to say so, Bolly, but I'm afraid she may be right, you know. I'm twenty-four and I've never had a proposal—nothing even approaching one. I'm a sort of universal sister, you know, because I'm plain.'

'You're talking nonsense, Miss Abby. You just haven't met the right man, that's all. He'll come, don't you fret.'

'Yes? Well, when he does I shan't marry him unless he lets you come along too,' she said firmly. 'Now let's go and see this room of yours and then I'll treat us to the pictures.'

A remark which would have shocked Uncle Sedgeley if he could have heard it; to go to the cinema barely a week after her mother's funeral—unthinkable! She could just hear him saying it, but it didn't matter what he thought; her mother would have been the first one to suggest it. Life went on and you didn't forget someone just because you sat in the stalls and watched some film or other without seeing any of it, and at least it would be warm there and infinitely better than sitting in the little flat talking, inevitably, of old times with Bolly, something she couldn't bear to do.

She said goodbye to him the next morning and started her journey. She had booked her flight when she had left the agency, obedient to the severe woman's instructions, and had packed her case with the sort of clothes she considered she might need, adding the blue uniform dresses and caps and aprons she had been forced to buy, and now on the plane at last, she got out her little notebook again and did some anxious arithmetic. With luck she wouldn't have to spend more than the equivalent of a few shillings; stamps for her letters to Bollinger, small odds and ends for herself. She hoped that her patient might need her for more than two weeks—three, or even four weeks at twenty pounds a week would mount up nicely, and they were going to pay her fare too. She closed the little book, opened the newspaper the air hostess had handed her and read it with grave attention, fearful of allowing her thoughts to wander, and was surprised when far below she saw the flat coast of Holland, glimpsed through the layers of cloud.

Schiphol, she discovered, was large, efficient and pleasantly welcoming. With hundreds like her, she was passed along the human conveyor belt which eventually spilled her into the open air once more, only to be whisked up once more into the waiting bus which would take her to Amsterdam. It covered the ten miles to the capital with a speed which hardly gave her time to look around her and she got out at the bus terminus, still not quite believing that she was in Holland. It seemed such a very short time ago since she had said goodbye to Bollinger, as indeed it was.

Mindful of her instructions, she took a taxi to the address in the Apollolaan. It was, she quickly discovered, away from the centre of the city, for they quickly left the bustling, older part behind, to drive through modern streets lined with blocks of flats and shops. When they stopped half way down the Apollolaan, she got out, paid the driver from her small stock of money and crossed the pavement to enter the important-looking doorway of the building he had pointed out to her. It was of a substantial size, and from the cars parked before it, inhabited by the well-to-do, and inside the thickly carpeted foyer and neatly uniformed porter bore out her first impression. He greeted her civilly, and when she mentioned her name, ushered her into the lift, took her case from her and escorted her to the fourth floor. Here he abandoned her, her case parked beside her, outside the door of number twenty-one—occupied, according to the neat little plate at the side of the door, by Mr and Mrs E. Goldberg. Abigail drew a heartening breath and rang the beautifully polished bell.

The door was opened by a maid who, in answer to Abigail's announcement of her name, invited her to enter, waved her to a chair, and disappeared. Abigail looked at the chair, a slender trifle which she felt sure would never bear the weight of her nicely rounded person, and stood looking around her. The hall was carpeted even more lushly than the foyer; the walls were hung with what she considered to be a truly hideous wallpaper, embossed and gilded, and as well as the little chair she had prudently ignored, there was a small settee, buttoned fatly into red velvet, and another chair with a straight back and a cane seat which looked decidedly uncomfortable. A wall table of gold and marble occupied the space between two doors, burdened with a French clock and matching vases. Abigail, who had a nice taste, shuddered delicately and wished that her mother could have been with her and share her feelings. For a moment her opulent surroundings faded to give place to the little flat in the Cromwell Road, but she resolutely closed her mind to her memories; self-pity helped no one, she told herself firmly, and turned to see who was coming through the door on the other side of the hall.

It had to be Mrs Goldberg, for she looked exactly like her name. She was middle-aged, with determinedly blonde hair, blue eyes which were still pretty and a baby doll face, nicely made up, which, while still attractive, had lost its youthful contours. She smiled now, holding

out her hand, and when she spoke her voice was warm
even though its accent was decidedly American.

'Well, so you're the nurse, my dear. I can't tell you
how glad we are to have you.' She added dramatically,
'I am exhausted, absolutely exhausted! Night and day
have I been caring for our dear Clara—she is so sensitive, you know, we couldn't leave her in hospital, although I'm sure they were kindness itself to her, but
she's used to the little comforts of life.' The blue eyes
looked at her a shade anxiously. 'We hope that the worst
is over; Doctor Vincent will be in after lunch and this
evening he'll bring a specialist—the very best to be
got, I assure you—to see dear Clara, and he'll decide
whether to operate or not.' She paused to take breath
and Abigail asked quickly: 'You'd like me to take over
immediately, I expect? If I could go to my room and
change...'

Mrs Goldberg smiled widely, showing a hint of gold
tooth. 'My dear, will you? I simply must rest. We lunch
at half past twelve—so early, but when in Rome, I always say—If you could get into your uniform and make
poor Clara a little more comfortable?'

'Of course.' Abigail smiled understandingly, hoping at the same time that Mrs Goldberg might suggest
a cup of coffee or tea. Half past twelve was an hour
away and she was, while not exactly tired, in need of a
few minutes to collect herself, but Mrs Goldberg made
no such offer, but followed her from the hall and into
a short passage and so to her room. It was nice, with a
view over the Apollolaan and comfortable anonymous
furniture so often found in guest rooms, and it had the
added attraction of a bathroom next door. As soon as
she was alone Abigail unpacked her uniform, washed

her face and hands, put her mousy hair up into its tidy bun, perched her frilly cap on top of it, buckled her belt around her trim waist and with a nicely made-up face, went back into the hall.

Mrs Goldberg must have been waiting for her; she appeared suddenly, like a cheerful outsize fairy, from one of the doors and said approvingly:

'My, how quick you've been, and what a quaint outfit—that cap, it's not a bit like our nurses wear back home.'

Abigail explained quickly that her hospital took pride in allowing its trained nurses to wear that particular headgear—it had been worn for a very long time and no one, least of all the nurses, wanted it changed.

'Mighty becoming,' commented Mrs Goldberg, 'it sure will tickle poor Clara pink.'

Abigail, following her companion through another door, wondered if her patient felt well enough to be tickled by anything. At first sight it seemed not. Mrs Clara Morgan lay uncomfortably hunched against far too many pillows. Some of these she had tossed to the floor, the remainder were crowding into her back, which probably accounted for her petulant expression. She acknowledged Mrs Goldberg's introduction languidly and said tiredly, 'I'm glad you've come, Nurse, I'm very poorly and I need a great deal of skilled care and attention.'

Abigail murmured suitably and enquired if the doctor had left any message for her.

'No,' said Mrs Goldberg, 'because he'll be here in a couple of hours. Clara will tell you all about herself, won't you, Girlie?'

Abigail judged it a good idea to get her oar in be-

fore her patient did, for she looked ill and tired and that
was probably why she looked peevish. Her voice was
persuasive. 'Would you like me to give you a bed-bath
and a fresh nightie and make you more comfortable?
You'll feel better for it.'

Her patient agreed, and while she submitted to Abigail's kindly hands, discoursed at length upon her condition, its seriousness, the possibility of an operation, the
need for her to return to the States as soon as she could,
and the kindness of her friends the Goldbergs. That
there was a thick thread of self-pity winding through
her narrative was natural enough; it hadn't taken Abigail long to gather that her patient was rich, spoilt and
self-indulgent. She had, it transpired, been widowed
twice, and, a still attractive woman in her early forties,
was prepared to marry again should she find someone
she liked sufficiently. Abigail listened without envy,
because it wasn't in her nature to be envious, and a
certain amount of pity, because it seemed to her that
Mrs Morgan was lonely too, despite her silver-backed
hairbrushes and silk nighties and enormous bottles of
perfume. But talking cheered her up, and by the time
Abigail had smoothed the last wrinkle from the sheets,
she declared that she felt a new woman.

'I do believe we're going to get on just fine,' she declared. 'I must admit that the idea of an English nurse
didn't appeal to me, but I'll admit to being mistaken,
though your uniform is pretty antiquated, isn't it?'

Abigail admitted that perhaps it was. 'They're trying
to change the uniforms in England, but you see, some
of the hospitals are very old and they like to keep their
own, however old-fashioned. Especially the caps—it's

like a regimental badge, everyone knows which hospital you were trained at just by looking at your cap.'

'Well, I must say whoever thought of yours had a nice eye for something sexy.'

Abigail was folding towels neatly. No one had ever called her cap sexy before! She remained silent, non-plussed, and then said:

'I think a nice milky drink, don't you? I'll go along and see about it.'

Milk and water, in equal proportions with afters of Mist. Mag. Tri., were her patient's portion for lunch. Abigail measured carefully, arranged the two glasses on a little tray with a pretty cloth and bore them away to the sickroom, where she put the tray on the bed table, together with a selection of novels, the daily paper and a handful of glossy magazines, and then, quite famished, found her way to the dining room.

Mr Goldberg had come home to lunch. A small fat man with large glasses and a fringe of greying hair, possessed of a charming smile. Abigail liked him at once and wasn't surprised to hear that he was something important to do with a permanent trade mission—anyone with a smile like that deserved to have a top job! They sat her between them at a large rectangular table and plied her with food. It was cold and grey outside, but here in the warm, over-furnished room, there was no need to think about the weather. She drank her soup, accepted a glass of wine and embarked on beef olives while she listened to her host and hostess and made polite replies to their questions whenever they asked them, which was frequently. She would have liked to have lingered over coffee with them, but she was on a job, after all. She excused herself and went back to her patient to find her asleep.

It seemed a good opportunity to unpack her few clothes and scribble a quick note to Bolly; most likely she would have the chance to post it before bedtime; if not, surely the hall porter would do it for her. She wrote the address with a little lump in her throat, because Bolly would probably be sitting by himself in that dreadful little back room with no other view than the house behind.

Dr Vincent came shortly afterwards. He was a tall man in his thirties, with regular features and an excellent command of the English language. He was obviously relieved to see Abigail and after he had examined Mrs Morgan and talked to her for a little while, he retired to the sitting room with Abigail so that he might discuss their patient. They sat opposite each other, on the edge of over-stuffed and very large easy chairs, because to sit back in them would have meant a complete loss of dignity on both their parts and the doctor was nothing if not dignified. He took her carefully through the ins and outs of Mrs Morgan's illness. 'This evening a specialist will come, Nurse—I shall of course accompany him. He is a consultant surgeon at several of our big hospitals and very well known. I feel that his opinion will be invaluable. It would be a pity for our patient to undergo an operation unless it is absolutely necessary. If we can get her well enough, she would much prefer that she should return to the United States with all speed. You are prepared to stay here until she returns, I hope?'

Abigail said that yes, she was. 'What have they in mind?' she wanted to know. 'A gastrostomy? Surely if

it's a bad ulcer they'll have to do an end-to-end anas-
tomosis.'

Dr Vincent eyed her warily. 'I think, Nurse, that we
must leave such things for Professor van Wijkelen to
decide.'

With a name like that, Abigail thought flippantly, a
man ought to be able to decide anything. He would have
a beard and begin all his remarks with -er. She would
probably dislike him. Dr Vincent was speaking again,
so she listened carefully to his instructions and forgot
about the professor.

He came that evening, an hour or so after her patient
had had another glass of milk and water with its attendant powder, and Abigail herself had had a short break
for her own tea. Mr and Mrs Goldberg were out, and it
had been brought to her on a tray in the sitting room. It
had been pleasant to sit down for a little while on her
own, while she had it, and then have the time to tidy
herself, powder her ordinary nose and put on more lipstick. The results weren't very encouraging, she considered, looking in the bedroom mirror. She had gone back
to her patient's room and taken her temperature and
pulse, and sat her up more comfortably against her pillows, and was on a chair in her stockinged feet, reach-
ing for a vase of flowers which someone had placed
out of reach, and which, for some reason, Mrs Morgan
had taken exception to, when there was a knock on the
door and Doctor Vincent came in. The man who came
in with him eclipsed him completely. He was a giant
of a man, with a large frame which radiated energy despite the extreme leisureliness of his movements. He
was handsome too, with pale hair, thickly silvered at
the temples, a high-bridged nose and a well-shaped,

determined mouth. His expression was one of cold ill-humour, and when he glanced up at her, still poised ridiculously on the chair, Abigail saw that his eyes were blue. It struck her with something of a shock that they were regarding her with dislike.

She got down off the chair, the flowers clutched in one hand, hastily put them down on one of the little tables which cluttered the room, crammed her feet into her shoes and reached the bedside at the same time as the two men. Doctor Vincent introduced the professor, adding a corollary of his talents, and Mrs Morgan, suddenly interested, shook hands. 'And our nurse,' went on Doctor Vincent, 'arrived from England today and is already, I see, attending to the patient's comfort. Miss Trent, this is Professor van Wijkelen, of whom I spoke.'

She held out her hand and he shook it perfunctorily and said nothing, only looked at her again with the same cold dislike, before sitting on the side of Mrs Morgan's bed and saying, 'Now, Mrs Morgan, will you tell me all your troubles, and perhaps Doctor Vincent and I can help you to get well again.'

His voice was charming, deep and quiet and compelling, and Mrs Morgan was nothing loath. Her recital, with various deflections concerning her own personal courage in the face of grave illness, her fears for the loss of her good looks and the fact that she had been twice widowed, took a long time. The professor sat quietly, not interrupting her at all, his eyes upon her face while she talked. He seemed completely absorbed and so, to his credit, did Doctor Vincent, who, Abigail guessed, must have heard the tale at least once already. She herself stood quietly by the bed, a well-trained mouse of a girl, her eyes, too, on her patient, although she would very much have preferred to fix them upon the professor.

Mrs Morgan finished at length and the professor said, 'Quite, Mrs Morgan,' and went on to ask her several questions. Finally, when he was satisfied with the answers, he turned to Abigail and asked her to prepare Mrs Morgan for his examination. He asked courteously in a voice of ice; Abigail wondered what had happened to sour him and take all the warmth from his voice as she bent to the task of getting Mrs Morgan modestly uncovered while the two men retired to the window and muttered together in their own language.

'He's ducky,' whispered Mrs Morgan, and then sharply, 'Don't disarrange my hair, honey!'

She lay back, looking, to speak the truth, gorgeous. Abigail, obedient to her patient's wish, had been careful of the hair; she had also arranged her patient's wispy trifle of a bedjacket to its greatest advantage. Now she stood back and said briskly, 'Ready when you are, sir,' and watched while the professor conducted his examination. He prodded and poked gently with his large, square hands while he gazed in an abstracted fashion at the wall before him. At length, when he had finished and Abigail had rearranged Mrs Morgan, he said: 'I think that there will be no need for an operation, but to be quite sure there are several tests which it will be necessary to do, and I am afraid that they must be done in hospital.' He paused to allow Mrs Morgan to pull a pretty little face and exclaim:

'Oh, no, Professor—I was so utterly miserable when I was there just a week ago, that's why I engaged Nurse Trent here.'

'In that case, may I suggest that you take her with

you to hospital? She can attend you during the day
and I am sure that we shall be able to find an English-
speaking nurse for night duty. I should suppose that
three or four days should be sufficient, then you can
return here to await the result of the tests. If they are
satisfactory, a week or so should suffice to see you on
your feet again and well enough to return home.'

'If you say so, Professor,' Mrs Morgan's voice was
just sufficiently plaintive, 'though I'm sure I don't know
how I shall get on in that hospital of yours. Still, as you
say, if I take Nurse with me, I daresay I'll be able to
bear a few days.'

She smiled at him after this somewhat frank speech,
but he didn't smile in return, merely inclined his head
gravely and offered his hand.

'You'll come and see me again, Professor?' Mrs Morgan was still smiling. 'I sure feel better already, you've
a most reassuring way with you.'

If the professor was flattered by this remark he gave
no sign. 'Thank you, Mrs Morgan. I think that there is
no necessity to see you again until you enter hospital.
I will arrange that as soon as possible and you will of
course see me there.'

'I look forward to that—and be sure that I have a private room. I'm so sensitive, I can't bear the sights and
sounds of hospital, Professor.'

He walked to the door and then turned to face her
with Doctor Vincent beside him. 'I feel sure that Doctor Vincent will arrange everything to your liking, Mrs
Morgan, and you will have your nurse to shield you
from the—er—sights and sounds you so much dread.'
His smile was fleeting and reluctant, a concession to

good manners, and it didn't last long enough to include Abigail. He nodded curtly to her as he went away.

Surprisingly, he came the following day, late in the afternoon when Abigail had returned from her few hours off and was sitting with her patient, reading the *New York Herald Tribune* to her. She read very nicely in her quiet voice, sitting upright in a truly hideous reproduction Morris chair. She had enjoyed her afternoon off, and wished that her patient lived in one of the old houses beside the canals, because she would have dearly loved to see inside one of them. The flat in the Apollolaan was comfortable to the point of luxury, but all the same, she wouldn't have liked to live in it for ever, but the brick houses with their gabled roofs reflected in the still waters of the *grachten*—they were a different matter; it would be wonderful to live in their serene fastness.

The morning had been successful too; Mrs Morgan seemed to like her, for she had chatted animatedly while Abigail performed the daily nursing chores, talking at great length about Professor van Wijkelen. 'A darling man, Nurse,' she mused. 'I must find out more about him—such good looks and such elegance.' She smiled playfully at Abigail. 'Now mind, dear, and tell me anything you should hear about him. You're bound to find out something in the hospital, aren't you?'

Abigail had said that probably she would, provided she could find someone who could speak English. She had gone to lunch with Mr and Mrs Goldberg after that, and they had asked her a great many questions about her patient and seemed, she thought, a little relieved that dear Clara was to leave them for a day or two. Without someone in constant attendance, she must have put quite a strain on their good-natured hospitality.

Mrs Goldberg had asked her kindly if she had everything she needed and to be sure and say if she hadn't and then told her to hurry out while she had the chance. And Abigail had, wrapped in her well-cut but not new tweed coat against the damp cold winds of Amsterdam. She hadn't been able to do much in two hours, but at least she knew where she would go when next she was free; the complexity of *grachten,* tree-lined, their steely waters overlooked by the tall, quaintly shaped houses on either side of them, needed time to explore. There was no point in looking at the shops, not until she had some money to spend, but there was enough to see without spending more than the price of a tram fare.

The knock on the bedroom door had taken them both by surprise. Mr and Mrs Goldberg were both out, neither Abigail nor her patient had heard the maid go to the front door. She came in now and said in her basic English, 'A person for the *Zuster.*'

Abigail put down the paper, which she was a little tired of anyway, saying: 'Oh, that will be instructions from the hospital as to when we're to go, I expect. I'll go and see about it, shall I?' and followed the maid out of the room. The visitor was in the sitting room. Abigail opened the door and went in and came to a standstill when she saw the professor standing before the window, staring out.

'Oh, it's you!' she declared, quite forgetful of her manners because of her surprise, and was affronted when he answered irritably:

'And pray why should it not be I, Nurse? Doctor Vincent has been called out unexpectedly and finds himself unable to call, and I had to come this way.'

'Oh, you don't have to explain,' Abigail said kindly, and went on in a matter-of-fact voice, 'You'll want to see Mrs Morgan.'

'No, Nurse, I do not. I wish merely to inform you that there will be a bed in the private wing tomorrow afternoon. Be good enough to bring your patient to the hospital at three o'clock. An ambulance will fetch you— you will need to bring with you sufficient for three days, four perhaps. Be good enough to see that Mrs Morgan fasts from midday tomorrow so that no time is wasted.'

He spoke shortly and she wondered if and why he was annoyed, perhaps because he had had to undertake Doctor Vincent's errand, although surely he had a sufficiency of helpers to see to such mundane things as beds... He looked very arrogant and ill-humoured standing there, staring at her. She said briskly, 'Very well, sir—and now if you'll excuse me, I'll go back to my patient.'

He looked faintly surprised, although he didn't bother to reply. Only as she started for the door did he ask, 'What is your name?'

She barely paused. 'Trent, sir.'

He said impatiently, 'I am aware of that—we met yesterday, if you care to remember. What else besides Trent?'

It was on the tip of her tongue to tell him to mind his own business, but she wasn't given to unkindness and perhaps he had some very good reason for looking so irritable all the time. 'Abigail,' she offered, and watched for his smile; most people smiled when they discovered her name; it was old-fashioned and quaint. But he didn't smile.

'Why?'

'I was born on a Saturday,' she began, a little worried because he wasn't English and might not understand. 'And Abigail...' She paused. 'It's rather a silly reason and I don't suppose you would know...'

He looked more annoyed than ever, his thick almost colourless brows drawn together in a straight line above a nose which to her appeared disdainful.

'You should suppose nothing. I am sufficiently acquainted with your English verses—Saturday's child has to work for her living, eh? and Abigail was a term used some hundreds of years ago to denote a serving woman, was it not?'

'How clever of you,' said Abigail warmly, and was rewarded with another frown.

'And were your parents so sure that you would be forced to work for your living that they gave you this name?'

She said tight-lipped, because the conversation was becoming painful:

'It was a joke between them. You will excuse me now, sir?'

She left him standing there and went back to her patient, who, on being told who the visitor was, showed her displeasure at not receiving a visit, although she brightened again when Abigail pointed out that she would see a good deal of him in hospital once she was settled in there. They spent the rest of the day quite happily, with Abigail opening and shutting cupboards and drawers in order to display various garments to her patient, who, however ill she felt, intended to look as glamorous as possible during her stay in hospital. It was much later, when Abigail had packed a few things for herself that, cosily dressing-gowned, she sat down before her dressing-table to brush her hair for the night. She brushed it steadily for some time, deep in thought, and she wasn't thinking about herself, or her patient or Bollinger, but of Professor van Wijkelen. He was the handsomest man she had ever seen, also the most bad-tempered, but there had to be a reason for the look of dislike which he had given her when they had met—as though he had come prepared to dislike her, thought Abigail. She finished plaiting the rich thickness of her mousy hair and stared at her face in the mirror. Plain she might be, but in an inoffensive manner—her teeth didn't stick out, she didn't squint, her nose was completely unassuming; there was, in fact, nothing to cause offence. Yet he had stared at her as though she had mortally offended him. She put the brush away and padded over to the bed, thinking that she would very much like to get to know him better, not because he was so good-looking; he looked interesting as well, and for some reason she was unable to explain she found herself making excuses for his abrupt manner, even his dislike of her. She got into bed wondering sleepily what he was doing at that moment—the idea that he was a happily married man dispelled sleep for a few minutes until she decided that he didn't look married. She slept on that surprisingly happy thought.

Chapter 2

The hospital was hidden away behind the thickly clustered old houses and narrow lanes of the city. It was itself old, although once inside, Abigail saw that like so many of the older hospitals in England, it had a modernised interior despite the long bleak corridors and small dark passages and bare enclosed yards which so many of its windows looked out upon. Mrs Morgan's room was on the third floor, in the private wing, and although small, it was well furnished and the view from its window of the city around was a splendid one. Abigail got her patient safely into bed, tucked in the small lace-covered pillows Mrs Morgan had decided she couldn't manage without, changed her quilted dressing-gown for a highly becoming bedjacket, rearranged her hair, found her the novel she was reading, unpacked her case and after leaving the bell within reach of her, went to find the Ward Sister.

Zuster van Rijn was elderly, round, cosy and grey-haired, with a lovely smile and a command of the English language which Abigail found quite remarkable. They sat together in the little office, drinking the coffee which one of the nurses had brought them, while Zuster van Rijn read her patient's notes and charts and finally observed:

'She does not seem too bad. Professor van Wijkelen never operates unless it is necessary—he is far too good for that, but she must have the tests which have been ordered—she can have the X-ray this afternoon and the blood test—tomorrow the test meal—just something milky this evening for her diet. You're to stay with her, the professor tells me.'

'Yes, Mrs Morgan is a little nervous.'

Zuster van Rijn smiled faintly. 'Yes,' her voice was dry. 'There's a room ready for you in the Nurses' Home—would you like to go there now? There is nothing to do for Mrs Morgan for half an hour and one of the nurses can answer the bell. I will tell Zuster de Wit to go over with you.'

Abigail went back to her patient, to explain and collect her bag, and then followed the nurse down one flight of stairs, over a covered bridge, spanning what looked like a narrow lane of warehouses, and so into the Nurses' Home. Zuster de Wit hurried her along a long passage and then a short one to stop half way down it.

'Here,' she said, and smiled as she flung open a door in a row of doors. The room was comfortable although a little dark, for its window overlooked another part of the hospital, but the curtains were gay and it was warm and cheerful. Abigail smiled in return and said, 'How nice. Thank you,' and Zuster de Wit smiled again, said

'Dag' and hurried away. Obviously she had been told to waste no time. Abigail, listening to her rapidly disappearing feet, hoped that she would be able to find her own way back to the ward again as she began to unpack her things. She had bought only a modicum of clothes—mostly uniform and her thick winter coat and a skirt and sweater, boots and the knitted beret and scarf she had made for herself during the weeks she had nursed her mother. It took only a few minutes to put these away and another minute or so to powder her nose and tuck her hair more tidily under her cap. It was almost four o'clock, as she shut the door she wondered about tea—perhaps they didn't have it; there were several things she would have to find out before the day was over. She went back over the bridge and found her way to her patient's room, to find her asleep.

Working in an Amsterdam hospital was almost exactly the same as working in her own London hospital; she had discovered this fact by the end of the day. Once she had become used to addressing even the most junior nurses as 'Zuster' and discovered that she was expected to say 'Als t'U blift' to anyone she gave something to, and 'Dank U wel' each time she was given something, be it instructions—mostly in sign language—or a thermometer or a holder for the potted plant someone had sent her patient, she felt a little less worried about the problem of language. She had had to go without her tea, of course—they had had it at three o'clock, but she went down to supper with the other nurses at half past six; a substantial meal of pea soup, pork with a variety of vegetables, followed by what Abigail took to be custard and as much coffee as she could drink.

She went back to the office to give her report and

then returned to sit with Mrs Morgan who was feeling a little apprehensive about the test meal. At half past eight, just before the night nurse was due on duty, a house doctor came to see the new patient and a few minutes later Doctor Vincent. He listened patiently to her small complainings, soothed her nicely, recommended her to do as Abigail told her, and went away again, and presently when the night nurse came and Abigail had given her a report too, she went herself, over the bridge to the Nurses' Home and to her room.

She hadn't been in it for more than a minute when there was a knock on the door and the same nurses she had seen at supper took her off to their sitting room to watch TV which, although she was tired, Abigail found rather fun because Paul Temple was on and it was amusing to watch it for a second time and listen to the dubbed voices talking what to her was nonsense. For so the Dutch language seemed to her; she had been unable to make head or tail of it—a few words and phrases, it was true, she had been quick enough to pick up, but for the most part she had had to fall back on basic English and signs, all taken in very good part by the other nurses. It had been a great relief to find that the night nurse spoke English quite well; enough to understand the report and discuss Mrs Morgan's condition with Abigail, and what was more important, Mrs Morgan seemed disposed to like her.

After Paul Temple she was carried off once more, this time to one of the nurses' rooms to drink coffee before finally going to her own room. She slept soundly and got up the next morning feeling happier than she had done for some time; it was on her way down to breakfast that she realised that the uplift to her spirits was largely due to the fact that she would most probably see the professor during the course of the day.

Her hope was to be gratified; he passed her on the corridor as she made her way to her patient's room after breakfast. She saw him coming towards her down its length and watched with faint amusement as the scurrying nurses got out of his way. When he drew level with her she wished him a cheerful good morning and in reply received a cold look of dislike and faint surprise, as though he were not in the habit of being wished a good day. Her disappointment was so sharp that she took refuge in ill temper too and muttered out loud as she sped along, 'Oh, well, be like that!'

She found her patient in good spirits; she had slept well, the night nurse had understood her and she had understood the night nurse, and the Ryle's tube had been passed and the test meal almost finished. The night nurse, giving the report to Abigail in the privacy of the nurses' station further down the corridor, confided in her correct, sparse English that she herself had enjoyed a quiet night and had got a great deal of knitting done. She produced the garment in question—a pullover of vast proportions and of an overpowering canary yellow. They had their heads together over the intricacies of its pattern when the professor said from behind them:

'If I might have the attention of you two ladies—provided you can spare the time?' he added nastily.

The Dutch girl whipped round in much the same fashion as a thief caught in the act of robbing a safe, but Abigail, made of sterner stuff and unconscious of wrongdoing, merely folded the pullover tidily and said:

'Certainly, sir,' which simple remark seemed to annoy him very much, for he glared at her quite savagely.

'You are both on duty, I take it?' he asked.

'No, me,' said Abigail ungrammatically in her pleasant voice. 'We've just discussed the report and Night Nurse is going off duty.'

'When I need to be reminded of the nurses' routine in hospital, I shall say so, Nurse Trent.'

She gave him a kindly, thoughtful look, her previous temper quite forgotten. Probably he was one of those unfortunate people who were always ill-tempered in the early morning. She found that she was prepared, more anxious to make excuses for him.

'I didn't intend to annoy you, sir,' she pointed out to him reasonably, and was rewarded with a sour look and a compression of his well-shaped mouth.

'The test meal,' he snapped, 'when is it complete?'

She looked at her watch. 'The last specimen is due to be withdrawn in fifteen minutes' time, sir.'

'If the patient doesn't tire of waiting for your return and pull the Ryle's tube out for herself.'

'Oh, no,' said Abigail seriously, 'she'd never do that—you see, I explained how important it was for her to do exactly as you wish. She has a great opinion of you.'

Just for a moment she thought that he was going to laugh, but she must have been mistaken, for all he said was, 'I want Mrs Morgan in theatre at noon precisely for gastroscopy. The anaesthetist will be along to write her up. See that she is ready, Nurse Trent.'

He turned to the night nurse, who had been silent all this while, and spoke to her with cold courtesy in his own language. She smiled at him uncertainly, looked

at Abigail and flew off down the corridor, leaving behind her the strong impression that she was delighted
to be free of their company. Abigail picked up the report book and prepared to go too, but was stopped by
the professor's voice, very silky.

'A moment, Nurse Trent. I am interested to know
what it was you said in the corridor just now.'

She wished she could have looked wide-eyed and innocent, or been so pretty that he really wouldn't want an
answer to his question. She would have to tell him, and
probably, as he seemed to dislike her so much already,
he would say that he wanted another nurse to work for
him and she would have to go back to England. Did one
get paid in such circumstances? she wondered, and was
startled when he asked, 'What are you thinking about?
I assure you it is of no use you inventing some excuse.'

'I'm not inventing anything. What I said was,' she
took a deep breath, '"Oh, well, be like that."'

'That is what I thought you said. May I ask if you are
in the habit of addressing the consultants in your own
hospital in such a fashion?'

She considered carefully before she answered him.
'No, I can't remember ever doing so before, but then,
you see, they always said good morning.'

She studied his face as she spoke; perhaps she had gone
a little too far, but she didn't like being treated in such a
high-handed fashion. He looked very angry indeed—she
waited for the outburst she felt sure would come and was
surprised when all he said, through a tight mouth, was:

'Young woman, you disturb me excessively,' and
stalked away, leaving Abigail with her eyes opened very
wide, and her mouth open too.

She didn't see him again until she entered the theatre and she thought it unlikely that he would notice her, disguised as she was in theatre gown of voluminous size and nothing visible of her face, only her nice eyes above the mask.

The morning's work had gone exactly to plan. It was precisely noon. Theatre Sister and two nurses were there and of course the anaesthetist—there was to be no general anaesthetic, but Mrs Morgan had had a pre-med and would need a local anaesthetic. He was a nice sort of man, Abigail thought; his English was fluent if a little difficult to understand and he had smiled kindly at her. Mrs Morgan, her hand held in Abigail's comforting grasp, was dozing in her drug-induced sleep; she had joked a little about it before they went to theatre because she would miss seeing Professor van Wijkelen, and Abigail had consoled her with the prospect of further visits from him, for there were still one or two more tests to carry out, though once the professor had done the gastroscopy and had made up his mind whether he needed to operate or not, there wasn't much more to be done.

Abigail arranged the blanket over her patient, turning it down below her shoulders so that it wouldn't get in the surgeon's way once he started. Mrs Morgan made a little whimpering sound and opened her eyes, and Abigail said instantly in a soothing voice, 'It's all right, Mrs Morgan, the professor is just coming.'

He was in fact there, standing behind her, talking quietly to Sister. He finished what he was saying and went closer to his patient, ignoring Abigail completely—something she had expected.

He spoke quietly to his patient. 'You feel sleepy, don't you, Mrs Morgan? We are going to spray your throat now and it will feel numb, but you will feel nothing else—a little uncomfortable perhaps, but that is all. It will take only a short time. Your head will be lifted over a pillow now and I am going to ask you to open your mouth when I say so.'

The small examination went well and Mrs Morgan, whom Abigail had expected to be rather difficult, didn't seem to mind at all when the professor inserted the gastroscope and peered down it, his great height doubled, his brows drawn together in concentration. At length he said, 'That will do. Kindly take her back to the ward, Nurse.'

Which Abigail did, to spend a rather trying few hours because Mrs Morgan was under the impression that the local anaesthetic would wear off in ten minutes or so, and when it didn't she was first annoyed and then frightened. Abigail, explaining over and over again that the numbness would disappear quickly and that no, Mrs Morgan couldn't have a drink just yet, longed for an hour or so off duty. It was already three o'clock; she had been relieved at dinner time, but no one had said a word about her off-duty. Probably the Ward Sister thought that she wouldn't mind as long as someone relieved her for a cup of tea.

The door opened and she looked up hopefully, unaware that her face plainly showed her disappointment at the sight of the professor standing there, for he certainly hadn't come to release her from her duties. She got to her feet, wondering why he stared so, and fetched the chart for him to study. He hadn't spoken at all and since he seemed to like it that way, she hadn't either. She had half expected to hear more about their morning's meeting, but now she rather thought that he wasn't going to do anything more about it. She took the chart back again and stood quietly while he spoke briefly to Mrs Morgan. Presently he turned away from the bed. 'Nurse, I shall want another blood count done and the barium meal will be done tomorrow at two o'clock. Attend to the usual preparations, please. I can find nothing very wrong, but I shall need confirmation of that before I make my final decision.'

She said, 'Yes, Professor,' and admired him discreetly. Forty or more, she concluded, and unhappy—though I don't suppose he knows it.

His voice, cutting a swathe through her half-formed thoughts, asked:

'You are comfortable here, Nurse? Everyone is kind to you? You have your free time?'

'Yes, thank you,' she answered so quickly that he said at once, 'Today?'

'Well, not yet, but I'm perfectly all right. Mrs Morgan is my patient, isn't she, and the ward is very busy. I'm quite happy.'

He said surprisingly, 'Are you? I should have supposed otherwise, although I daresay you do your best to disguise the fact.'

She was appalled, and when had he looked at her long enough to even notice? 'I—I…' she began, and was instantly stopped by his bland, 'No need to excuse yourself, Nurse Trent—we all have our worries and sorrows, do we not—and never as important as we think they are.'

Abigail went brightly pink. She blushed seldom, but when she did, she coloured richly from her neck to the roots of her hair. He watched her now with a detached interest, nodded briefly, and went away.

She was relieved shortly after that and after a cup of

tea in the dining room she tore into her clothes and went out into the city. The night nurse had explained how she could get to the shops in a few minutes; now she followed the little lanes between the old houses, pausing frequently to make sure that she could find her way back again, and came all at once into a brightly lighted street, crowded with people and lined with shops. She spent half an hour peering into their windows, working out the prices and deciding what she would buy when she had some money. That wouldn't be just yet; as soon as she had her first pay she would have to send it to poor old Bollinger. She wasn't happy about his room—it had looked cold and bare and although the landlady seemed kind enough she hadn't looked too clean, and supposing he were to become ill, who would look after him? She stood in the middle of Kalverstraat, suddenly not sure if she should have left him.

Mrs Morgan stayed in hospital for another three days, becoming progressively more cheerful because it seemed unlikely that she would need an operation after all. Besides, the professor visited her each day and she made no secret of her liking for him. He spent ten minutes or so listening gravely while she explained some new symptom she feared she might have, and then courteously contradicted her, impervious to her undoubted charm and quite deaf to her suggestions that he might, in the not too distant future, pay her a visit at her Long Island home. He seldom spoke to Abigail and when he looked at her it was with a coldness which she admitted to herself upset her a great deal more than it should have done.

They went home on the sixth day, this time in Mr Goldberg's Buick motor car; the professor had paid a visit the evening before and had stayed a little longer than usual, reassuring Mrs Morgan as to her future health, and had bidden her goodbye with his usual cold politeness, nodding briefly to Abigail as he went away. On her way off duty, half an hour later, she had seen him in the main ward, doing a round with his registrars and housemen, Sister and attendant satellites of students, nurses, physiotherapist and social worker. He looked very important but completely unconscious of the fact, an aspect of his character which she found strangely endearing.

The days following passed pleasantly enough. Mrs Morgan was out of bed now, although she preferred to keep to her room, walking a little and talking incessantly about her flight to the States, which she anticipated with all the impatience of someone who always had what they wanted when they wanted it. Abigail was impatient too—although she damped it down—for payday. She had had several letters from Bolly and from the sparse information they contained as to how he fared, she guessed that life was being difficult for him. She had already decided that she would send almost all her money to him, for she was almost certain that Mrs Morgan would ask her to stay another week, perhaps longer, and she didn't want him to wait any longer for it. The moment she got back to London she would go to the agency again and ask for another job. She reviewed her plans almost daily, and behind all this careful scheming was the thought that she would never see the professor again once she had left Holland. A ridiculous thing to worry about, she told herself scornfully, for she very much doubted if he would notice if she were there or not. She dismissed him firmly from her thoughts and went out each day, exploring Amsterdam.

It was on the morning that she was due to be paid that Mrs Morgan asked her if she would stay another week. 'I know I don't really need you, honey,' she said, 'but you are such a comfort to have around, and Dolly and Eddy don't need to worry about me at all. I've booked a flight for next week—a week today—if you would stay and see me safely away?'

She opened the crocodile handbag with the gold fittings which looked almost too heavy for her to carry and took out an envelope. 'Here's your salary, honey—I got Eddy to see to it for me. You'd rather have the cash, I'm sure. I bet you've got your eye on something pretty to buy with it.'

Abigail agreed pleasantly. She had grown quite fond of her patient while she had been looking after her and she saw no point in disturbing her complacent belief that the rest of the world lived in the same comfortable circumstances as herself. She put the envelope in her pocket and picked up the guide book of Holland which she had been reading to Mrs Morgan. Later, when she was free that afternoon, she would go to the post office and send the money to Bollinger, and perhaps now that she knew when she would be finished with the case, she should write to the agency and ask if they had anything else she could go straight to. The problem remained at the back of her mind while she read aloud about the delights of Avifauna and the best way of getting there, she was interrupted half way through by her companion telling her with enthusiasm that she intended to return. 'Because,' said Mrs Morgan, 'this is a sweet little country and I must say some of the people I've met are well worth cultivating.' She giggled happily and Abigail, who knew that she was talking about Professor van Wijkelen, smiled politely and wondered what success she would have in that quarter.

With her patient tucked up for her afternoon nap, Abigail was free to go to her room and open the envelope. There was two weeks' salary inside and her fare—but only her single fare. She had expected to be given the return fare and had neglected to ask anyone about it. Perhaps she was only entitled to half her travelling expenses; on the other hand, Mrs Morgan might give it to her with her next week's pay. She put the fare away in her bag, popped the rest into the envelope she had ready and got into her outdoor clothes.

It was cold outside and bleak with the bleakness of January. The clouds had a yellow tinge to them and the wind was piercingly cold. She hurried to the post office some streets away, where there were clerks who spoke English and would understand her when she asked for a registered envelope.

The post office was warm inside. The walk had given her eyes a sparkle and put some colour into her cheeks. She had perched her knitted beret on top of her head and wound its matching scarf carelessly round her throat. She took her gloves off and blew on her cold fingers and went up to the counter.

It took a little while to understand the clerk and then she was so disappointed that she could hardly believe him. She had taken it for granted that she could send either the cash or a money order to Bolly and it seemed she had been hopelessly at fault—she could do no such thing. Go to a bank, suggested the clerk helpfully, where there would be forms to be filled in and a certain amount of delay. But she wanted Bolly to have the money now—within the next day or two. If she waited until she went back herself that was a whole week away—besides, she had promised Bolly. She sighed and the clerk sighed in sympathy and she said, 'Well, thank you very much for explaining. I should have found out earlier, shouldn't I?'

'Can I help?' The professor—she would have known his icy voice anywhere. She whirled round to face him.

'Oh, how funny to meet you here, sir. I don't think so, thank you. It's just something that was my own silly fault anyway.'

'Why should it be funny, Nurse Trent? I also write letters, you know.'

'Yes, I'm sure you do, only—only I should have thought that you would have had someone to post them.'

'Indeed? I am not particularly interested in your suppositions, but I find this one extraordinary. How can I help you?'

Persistent man, he wasn't going to take no for an answer. She explained in a matter-of-fact voice and apologised again for being stupid.

'Why should you be stupid?' he asked irritably. 'You were not to know before you asked. How much money did you want to send?'

'Forty pounds. No—I've got to take some off…' she began to reckon twelve and a half per cent of forty pounds in her head and the amount came different each time she did it. Finally she asked, because he showed signs of impatience, 'How much is twelve and a half per cent of forty pounds?'

'Five pounds. Why?'

'Well, that's what I have to pay the agency for as long as I work for them.'

'Iniquitous! It so happens that I am going over to London this evening. I will take the money, since you seem so anxious to send it.'

She stared at him, astonished. 'But you don't even... you're very kind, but I couldn't trouble you. I shall be going back myself in a week's time.'

The professor tweaked her out of the queue forming behind her.

'Ah, yes—I should be obliged if you would remain in Amsterdam for a further few weeks. I have a patient upon whom I shall be operating in ten days' time, and he will need a special nurse in hospital and probably to accompany him home when he is sufficiently recovered. Your usual fee will be paid you.'

Abigail's voice sounded a little too loud in her own ears. 'But you don't...' She stopped—what had his personal opinion of her got to do with it anyway? He wanted a nurse and she was available. She answered him with her usual calm good sense, 'Yes, Professor, I should be quite willing to stay on for as long as you require me.'

He nodded carelessly, as though he had known all along that she was going to say yes.

'Very well, we will consider the matter settled,' and when she looked at him it was to find him smiling. Perhaps it was because she had never seen him smile that her heart lurched against her ribs and her breath caught in her throat. It transformed his handsome face into one of such charm that if he had at that moment suggested that she should remain in Holland for the rest of her life, she would probably have agreed without further thought. But her idea wasn't put to the test; the smile vanished, leaving him looking more impatient than ever.

'Give me the address of the person who is to receive the money,' he suggested, 'and I will see that it reaches him—or her.'

'Him,' said Abigail, and would have liked to tell him about Bolly, but quite obviously her companion was anxious to be gone. She handed him the envelope with the letter inside and the forty pounds hastily pushed in with it. She had forgotten about the agency fee, but he hadn't.

'Twelve and a half per cent?' he wanted to know.

He really was in a hurry. 'I'll—I'll take it out of my pay next week. You're sure…?'

He interrupted without apology, 'Stop fussing, Miss Trent.' He stuffed the envelope into a pocket with a non-chalance, Abigail thought vexedly, of a man who found forty pounds chicken feed, wished her a curt goodbye and walked away. She began to walk back to the flat, her head bent against the sneering wind, telling herself that the reason she felt so happy was because Bolly would have the money by the following evening, or at the very least, the morning after.

The professor came to see Mrs Morgan three days later. He paid his visit while Abigail was out for her afternoon walk and left no message for her at all. It wasn't until the evening previous to Mrs Morgan's departure that he came again. Abigail was packing her patient's clothes, surrounded by tissue paper, orderly piles of undies, innumerable hats and an assortment of suitcases. Evidently Mrs Morgan never worried about excess baggage. That lady was reclining on the couch, directing operations; she looked very well and remark-

ably attractive, which was more than Abigail felt, for her
head ached and her usually neat hair was a little untidy,
nor had she had the time to do anything to her face for
some time, and over and above these annoyances she
was worried about Bolly; she had had a cheerful letter
from him, thanking her for the money, but she sensed
that he was hiding something from her. She was thinking about it now and frowning—she was still frowning
when there was a knock on the door and Doctor Vincent
and the professor walked in. They both wished her a
good evening and she flushed a little under the professor's brief, unfriendly glance, very conscious that she
wasn't looking her modest best. They stayed perhaps
ten minutes, made their farewells and started for the
door. But this time Professor van Wijkelen made a de-
tour and came to a halt by her and her pile of luggage.

'I understand that you will be taking Mrs Morgan to
Schiphol tomorrow morning. You will be fetched from
there and taken straight to the hospital. Perhaps you can
arrange to have your luggage with you.' His eyes strayed
over the ordered chaos around them. 'I trust you have
a good deal less than this.'

'One case,' Abigail told him briefly, and he nodded.
'I will leave a message for you at the hospital tomorrow,' he stated. 'Good evening, Nurse.'

He had gone before she could thank him for posting her letter.

Mrs Morgan was actually bidding Abigail goodbye
at Schiphol when she interrupted herself to exclaim,
'There, I knew there was something, honey! I've clean
forgot to give you your money.' She made to open her
unwieldy bag, but it was too late; a smiling official indicated the passenger conveyor belt which would take

her one stage nearer the plane. 'I'll post it to you,' she called, waved and smiled and nodded, and was borne swiftly away; so easy for her to say it, thought Abigail a little forlornly, but where would she send the money to? Mrs Morgan knew that she was going to another job, but she hadn't asked for any details and Abigail hadn't volunteered any. Perhaps she would send the money to the agency. If so, would the severe woman who had interviewed her send it on, or would she keep it and expect Abigail to call for it? And what about the rest of her fare—she hadn't had it yet.

She stood pondering, pushed to and fro by the hurrying people around her. She had been silly; she should have asked for her salary and her fare sooner. But she hadn't liked to, even though the money was rightly hers. And now she had landed herself with only a few pounds. Supposing the professor had changed his mind about employing her for his next patient? She had been rash enough to buy herself a pair of shoes the day before, and now she was left with less than her fare to England. She moved at last, back to the reception area to fetch her case. She had been foolish twice over; the professor had said that she would be fetched from the airport, but how was she to know who was looking for her? Supposing they couldn't find her and she was left—supposing they forgot all about her, supposing… Her gloomy thoughts were cut short by the professor's voice. She hadn't seen him, but here he was beside her, taking her case from her as relief as well as delight flooded through her, although her quiet 'Good morning, Professor,' was uttered in her usual voice. She received an ill-tempered grunt in reply and a brief, 'Come along, Nurse,' as he made for the door.

She trotted beside him because otherwise she could never have kept up with him, and to lose him now would be unthinkable. There were a great many cars outside and she wondered which of them was his.

He stopped in front of a black Rolls-Royce Silver Shadow, sleekly and unobtrusively perfect among the other cars, opened its doors, told her to get in with the cold courtesy she had come to believe was the only alternative to his ill-humour, and went to put her case in the boot. He didn't speak when he got in beside her, and was still silent as he edged the car away from the crowded bustle of the airport and on to the main road. They were tearing along the motorway to the capital when she ventured helpfully:

'I expect you came yourself so that you could save time telling me about the patient.'

She looked at him as she spoke and he turned to meet her gaze briefly. She wished that he would smile again, but he didn't, although when he did speak she had the impression that somewhere, deep down inside him, he was laughing. Imagination, she told herself roundly; why should he laugh?

'A doctor,' he stated flatly. 'Professor de Wit, seventy years old. He's to have a gastroenterostomy—CA, of course, but everything's in his favour, he's got a sound heart and chest and a great desire to live. He is to have a room in the private wing and you will be working under Zuster van Rijn with whom you will arrange your off-duty, please.'

Having thus given her the bare bones of the case he fell silent once more, and Abigail, not knowing if he was occupied with the intricacies of the day's operating list, forbore from disturbing him. It was only when he drew up in front of the hospital entrance and called to the porter to come and collect her case that she said:

'Thank you for posting my letter. I heard from—that is, it arrived safely. I'm very grateful to you.'

He looked at her with quick annoyance. 'There's no need to say any more about it,' he stated with such finality that she felt snubbed, so that she too was annoyed. 'I shan't,' she told him crisply. 'Obviously gratitude and thanks are wasted upon you, sir.'

She walked briskly into the hospital, not waiting to see what the porter was going to do about her case. She was half way across the width of the entrance hall when she was amazed to hear the professor laughing. It was a deep bellow and sounded perfectly genuine.

It was surprising to her how quickly she slipped back into the routine of hospital. She had been given the same room again and this time it was so much easier because she knew some of the nurses and they greeted her as an old friend. Zuster van Rijn seemed glad to see her again too; they were short-staffed on the surgical side, she told Abigail, and specialling could be awkward unless there were enough nurses.

'Will you work as you did before,' she asked, 'and take an afternoon off? I know it's not quite fair that you shouldn't work shift hours as the other girls do, but that way I can spare a nurse to take over while you're off duty. There will be the same night nurse as you have already worked with, and you shall have your days off, of course, but how or when I do not know at the moment. You are content?'

'Quite content,' Abigail told her. Days off didn't matter, not for the first week at any rate, for she hadn't any money to spend. The problem of how to get the money

over to Bolly was looming heavily again too; she had
done nothing about it because she had expected to return to England, now she would have to start all over
again. She dismissed her problems and followed Sister,
prepared to meet her patient.

She liked him on sight. He was lying in bed and although his face was pinched and white with his illness,
he was still a remarkably good-looking old man. Ex-
cepting for a thick fringe of white hair, he was bald, but
the fringe encircled his face as well in rich profusion
and his blue eyes were youthful and sharp. She shook
his hand—gently—because she could see that he was
an ill man, and despite his alert expression and merry
eyes, probably in pain as well.

Zuster van Rijn left them together after a few minutes and Professor de Wit said, 'Pull up a chair, my
dear, and let us get to know each other. I believe Dominic wishes me to spend a week in bed before he operates, physiotherapy and blood transfusions and all the
other fringe benefits of his calling which he so generously offers.'

Abigail laughed with him. So the professor's name
was Dominic—she stored the little piece of information away, though what good it would do her she had yet
to discover. She listened to the old man's placid talk in
his slow, almost perfect English and by means of gentle
questions of her own found out that he slept badly, ate
almost nothing, had lost his wife twenty years previously, had a doting housekeeper to look after him, and
a dog and a cat to keep him company, as well as a half-
tamed hedgehog, a family of rabbits and a pet raven.
They were discussing a mutual dislike of caged birds
when Professor van Wijkelen came in.

The two men, she saw at once, were old friends. It was also apparent that the older man trusted the younger completely. He lay listening quietly while the professor told him exactly what he was going to do and why.

'It sounds most promising, Dominic. I gather I am to be a new man by the time you have finished with me.'

'Shall we say soundly repaired, and fit for another ten or fifteen years—and that's a conservative estimate.'

'And what does Nurse say?' It was her patient who spoke.

Her smile lighted her ordinary face with its gentleness and sincerity.

'I never think of failure—Professor van Wijkelen will operate and it will be a complete success, just as he says.' She looked across at him as she spoke and found him staring at her, and there was no mistaking the faint sneer on his face, but because she liked him, she saw the hurt there too. Someone at some time had turned him into a cold, embittered man; she wondered who it was and hated them. Once, just once, he had smiled at her and she wanted him to smile like that again, but that, at that moment, seemed unlikely.

She settled down to a steady pattern of work, the same work as she would have been doing in a London hospital, even though the language was different, but all the doctors and a good many of the nurses spoke English and she herself, with the aid of her dictionary and a good deal of good-natured help from everyone else, managed to make herself understood. The days passed quickly. Under her patient's kindly direction she went each afternoon to some fresh part of the city, sometimes to a museum, sometimes to gaze at the outside of some old house whose fascinating history he had described to her delighted ears while she was fulfilling the various duties which made up her day. He was looking a little better, mainly due to the blood transfusions, to which he submitted with an ill grace because they interfered with his movements in bed. He was a great reader and an even greater writer and a formidable conversationalist. Abigail became fond of him, as indeed did anyone who came in daily contact with him. The day before his operation he paid her, handing her an envelope with a word of thanks and a little joke about him being strong enough to do it the following week, which touched her soft heart because although she had complete faith in Professor van Wijkelen, things quite outside his control could go wrong. She tucked the envelope away under her apron bib and as she did so wondered for the hundredth time why Bolly's last letter had been so strange; asking her not to send him any more money for at least another week. A good thing in a way, because she had not yet discovered the best way of sending it to him, all the same, she felt a vague disquiet.

Professor van Wijkelen came each day, treating her with his usual polite chill, at direct variance to the obvious regard he had for his patient. She stood quietly by while they talked together and longed for the warmth of his voice to be directed just once at herself. A wish which was most unlikely to be fulfilled, she told herself wryly, handing him charts and forms and reports and at the end giving him her own report very concisely in her clear precise voice. He liked to take her report outside the patient's room and did her the courtesy of giving him his full attention. And now, on this day before he was to operate, he listened even more carefully than usual. When she had finished he said, as he always said: 'Thank you, Miss Trent,' and proceeded to give her detailed instructions as to what he wished her to do on the following day.

The operation was a success, although only the next few days would show if the success was to be a lasting one. Abigail had taken her patient to the theatre and remained there to assist the anaesthetist. For a good deal of the time she was free to watch the professor at work. He was a good surgeon completely engrossed in his work and talking very little. When at length he was finished, he thanked the theatre sister and stalked away without a word. He was in his old friend's room within minutes of his return to it, though. Abigail was still getting the old man correctly positioned and adjusting the various tubes and drip when he came silently through the open door.

'I don't want him left, Nurse. I have spoken to Sister— if you wish to go off duty, she will send someone to take over. Is that clear?'

'Perfectly, thank you,' said Abigail, and because she was checking the closed drainage, didn't say any more. She had no intention of going off duty; she had promised Professor de Wit that she would stay with him and she could see no reason why she shouldn't do just that. She was, when all was said and done, his special nurse. Professor van Wijkelen said abruptly:

'He'll do—with careful nursing,' and turned on his heel and left her.

She didn't leave her patient again, only for the briefest of meal breaks and the professor came in twice more as well as his registrar, a portly little man whom Abigail rather liked. He spoke a fluent, ungrammatical English and she got on famously with him and she was grateful to him too, because he came often to check on the patient's condition and cheer her with odd titbits of gossip so that the day passed quickly. It was half an hour before she was due off that Zuster van Rijn came rustling down the corridor to tell her that the night nurse had been struck down with a sore throat and a temperature and wouldn't be able to come on duty, and there was no one to take her place. 'I can put a nurse on until midnight, though, and then she need not come on until the noonday shift. Could you possibly…?'

'Yes, of course,' said Abigail. 'I'll go off at eight, have supper and a sleep and come back here at twelve.'

Zuster van Rijn looked relieved. 'That is good—tomorrow morning I will get someone to take over while you go to bed for a few hours.'

So it was that when Professor van Wijkelen came at one o'clock in the morning, it was Abigail who rose quietly from her chair near the bed. His glance flickered over her as he went to look at his patient; it was only when he was satisfied as to his condition that he asked curtly:

'Why are you on duty? Where is the night nurse?'

'It's quite all right, sir,' said Abigail soothingly. 'Nurse Tromp is off sick and there wasn't time to get a full-time night nurse. I've been off duty, I came back at midnight.'

'Until when?'

'Until I can be relieved. Zuster van Rijn will arrange something.'

'Have you had your days off?'

'I'd rather not have them until the professor is better.' She spoke uncertainly because he was looking annoyed again. 'I imagine that my days off can be fitted in at any time, as I'm not a member of the hospital staff.'

'You have no need to state the obvious, Nurse. You must do as you please and I daresay Zuster van Rijn will be glad if you remain on duty for a few days until Professor de Wit is on the mend.'

He spoke carelessly as though he didn't mind if she had her days off or not, and indeed, she thought wearily, why should he?

He went away then and she spent a busy night, because there was a lot of nursing to do and the professor had regained consciousness and wished to be far too active. But presently, after an injection, he dropped off into a refreshing sleep and Abigail was free to bring her charts up to date, snatch a cup of coffee and then sit quietly between the regular intervals of checking one thing and another. It was, she mused, a splendid opportunity to think quietly about the future, but perhaps she was too tired, for when she tried to do so, she seemed unable to clear her mind. She gave up presently, and spent the rest of the night idly thumbing through her dictionary, hunting for words which, even when she found them, she was unable to pronounce.

The professor came again at seven o'clock. Abigail, with the help of another nurse, had made her patient's bed and sat him up against his pillows; she had washed him too and combed his fringe of hair and his whiskers and dressed him in his own pyjamas. He looked very old and very ill, but she had no doubt at all that he was going to pull through, for he had a good deal of spirit. She was drawing up an injection to give him when Professor van Wijkelen arrived; he looked as though he had slept the clock round, and now, freshly shaved and immaculately dressed, he sauntered in for all the world as though he were in the habit of paying his visits at such an early hour. His good morning to her was brief; so brief that it seemed pointless, but she answered him nicely, smiling from a tired face that had no colour at all, unhappily aware that there was nothing about her appearance to make him look at her a second time.

He didn't say much to his patient but motioned her to give the injection, walked over to the window and sat down at the table there and began to study the papers she had laid ready for him. He had given her fresh instructions and was on the point of leaving when he remarked:

'You look as though you could do with a good sleep, Nurse.'

'Of course she needs a good sleep,' Professor de Wit's voice was testy even though it was weak. 'Just because you choose to work yourself to death doesn't mean that everyone else should do the same.'

'I have no intention of working anyone to death. Nurse is doing a job like anyone else and she has a tongue in her head. If she cannot carry out her duties, she has only to say so.'

He didn't look at her but flung 'I shall look in later,' over his shoulder as he went.

'Such a pity that...' began her patient, and fell asleep instantly just as Abigail was hopeful of hearing why something was a great pity—something to do with Professor van Wijkelen, she felt sure.

The next few days were busy ones. Her patient continued to improve, but there was a great deal of nursing care needed and Abigail was a conscientious nurse. She took her daily walk because she knew that she needed the exercise in the fresh air, despite its rawness and the bitter wind which never ceased to blow, but her days off she saved up; she would take them when the case was finished. There had, as yet, been no talk of sending Professor de Wit home although it had been made clear to her that she was to accompany him. They would be in hospital another week at least—two probably; if it hadn't been for the niggling worry about Bollinger, she would have been happier than she had been for a long time. She had made some friends in the hospital by now and she was battling on with her Dutch, helped a great deal by her patient, who now that he was feeling better spent a fair proportion of his waking hours correcting her accent and grammar.

It was the day after the drip came down for the last time and the old man had walked a few steps on her arm that Professor van Wijkelen had come to see him and on his way out again had said in his usual austere way:

'Nurse, if you are free tomorrow afternoon, I wish you to come with me—there is someone who wants to meet you.'

'Who?' asked Abigail, who liked to know where she was.

'Shall we say you must wait and see?' he enquired silkily, and then suddenly, as though he sensed that she was about to refuse, he smiled with such charm that she would have agreed to anything he wished. 'Please,' said the professor.

She nodded, knowing that when he looked at her like that she wanted nothing more than to please him. She was thoughtful after he had gone and Professor de Wit said nothing, although she had expected him to. When she saw that he didn't intend to discuss it with her, she launched into an argument on the subjunctive in the Dutch language, concentrating fiercely upon her companion's learned comments, because Professor van Wijkelen was taking up much too much of her attention these days.

Chapter 3

The professor was waiting for her when she reached the hospital forecourt the following afternoon. He greeted her with unsmiling courtesy as he opened the car door for her to get in, and because he so obviously didn't want to talk, she remained silent as he took the car through the gates and into the narrow streets beyond.

'You don't want to know where I am taking you?' he enquired blandly.

'Yes, of course I do, but I daresay you wouldn't choose to tell me, so I shan't ask.' Abigail spoke matter-of-factly and without rancour.

'We are going to my house.'

That startled her. 'What ever for?'

'There is somebody you should meet—it seemed the best place.'

'Oh, I see.' She didn't see at all and she was long-

ing to ask him who it was and didn't because he would
be expecting it.

'Very wise of you,' he commented silkily, answering her unspoken thought. 'I've no intention of telling
you. How do you find Professor de Wit?'

She obligingly followed his lead. 'Determined to get
well as soon as possible.'

'Yes—I have every hope that he will. The operation
wasn't quite straightforward.' He launched into details
and then said to surprise her:

'He likes you, Nurse Trent. I hope that you will be
prepared to go home with him for a few days?'

'Certainly,' said Abigail. There was nothing she
would like better, for a variety of reasons, which for
the moment at least, she didn't intend to look into too
deeply. She looked about her. They were travelling along
the Herengracht, beautiful and picturesque with its old
houses on either side of the tree-lined canal. Some way
down its length the professor turned the car into a short
arm of the canal—a little cul-de-sac, spanned by a narrow footbridge half way down its length. Houses lined
the cobbled streets on either side of the water and across
its far end, and trees, even in their winter bareness,
crowded thickly along its banks.

The Rolls slid sedately along its length and came to
a halt outside one of the houses at the end, facing the
canal. It was a very old house, with double steps leading to a great door and another, smaller door tucked
away under those same steps. The windows were high
and narrow and climbed up the front of the house. The
higher they climbed the smaller they became, until
they terminated in one very large one, heavily shut-
tered under the steep gable of the house. There was a

tremendous hook above it, because that was the only way to get anything in or out of the houses' top floors.

It was peaceful in the small backwater, away from the traffic, with only the wind sighing around the steeple roofs. Abigail got out and looked around her while the professor opened his house door, and then at his bidding went inside.

It was all she had expected and hoped for, with its black and white tiled floor, its plasterwork ceiling and plain white walls, upon which were hung a host of paintings, and its carved staircase rising from one side.

The furnishings were in keeping—a heavy oak table along one wall, flanked by two carved oaken chairs which Abigail thought looked remarkably uncomfortable, while the other wall held an oak chest upon which reposed a great blue and white bowl, filled with spring flowers.

Abigail rotated slowly, trying to see everything at once. 'How absolutely beautiful—it's quite perfect,' she said, and was instantly sorry she had spoken, because when she looked at her companion he was looking down his long nose at her as though she had been guilty of some offending vulgarity. She went a faint, angry pink, which turned even brighter when he remarked austerely:

'I feel sure, from the ferocious expression upon your face, that you are on the point of bidding me not to be like that, or some such similar phrase, Miss Trent. May I beg you not to do so—I am easily irritated.'

'So I've noticed,' Abigail told him tartly. 'The smallest thing… And now, Professor, if I might meet this person.' Her eyes swept round the empty hall; the house was very quiet, she allowed her thoughtful gaze to rest upon the man beside her and was on the point of speaking when he interrupted her:

'No, Miss Trent, I can assure you that there is nothing of sinister intent in my request to you to accompany me here.' He smiled thinly. 'You surely could not have seriously supposed that?'

It was annoying to have her thoughts read so accurately. Abigail said crossly, because that was exactly what she had been thinking, 'No, of course not. I'm not such a fool—you have to be joking.'

He said nothing to this but opened a door and said: 'Perhaps you would like to wait in here?'

She went past him into a small panelled room, warm and snug in the light of the fire burning in the steel grate. It was furnished in the utmost comfort with a number of easy chairs, leather-covered; a charmingly inlaid pier table against one wall, one small round table, inlaid with coloured mosaic work, conveniently close to the hearth, a revolving bookcase filled with books and a small Regency work-table. The professor pressed a switch and a number of table lamps bathed their surroundings in a delicate pink, highlighting the walls, which she could see were covered with red embossed paper, almost hidden along two sides of the room by the pictures hung upon it, and completely hidden on its third side by shelves of books. The room called for comment, but this time she held her tongue, walking to the centre of the room and standing quietly, waiting for him to speak first.

He didn't speak at all, but went out of the room, shutting the door behind him, and Abigail for one split second fought an urge to rush to the door and try the handle. Instead, she turned her back on it and went to examine the paintings on the walls. Mostly portraits of bygone van Wijkelens, she decided, who had undoubtedly passed on their good looks with an almost monotonous regularity. She was peering at a despotic-looking old gentleman in a tie-wig, when the door opened behind her and she turned round to see who it was.

Bollinger stood there. She cried on a happy, startled breath: 'Bolly—oh, Bolly!' and burst into tears. He crossed the room and patted her on the shoulder and said: 'There, there, Miss Abby—I gave you a shock, eh? Thought you'd be pleased and all.'

'Oh, Bolly, I am! I'm so happy to see you, that's why I'm crying—aren't I a fool? But how did you get here?' A sudden thought struck her. 'In the professor's house?' She whisked the spotless handkerchief he always carried out of his pocket and blew her nose and wiped her eyes. 'Does he know?'

'Course he knows, love. It's him as thought to do it. You see, he comes along one night and gives me your letter and the money, and I asks him to have a cuppa, seeing as it's a cold night, and we gets talking and I tells him a bit about us, and he says to me, "Well, Bollinger, seeing as how Miss Trent's going to be in Amsterdam for a week or two yet, why don't you get yourself a little job and be near her?"'

'"Well," I says, "that's easier said than done," and he says: "I'm looking for a gardener and odd job man for a week or two while my man has his bunions done—how about it?" So here I am, Miss Abby, came yesterday. He paid me fare and I'm to get my wages, so I'm in clover, as they say—no need for you to give me any more money.'

'It's fantastic,' declared Abigail. 'I simply can't believe it—do you like him, Bolly?'

'Yes, that I do, Miss Abby—a bit of a toff, you might say, but a gent all right.'

Abigail blew her nose again to prevent herself from bursting into another bout of tears. 'Oh, Bolly, it's like being home again. And of course I shall go on paying you your money—have you any idea how much it is we owe you? Don't you see, Bolly, I must pay you back now that I know about it and can afford to do so?'

'Well, if it makes you happy, Miss Abby. How long do you think you'll be here?'

'I'm not sure. Another two weeks, perhaps three. What have you done about your room?'

'I give it up, it wasn't all that hot. This professor, he says he knows someone in London lets rooms, very nice—a bit more than I got, but if I save me wages…'

'And I pay you each week while you're here, and by the time I get back to London and you're running a bit low, I'll be in another job and be able to send you something each week.' She hugged him. 'Oh, Bolly, it's all so wonderful, I can't believe it. Are you happy here? Where do you live?'

'Here, of course, Miss Abby. I got a room at the top of the house—very snug and warm it is too.'

'You don't have to work too hard?'

'Lord love you, no, Miss Abby—nice little bit of garden behind, and I does the odd job—and I'm to go to his other house in the country once a week and see to the garden there.'

Abigail stood silent, digesting this new aspect of Professor van Wijkelen. 'Well…' she began, and was interrupted by the door opening to admit a small round dumpling of a woman with a pleasant face. She shook Abigail by the hand and said in very tolerable English, 'The housekeeper, Mevrouw Boot,' and Abigail, mindful of her Dutch manners, replied: 'Miss Abigail Trent.'

Mevrouw Boot eyed her with kindly curiosity as she spoke. 'The professor begs that Miss will return to hospital when she must. There is a car at the door in five minutes. He excuses himself.'

She smiled again and went quietly out of the room, and Abigail looked at Bollinger and said with unconscious sadness, 'He doesn't like me, you know,' and had this statement instantly repudiated by Bolly who exclaimed in a shocked voice:

'That I can't believe, begging your pardon, Miss Abby—a nice young lady like you…'

'Well, it doesn't matter in the least,' said Abigail with such firmness that she almost believed what she was saying—but not quite, because it mattered out of all proportion to everything else. 'I'd better go, I suppose it's a taxi and I oughtn't to keep it waiting. Come to the door with me, Bolly.'

They crossed the hall, lingering a little. 'The professor says you're to come whenever ye're inclined,' Bolly explained, 'but not the days I go to the country.'

She nodded and stopped. 'All right, Bolly, I'll remember. I'm very grateful to him. Do you suppose I should write him a letter?'

He looked astonished. 'You see him, don't you, can't you do it then?'

She shook her head. 'I told you he doesn't like me,' and as if to underline her words one of the doors opened and Mevrouw Boot came into the hall and before she closed the door behind her, Abigail and Bollinger had

an excellent view of the professor sitting at a desk facing it—the powerful reading lamp on it lighted his face
clearly; he was staring at Abigail with no expression,
giving her the peculiar feeling that she wasn't there, and
then lowered his handsome head to the papers before
him. The door closed and when the housekeeper had
gone, Abigail said softly:

'You see, Bolly? He doesn't even want to see me,
let alone speak.'

She smiled a little wanly, wished him a warm goodbye and went outside. The Rolls was before the steps,
an elderly man at the wheel. He got out of the car when
he saw her and opened the door, smiling nicely as he
did so although he didn't speak, and she returned the
smile, for he had a kind face, rugged and lined—like a
Dutch Bolly, she thought as she settled herself beside
him for the journey back to the hospital. During the
short ride she tried her best to reconcile the professor's
dislike of her with his kindness to Bollinger. There had,
after all, been no need to offer the old man a job, even
a temporary one. She hoped that Bolly hadn't told him
too much, although she discounted as ridiculous the
idea that he might have acted out of sympathy to herself
as well as Bollinger. It was all a little mysterious and
she gave up the puzzle and began to ask her companion some questions about Amsterdam, hoping that he
could understand. It was an agreeable surprise to find
that he could, and moreover, reply to them in English.

At the hospital, she thanked him for the ride, wondering who he was and not liking to ask for fear the
professor would hear of it and consider her nosey. She
went back to her patient with her curiosity unsatisfied,
to find him feeling so much better after a refreshing

nap that he wanted to know what she had been doing with her afternoon. She told him, skating over the more unexplainable bits, and rather to her surprise he made very little comment, and that was about herself and Bollinger. About the professor he had nothing to say at all.

The days slid quietly by, each one bringing more strength to Professor de Wit. He was to go home in a week's time, said Professor van Wijkelen when he called one morning soon after Abigail had been to his house, and as he had said it, both he and his patient looked at her.

'You'll come with me, Abby?' asked her patient, who considered himself on sufficiently good terms with her by now to address her so. The professor's cool, 'I hope you will find it convenient to go with Professor de Wit for another week, Nurse Trent,' sounded all the more stilted. She said that yes, of course she would, hiding her delight at the idea of seeing the professor, even if he hated her, for another few days, and the lesser delight of knowing that she would be able to repay Bolly quite a lot of money. She went away to fetch the latest X-rays the professor decided to study, walking on air.

She told Bollinger about it the next day when they met, as they often did, for a cup of coffee and half an hour's chat. Bollinger, she was glad to see, looked well, and he was happy with his gardening and the odd jobs he was doing around the house. He had been to the country too, but Abigail didn't press him with questions about this; somehow she felt that the less she knew about the professor's private life, the better it would be.

She hadn't been back to the house on the *gracht*—not since the time when he had looked right through her, as though she were someone he didn't want to see there. Each time Bollinger suggested it, she had some excuse, but when she went home with Professor de Wit, she would have to do better, for she discovered that the older man had a small house within walking distance of the professor's home, and Bolly would expect her to go and see him quite often and she could think of no good reason why she shouldn't. The professor had even told Bollinger to use the small sitting room where they had met, and offer Abigail tea if she wished, which, considering the lack of friendliness he showed towards her, puzzled her very much.

She took care during the next few days to keep herself busy, both in her work and her leisure; under her patient's tuition, she was beginning to make a little headway with her Dutch, and because it pleased him excessively and kept him interested in something while he struggled through the unrewarding days of convalescence, she spent a good deal of time outside her working hours with him, not admitting to herself that it served her purpose very well and gave her a real excuse for not going to the house on the *gracht*.

The professor came daily, sometimes twice, but beyond wishing her a good day and asking her in a strictly professional manner how his patient did, he made no effort to talk to her. About Bollinger he had said nothing at all, and the short, painfully careful note she had sent him had been ignored.

But she was not able to follow this rather cowardly scheme for any length of time; Professor de Wit took her to task for not going out enough, and dispatched her to Kalverstraat on her next free afternoon to fetch him some books he had ordered. She knew her way about by now and hurried down the narrow lanes, wrapped warmly against the snarling wind and the first powdering of snow from a heavy sky. There were several ways in which she might reach the bookshop; she chose the longest of them, because although it didn't pass Professor van Wijkelen's house, it went close to it, which, she told herself sternly, was the silliest reason for taking it.

There were several alleys connecting one *gracht* with the next. She went down one of them now, her head bent against the quickening snow, her feet sounding loudly on the uneven cobbles and echoing against the silent warehouses, leaning, crooked with age, against each other on either side of her. She was nearly at the end when a movement in the gutter drew her attention—a slight movement, made without sound. She slowed her pace to investigate, crossing the road gingerly; it might be a rat, and she was afraid of rats. But it wasn't a rat, it was a kitten, a very small one, its dirty black and white fur clinging wetly to its bony body, a few drops of blood on its filthy white shirt-front. She stooped and picked it up with care, fearful of hurting it, and exclaimed with pity at its pathetic lightness. It was an ugly small creature, with a large nose; even when clean and well fed, she doubted if it would be worth a second glance. It gave her a penetrating glance from blue eyes and mewed, and all thought of fetching her patient's books went out of her head. She wrapped the waif in the ends of her long scarf, cradled it against her and hurried on. The professor's house was only around the next corner. She would go there and get Bolly to take care of it after she had examined it to see where it had been hurt.

At the house she hesitated. To ring the front door bell and ask to go in so that she might attend to a stray kitten seemed to her to be taking advantage of the pro-

fessor's message that she might stay for tea with Bolly—
and probably it had been mere civility on his part, with
no thought of her accepting. She didn't think he was
at home—there was no car to be seen and the house
stood silent in the snow. She knocked on the little door
beneath the steps and waited.

Bollinger opened the door, his face lighting up at the
sight of her. 'There, Miss Abby,' he exclaimed, 'I knew
you'd be along—on such a nasty day too. Come in and
we'll have a cuppa.' He opened the door wider, saying:
'But I don't know if you should come in this door. The
one above's for you.'

'Well, no—I shouldn't think so,' Abby stated. 'I
haven't been invited you know—besides, I've got something—look.'

They carried the kitten to the kitchen at the back
of the house, a surprisingly bright room overlooking
a small walled garden, now shrouded in snow. There
was no one there; Bolly explained that Mevrouw Boot
had gone out to see some relative or other and the daily
woman who came in to do the rough work had gone
home. 'Let's put the little beggar in front of the stove,'
he suggested, 'get him warm, then we can have a look.'

Which they accordingly did, to be rewarded after a
few minutes by a faint movement from the small creature, who put out a pink tongue and weakly tried to
lick its fur. 'There,' said Bolly, who knew every old
wives' tale and believed them all, 'she'll get better—
she's licked herself.'

Looking at the bedraggled kitten, Abigail refrained
from saying that she considered that a too optimistic
statement. Nevertheless, they must try to do something.
Because there had been nothing else, she had wrapped

it in her scarf; now she produced a handkerchief and started to clean its dirty fur. She did it very gently because she was afraid of hurting it, but she managed to get off enough of the muddy wet to discover where it was hurt. There was a cut on its puny chest, not a large one, but probably deep.

'If I had a pair of scissors…' she began.

Someone had come into the kitchen and joined them. 'If I might take a look?' the professor enquired almost apologetically.

It was Bolly, who had gone to the stove to warm some milk, who answered him. 'Ah—good thing you've come, sir—this here beast don't look too good, Miss Abby found him in one of them alleys round the back.' His tone implied that the alleys in question failed to win his approval. 'She brought him here.'

'And quite right too.' The professor was on his knees beside the scrap stretched on Abigail's scarf, his capable hands busy. 'I didn't hear the house door bell,' he commented mildly, and looked at Abigail.

'No—well, I didn't come in through the big door.' At his raised eyebrows she hurried on, 'I—I had to take the kitten somewhere and I was close by and I thought that Bollinger might help—so I rang the bell of the little door under the steps.'

He had picked the kitten up and was inspecting the cut. 'It is, of course, no concern of mine, Miss Trent,' his voice was smooth, 'but I can assure you that you have no need to—er—creep in the tradesmen's entrance of my house.'

'I didn't creep…' began Abigail indignantly. 'I didn't know you were here.'

'And if you had known?'

She went pink, longing to tell him that ringing the door bell of his house was something she would never willingly do, knowing herself unwelcome in it. She said nothing, but took the saucer of milk from Bolly. She asked:

'Can it have this? Is it likely to need an anaesthetic?'

His mouth twitched, but he said gravely enough, 'I think there will be no need of that. Give him a little of the milk and I'll put a stitch in. He'll be all right in a day or so—he's nearly starved to death.'

He got to his feet and went away, to return presently with a needle and gut, scissors and a spray of local anaesthetic. 'Bring him over here,' he commanded Abigail, 'and hold him still on the table. Bollinger, turn on the light, if you please.'

He was very quick and the kitten lay still, licking the last drops of milk from its small chops. When he had finished, the professor unbent himself and gathered up his odds and ends.

'And now what is to become of the creature?' he wanted to know blandly. 'You intend to take him back with you, Miss Trent?'

Abigail removed her finger from the kitten's clutches and stared down at it. It was unthinkable that it should be turned into the streets; she would have to take it with her, and heaven knows what they would say about it in hospital—perhaps she could keep it in her room and take it back to England when she went… Her thoughts were interrupted by the professor's voice. 'No doubt you think that he should remain here?'

She looked at him then. He had never been particularly pleasant to her, but she refused to believe that he was an unkind man. 'I don't think you would turn anyone or anything away if they needed help,' she stated flatly, and added, 'That's if you don't mind.'

The stare from his blue eyes was shrewd; when he didn't answer she went on quietly, 'It's quite all right if you don't want to be bothered. I'll manage. Thank you very much for being so kind.' She smiled at him and the plainness of her face was changed to a kind of beauty. She picked up her scarf and began to arrange it around the kitten, then buttoned up her coat. Her fingers faltered at the top button when the professor spoke.

'I beg your pardon for teasing you. Of course the animal shall stay here.' His manner changed to a fierce mockery. 'In any case, how could I refuse after your pretty speech?'

'I meant it,' said Abigail, trying to keep the hurt out of her voice. 'Thank you, Professor. It won't be any trouble to you, I know Bollinger will keep it out of your way, won't you, Bolly?' she besought the old man, who said at once, 'Of course I will, Miss Abby, don't you fret your pretty head, I'll do me best—you won't know him when you come.'

'Your thoughtfulness does you credit, Miss Trent, but I assure you that the kitten will be welcome. I have a dog who will be delighted to have company when I am not here, and as the kitten is a female, I foresee no difficulties.' He started for the door. 'Bollinger, perhaps you would be so good as to make a pot of your excellent English tea and bring it to my study. Miss Trent, be so good as to accompany me.'

Abigail was astonished to a state of speechlessness. 'Me?' she wanted to know, and then, remembering, 'But I can't—I've got to go to the Kalverstraat and get Professor de Wit's books.'

Her host's eyes flickered to his watch. 'No matter, I have to go there myself this afternoon—I'll bring them with me when I call in later.'

He held the door open for her, so certain that she would do as he wished that she saw no other course open to her. She went past him and up a few steps, old and worn uneven by countless feet over the years. There was a door beyond them which he pushed open and they were, as she had guessed, in the back of the hall, which they crossed to enter a room she took to be his study. The walls were lined with books, a large circular table standing in the centre of the room held more books as well as papers, unopened letters as well as opened ones, several copies of *World Medicine* and *The Lancet* and a great many journals in the French and German tongues. She turned, round-eyed, from this businesslike disorder, to view the desk in one corner, very tidy, although there was a sheaf of papers pushed to one side as though he had risen from his chair in haste. That same chair was tall and straight and definitely not for lounging, but there were two leather armchairs on each side of the brightly burning fire, and a table lamp beside one of them cast an inviting glow. It was a well-lived-in room; she could imagine the professor sitting here working and reading; the thought conjured up a picture of a lonely, bookish life, which she felt sure was quite erroneous; with his good looks and unmarried state, not to mention the fact that he was undoubtedly wealthy, he would be much in demand among his friends and acquaintances. She frowned because it was foolish of her to speculate upon his private life, but the frown turned to a delighted smile as a Great Dane came from behind the desk and offered a paw. Abigail shook it and hugged him as well. 'Beautiful,' she addressed him, 'and so…' she remembered just in time how vexed the professor had looked when she had admired the hall. She said instead, 'What's his name?'

'Colossus.' And she, forgetting to be wary of him, chortled: 'Oh, how apt—Julius Caesar, isn't it? Something about petty men walking under his huge legs,' she added admiringly. 'How very clever of you.'

She smiled at him and encountered a look of such fierce derision that she got to her feet and said instantly, 'I don't think I'll stay for tea, if you don't mind.'

The look had gone. 'I must beg your pardon for the second time this afternoon,' he smiled unexpectedly and she felt her heart tumble. 'Please stay, Abigail.'

She would never understand him; it was like going along a winding road wondering what would be around the next corner. She sat down in one of the chairs and asked in a voice which forgave him, 'What will you call the kitten?' She pulled Colossus's ear and heard the dog sigh with pleasure, and at that moment Bollinger came in with the tea-tray and the professor said:

'We want a name for the kitten, Bollinger. Any ideas?'

Bollinger put the tray down by Abigail, smiled at her and then frowned in thought. 'Well,' he said at length, 'she's an orphan, isn't she? So she'll be Annie.'

He looked at them hopefully. 'Little Orphan Annie,' he explained, and beamed at the professor when he declared: 'A splendid name for her, Bollinger. Annie it shall be. When she's a little more herself, Colossus shall go down to the kitchen and make friends.'

'She's having a nap,' continued Bollinger, 'I haven't moved her, so snug she lies. I'll feed her presently.'

'Every two hours—milk, Bollinger, and not too much of it.'

'OK, boss,' said Bollinger comfortably. 'I'll say bye-bye for now, Miss Abby.' He sounded wistful and she was quick to hear it.

'I'll meet you for coffee—tomorrow, Bolly, and you can tell me about Annie.'

The professor's voice was blandly polite. 'May I suggest that you come here? I shall be away for a couple of days and I think it would be as well if you kept an eye on Annie until I return.'

'Now that's an idea,' said Bollinger enthusiastically. 'No reason why you shouldn't, is there, Miss Abby?'

Abigail said that no, there wasn't, in a rather prim voice which concealed sudden delight. She wanted to come to this old house again; she could think of nothing nicer than living in it for ever and ever. She lifted the teapot and almost dropped it again, struck by the knowledge that the house meant nothing at all without the professor in it—bad temper, frowns, sneers and all. Somewhere behind that forbidding manner must be the man she had fallen in love with—once or twice he had allowed himself to be glimpsed and she dearly wished that he would allow it again. She had no illusions about herself; the professor was as likely to fall in love with her as the moon would turn to cheese, although miracles did happen… She handed him his tea and poured some for herself, asking in a matter-of-fact voice whether Colossus found city life a little trying.

'No—not really. He has a good walk each morning and another some time in the evening and he goes with me to Friesland, where I have another home. He can exercise there to his heart's content.'

'Friesland,' wondered Abigail, 'isn't that a long way?'

'No, a hundred and thirty odd kilometres. An hour and a half's driving—less.'

'Is that where Bollinger went?'

'Yes—there is quite a large garden there. He enjoyed himself enormously.'

He handed Abigail a dish of little cakes and she took one and bit into it. It tasted as delicious as it looked. 'Yes, he loves gardening, but I expect you know that. He has green fingers.'

'Green...? What does that mean?'

'He can grow things and they grow for him because he understands them.'

The professor sipped his tea. 'How interesting. I shall look forward to a beautiful garden this spring.'

Abigail put down her cup and saucer—delicate, paper thin and transparent with a white and purple pattern; she would make a note of them and ask Professor de Wit about them later on—the teapot too; silver and very plain with a rounded lid. 'I think I'd better go,' she said politely, while she longed to stay, but her companion, while making pleasant enough conversation, had shown no great delight in her company, nor did he press her to stay. He got up as she did and went with her into the hall. There were red tulips, dozens of them on the chest today, she noticed. They were half way to the front door when the professor stopped.

'One moment, Miss Trent—your scarf. You made a bed for the kitten, did you not?'

'Yes, but it doesn't matter. I'm not cold and it's a short walk.'

He ignored this and turned on his heel and went to a pillow cupboard at the back of the hall and came back with a silk square. 'This will do.' He unbuttoned her coat, tied the scarf round her neck and buttoned the coat up again, and when she murmured her thanks made no reply, but went ahead of her to the door and flung it open on to the snow outside. The Rolls was by the steps.

'Jan will take you back. Goodbye, Miss Trent.' As she went down the steps she thought indignantly that he sounded relieved that she was going, and possibly he was, but he might have had the decency to pretend— and he had lent her his scarf, but then he would have lent a scarf to anyone in an emergency. She refused to tease herself any more and began a determined conversation with Jan, which lasted until they reached the hospital entrance.

She had spent two happy afternoons at the house on the *gracht,* playing with a slowly recovering Annie and listening to Bollinger's cheerful talk. She had been able to give him some more money too, which he had refused to take until she had pointed out that the quicker she paid her debt to him the quicker she could make a fresh start.

'There's nothing you can do about it, Bolly,' she told him, 'so don't argue. Besides, I'm to be a week at Professor de Wit's house and I've got my fare back to England and some money besides.' She didn't mention that she had heard nothing from Mrs Morgan—she could always go to the agency and ask what to do about it. The prospect of going back to England depressed her, but she was too level-headed to allow it to dominate her thoughts. She had told Bolly that when she knew for certain when she was leaving, she would let him know and he could either come with her or follow when it was convenient. As far as she could make out, he and the professor had a very easy-going agreement between them, and Bolly had said that the man whose work he was doing wouldn't be well for a few weeks yet; he might stay until he was and that would give her time to find another job, this time where she could live out and get a small home together for them both.

The transfer of her patient went without a hitch. Professor de Wit's house was much smaller than his friend's but just as old. It had no garden though, just a few square feet of paving stones and a high wall, but the rooms were delightful. His bedroom was on the first floor and hers next to it, because, as he pointed out to her, after his stay in hospital he was a little nervous of being quite by himself. His housekeeper, Juffrouw Valk, seemed to Abigail to be a sensible and kind woman and perfectly able to look after the professor once she had been told about his diet and what he might and might not do. She spoke no English, which, Professor de Wit pointed out with some glee, was splendid for Abigail's Dutch. And so it was; by the end of the afternoon Abigail had managed to communicate quite a lot to Juffrouw Valk, who smiled and nodded and encouraged her and went to a great deal of trouble to have things just so.

Abigail and her patient ate their dinner together in the small dining room at the back of the house after she had spent some time in the kitchen showing the older woman what Professor de Wit might eat and how much, and immediately the simple meal was finished, she helped him climb the stairs and got him to bed, for he was tired and happy and exhausted. She had settled him nicely in his bed and was getting his spectacles and newspaper for him when Professor van Wijkelen arrived. He stood in the doorway of the bedroom, looking larger than ever, and, Abigail was quick to perceive, very out of humour. Or perhaps it was only herself who caused that expression on his face, for it cleared as he went over to sit by his patient's bed, and after a minute, seeing that she wasn't needed, she slipped away, downstairs to the kitchen, to help Juffrouw Valk with the washing up and improve her Dutch at the same time. She was forced to go back upstairs very soon, though, because the professor called to her briskly from the head of the narrow little staircase. She followed him into his patient's bedroom and stood, very neat in her uniform, waiting to hear what he had to say.

'We have been discussing you, Miss Trent. Professor de Wit agrees with me that another week of your excellent nursing and he will be able to dispense with your services—with regret, I must add.'

He sounded not in the least regretful himself. Abigail fastened her eyes on the glowing silk of his tie and remembered, for no reason at all, that once, quite by accident, he had called her Abigail.

'This suits me very well, however,' went on the professor, 'for I have another patient in need of your care for a week or so. A Scotswoman who lives in one of the houses in the Begijnhof—you have probably been there?'

Abigail nodded. It was peaceful and beautiful and the little houses couldn't have changed much since they had been built centuries before. 'A week should suffice,' went on the professor smoothly, 'a short delay for you, I know, Nurse, but you would be doing her a great kindness—she is a charming person.'

He smiled at her, and even as she heard her own voice saying that yes, she was quite prepared to take another case for him, she was chiding herself for being a fool. Now that he had got what he wanted he would doubt- less be as morose and irritable as before; it was an ever- recurring pattern which she weakly never attempted to alter. She only had to say no. She peeped at him—he wasn't smiling now and she saw that he looked very tired, so that his hair looked more grey than it really was and the lines of his face were etched more deeply. He looked up and his eyes held hers for a brief moment and the smile on her lips froze before their coldness. She looked away quickly and he turned back to Profes- sor de Wit, and presently got up to go. It hardly seemed the right moment to give him back his scarf, but she went and fetched it all the same and handed it to him with a word of thanks, remembering how gentle his hands had been when he had tied it round her neck. He took it carelessly now and stuffed it in a pocket. Abi- gail went downstairs with him and let him out into the coldness of the winter evening. He didn't reply to her sober good night.

'I shall miss you, Abby,' declared her patient when she went back upstairs, 'but Dominic is quite right, I shan't really need you. I've surprised even him, I be- lieve. But I'm glad you will still be in Amsterdam. You must come and see me when you can.'

'I should like that, though I shall only be here for another week after I leave you, shan't I? I must write to the agency in London and see if they have another job for me.' She smiled at him. 'Otherwise I might have to wait a few days for a case and I should prefer to go straight to a patient.'

'What—no days off, Abby?'

'Yes—that is, no, I can't…don't let's talk about me, it's so dull.'

'Dull? My dear Abby, you are the last person I should describe as dull. Tell me, how is that ridiculous kitten you wished on Dominic?'

They spent the rest of the evening talking about nothing in particular and when she had finally tucked the old man up for the night she went to her own room and got ready for bed too. It was marvellous, she told her reflection in the little shieldback mirror on the dressing-table, that she had another patient to go to, and marvellous, said her heart, that she would see the professor for a further week. 'And a lot of good that may do you,' she admonished her mirrored face, 'for he only speaks to you when he's got something unpleasant to say or when he wants something.' Her face reflected sadness; she made a derisive face at it and got into bed and lay awake, thinking about Dominic van Wijkelen. He had looked so very tired that evening, and although the house on the *gracht* was a beautiful home and his housekeeper everything she should be, it surely wasn't quite the same as going home to a wife and children. Even if he were tired to death, he would open the great front door and find them waiting for him. It would be lonely in that house…a tear slid beneath her lids and she blinked it away. 'At least he's got Annie,' she reminded herself, and went to sleep on that ridiculous thought.

The week went pleasantly by. Professor de Wit, now that he was home again, began to take up the thread of his life once more; he was still weak, but he managed the stairs on his own now and spent an hour or more each day working on the book he was writing—a lengthy treatise on biochemistry, which Abigail strove to understand, when, carried away by some theory or other, he would talk at great length about the fascinations of cell life. And his friends came; learned gentlemen who spoke kindly to her and drank a great deal of coffee while her patient sipped his milk.

Juffrouw Valk had proved a treasure; not only had she obtained extra help in the house, she had proved a quick and willing learner when it came to Abigail explaining her patient's diet and what he might and might not do. She wrote it all down in laborious Dutch too so that Juffrouw Valk couldn't forget, and that lady, far from laughing at Abigail's efforts, praised her kindly and tactfully pointed out the mistakes. Abigail could see that she would be leaving Professor de Wit in excellent hands.

Professor van Wijkelen came daily, sometimes briefly, sometimes to stay long enough to play chess with his old friend, and each time he came he brought news of Annie and Bollinger—both, it seemed, in the best of health and firm friends. On one of his visits he suggested that she should go to see them and when she replied quietly that she had been that very afternoon he answered dryly, 'Ah, yes—while I was away from home on operating day, as you very well know.'

The afternoon before she was due to leave Professor de Wit's house, she walked round to see Bollinger once more and enquire after Annie. Despite the professor's words, she had formed the habit of ringing the bell of the little door under the steps, with the vague, half-formed idea that if the professor were home she could, if she wished, beat a hasty retreat. But he was out that afternoon, she had a cup of tea with Bollinger, admired Annie, who had turned from the miserable little waif she had been into a plump, enchanting kitten, and petted Colossus, who chose to have tea with them, taking up a good deal of room before the fire. He stretched out now with Annie balanced on his paws while she tidied away her whiskers after the saucer of milk Bollinger had given her.

'So you're off again, Miss Abby,' he commented, and Abigail detected the satisfaction in his voice. 'The boss says it's a Scotch lady this time—very nice too, specially as his gardener ain't going so fast as he might with his bunions.' He sighed happily. '"No hurry," he tells me, '"you're far too useful a man to go before you need."' He added proudly, 'I help Jan with the cars—cleaning 'em, you know.'

Abigail hadn't seen him so happy for a long time, not since her father had been alive and Bolly had seen to the garden and driven and serviced their old-fashioned, solid car, and between whiles made himself useful in the house. She wondered how he would like London again; even if she was very lucky and got a job where she could live out, it would have to be a furnished flat, and a small one at that. She said now, her nice voice urgent:

'Bolly, when I go back to London, don't come with me, not if there's still a job for you here. Stay on a little while, until I can get a home for us.'

'And who's going to look after you?' he demanded fiercely.

'I'll be fine, Bolly. I'll get a job where I can live in for a couple of weeks, that'll give me a chance to look round.'

It sounded easier than it would actually be, but it lulled the old man into a sense of security; he needed very little persuasion to do as she asked and she knew that secretly he was happy to be staying.

When she got up to go she said, 'I don't know exactly when I'll be here again, Bolly. I'll have to see how the new patient is, but I'll come as soon as I can.'

'Right, Miss Abby. The boss'll tell me how you go on, he always does.'

Abigail, on her way out, stopped. 'Does he? Does he really? I shouldn't have thought...' She walked on again, having uttered these rather obscure remarks, said her goodbyes and went back to her patient.

The professor came early that evening. They had barely finished their simple dinner when he was announced by Juffrouw Valk, who in the same breath offered coffee and perhaps, if the professor was a hungry man, a little something to eat. He declined the little something but accepted the coffee, which Abigail poured for him, listening with a sympathetic ear to his patient's gentle complaints about not being allowed to drink that beverage. Abigail offered him his milk with such a motherly air, explaining how good it was for him, that he chuckled and said:

'Abby, I find I do a great many things I don't care about, as a consequence of your persuasive ways. I can see that in due course you will wheedle your husband and children most shamefully into doing exactly what you want.'

Abigail laughed at his little joke and hoped that it didn't sound hollow. She saw no prospect of marriage, and even if she did, she only wanted to marry the professor, sitting beside her now, drinking his coffee and taking no notice of her at all. She got to her feet.

'I expect you would like to talk, and there are several things I have to do.'

'Stay where you are,' the professor's voice was a little sharp and when she looked at him in surprise he added: 'Please.'

So she sat down again, looking at him with a calm face, wondering what it was he had to say.

'I shall fetch you tomorrow,' he spoke in a no-nonsense voice. 'Kindly be ready by three o'clock. My patient is nervous of returning home alone, and it seems to me that getting to know each other over a cup of tea might be best for you both. I should imagine that you will be with her for a week or ten days and I have told Bollinger this—he knows that he is free to leave when he wishes. I don't know what arrangements you have made, but he seemed to think that he would stay here while you—er—find a home.'

'Yes,' said Abigail briefly. It was, she told herself, no concern of his.

'Which is no concern of mine, is it?' concluded the professor with uncanny perception. He turned back to Professor de Wit. 'I'll be in to see you each day, but you are making good headway now and you have Juffrouw Valk, who, Nurse tells me, has proved an apt pupil in the compiling of your diet and so on.'

Abigail perceived that he had finished with her. She was still not sure what her patient was suffering from and if he didn't choose to tell her, then she wasn't going to ask. She got to her feet again, and this time no one suggested that she should stay.

She was quite ready by three o'clock, with her case in the narrow hall and her outdoor clothes on. She had said goodbye to Juffrouw Valk, promised Professor de

Wit that she would visit him before she went back to England, extracted a promise from him to be good and do exactly what he should and thanked him with charm for the gloves he had given her. They were lovely ones, warm brown leather, fur-lined. She hadn't had such a pair for a very long time. She put them on and declared that as long as winter lasted she would wear them every day, and because he looked so lonely sitting there she put her arms round his thin shoulders and kissed him, just as the professor came into the room.

'Ah, Dominic, envious?'

His visitor smiled bleakly and turned such a look of ice upon Abigail that she blinked under it. He said briefly to his patient, 'Hullo,' and advised him that he would call in later, and then asked, in a voice to freeze her marrow, 'You're ready, Nurse?'

She told him yes, she was, in a voice as cold as his own, though it warmed as she bade her patient goodbye and followed the professor out to his car.

She sat silently beside him because it was obvious that he was in a towering rage about something or other. He had woven the car through the traffic on the Herengracht before he spoke.

'Your patient,' he began, 'Mrs Macklin—she has been ill for some time. A peptic ulcer—I operated some six weeks ago, but she has been slow to recover. She is now much better, but naturally after so long a stay in hospital, she's nervous of going home alone. She has no relations and isn't the type to bother her friends. She has very little money, by the way—you will be good enough to say nothing to her about your fee. If she should ask tell her that it will be settled later. I will see that you are paid.'

Abigail took a quick look at him. He was staring ahead, his profile fierce and unfriendly, as though daring her to make any comment, so she said in a matter-of-fact voice, 'Just as you wish, sir. How old is Mrs Macklin?'

'Sixty-five. She is the widow of a Scottish Presbyterian parson.'

He didn't speak again, even when he pulled up in the Begijnsteeg, got her case from the boot of the car and crossed the quiet Begijnhof to the end house on the semi-circle of quaint dwellings surrounding the church. The steps leading to its door were narrow and worn, and the front door creaked with age as he turned its handle and walked in, saying, 'Hullo there,' in a cheerful voice, the sort of voice he never used towards Abigail. She stifled a sigh and followed him into one of the smallest houses she had ever been in.

Chapter 4

The hall contained two doors and a small circular staircase at its end, its wooden steps worn crooked with age, its floor was brick with a hand-made rug upon it, the walls were white plaster, upon which was displayed a fine plate of Delft Blue and nothing else. The professor opened the door nearest him and ushered Abigail inside, into a room which was small, low-ceilinged and rather dark, although the early February afternoon largely accounted for this.

It was an attractive room, though cluttered, with small tables laden with photographs in silver frames, a writing bureau against one wall and a display cabinet on the other. There were footstools and several small comfortable chairs; there was one large easy chair by the small old-fashioned pot stove set in its traditional tiles; the woman sitting in it spoke to them as they entered.

'Dominic, my dear, how punctual. I won't get up—you won't mind? And is this my nurse?'

'It is. Miss Abigail Trent—Mrs Macklin. I'll take the bags up, shall I?'

He went out of the room again and it seemed much larger without his bulk half filling it. Abigail said how do you do and stood quietly while she was inspected, carrying out her own inspection at the same time. Mrs Macklin was tall, though how tall it was hard to say until she stood up, she was also very thin, with a long, sharp-nosed face and bright dark eyes. Her iron grey hair was screwed into an old-fashioned no-nonsense bun, skewered with equally old-fashioned hairpins. After a moment they smiled at each other and Mrs Macklin said, 'You're exactly as Dominic described you. Shall we have a cup of tea together? Could you put the kettle on? The kitchen is behind this room and you'll find the tray already laid. A neighbour kindly did it for me—she was here waiting when Dominic brought me home a couple of hours ago.'

Abigail took off her gloves and unwound her scarf and went to find the kitchen, small and a little old-fashioned, with a gay gingham frill round the mantelshelf above the small electric cooker and a row of pot plants on the windowsill. She filled the kettle and put it on, listening to the creak of the stairs as the professor descended them with measured tread. He had very large feet, thought Abigail lovingly, but then he was a very large man. She could hear the murmur of their voices in the room next door as she made the tea in the brown earthenware pot, put it on the tray and carried it through to the sitting room.

The professor took the tray from her at the door and

Mrs Macklin smiled at her and said, 'My dear, there's a fruit cake in the tin on the middle shelf of the cupboard,' so Abigail went back and found the cake, a plate to put it on, a knife and three little porcelain tea plates, all different in design and, she guessed, very old.

They had tea to the accompaniment of cheerful small talk, and Abigail, under the impression that she now knew the professor quite well, discovered another side of him entirely. It was as though Mrs Macklin had charmed away his ill temper and coldness, and although he spoke seldom to her, and then only briefly, she was aware of this. She didn't talk much herself, but sat listening to her new patient and the professor mulling over the city's news.

The professor got up to go presently, saying as he did so: 'Be good enough to come with me to the door, Nurse Trent, I have one or two instructions for you.' He wasn't looking at her and his voice was as cold as ever it had been, but at the door, just as he was going, he halted and said in quite a different voice: '*Hemel,* I forgot the cat—I intended to fetch him...'

'You have enough to do,' called Mrs Macklin from the sitting room, 'you know you haven't a minute to spare this evening.'

'I'll get him,' Abigail offered. 'I know my way around Amsterdam very well now and I'm sure there'll be plenty of time this evening.' She had a sudden unsatisfactory picture of the professor, spending his evening wining and dining some gorgeous girl who could make him smile instead of scowl as he was at that moment.

'I can't allow you to go trudging all over Amsterdam after a cat.' His voice was polite and quite impersonal.

'You exaggerate,' Abigail pointed out reasonably. 'I

never trudge anywhere—you make me sound like Little Orphan Annie…' She stopped, because although she wasn't Annie she was an orphan. She fixed her gaze on the fine cloth of his car coat and clenched her teeth to stop the tears coming into her eyes. She gulped back the lump in her throat and said:

'I shall enjoy it.'

'And will you enjoy the shopping and housework and the cooking?' he enquired.

'Yes. There isn't much nursing for me to do, is there? And it's such a tiny house.'

'I will get some kind of household help for Mrs Macklin by the end of the week. In the meantime I should like you to restrain her from doing everything. She has always been a very active woman and likes to have her own way.'

'Most people do,' remarked Abigail, and looked at him, to surprise an expression on his face which set her pulse racing—it was such a peculiar look, half wonder, half amusement, wholly tender. She met his eyes squarely and waited for him to speak.

'I didn't know that there were girls like you left in the world,' he said slowly, and put up a hand and lifted her chin gently with his forefinger and scanned her face as though he hadn't really looked at it before. 'You've almost restored my faith in women, Abigail.'

He dropped his hand, turned on his heel and was out of the door, wishing her good afternoon in a perfectly ordinary voice before she could draw a difficult breath.

She had no time to ponder his remark because she went to fetch Jude the cat soon afterwards, and when she got back and had settled him with his mistress, Mrs Macklin began at once to talk.

'Sit down, my dear. You must be wondering about me and why I should need a nurse, for I'm sure Dominic neglected to tell you anything at all, except the number of pills I'm supposed to take each day. I was his mother's dearest friend, you know, and when she died I promised that I would keep an eye on him, because I've known him ever since he was a baby, but now I'm older and the boot is on the other foot. It's he who keeps an eye on me now, although I will say that he still listens to me with a fair amount of patience and even takes my advice from time to time. When this silly ulcer business started, nothing would do but that I must go into hospital, and when he saw that medical treatment wasn't going to cure me, he operated himself and insisted on me staying there much too long, I consider. He seems to think that I need a nurse for a short time, though I told him that I was as fit as a fiddle, and now he tells me that he's arranging for someone to come each day and help in the house when you go.' She snorted delicately. 'I never heard such nonsense, though I must admit, my dear, that I'm going to enjoy your company—to tell you the truth, I was just a little nervous, and since he tells me that it will cost me nothing… I didn't know that the *Ziekenfonds* paid for private nurses, but they've improved these things so much in the last few years, haven't they, and I've never had occasion to make use of them before.'

Abigail made a sympathetic murmured reply. So that was what the professor had told her patient, and that was why she was to say nothing about fees. He was paying them out of his own pocket. She reflected with brief tenderness upon him, then remarked calmly:

'I'm sure the professor knows best; it really does

seem a bit strange when one comes back from hospital. We could use this week finding out just how much you can do without getting tired, don't you think? Then if you have someone in to do the housework, you'll be able to cope with the cooking and perhaps the shopping—isn't that a good idea? Now, shall I get some supper for us—and what about Jude, he'll want a meal, I expect—supposing you sit there and enjoy his company for a while and I'll explore the kitchen.'

Mrs Macklin agreed to these suggestions readily enough and Abigail retired to the kitchen; her patient was more tired than she wished to say, and a week of cosseting would do her good. Abigail nodded her neat head in confirmation of her own opinion and began opening cupboard doors and peering at their contents.

She saw her patient into bed quite early that evening, with Jude on his own shawl at her feet and a bell within reach, and then crossed the landing to her own room. It was extremely small and rather sparsely furnished, but the bed and the chest in the window and the chair beside it were very old and glowing with the loving polishing of many decades of housewives. She undressed slowly, despite the chill, thinking about the professor and wondering what exactly he had meant that afternoon. Why had he lost his faith in women in the first place—or had he been joking? That was unlikely—he wasn't a man to make that kind of joke. She went downstairs, dressing-gowned and slippered, and had a shower in the cubicle squeezed in beside the kitchen, then crept upstairs again and into bed, her thoughts still centred on him. Perhaps he was in love with someone who didn't love him, although this seemed to her to be quite inconceivable—she was still worrying about it when she went to sleep.

She got up early the next morning to find a light powdering of snow once more and a snarling wind whining round the little square. She made tea and took Mrs Macklin a cup, suitably weak, then let Jude out for his morning prowl. Mrs Macklin, sitting up in bed to eat her breakfast, said cheerfully that she had slept like a top and she hoped that Abigail had too. 'And my dear,' she went on. 'I really cannot call you Nurse or Miss Trent—I shall call you Abigail, such a pretty name and seldom heard these days. Was there a reason for it?'

Abigail explained, and her companion said admiringly: 'What a good idea—how imaginative some people are.' She bit into a slice of paper-thin bread and butter with relish. 'I was sorry to hear about your mother, child.'

Abigail almost dropped an empty porridge plate she was removing to the kitchen. 'My mother?' she faltered. 'How could you possibly know?'

Mrs Macklin gave her an innocent look. 'Dominic told me, of course—should he not have done so?'

Abigail shook her head. 'No, it's not that—it's just that I didn't think he knew…!'

'Dominic knows everything,' remarked her patient complacently, 'as you will discover for yourself, no doubt.'

She spent the morning tidying the house and shopping and cooking their simple meal, which they had barely finished when the professor arrived. The visit seemed more social than professional; he greeted Abigail with his usual distant manner and then sat for ten minutes with Mrs Macklin, talking about nothing in particular. As he got up to go he remarked to Abigail, 'I see you brought Jude safely back. You had no difficulty in finding the place?'

Abigail said that no, she hadn't, thank you, and forbore from mentioning that she had had to pay a week's board for the animal before they would let her have him. The professor had paid all the previous bills; he had forgotten this, the final one; a mere thirty gulden for him perhaps, but a large slice of the money she had left in her purse. She hoped that he would remember it when he paid her, for she had given Bollinger most of the money she had earned from looking after Professor de Wit. She still had her fare to England, but not a great deal besides.

He nodded carelessly in reply. 'I imagine Mrs Macklin is going to rest for a couple of hours. Get your hat and coat and I will take you along to see Bollinger—and Annie.'

Abigail opened her mouth to refuse this high-handed disposal of her free time, but was thwarted by her patient.

'What a splendid idea!' declared that lady. 'I shall lie down here on the sofa and take a nap until you return. Run along and put on your things, Abigail, Dominic can make me comfortable.'

Abigail, running a professional eye over Mrs Macklin when she came downstairs again, had to admit that he had done his work very well—the old lady looked not only comfortable, but pleased with herself. She wished her goodbye and followed the professor out of the house and walked with him across the cobbled square and into the car. He didn't speak for the entire journey, and she, who had hoped that perhaps his remark of the previous day might have meant a breaking of the ice between them, was disappointed. They got out, still silent, at his front door and went inside, where he cast his coat in an untidy heap into one of the chairs, his gloves after it, and strode across the hall to the room where she had had tea with Bollinger. And all he said was: 'Bollinger will be in directly,' as he went away.

It was nice to see Bolly again—and Annie, tucked cosily under his arm. They sat by the fire and drank their coffee which Mevrouw Boot had brought to them and Abigail listened to Bolly's account of his day in Friesland and saw how happy he was. It seemed a pity that he couldn't stay for always. She voiced the thought. 'Bolly, if the professor asked you, would you stay here? It's just what you like, isn't it, and it suits you, doesn't it? I should be perfectly all right in England—you know what private nursing is, first one place, then the other. I shall be away from home a great deal.'

He looked shocked. 'Miss Abby, what's ever come over you?' he wanted to know. 'I must own it's nice here, but the other bloke'll be back before long anyway and I doubt if the professor would want me. Besides, we want a home, don't we?'

'Yes, of course, Bolly,' she agreed hastily, 'it was only an idea. How's Annie?'

'See for yourself, Miss Abby. Flourishing, and such friends with Colossus; sleeps with him too, and sits in the dining room while the boss has his meals. He's that fond of her.'

'I'm so glad.' She stroked the kitten on her lap. 'I didn't think he would be—I mean, I knew he'd be kind to her and give her a home...'

'Lord love you, miss, the boss ain't a bit like he

seems—very soft-hearted, he is. Does a lot, quiet like, so I hear.'

'I'm sure he does, Bolly—and now I must go because I don't want to be too long away from Mrs Macklin. I'll come again very soon. I still think it would be the best thing for me to go back alone and you follow me when I've found something.'

He nodded reluctantly. 'OK, Miss Abby, anything you say, and you're to go out the front door, the boss says. Real narked, he was, that you should use the servants' entrance.'

Abigail's nice eyes rounded with surprise. 'Was he? I should think that would be the last thing to worry him.' A thought struck her. 'Bolly, did you tell him much about us—I mean Mother and...'

'Only a trifle, here and there, so to speak.'

With which remark she had to be content. She wished him a warm goodbye and went, obedient to the professor's wish, through the house door. At the bottom of the steps stood the Rolls with Jan at the wheel. He got out when he saw her and said: '*Dag,* miss. I take you back, the Professor's orders.'

She wondered how long he had been waiting there and why the professor hadn't told her. Probably he hadn't given it a thought after he had given Jan the order. She got in and immediately embarked on a conversation with Jan in her laborious Dutch, without mentioning his master; she knew without being told that Jan would hear no word of criticism against him.

She was out shopping when the professor called the next day. Mrs Macklin told her in a satisfied voice when she returned that he was sufficiently pleased with her progress to allow her to do a little cooking. 'So I shall cook supper, my dear, though I doubt if I shall feel much like washing up the dishes afterwards. And tomorrow if it is fine, I should like to come with you, just to the grocers in the Begijnsteeg. Dear me, how pleasant it is to get back to normal life, and with you here, not nearly as frightening as I had imagined.' She added hastily as if to explain her change of attitude, 'One gets lazy in hospital and too secure.' She smiled at Abigail. 'How pretty you look in that woolly thing, dear, and such pink cheeks. Oh, I nearly forgot to tell you, Dominic has got someone to do the housework, a Mevrouw Rots, she'll be coming in a week's time. What happens to you then, Abigail?'

'I go back to England, Mrs Macklin.'

'You have a home to go to—relatives?'

'No—cousins in Canada and an uncle and aunt who don't want to know about me. But don't worry, all I have to do is to go to the agency and they'll find me another job—at once, the same day, perhaps.'

'How appallingly efficient,' said Mrs Macklin dryly, 'and how very dull for you. All work and no play...'

'Oh, I daresay I'll take a day off.'

'Big deal,' commented her patient unexpectedly, and Abigail laughed with real amusement. 'That's better. You should laugh more often, Abigail.'

Abigail had nothing to say to this and her companion went on in the most casual manner, 'Dominic doesn't laugh enough either. Did you get all the shopping?'

The day passed at a gentle pace, for although Abigail found enough to do in the little house there was no hurry over the doing of it; during the morning Mrs Macklin told her its history and added, 'I was lucky to get it, because they're really alms-houses, I suppose.

It's so central and the rent is low—besides, it's close to my friends. Are you going to see Bollinger today?'

'I thought I might go and see how Professor de Wit is—he was my last patient, you know.'

'Yes, Abigail, a good idea. He's an old acquaintance of mine too. Dominic has promised to take me to visit him one day soon—he has been very ill, I understand, but you know more about that than I do. Dear me, how dull life would be for us elderlies if we were without Dominic to keep a watchful eye upon us. He has never allowed me to be lonely—he was fond of my husband.'

Abigail made some reply; Mrs Macklin must know the professor very well; perhaps during this week she might tell her a little of his life. It would be nice to know; she mused over the interesting fact that he appeared to be Doctor Jekyll and Mr Hyde, for according to her patient there never was a better man. Undoubtedly there was a great deal more than met the eye. She said now: 'Bollinger thinks the world of him and I can quite understand why, for he made it possible for him to leave the most dreary room imaginable—he was so lonely, too, and here in Amsterdam he's happy.'

'Yes?' Mrs Macklin sounded interested. 'Dominic mentioned in the vaguest way that he had been lucky enough to find someone to take Jaap's place until he got back to work, but he didn't tell any of the circumstances.' She gave Abigail a shrewd glance. 'Sit down, dear, and tell me about yourself and Bollinger, and your parents too, that is if you can bear with an old woman's curiosity.'

It was a delight and a relief to be able to talk to someone about Bolly and her mother and their life in London and how she missed the hospital; she told about the agency too and made Mrs Macklin laugh with her description of the stern woman in charge of it. At length when she had finished, Mrs Macklin leaned back in her chair and sighed. 'You poor child, life hasn't been very kind to you in these last few years.' She studied Abigail's face. 'But you're not sorry for yourself, are you?'

'No—well, almost never. Sometimes when I see a lovely dress or some fab jewellery, or a girl with everything, you know—lovely face and hair and up-to-the-minute clothes and the men looking at her—then I wallow in self-pity.' She laughed as she said it and her companion laughed with her.

'Bunkum,' said Mrs Macklin firmly. 'Go and put on your hat and coat and visit Professor de Wit and give him my best wishes.'

Abigail spent a pleasant hour with the old man; he was as thin as ever and still pale, but he had lost none of his zest for life; he wanted to know exactly what she was doing and if she was happy, and listened to what she had to say about Mrs Macklin. 'She's a dear,' said Abigail. 'You know with some people you can be friends at once, just as with others it's quite impossible.' Of course she was thinking of the professor and her elderly companion gave her such a penetrating look that she went a guilty red, although he had said nothing, and changed the conversation. 'I'm going back to England next week,' she volunteered.

He looked surprised. 'You'll like that?'

'I—I suppose so. I like Amsterdam, though at first I thought it would be a bit difficult and lonely, but it's not—there are Bolly and Annie and you and Mrs Macklin, as well as the nurses in the hospital.'

She omitted the professor and her listener appeared

not to notice, for he said jokingly, 'Quite an impressive list! We shall all miss you. And now, my dear, run along to the kitchen and see if our good friend Mevrouw Valk has made that abominable weak tea I am forced to drink.'

Abigail, who liked her tea strong, sipped the tasteless beverage with him and listened intelligently to his theories on cell life, while at the very back of her mind she wondered what the professor was doing. He was, in fact, in the act of pulling the door bell and appeared a moment later before them, dwarfing everything in the room behind him. He greeted his old friend warmly and Abigail with the cold courtesy she had come to expect. She offered him tea and took care not to catch his eye because she happened to know that he detested weak tea, and this was pale and insipid and, what was more, tepid. She sat for another ten minutes for the sake of good manners, then rose to go with the excuse that she should return to Mrs Macklin before that lady, refreshed from her afternoon nap, decided to do something beyond her strength.

The professor got up too, observing that he would show her out, and when she assured him that she was very well able to see herself to the door, he remarked, 'Don't be bird-witted, I have something to say to you.'

She bade Professor de Wit goodbye with the hope that she would see him again before she left Amsterdam, and went out of the room closely followed by the professor. In the dark, panelled hall which was barely big enough for the two of them, he said to surprise her into speechlessness:

'It is the hospital dance in five days' time. I should like you to come—it is to commemorate its foundation.'

Abigail's heart tripped, steadied and turned right over. She spoke quickly before that treacherous organ should make her change her mind.

'Thank you, Professor, but I don't think I'll accept your kind...'

'Why not?'

She stared up at him, looming over her in the dimness and much too near for her peace of mind, trying to think of a really good excuse. 'Well...' she began, not having the least idea what she would say.

'Don't tell me that you have nothing to wear,' he remarked with faint amusement, and she, who had been on the point of saying just that, exclaimed roundly, 'Certainly not, I have several...' She paused, unwilling to utter such a trivial lie to him. 'I don't know anyone,' she offered with sudden inspiration.

'Me?' he queried.

'Oh, don't be ridiculous!' Abigail's voice was a little gruff and she had the uneasy feeling that she was being rude; all the same she went on: 'You're hardly likely to spend the entire evening...' She broke off.

'No, probably not,' he agreed with infuriating readiness, 'but my junior registrar professes a desire to get to know you, and Professor de Wit will be there...'

'You're never allowing him to dance?' Her voice squeaked in protest.

'I should have thought a woman of your good sense would have known better than to have asked such a silly question.'

It was annoying to be addressed as a woman of good sense; if that was how he thought of her then she would go to this dance and she would find a dress to fit his detestable opinion. Something grey or mousey with a high neck and one of those awful shapeless draped fronts.

He asked sharply, so that she jumped guiltily, 'What are you plotting? You will buy a dress— pink, I think, deep pink and of a style to suit you. I believe that I shall come with you to buy it.'

'Indeed you will not,' declared Abigail, her fevered imagination picturing him selecting delectable gowns without once looking at their price tickets.

'And who will carry all the parcels?' he enquired silkily. 'There will be shoes as well.'

'No, thank you, Professor, I would far rather go alone—it would be distracting.'

'Do I distract you, Miss Trent?'

She fumed silently at his awkward questions. 'No— yes, I don't know—you see, I shall want to have a good look round first.'

'Yes? I should have thought that you could have found what you wanted within minutes at Dick Holthaus or Max Heymans.' Two dress shops which she, after only a short stay in Amsterdam, had discovered matched high prices with high fashions—they were the sort of shops she would have loved to have gone to. She frowned, wondering how it was that the professor knew about them, and then remembered to look casual as she said carelessly:

'Oh, I daresay they have, but I still want to look everywhere first.'

He opened the door for her. 'As you wish, but pink, remember, and pretty.'

She walked back to the Begijnhof with a head full of ideas pushing each other round and round; she would never be able to buy a dress with the money she had.

True, she had been paid the day before, but the professor had obviously forgotten about Jude's fees and she wasn't going to ask him for them. And she, like a fool, had given Bolly half straight away. She could borrow on her fare, for she would be due another week's salary when she left Mrs Macklin and there was still the money from Mrs Morgan, surely waiting for her at the agency. She did some rapid sums in her head, and when she got back to Mrs Macklin, asked that lady if she knew of a dressmaker.

'Of course, my dear,' said that lady without hesitation. 'There's Juffrouw Blik, three doors down—a *dominee*'s daughter and crippled in one foot, poor woman, but charming. Don't be put off at the sight of her, Abigail, she's not a very fashionable sort of woman, but she's very good with clothes, especially with something pretty.'

She gave Abigail a questioning look and was instantly told all about the invitation. 'I'd rather like to have the dress made,' said Abigail, 'then I can get exactly the material and shade I want.' Quite unconsciously she spoilt this by adding, 'Is she expensive?'

Mrs Macklin bent her head over her knitting. 'No, dear, about twenty-five gulden, I should think, and for these days it's ridiculously cheap. Why not go to the Bijenkorf tomorrow and see if you find what you want? I know they have a silk sale on, but there'll be other materials, not in the sale.'

They spent the evening discussing the sale, the dance, the dress, the most suitable shoes to go with it and Abigail's hair.

'Leave it as it is,' urged Mrs Macklin. 'It suits you, it's pretty.'

'Pretty? It's mousy and straight.'

'Mice are pretty little creatures,' her patient pointed out, 'and they have straight hair.' She began to talk about the numerous dances she had been to in her youth and not once during the evening did they mention the professor, although Abigail thought about him a great deal.

She found just the material she wanted in the Bijenkorf—rose pink chiffon and a matching silk to line it, both at sale price too, although even then their purchase made a great hole in her purse. But she was feeling reckless by now; drunk with the prospect of spending an evening in the same company as the professor, she purchased some silver slippers and a handbag and walked back happily clutching her purchases, and after getting the lunch for her patient and herself and settling her for a nap, went to see Juffrouw Blik.

Juffrouw Blik's house was really a flat, for she lived on the ground floor; the floor above was rented to a retired schoolteacher. Her sitting room was the same size as Mrs Macklin's but seemed even smaller, if that were possible, because of the number of half-finished garments hanging around its walls and over the chairs, and the old-fashioned treadle sewing machine taking up all the space under the window.

Abigail, eyeing Juffrouw Blik's dumpy, unfashionable person, felt a little dubious about handing over her precious material to the dowdy little woman, then took heart when she remembered that Mrs Macklin had recommended her very highly. In her difficult, halting Dutch she explained what she wanted, showed the pattern she had bought, made a date for a fitting and, with an eye to the urgency of the matter, allowed herself to be measured.

The dress was a success. Abigail, trying it on the day before the dance, had to admit that the professor's demand for rose pink had been completely justified, for the soft colour of the gossamer fine material gave her face a glow and Juffrouw Blik had cut it with panache so that it fitted where it should and the wide, wide skirt swirled around her as she turned and twisted before the mirror. And to complete the outfit, her patient had produced a Russian sable coat, its Edwardian cut exactly right for the dress, and when Abigail protested that she couldn't possibly borrow so valuable a fur she had declared, 'Nonsense, child—I wear it once, perhaps twice a year—it needs an airing. You will be the belle of the ball.'

At which remark Abigail had looked very doubtful, but since she had been invited to go, the least she could do was to look her best. She had seen very little of him during the past few days—true, he had spoken to her during his visits to his patient, but only upon matters which concerned that lady's welfare. Not once had he mentioned the dance, nor for that matter had he given her any sign that he had invited her to attend, which had such a damping effect on her spirits that by the day of the dance she felt no excitement at all, only a secret fear that he had forgotten all about it, and she would dress and then sit and wait in Mrs Macklin's little sitting room, watching the clock ticking through the hours, and he would never come.

It was the morning of the dance, after he had paid his visit to Mrs Macklin, professed himself pleased with her condition, reiterated that the daily help would come in three days' time and reminding her that she was no longer a young woman, that he turned to Abigail, standing like a silent, well-trained shadow beside him.

'You will be called for at nine o'clock,' his voice was pleasant and completely disinterested. 'The dance will not end until the small hours; if you become tired or wish to return here you have only to say so.'

As though she were an old lady or a cripple like poor Juffrouw Blik! thought Abigail, bursting with indignation. Perhaps he was hoping that once having done his duty in inviting her, she would choose to leave early, leaving him unencumbered to dance with the countless lovelies who would most certainly be there. She said coolly, 'I shall be ready, Professor,' and went with him to the door and showed him out with a convincing and utterly false calm.

She was ready by a quarter to nine that evening; she had cleared away the supper, made everything ready for her patient's night and then gone upstairs to the little room of which she had become so fond, to dress. The result was gratifying; she was no beauty, nor would she ever be, but there was no doubt at all that pretty clothes did a lot for a girl. She had taken Mrs Macklin's advice too, and put her hair up in its usual simple style and used the very last of the Blue Grass perfume she had been hoarding for just such an occasion as this one. Wrapped in her borrowed sables, she stood in front of the mirror and promised her reflection that she would enjoy herself and what was more, stay until the very last dance, despite the professor's offer to send her home early. Anyone would think that I was ninety! she told her face in the mirror. You go and enjoy yourself, my girl.

When the doorbell rang at exactly nine o'clock she

flounced downstairs rather defiantly. That would be Jan, she supposed, or a taxi. She flung open the sitting room door, exclaiming: 'Will I do?' and stopped short at the sight of the professor, very grand in his white tie and tails, warming himself before the stove. He inclined his head by way of greeting and said nothing at all, which she found so disconcerting that her defiant mood ebbed away and she looked appealingly at Mrs Macklin, who said satisfyingly:

'Abigail, you'll have a lovely evening, no doubt of it. You look delightful.'

A sentiment hardly echoed by the professor, judging by the expression of his face, for he was glaring down his long nose at her and just for a moment she was tempted to turn round and go upstairs again and tear off her finery and not go at all, but common sense prevailed—there was no reason why she shouldn't have a good time once she got there. She glared at him, disappointment raging under the pink chiffon, to lose all other feelings but one of delight as he told her:

'You take my breath away.' He sounded his usual austere self, but at least he was paying her a compliment. 'I hardly recognised you,' which rather spoilt the compliment, but he actually smiled and she smiled warmly back, her eyes shining. 'Abigail pink and pretty,' he murmured surprisingly, and spoilt that too by adding, 'My registrar will be in the seventh heaven!'

The dance had already started, by the time they had arrived the dance floor was crowded and everyone, in Abigail's feverish imagination, knew everyone else, except her. The professor waited for her while she disposed of the sables and then danced with her. He danced very well, but with a remoteness which was decidedly chilling, so that after one or two attempts at conversation, successfully squashed by his gravely polite replies, she took refuge in silence and was relieved when the dance finished and she was introduced to the junior registrar— a young man of a most friendly disposition even if he was a little on the short side and inclined to be fat. He in his turn introduced her to friends of his own so that presently she began to enjoy herself despite the lack of interest shown by the professor. It was all the more surprising, therefore, when he sought her out and asked her to go in to supper with him. She had already been asked by Henk, the registrar, and was on the point of saying so, for the professor didn't look over-enthusiastic at the prospect of partnering her anyway, when Henk said, 'That's OK by me, Abigail—Professor van Wijkelen has first pick, since he brought you. We'll dance again after supper.'

The professor led her away towards the supper room, chose a small table for two, and only when he had seated her and fetched two plates of food did he speak. 'That was a little unfair of me, I'm afraid,' he observed coolly, 'but I haven't seen you for some time.'

'I've been here all the evening,' stated Abigail flatly, 'and it was very unfair.'

'Meaning that you prefer Henk's company to mine? I can well believe it, Miss Trent—he's still a young man and good fun, I should imagine, do you not agree?'

Abigail bit into a small sausage on a stick. 'Quite nice,' she answered. 'Why do you pretend to be Methuselah? I've no intention of pitying you.' She watched his eyebrows lift and went on recklessly, 'You really had no need to bring me in to supper, you know—I didn't expect it.'

His voice was all silk. 'The reason I did so was because I have something to say to you and this seems a good opportunity to say it.'

Abigail finished the sausage and started on a minute vol-au-vent. Surely he wasn't going to tell her she looked nice, or was being a success or something of that sort? Hardly twice in one evening. She took another bite and asked, 'Yes, sir?' She added the sir from sheer naughtiness because he looked so remote, just as though they were on a ward, discussing a patient and she in uniform. If he preferred her in her cap then she would wear it, metaphorically speaking.

'You leave Mrs Macklin in three days' time,' it was a statement, not a question. 'Unless you are committed to returning to England, you would oblige me greatly by remaining for a further week or so and working in the hospital. There is an outbreak of salmonella on the children's ward, both nurses and patients, I am afraid. We are short of nursing staff as a consequence just when they are most needed. I have a number of beds on the ward and we—that is, I and my colleagues agreed that it would be a good idea if you would be kind enough to help fill the gap while the emergency lasts. You will be paid your usual fee. As to where you will live, I am of the opinion that Mrs Macklin would be delighted if you were to remain with her as a paying guest—and it would be excellent for her to have an interest in life after her long illness.'

How like him, thought Abigail, everything worked out beforehand. She wondered what he would say if she refused. She chose a cheese straw and nibbled at it while she studied him across the table. He looked as impassive as ever, although he was staring at her in a rather disconcerting way. He said suddenly, 'Please, Abigail,' and she gave him a reassuring, almost motherly smile because she sensed anxiety behind the blandness of his face and she loved him far too much to allow him to be worried or anxious even when he was annoying her so excessively.

'Of course I'll come. I like children—besides, it will do me good to do some work for a change. Do you want me to come straight from Mrs Macklin's?'

'Thank you, Abigail. Yes, if you could manage it—I don't know about your days off.'

She shrugged. 'I have plenty of free time and I shall get two days each week in hospital, shan't I? If you will tell me the name of the ward to go to and what time.'

'The Beatrix ward, it's in the oldest part of the hospital, on the top floor. Could you manage ten o'clock? I'll see Zuster Ritsma—you will do staff nurse's duties, of course.' And when she nodded briefly, he went on:

'Can I get you anything else to eat?'

She shook her head; he had got what he wanted—he hadn't eaten anything himself, probably he was waiting to take one of the pretty girls she had seen him dancing with down to supper—it had been an excuse to get her alone and pin her down. 'When did the epidemic start?' she asked him.

He looked faintly surprised. 'Six days ago.'

The day before he had invited her to the dance. She managed a smile as she got up and her voice was a little high. 'Well, I think I'll go and find Henk—he'll be looking for me...' Which wasn't quite true but saved her pride a little, only to have it trampled upon a moment later by the professor.

'You look charming, that dress is most becoming.'

He smiled a little as he spoke and she was conscious of a stab of humiliation. As they went back to the dance floor she said a little unsteadily, 'You didn't have to say that—I would have come to the hospital without any—any softening up.'

It wasn't until that moment the idea took shape that the whole thing had been a softening-up process—the invitation to the dance and the interest in what she would wear, being fetched by him and danced with and supped with. She went a little white and said in a voice that was almost shrill:

'Oh, there's Henk—I daresay I shall see you later.' She smiled with forced gaiety, ignoring the fact that the professor was about to say something, and lost herself in the crowd.

She danced for the rest of the evening and once more with the professor, with whom she kept up such a steady flow of chatter that he was hard put to it to get in a yes or no. He did indeed manage to say: 'There is something I should make clear...' before she interrupted him with: 'Oh, please need we talk shop—I'm having such fun.' She spoke to his shirt front in a brittle voice and avoided his eye, fearful that he was going to pay her another insincere compliment or launch into her hospital duties, neither of which she felt she could bear at that moment.

She had spent some time with Professor de Wit, sitting in a good deal of state, surrounded by friends and admirers and watching the dancing with a good deal of amusement. He welcomed Abigail with a delighted smile and urged her to sit with him. 'You look delightful my dear,' he said happily. 'What a pretty girl you are, to be sure—that pink dress is just your colour,' and he spoke with such sincerity that she very nearly believed him. 'You have danced with Dominic?' he asked, and she said yes, she had, and wasn't it a fab dance and how was he feeling. They talked cosily together until several elderly gentlemen, heavily bespectacled and delightfully mannered, presented themselves with the wish to spend a little time with their old friend, but on no account must the young lady feel called upon to desert them. Which she rightly interpreted as a flowery way of hinting that she should go. Which she did, leaving them prosing gently over Professor de Wit's book, oblivious of the gay scene around them. She was dancing the last dance with Henk when he remarked:

'We shall be seeing you in a day or two, so the Prof tells me. He's got beds in the other wards as well, but Children's is his pet. Very soft-hearted is our Prof, though you wouldn't think it sometimes—got a tongue like a razor and a voice like a deep freeze most of the time.' He glanced at her and added, 'He's a fine man, though. I wouldn't like to work for anyone else.'

Abigail nodded understandingly. 'I'm sure you wouldn't. I've seen some of his kindness.'

There wasn't much kindness evident in the professor's face when they met presently, however. She was wrapped once more in the sables, her plain little face radiant with the pleasures of the evening and her modest success. She saw him waiting by the entrance and exclaimed as she reached his side,

'Oh, it was fun. Thank you very much for inviting me.'

'You thank me when you believe that I did it merely to—what was the expression? Soften you up? How generous of you, Miss Trent!'

He led the way to the car and she got in silently and sat, still silent, while he drove through the quiet streets of the city to the Begijnsteeg. They didn't speak as they got out of the car either. They were half way across the square when at length he broke the silence, at the same time coming to a halt in the dim light of the street lamps.

'I wished to say something to you, to explain, while we were dancing, but I was unable to get a word in edgeways for your ceaseless chatter. I shall do so now, at the risk of us both catching a chill, but as the cold will doubtless preclude you from either interrupting me or answering me back, I feel the risk is worth taking.'

Abigail, from the depths of the sables, eyed him with her mouth open. She had become used, in the last few weeks, to the professor's deliberate way of expressing himself, and indeed, could not imagine him doing anything else, but she hadn't liked that bit about the ceaseless chatter, although she was fair enough to own that it was perfectly true. 'Yes, sir?' she prompted him encouragingly.

'Stop calling me sir,' said the professor nastily. 'You do not need to throw my age at me every time you open your mouth.'

Abigail, perhaps because it was darkish and his face was in shadow so that she couldn't see its usual harsh expression, said boldly:

'Don't talk rubbish! You're far too sensitive about your age—you're in your prime and extremely handsome and you must know that women adore men who are a little bit older.' She stopped, appalled at her own words, and hastened to rectify her mistake by adding belatedly, 'Well, most women.'

'Are you toadying to me?' he asked her in a dangerously quiet voice.

'Toadying?' She was breathless with rage now. 'Why
should I toady to you? You—you…' the rage went as
suddenly as it had come. 'I was trying to help you,' she
said sadly, 'but I see I've made a mess of it.' She moved
away a few steps, towards Mrs Macklin's house. 'I'll
say good night.'

'No, you won't, not until I've done. You were wrong
this evening. I wasn't—er—softening you up, I wouldn't
stoop to such a trick. I meant what I said too—you do
look pretty in that pink gown, it becomes you and you
are charming. You're charming in whatever you wear.'

She couldn't see his face properly, but it didn't matter. She could hear the sincerity in his deep voice and
her heart sang, she wanted to throw her arms around
his neck and hug him, but all she said was: 'Thank you,
Professor' in a voice devoid of all expression. 'I'm glad
I was wrong.'

They walked on and at the door he took the key and
opened it for her, then with it still in his hand stood
looking down at her.

'Thank you for coming,' he said, and now his voice
wasn't cold or austere but warm. 'I told you, did I not,
that you had almost restored my faith in women. You
have done more than that; you have restored my faith
in human nature.'

He bent his head and kissed her on her mouth, a little
awkwardly as though he hadn't had much practice at it
lately. She longed to return his kiss, but didn't; with a
murmured good night she slipped inside.

She had a great deal to think about, she decided, as
she crept up to her room—the professor's contradictory

behaviour for a start. Why was it that at times he looked at her as though he disliked her—no, it wasn't dislike, it was disquiet, as though he expected her to do something which would upset him, and on the other hand, at times he was charming and more than that. She paused on the top step of the precipitous staircase and remembered his kiss. Out of gratitude perhaps, her common sense urged her, and indeed, when she got to her room and viewed herself in the mirror she had to admit that common sense was right; the sables were magnificent, but her face was still unremarkable and her hair had become loose. She lacked glamour or whatever it was that made a man kiss a girl. It had of course been almost dark—she smiled a little bitterly; in daylight she would have stood no chance at all.

Chapter 5

Three days later she reported for duty at the hospital.
Mrs Macklin had received her news with glee and an
instant offer of her room. 'Because, my dear,' she explained, 'it would be so very pleasant to have you living
here. I know I'm perfectly able to manage for myself
now, but I do so enjoy your company.' She added that
Abigail was to consider the house as her own home and
if she wanted to ask Bolly round at any time, she was
to do so, and anyone else she liked to invite.

'I don't know anyone else,' Abigail pointed out.

'That nice surgeon you were telling me about?' enquired Mrs Macklin, 'or perhaps one of the nurses—
or Dominic.'

Abigail had made some sort of a reply, trying to
imagine herself inviting the professor round for tea.
He had paid his usual visits during the three days, of

course, and he had been pleasant enough, though a little distant, and she had caught him eyeing her warily; probably wondering to himself what on earth had possessed him to kiss her; wondering too how she would react to it. Well, she had no intention of reacting at all, she resolutely buried the memory of it under the activities relative to her removal to hospital, and if her thoughts were wistful, she took care that they didn't show.

She had paid a visit to Bolly, of course, carefully choosing a day when she knew the professor to be operating and therefore away from home. She and Bolly, in company with Annie and Colossus, had tea in the little sitting room and discussed the turn of events.

'Things are looking up,' declared Bollinger, well content. 'I must say I like this city, Miss Abby, and you look pretty bobbish yourself. I hope you stay a week or two at the hospital.'

A sentiment to which Abigail heartily subscribed!

The sister of the children's ward was glad to see her; her staff had been severely depleted by salmonella, and worse, several of the small patients were ill with it too. The ward was closed to outsiders; a great effort was being made to find the source of the infection, but as Zuster Ritsma explained, it wasn't so easy, for this wasn't the salmonella due to infected food, which would have been comparatively easy to trace, but an insidious type so that a nurse would be working on the ward, unaware that she was already infected.

'I hope,' she continued in her excellent English, 'that you are a strong girl, Nurse Trent.' She eyed Abigail's small, nicely plump frame with some uncertainty, and Abigail made haste to assure her that she was as strong as a horse and very healthy. Zuster Ritsma took her word for it. 'At least I am grateful to have another nurse on the ward,' she observed with relief, and proceeded to delve into the report, carefully explaining each case as she went. It took some time, and when she had finished, Abigail followed her round the ward and in and out of the glass-partitioned cubicles.

The ward was full, with the infected children away from the rest at the end of the ward—six of them, in various stages of illness, three with drips up and the other three, Zuster Ritsma said, getting better. There were four more suspects in the next two cubicles, and in the last large cubicle there were four babies, each isolated and each very ill. They were post-operative and all were infected. They lay making no sound, dangerously lethargic. Zuster Ritsma adjusted a drip and said, 'We shall save them all, but it will be much hard work.'

She smiled at Abigail as she spoke, and Abigail, who liked her and sensed her anxiety, agreed bracingly. 'What do you want me to do?' she asked.

'These babies. There are four, you see. It will be a heavy task, but if you would stay here, in these cubicles, then the other nurses can stay in the ward.' She picked up a chart and they bent over it together while she explained what had to be done. 'If you need help, I will come—there is a bell and an intercom—also a red light. The night nurse comes on duty at ten o'clock—we work in three shifts.' She hesitated. 'Would you work until then, do you think? Just for today—I have no nurse until tomorrow, and the professor insists that there are *gediplomeerd* nurses.'

'Yes, of course I will, and if this doesn't go on for too long surely two of us could manage between us—I'm quite willing if the night nurse is.'

Zuster Ritsma brightened. 'Oh, that would be excellent. But I do not know if Professor van Wijkelen will allow it.'

'Does he have to know?' asked Abigail. 'As long as there's a nurse here—we can have the time made up to us later. After all, we shall each get twelve hours off and the sick nurses will be coming back in a few days, won't they?'

'It is, how do you say? emergency,' mused Zuster Ritsma. 'You do not dislike?'

'No, I don't dislike,' Abigail agreed quietly, 'and I don't suppose he'll notice.'

But her companion shook her head at this rash statement. 'The professor notices everything.' She was very positive about it.

He came half an hour later, looking thunderous, but not, Abigail guessed, because he was annoyed, rather because he was deeply worried about the infection on the ward, especially the babies, each of whom he had operated upon for pyloric stenosis and who should have by now been on the way to recovery. He ground to a halt beside Abigail and wished her a good morning in a voice which implied that as far as he was concerned there was no such thing, and then, with Zuster Ritsma by his side, examined the babies one by one with meticulous care, throwing suggestions and orders at Henk as he did so. Abigail stood silently by, wishing that she could understand even a quarter of what he said; and in the end she had worried unnecessarily, for he repeated everything he had said to the other two in clear and concise English as he dealt with each baby.

When he had finished he came and stood beside her, looming large in his gown and mask. 'You're quite happy to be doing this work?' he wanted to know, and he sounded so irritable that she wouldn't have dared to say anything but yes, though that was the truth anyway.

'You're off duty,' he snapped at her. 'There is a grave shortage of nurses for a few days, but I have asked for extra staff. You will take your usual time off, Nurse.'

Abigail said, 'Yes, sir,' before Zuster Ritsma, who was looking guilty, could speak; if there were extra nurses, well and good, otherwise they would carry on as she had suggested and he would be none the wiser. This thought allowed a look of complacency to cross her grave face and he was quick to see it. 'Why do you look like that?' he demanded, 'as though you had been clever about something.'

Abigail gave him an innocent look. 'Me?' she asked. 'What have I to be clever about?'

He grunted, nodded briefly and went away, followed by Henk, who winked cheerfully at her as he passed. She was left on her own then, busy with the babies—their drips, their charts, their tiny, feeble pulses, their unhappy vomiting and the continuous cleaning up and comforting. When Zuster Ritsma did appear again she looked as agitated as someone so calm could look.

'The nurses—the professor asked for them, you know? Two of them have the first symptoms…the other one has gone home at a moment's notice because her mother is ill.'

'That's OK—we'll carry on as we said we would, shall we, Zuster? Provided the night nurse doesn't mind, I certainly don't.'

The professor came again in the afternoon, looking preoccupied, but beyond studying the babies' charts and altering his instructions accordingly, had nothing to say to her. And early in the evening Henk came and stayed for ten minutes or so and, unlike the professor, asked her if she was managing and was there anything she needed. She was feeling a little tired by now and longing to get out of her enveloping gown and mask; she hadn't had them off since she had been relieved for her dinner; tea had been brought to her on a tray and she had had it while she wrote up the charts.

It was a quarter to ten when the professor came again. Only his eyes showed above the mask, staring at her coldly, although he had nothing to say until he had examined the babies at some length. But presently he straightened himself, professed satisfaction that they were at least holding their own, and then in a voice of withering chill demanded to know when she had been off duty.

'Well,' said Abigail carefully, 'you see, it's like this—I haven't. It seemed a good idea.'

'You disregarded my instructions, Nurse Trent?' His eyes narrowed. 'No, don't interrupt me. I am not in the habit of having my wishes ignored.' He went on disagreeably but without heat, 'I asked you to come to this ward to help out temporarily, nothing more. When I need advice from you concerning its management, I shall no doubt ask you. Until then, be good enough to refrain from interfering.'

Abigail adjusted a drip to a nicety and said kindly, as though she were reasoning with a bad-tempered child, 'There's no need for you to get into a nasty temper, Professor. You know very well that everyone here falls over their own feet to satisfy your every whim, and don't pretend you don't. Zuster Ritsma carried out your orders to the letter, but she couldn't prevent two of the nurses due on duty from sickening with salmonella, nor could she stop the third one from going home to look after her ill mother. She was so worried that I suggested that the night nurse and I should do a twelve-hour stint each until there are more nurses. That's all—nothing to lose your cool over.'

She stopped abruptly; she had said much more than she had intended, and none of it very polite. He was, after all, a consultant in the hospital and a well-known surgeon. She met the stare from his blue eyes and tried not to feel nervous.

'I have not—er—lost my cool, Miss Trent—it is not in my nature to give way to my feelings, although I am bound to plead guilty to a bad temper.' His eyes gleamed above the mask and she wondered if he was laughing, but decided that it was most unlikely. 'I am indebted to you for your help and I apologise for jumping to conclusions. I will see that your off-duty is made up to you as soon as it can be arranged.' He turned and walked away as silently as he had come, leaving her feeling bewildered. She had expected a good telling off at the very least; instead he had been—what had he been? It was difficult to know, but she suspected that he had been amused at her outburst.

The night nurse came and they spent the next twenty minutes poring over charts and studying the babies together, until finally Abigail was free to leave the ward. She tore off her gown and mask, threw them in the bin and hurried to the changing room where she took off her uniform and cap and tugged on a skirt and sweater without much attention as to how she looked, bundled her hair up under the woolly beret, flung on her coat and made her way to the front entrance of the hospital. It was very dark outside and the wind seemed, if anything, more bitter than a month ago when she had first arrived in Amsterdam. The winter was lasting a long time; she tucked her chin into her scarf and started down the steps.

The Rolls was at the bottom of them and the professor was at the wheel. He got out when he saw her and she made to pass him with a cheerful good night, but he put out a hand and stopped her. 'Get in,' he said.

There was nothing she would have liked more than to have sunk into the comfort of its leather-covered interior, but perversely she replied, 'The walk will do me good, thank you, sir. I need the exercise.'

Wasted breath. He urged her gently towards the open door. 'This is hardly the time of day to go walking around,' he said testily. 'As for exercise, we shall consider that presently.'

She saw that she had no chance against him. She got in and sat silent, fuming at his arrogance and wondering what he had meant about exercise. The journey was a short one. He turned the car silently into the Begijnsteeg and stopped and ushered her out, to fall into step beside her. 'I also need exercise,' he stated, and took her arm to lead her across the silent square. Abigail thought at first that he would stop at Mrs Macklin's door, but he didn't pause, striding briskly along, and she, perforce, keeping pace with his large well-shod feet. He didn't speak for a few minutes and nor did she; for one thing she had been surprised into speechlessness by his action and for another she was far too busy with her thoughts. She had been rude to him in the ward, so probably he was going to give her a telling-off. She sighed without knowing it and braced her tired shoulders.

He spoke at length. 'Have you the door key?' and when she said that yes, she had, he fell silent again. It must have been five minutes later before he asked her, 'How much terramycin are we giving Jantje Blom?'

Jantje was the smallest and the frailest baby. She told him the amount and they went on walking briskly over the cobbles, the wind creeping meanly through her coat so that she shivered.

The professor stopped and peered down at her in the dim light. 'I haven't done this for a long time,' he remarked thoughtfully, and she, thinking that he was talking to himself, said soothingly: 'No, I don't suppose many people do,' and was amazed when he burst into a bellow of laughter so that she said: 'Oh, hush, you'll wake all the old ladies!'

She shouldn't have spoken like that, she supposed, she stood still, waiting for him to snarl something nasty about young women being pert, but all he said was: 'That isn't what I meant, but you don't understand, it doesn't matter at the moment. I'm sorry I was ill-tempered this evening.'

'You had every right to be,' said Abigail fairly. 'I was abominably rude.'

'Yes. I didn't mind—at least you're honest.' His voice sounded bitter and she made haste to say, 'I expect it's worrying for you,' and he laughed again softly; she wondered why, shivering with cold, and he said at once,

'God, I'm thoughtless—you're cold.'

'Yes, but I enjoyed it.'

'Not if you catch a chill.'

She shook her head in the dark. 'I'm very tough.'

He walked her briskly to Mrs Macklin's house. 'Your spirit's tough,' he corrected her.

The house was in darkness. They stood very close in the hall while she found the light switch and then led the way to the kitchen, where, to her surprise, he said, 'I'll get the tea,' and sat her down by the table against the wall. Presently, with the teapot between them, sitting opposite her in one of the narrow wooden chairs, he began to discuss her small patients, and although she was very tired by now, she listened intelligently and even ventured one or two opinions of her own as to their treatment. It was a surprise to her when the Friese clock on the wall chimed midnight, and it surprised the professor as well. He got to his feet with the remark that he should be shot for keeping her from her bed, and although she protested, he washed the cups and saucers and tidied everything away before putting on his topcoat and going to the door. Abigail got up too, because she would have to lock it after him, and followed him out into the hall, but when she put out a hand to switch on the light his large one came down on hers and prevented it. 'No need,' he said very quietly, then caught her close and kissed her, and this time, she thought confusedly, he must have been putting in some practice. He was through the door and down the steps with a muttered good night before she could utter a word.

She went on duty the next morning with her thoughts in confusion—she had been too tired to do more than tumble into bed and fall asleep the night before, and there had been no time to think in the morning for Mrs Macklin had been full of questions about her work as they sat at breakfast together. Only at the end of Abigail's recital of the day's happenings had she said with something like complacency, 'I heard you come in last night, my dear, but Dominic was with you, wasn't he, so I knew you would look after yourselves and there was no need for me to come down.'

'Professor van Wijkelen was kind enough to bring me home,' said Abigail, with a composure she didn't feel. 'He came in for a cup of tea. It was very cold yesterday, wasn't it?'

Her companion ignored this red herring. 'He works too hard,' she observed, 'and I daresay he's worried about this infection—whatever it is. I hope you won't catch it, Abigail.'

Abigail assured her that she wouldn't, cleared the table, washed up, wished Mrs Macklin goodbye and set off for hospital. She went the long way round so that she could have a quiet think as she went, but somehow only one thing occupied her thoughts and that was the professor's kiss. As she went through the hospital gates she wondered how it would be when they met.

It needed only one look at his face as he came towards her in the ward to see that they were back to square one. He looked withdrawn and tired; she wasn't sure how old he was, but today there were lines she had never noticed before. He bade her good morning with the austere good manners which so daunted her, and went at once to work on the four babies.

They were a little better, she reported, her disappointment well hidden behind a professional manner not to be faulted. She gave chapter and verse of their progress during the night and since she had been on duty, adding that Jantje was not responding quite as well as the other three. His mother, she informed the professor, was waiting in the visitors' room on the landing and hoped for a word with him. He nodded without looking at her, got out his stethoscope and when he spoke again it was only to give her further instructions, and presently when Henk joined them, the two men talked together in their own language and it was Henk who turned to her at last and detailed the new treatment the professor had decided upon for Jantje. They went away together, with a cheerful wink and smile from Henk and the briefest of nods from the professor.

It wasn't until after the list that the professor came and then it was almost six o'clock, and although they discussed Jantje together he had little else to say. After he had gone she wondered sorrowfully what it was she had done to cause him to change so towards her. She had actually believed that at last he was beginning to like her, or at least to tolerate her, but she had been wrong. She tended the babies carefully and tried not to think about him.

Off duty at last, she changed rapidly, a little uneasy about the walk back to the Begijnhof; there was no bus going near enough to make it worth while to take one; it was only ten minutes' walk, but it was dark outside and looking out of the window she could see sleet beating upon it. She would get wet. She hurried through the hospital, her mind busy trying to remember some other way home which would save her going through the narrow dark lanes.

Long before she had reached the front hall she had given up the idea; the day had been long and she was tired and the effort was too great. She went through the door and down the steps and the sleet bit into her face like miniature knives and forced her to close her eyes. When she opened them a few seconds later, the Rolls was within a few feet of her and Jan was already getting out and holding the door open for her to get in. He said cheerfully, 'Good evening, miss, I am to bring you to Mrs Macklin's house.'

'Oh, Jan, how lovely! But who…? Did Professor van Wijkelen tell you…?'

'Yes, miss.'

His tone was fatherly and final, and indeed Abigail was too tired to argue. She sat back in her seat beside him, wondering why the professor should take care of someone he could barely greet civilly; perhaps he was afraid that if she was out in the rain and caught cold, she would be of no further use to him—but that hadn't bothered him the previous night. Because she was tired and rather unhappy the memory of it brought tears to her eyes, and when the car stopped she thanked him in a quiet, normal voice and would have got out, but he got out too and started to walk with her across the cobbles. When she protested, he said merely, 'The professor told me to, miss,' and waited while she went up the steps before he wished her good night and walked away, back to the car.

She hadn't expected Mrs Macklin to be up, but that lady popped her head out of the sitting room as she went into the house and without appearing to notice her woebegone expression, said cheerfully, 'There you are, dear—I didn't feel like going to bed, so I've made a jug of cocoa for us both. You're tired—come in by the stove and be warm and comfortable for half an hour.'

She turned her back and went and sat down again, leaving Abigail to take off her outdoor things and brush away the tears. When she was sitting opposite Mrs Macklin in the comfortable warmth of the little room, her companion asked, 'A bad day?'

'No, not really,' Abigail admitted. 'Three of the ba-

bies are much better and the fourth will do, I think, and
there aren't any fresh cases today and none of the con-
tacts are proved positive—I should think the worst's
over. Henk seemed to think so—they've found the
source—one of the porters.'

'Did you see Dominic?'

'Yes, he came to see the babies.'

'I heard the car—he didn't come in this evening.'

'No, Jan brought me home, actually. I hadn't expected…he was waiting for me…the professor had sent
him.' Abigail drew a determined breath. 'Mrs Macklin,
why is he so—so considerate of me, and yet he doesn't
like me at all?' She sighed, took a sip of cocoa and
looked enquiringly at the older woman.

'I've been hoping you would ask me that,' said Mrs
Macklin surprisingly. 'I didn't feel I could tell you, but
now that you've asked—' she nodded her grey head
in satisfaction. 'One can't gossip about one's friends,
but there comes a time… The reason Dominic dislikes
women is because he mistrusts them—young women,
that is.' She waited expectantly for Abigail to say something.

Abigail poured more cocoa for them both; all she
said was: 'You're sure you want to tell me?'

'Oh, yes, I'm going to tell you, my dear—he's far too
nice a man to be misjudged, especially by you, Abigail.'

Abigail let that pass. Mrs Macklin went on: 'He's—
let me see turned forty now. When he was a young man,
in his early twenties, he married—a lovely girl, tall and
dark, I remember she was most arresting. I don't think
that for one moment he loved her—infatuated perhaps,
and that passes for love for a little while, doesn't it? She
was the kind of girl men fall for, and because Dominic

was young and handsome and knew everyone, as well as being a wealthy man—you knew that, Abigail?—she married him. Within a few weeks he discovered that she was having affairs; before six months were out she was killed in a car crash with her current boy-friend. Dominic changed from that day—oh, he wasn't broken-hearted, he had long since lost all feeling for her, but his pride was hurt. He was still charming to the girls of his acquaintance, but it was as though he had resolved to live his life without them. He had—still has—his work. It absorbs him, doesn't it, and always will. Mind you, he keeps his true feelings well hidden,' she paused, 'at least I always thought so, but now I'm not so sure—he goes out a great deal, because he has many friends and he's well liked. He's still a very good-looking man, of course, he has almost everything; looks, brains, an excellent position in life, more money than he knows what to do with—but no love.'

Abigail's hands were clasped so tightly round her cup that the knuckles showed white. She said in a tight little voice, 'Yes,' and went on inconsequently, 'He loves little children, and he's good to his patients; they trust him. It's very sad that he has no one to love and won't allow anyone to love him.'

Mrs Macklin gave her a long thoughtful stare. 'Very,' she agreed, 'especially as every female under forty who can get within striking distance of him has done her best to remedy that fact.'

Abigail, who seldom blushed, went becomingly pink. 'Oh, is that why he?—surely he would never think that I—he gets irritated with me, all the time—well, almost all the time,' she amended truthfully. 'I didn't know— I'll try and keep out of his way as much as possible.

Perhaps he'll meet some girl who can make him happy. I hope so.'

She got up and went to the kitchen with the cups on a tray. 'You could make him happy,' her heart urged her silently, 'because you love him.' She drowned the lunatic thought with a gush of water from the tap and washed the cups and saucers with a deliberately empty mind, and when she went back to the sitting room, beyond thanking Mrs Macklin for her confidence, made no reference to their conversation. Instead she enquired how her companion felt and listened sympathetically to Mrs Macklin's small grumbles about her health. They went to bed soon after that, and Abigail lay trying not to think about the future, because it would be without Dominic and she couldn't imagine it without him, even though, because he had been let down once, so long ago, he wouldn't even allow himself to like her. After all, she told herself wryly, she had got used to his irritable manner and cold voice by now; they made no difference to her feelings, and now that she knew their reason, she wouldn't mind any more—well, not very much.

The days, with their strict routine and small crises, came and went. The weather became steadily worse, with little flurries of wet snow and leaden skies. Abigail's boots leaked and she didn't dare to buy another pair, since she had, as yet, had no money for her first week's work at the hospital and paying Mrs Macklin had made a hole in what she had. Possibly she would be paid when she had finished working for them, and borrowing from Bolly was out of the question, anyway. She didn't intend seeing him until the salmonella scare was over. The situation was improving fast now, although there were still a number of nurses off duty, but there had been no fresh infection for some days. The babies were out of danger too, although they still had a long way to go and needed a great deal of care. She had become very fond of them and delighted in their progress; even little Jantje was improving at last.

It was in the middle of the second week of her job at the hospital that the professor arrived alone one afternoon. He examined the babies, studied their charts and path lab reports, expressed his satisfaction and then asked her: 'When do you intend to revert to your normal working hours, Nurse Trent?'

She kept her voice coolly friendly. 'Tomorrow, sir. Zuster Ritsma may have told you that there are two more nurses returning to duty, and another one at the end of the week. Is it true that the ward is to come out of isolation in a day or two?'

'Yes. Which duty will you be taking?'

She knew that too, but she wasn't going to tell him. 'I'm not sure—Zuster Ritsma has it all arranged.'

'Your days off?' he persisted.

'I'm to have those as soon as possible. Zuster Ritsma has kindly said that I may choose.'

'Have you any plans for them? Do you wish to go away, or spend some time with Bollinger? He can be spared.'

'That's very kind of you. I hadn't begun to think about it. I think I should like to take him out for the afternoon—he loves the cinema.'

He looked at her unsmilingly, his eyes thoughtful, and she was hopeful that he had remembered that she was owed a week's salary, but all he said was, 'I see,' and stalked away.

She was to do an early shift; half past seven until four

each day, and as the professor invariably came before noon and after five, it meant she would see him only once a day, and not at all on operating days. Which, she told herself, was all for the best. It would leave her evenings free to keep Mrs Macklin company too and she could call and see Bolly on her way off duty. An excellent arrangement for all concerned, she reiterated, and began to wonder how much longer they would need her in the hospital.

She had mentioned it tentatively to Zuster Ritsma over coffee and had been told kindly that the professor had arranged that she should work there and would doubtless tell her when he no longer needed her. 'Although,' Zuster Ritsma had added, 'I hope it won't be just yet, for we shall be short-staffed for another week or so yet.' Abigail hugged that fact to her as she went about her work.

It had surprised her that Jan came to fetch her each evening; she had thanked the professor on the day following the first occasion and he had looked down his nose at her and remarked rather testily that as there were so many nurses off sick, it behoved him to take care of those who weren't. So she hadn't mentioned it again, but it was nice to find Jan waiting for her in the cold dark and she was secretly glad that she didn't need to walk alone through the dim, deserted lanes around the hospital.

She was a little tired on the morning of her new shift; it had meant getting up at six o'clock to get her breakfast and take Mrs Macklin a cup of tea before she left the house, and she had been late off duty the evening before, but she cheered up as she walked along the familiar little back ways in the semi-dark, replying to the milkmen and postmen and paper boys' cheerful *Goeden Morgen,* as she hurried by. The night nurse was cheerful too, for the night had been without worries. The babies were asleep, so Abigail helped with the older children's breakfasts, laughing a good deal with them because half the time she couldn't understand what they were saying and when she spoke herself they found her accent so comical. Jantje woke up presently and she went to give him his bottle. He was very slow still; she sat on the low chair by his cot, cuddling him close and encouraging him while he blinked up at her with eyes still lacklustre from his illness. 'Beautiful boy,' she urged him, 'drink up like a good lad.' She kissed the top of his small bald head. 'I wish you were mine.'

'You like babies—children?' The professor's voice sounded harshly from behind her and the bottle jerked in her hand so that Jantje, sucking half-heartedly, stopped altogether.

'Yes,' said Abigail, and hoped that he couldn't hear the uneven thud of her heart, and then to Jantje, 'Come along, my lovely boy, it's good for you.'

'No,' said Henk from the doorway, 'it's Guinness that's good for you, is that not so?' It sounded funny in his strongly accented English and she gave a chortle of laughter and laughed again when he said, 'Since he seems to understand English, can you not also say, "Time, gentlemen, please?"'

'That's an idea, he's such a slowcoach.' They were both standing by her now and she looked up and smiled, to meet Henk's cheerful face and the professor's bleak stare, which she ignored, saying cheerfully, 'He's better, isn't he, sir?'

'Yes, Nurse Trent.' He turned away to examine the

other babies as Zuster Ritsma joined them and they all talked babies for a few minutes while Abigail coaxed the last of Jantje's feed into him and popped him back into his cot. She was about to pick up the next baby when Zuster Ritsma said, 'Nurse Trent, there are nurses returning, is it not good? Today at one o'clock there will be two, one will work here tomorrow and you will take a day off. There are three days due to you, is it not, but the others you shall have when you wish. The professor wishes it so.'

Abigail looked at the professor who was frowning at nothing in particular. When he looked at her the frown turned into a scowl. 'We are still not fully staffed,' his voice was stiff. 'I do not wish you to be overtired, otherwise you will be of no use here. Also it is convenient.'

'Charming!' Abigail's voice rang with annoyance. 'Such thoughtfulness does you credit, I must say.' Her usually soft voice had an edge of sarcasm. 'It's nice to know I'm useful, even if only as a cog in your machine.'

She would have liked him to have looked uncomfortable or even ashamed—had she not, only the day before, told him that she was to choose her days off?—and now they were being thrust upon her without a by-your-leave. He appeared to be neither; there was a gleam in his blue eyes which might have suppressed temper, but his expression remained bland; beyond a faint lift of the eyebrows he might not have heard her. She turned her back, picked up the baby she was going to feed and bore it away to change its nappy. She hated him! The hate lasted a good five minutes and was then wiped out by a flood of love which made nonsense of her own bad temper and his own disregard of her as a person. She fed the baby and thought of all the good reasons why he should be so horrible, then forgave him for all of them.

He didn't come again that day. The two nurses, Zuster Vinke and Zuster Snel, came on at noon; the three of them worked together until it was time for Abigail to go off duty.

It was still cold and it didn't seem to have got light all day and now that was fading, making the lighted shops she passed seem very cheerful. Almost home, she stopped at a *banketbakkerij* and bought some crisp little biscuits, which would be nice for tea, for she had no doubt that Mrs Macklin would be waiting for her. She couldn't afford the biscuits, her store of money was now so low that even that small luxury was an extravagance, but she was feeling reckless and a little defiant. She turned into the square with the windows of its little houses shining a welcome, her head full of plans for the next day. She wouldn't be able to do much—visit Bolly, naturally, and perhaps take Mrs Macklin to see Professor de Wit. He didn't live very far away; she wondered uneasily if it was too far for the old lady, or would she have to have a taxi? She decided to break into her fare which she still had saved; after all, she would be paid soon, especially as she made up her mind, there and then, to ask about it at the hospital the moment she returned.

She opened the little house door and shut it thankfully upon the dark outside, calling, 'It's me, Mrs Macklin,' as she cast her outdoor things on to the banister of the little staircase. 'I'll get the…' she began as she went into the sitting room, and stopped, because the professor was standing before the stove.

His 'Good evening, Miss Trent,' was very stiff. 'I

am just about to go—I am already late. I called to see how Mrs Macklin does and find her very well, so well, in fact, that she is going on a small outing tomorrow. There is a concert of Viennese music tomorrow evening in the Concertgebouw which she is anxious not to miss. Perhaps you would care to accompany her?' he added carelessly. 'I don't suppose you are interested.'

'Why should you suppose that?' enquired Abigail, falling neatly and unwittingly into his trap. 'I should enjoy it very much!'

'Yes?' If she had any doubts about accepting, the one syllable would have decided her; it contained enough faint mocking disbelief to furnish a whole scathing sentence.

'Yes,' she reiterated, and realised too late why he had been so adamant about her day off—she would be company for Mrs Macklin who he would not wish to go alone. If it hadn't been that she liked her erstwhile patient far too much to disappoint her, she would have said a decided no. She gave the professor a smouldering look and saw that he knew exactly what she was thinking. She said hastily before her temper got the better of her, 'Shall I get the tea, Mrs Macklin? And does the professor intend to stay?'

It seemed that he didn't. She showed him to the door, wished him a chilly goodbye and went to put the kettle on.

They had almost finished tea, talking trivialities in which the professor had no part, when Mrs Macklin observed, 'Dear me, Abigail, I almost forgot. Dominic asked me to tell you that Jan would be here with the car at ten o'clock tomorrow morning and he will take you wherever you wish. Dominic will be away all day and if you would care to lunch with Bollinger at his house, he hopes that you will do so—he has already mentioned it to Bollinger, I believe.'

Which meant, thought Abigail, that Bollinger would be expecting her and she couldn't disappoint him. She might as well go straight there in the morning; it would be pleasant to have a long talk to him and having lunch there would solve the vexed question of her shortage of cash. Perhaps the professor was making amends, although he hadn't seemed particularly friendly just now. On the contrary; he had got his own way again. She said aloud, 'That will be very nice. I would have gone to see Bolly anyway, but I had thought that perhaps you and I could have gone round to see Professor de Wit in the afternoon.'

'A very kind thought, Abigail, but as it happens, he will be at the concert with us, so we shall be able to have a good chat there. I'm greatly looking forward to it. What will you wear?'

'Oh, lord,' exclaimed Abigail, dismayed, 'I haven't got anything—at least only a very plain velvet dress—it's brown and I've never liked it. I only packed it at the last minute because I thought it might be useful—it's that sort of a dress. Will it do, you think?'

'I'm sure it will. You're not a girl to need frills and flounces. Look how well that pink dress becomes you, and that's simple enough.'

Abigail agreed reluctantly and wished wholeheartedly for a new dress, although no one would see her at the concert and her two patients were much too kind to criticise her appearance. 'What will you wear?' she asked in her turn. The two ladies spent a delightful evening discussing clothes.

By the time Jan came she had breakfasted, taken Mrs Macklin hers on a tray, tidied her own room and dressed herself ready to go out. The weather showed no signs of improving, but in the comfort of the big car, it didn't matter. She spent the short journey practising her Dutch upon Jan, who obligingly corrected her many mistakes and helped out when she lacked a word. She thanked him nicely, as she always did, when they arrived at the professor's house and got out, to be admitted by a delighted Bollinger.

It was only a week or so since she had seen him, but it seemed much longer than that. He led her into the small sitting room and poked up the bright fire in the grate, then went away to return a few minutes later with a tray of coffee and with Colossus and Annie at his heels. They made much of her and then planted themselves side by side before the fire.

'Regular little charmer, is our Annie,' observed Bollinger, 'makes rings round the boss, she does, sits on his lap the instant he takes a chair. Lucky Colossus don't mind—fair spoils the little beast does that dog.'

'I'm glad. She's quite a beauty now she's plump and well fed. And now tell me, Bolly, how are you getting on?'

She listened patiently to the recital of his days. Not exciting, but she could see that he had enjoyed every minute of them, and when he had finished she explained carefully about not getting her pay and why she couldn't give him any money. As she had known he would, he offered to lend her all he had, but she refused gently and with gratitude, telling him that she would certainly be paid at the end of the week. And that awkward fact negotiated, she went on to give him a lighthearted account of her own week, making it out to have been much easier than it was.

Bolly, who was no fool, shook his elderly head and said, 'It can't have been much fun, Miss Abby—the boss told me each evening how you was getting on—real hard work, he said it was, and you not saying a word of complaint.'

'Well,' Abigail replied reasonably, 'I really didn't have much to complain about, you know,' at the same time swallowing surprise because the professor should have said that.

There was a great deal to talk about. Somehow sitting there in the comfortable room, life seemed suddenly secure and pleasant, with the dog and kitten between them and the cheerful firelight turning the silver coffee service to gold; for all the world as though it were home, thought Abigail wistfully.

Presently Bolly went away to return with Mevrouw Boot, both carrying loaded trays, the contents of which they proceeded to arrange on the small rent table under the window, and when, after a short chat, the housekeeper went away, Bolly said diffidently: 'Miss Abby, here's your lunch. The boss said you was to have it here. I usually eat with Mevrouw Boot, but the boss, he suggested you might like me to stay with you.'

'Well, of course I should love you to stay,' Abigail went round the table to give the old man a hug. 'You're my friend, Bolly, I don't know what I'd do without you.'

He beamed at her. 'That's the very words the boss used,' he commented, and pulled out a chair for her to sit down.

'Oh?' she tried not to sound interested. 'Did he?'

Bollinger placed a pipkin of soup before her and removed its lid, and its fragrance caused her small nose to twitch in anticipation of it.

'That's right,' he agreed. 'He's a fine gentleman, is the boss, once you get to know him.'

And that was something in which Bolly had been more successful than she—for she didn't know him at all and it didn't seem likely that she ever would. She sighed, dismissed the unhappy thought and applied herself to her soup.

They went for a walk when they had finished lunch, taking Colossus with them and leaving Annie curled up before the fire, and although it was cold and windy, Abigail enjoyed it, just as she enjoyed the tea they found waiting for them when they got back, for it was like the teas she remembered when she was a child—hot buttered muffins in a silver dish, tiny sandwiches and a sponge cake as light as a feather.

'What a marvellous cook Mevrouw Boot is,' she commented, licking a jammy finger.

'You're right there, Miss Abby—made the muffins, she did. The boss said you was to have a good English tea—muffins, he says, and an English cake, and see there's plenty of milk in the jug. We done our best.'

'It's marvellous,' Abigail praised him, much struck by the professor's attention to detail—for instance, knowing that there was never enough, if any, milk served with tea in Holland. 'I must go to the kitchen and thank Mevrouw Boot.'

Which she did before setting out for the Begijnhof once more, after promising that she would meet Bolly for coffee in a day or two's time.

She found Mrs Macklin in her bedroom, doing things to her hair.

'Heavens, am I late?—it's not till eight o'clock, is it?—there's still supper…!'

'Yes, dear,' said Mrs Macklin, 'there's plenty of time. I thought I'd get all ready except for my dress; I can put that on after supper. *Erwten* soup—it's been on all the afternoon—and yoghurt for afters.'

'Very nice.' Abigail, who wasn't fond of pea soup, remembered her splendid lunch, went downstairs again to lay the supper table.

She dressed after supper when everything had been tidied away and she had laid her breakfast ready for the morning, but first she fastened Mrs Macklin into the handsome black dress, laid the table wrap ready and then went to her own room. Twenty minutes later she was standing before her mirror, eyeing her reflection with distaste, intent on her face and quite failing to see that the brown dress matched her eyes exactly and showed off her pretty figure to advantage. She had made up her face with care and had done her hair with even more attention to detail; now she put on her tweed coat over the despised brown velvet and went downstairs. She found Mrs Macklin already there, looking very *grande dame,* even though, as she pointed out to Abigail, she had lost so much weight that the dress was loose-fitting.

'And mine's a little too tight,' said Abigail, 'which is far worse.' She looked down at her person rather anxiously. 'I hope the seams don't pop. How lucky there won't be anyone there to see, though I expect you'll be bound to meet someone.'

'Certainly,' said Mrs Macklin, and her dark eyes snapped with amusement, but Abigail, with her head twisted over one shoulder trying to see if she looked all right from the back, missed that.

They were to be fetched by Jan, who would collect Professor de Wit first, Mrs Macklin told her and at ten to eight, Jan rang the door bell and escorted the older lady to the car, while Abigail made a few last-minute arrangements for Jude's comfort, she hurried after them and got into the seat beside Jan, leaving the two older members of the party to greet each other on the back seat and then talk non-stop throughout the entire short journey.

Jan seemed to know exactly where they were to go. He gave Mrs Macklin an arm up the stairs in the Concertgebouw, and Abigail, her arm tucked protectively in Professor de Wit's, followed him happily. They had a box and once the party was seated Abigail looked around her with a good deal of interest.

The auditorium was full and, from what she could see of the audience, it was smartly dressed. It was all much more splendid than she had anticipated and she thanked heaven silently that the brown dress, although not exciting, was at least passable, but she forgot that presently when the music started. She was sitting beside Mrs Macklin with an empty chair beside her, but she forgot her companions too, leaning forward, her elbows on the red plush of the box, her chin in her hands, staring down at the orchestra. It was the faintest of sounds which caused her to turn her head. Dominic van Wijkelen was sitting beside her in the chair which had been empty; he nodded briefly into her surprised face and became at once absorbed in the music, and most unreasonably the thought that she might just as well not be there for all the notice he had taken of her crossed her mind, then she stifled a laugh, because she herself had been completely absorbed not a minute since, and anyway, what was there about her to rival the music? She focused her attention once more and found that although the magic was still there it was tempered by the presence of the professor, sitting so close and so withdrawn.

The music came to an end and the lights went up and in the general buzz of clapping and talk the professor got up and went to bend over Mrs Macklin's chair; he didn't take his seat again until the lights were lowered and he hadn't spoken one word to Abigail. She sat like a statue, wondering if she hadn't been meant to come with Mrs Macklin—whether she had misunderstood, and this, mixed with a rising hatred of the miserable brown dress, caused her calm face to assume an expression of extreme disquiet, which was perhaps the reason for the professor to place a hand quietly over her own, clasped in her lap. The expression on her face turned to one of great surprise; she turned her head slowly to look at him, her mouth a little open, her eyes saucer-round, and met a look to melt her bones, a look she had only seen on his face when he had been bending over a patient—kind and gentle and faintly smiling, and when she attempted to pull her hand away, he merely held it in a firmer grip, and the smile widened. There was nothing to do but leave it where it was, tear her gaze away from his and stare at the orchestra below.

He gave her her hand back when the lights went up and asked, still smiling: 'You are enjoying your day off, Abigail?'

She found her voice, a little high and squeaky. 'Yes, thank you. It was lovely to see Bolly—thank you for letting me spend the day at your house and giving me lunch and tea.'

'A pleasure which I was unfortunately prevented from sharing,' he replied. 'What do you think of our Annie?'

They talked about commonplace things and soon her heart stopped its absurd racing, and she was able to tell herself that probably the music had made him feel romantic and she was the nearest woman—a tale which held no water at all when presently the lights went out and he possessed himself of her hand again.

The evening was like a dream—a dream from which she had no desire to waken, but the concert came to an end and Abigail put on the serviceable winter coat once more, took Professor de Wit's old arm and walked slowly in the wake of the others, down to the car. Jan wasn't there this time. The professor stowed his passengers comfortably and got behind the wheel himself, disentangled the Rolls with remarkable patience from the multitude of cars around them and drove without haste through the city. They had stopped before his house before Abigail had even begun to wonder where they were going, and she found herself, in company with the two older members of the party, being ushered into the welcoming warmth of the hall, where Bolly, who had opened the door to them, took their coats and invited them to enter the drawing room—a room Abigail had not yet seen. She smiled at Bolly and paused a moment to have a word with him before following the others inside, and became aware that the professor was beside her, but beyond giving her a quick glance he didn't speak to her but to his guests in general.

'It seemed a good idea if we had a drink and a sand-

wich before we part,' he said pleasantly, and piloted
them to the chairs scattered around the great fireplace,
and as though she had been given her cue Mevrouw
Boot came in with a trolley and Bollinger behind her.

Abigail, eating tiny hot sausages, *bitterballen* and
vol-au-vents and drinking the Cinzano she had asked
for, made conversation with Professor de Wit and contrived at the same time to look around her. The room
was large and lofty with an ornate plaster ceiling and
panelled walls painted white, divided by gilded col-
umns. The floor was completely covered by a fine carpet of a delicate, almost faded pink, and the chairs, of
which there were a considerable number, were upholstered in a variety of shades in that colour, as well as
muted blues and greens. There was a chandelier hanging from the ceiling's centre, reflecting light into every
corner, and a number of matching wall chandeliers. The
curtains were of the same dull pink as the carpet, and
the only dark colours in the room came from the paintings on the walls, family portraits and landscapes for
the most part. It was a delightful room, restful as well
as beautiful; it made her feel dowdy, and the knowledge
that her host's eyes were upon her did little to make her
feel anything else; she and her brown dress stuck out
like a sore thumb in the beautiful pastel-tinted room.
She turned her shoulder to the professor and listened
attentively to the old man's dissertation on the music
they had been listening to.

They stayed an hour before the professor drove them
home, Professor de Wit first, to be handed over carefully to the ministrations of Juffrouw Valk and then on
to Mrs Macklin's house. The professor accepted Mrs
Macklin's offer of a cup of coffee with the air of a man

who had had no refreshment for a considerable time, and sat down to talk to her while Abigail went to the kitchen to make it. But Mrs Macklin took only a few sips, declaring that she was now too tired to enjoy it and would go to bed at once, but despite this she refused Abigail's help, merely allowing her to help her off with her dress when she got to her room and then sending her downstairs again. Abigail had expected the professor to be on his feet, coated and ready to go home, but he was still sitting where she had left him, and now as she entered he got to his feet and fetched the coffee pot from the top of the stove and refilled their cups. Abigail sipped in silence, while her thoughts, like mice on a wheel, spun round, trying to find a suitable topic of conversation.

There was no need. The professor put his cup down and said in the kind of voice he used when he was giving her details of a patient: 'You look very pretty, Abigail.'

He was of course either being kind or joking—she thought the former. She was not in the least pretty, certainly not in the brown velvet. Probably her nose was shining too. She said in a small voice:

'Thank you, I don't know why you said that because it's not true, but thank you all the same.'

She gasped when he answered her blandly, 'No, it's not true. You're not pretty, you're beautiful, because you're honest and kind. I told you, did I not, that you had restored my faith in women, and now I'm a little afraid.'

'Why?'

'Because it may not be true…'

She got to her feet and walked over to him. 'It's quite true,' she assured him, and smiled up into his face. She only just stopped herself in time from telling him how much she loved him. But perhaps he didn't want love—not from her—perhaps she was just a stepping stone to some other girl, a girl who really was pretty and led his kind of life. She kept the smile there, though, and he smiled slowly back, towering over her. For the third time he kissed her, and this time it was a kiss to keep her awake for a very long time after he had gone.

Chapter 6

She was talking to Henk when the professor came on to the ward the next morning. They had been laughing about something or other together and she turned a still smiling face to him, and although her good morning was quiet, her eyes were warm; a warmth dispelled instantly by the austerity of his face and his own dry, 'Good morning, Miss Trent.' He looked as though he had been up all night, she thought, which might account for his withdrawn air. When he asked for the reports on the babies, she gave them in a brisk friendly voice, not smiling at all. Perhaps when Henk went... Henk didn't go; he suggested it, for he was wanted on another ward, but the professor told him rather sharply to remain where he was, so that it was impossible to say anything, even if Abigail had known what to say. Which she didn't.

After a night of thinking, sometimes very muddled because she had dozed off from time to time and the thoughts became dreamlike and quite unmanageable, she had come to the conclusion that in some way she had been the means of making him realise that not all women were like the girl he had so disastrously married. She doubted if he had any feeling for her—gratitude perhaps, a slow dawning friendship which was destined to come to a premature end once she was back in England, and right at the back of her mind, hardly to be thought of, was the possibility that he had, much against his will, fallen a little in love with her.

She watched him stalk away from the ward after a blandly polite goodbye and admitted that the possibility of him entertaining any feelings for her was so slight as to be non-existent. She picked up Jantje and put him on the scales. He was beginning to gain weight now and looked like a baby once more. He smiled windily at her and she said aloud:

'He's going to send me away, dear boy. I'll bet you my month's money on it, for either he has set his sights on some blonde lovely and wants me out of the way, or I embarrass him.'

She was right, of course. She didn't see him the next day and the following afternoon, just before she was due off duty, he turned up, with Henk and Zuster Ritsma. The babies were examined, a fairly short business now, and then he turned round to address Abigail.

'We seem to be over our emergency, Nurse. I must thank you for your help, we are all deeply appreciative of it. Shall we say that you can go at midday tomorrow?'

She had expected it, and now it had happened it wasn't as bad as she had thought it would be. She said matter-of-factly, 'That suits me very well, thank you.' She glanced at him and managed to smile briefly, then found his eyes upon her in a thoughtful stare. But when he spoke it was abruptly. 'I'll say goodbye, Nurse.' He offered his hand and she took it and remembered vividly how he had held it at the concert and how, later, he had kissed her. She smiled again, too brightly, quite unable to speak.

Mrs Macklin, when she was told, was so astonished that she could think of nothing to say for several seconds. 'I thought you would be here for weeks—months even,' she managed at last. 'I knew you wouldn't be at the hospital for ever, but Dominic always has so many private patients and he has often told me how difficult it is to get a nurse for those who want to stay at home. You're not mistaken, my dear?'

'No, I expected it—at least for the last two days I've been expecting it.'

'Since we went to the concert,' commented Mrs Macklin sharply.

'Well, more or less.' Abigail got up from her chair, 'If I'm to leave at midday I'll go back to England by the night boat, if I can get a ticket.'

It would be better that way, for she would be able to sleep on board and when she got to London she could go straight to the agency and get another job. She went up to her room and started to pack in a halfhearted fashion. She would have liked a good weep, but there was really no time; she had to see Bolly before she went and got her ticket and say goodbye to Professor de Wit, and what was the use of crying anyway? She screwed up the brown velvet dress into an untidy bundle and rammed it into her case. She didn't care if she never wore it again, but the pink dress she folded carefully in tissue paper and tucked it away, out of sight, under her spare uniform. It was a pity, she told herself, that she couldn't tuck her dreams away as easily.

She left the hospital the next day, handing over to the nurse who was to relieve her before going to say goodbye to Zuster Ritsma, who shook her fervently by the hand, wished her well and told her that any papers concerning her work would be posted on and what was her address.

Abigail gave the name of the agency, and when Zuster Ritsma, not quite understanding, persisted that she wanted Abigail's home address, explained that just for the time being she had no home. Zuster Ritsma, the eldest of a large family to whose welcoming bosom she retired on her days off, gave her a deeply pitying look, and Abigail, to forestall the sympathy she could see in the sister's eye, asked for her money.

Her companion looked blank. She knew nothing about it, she said. She had understood that the professor would be paying her as he had engaged her in the first place.

'I think you had better ask him, Nurse Trent—if you would like to go to the consultants' room and see if he is there?'

Abigail liked no such thing; to ask him meekly for her salary after he had so thankfully wished her goodbye was more than enough. She had just sufficient money to get to London and a pound or two besides; she would manage until he sent it on to her. In any case, she consoled herself, Mrs Morgan's money would have arrived at the agency by now. There remained only Bolly to worry about; she was glad now that they had already discussed her return to England, leaving him behind for a little while. She made her way to the house on the *gracht,* doing hopeful, inaccurate sums in her head.

Bolly was surprised and disconcerted at her news. 'A bit quick,' he observed. 'I don't like the idea, Miss Abby—you on your own.'

'But, Bolly,' she made her voice reasonable and cheerful too, 'we did agree that it was the best thing, remember? I shall be quite all right, with any luck I'll get a job straight away and then I can start looking for a flat. I shall be much happier knowing that you're here while I'm doing it.'

And seeing Dominic each day, she added silently. Still determinedly cheerful, she went on: 'I must go now, Bolly dear. I'll write to you the minute I get fixed up, I promise.' She gave him an affectionate hug, bade farewell to Annie and Colossus and went round to Professor de Wit's house, where she told him her news and wished him goodbye. Unlike Bollinger, the old man didn't seem in the least surprised to hear that she was leaving.

'A natural sequence of events,' he called it, and when she enquired what he meant he told her she would have to wait and see, but she could mark his words. Abigail smiled and murmured and decided he didn't mean anything at all; he was old and so clever as to be a little eccentric at times. She kissed him goodbye with real affection.

She had plenty of time when she got back to Mrs Macklin's. The boat train didn't leave until the late evening. She ate a simple supper with Mrs Macklin, who was frankly tearful at the prospect of her leaving and only cheered up when Abigail pointed out that she would most certainly return one day, 'For if I can come once I can come again,' she pointed out, knowing that she never would, because then she might meet the professor again and she wouldn't be able to bear it. A clean break, she told herself silently, was by far the best.

She cleared the supper things away and made coffee, then sat by the stove, chatting with false gaiety until it was time for her to put on her outdoor things and fetch her case. She had refused Bolly's offer to take her to the station; he was an old man and she didn't like the idea of him being out in the cold darkness. She would go to the Spui and find a taxi. She told Mrs Macklin what she was going to do as she went to the door. It opened as she got to it and the professor, looking more irritable than ever, came in. He said without preamble, 'I intended to take you to the boat, but I'm expected in theatre in an hour. I'll take you to the station.'

Abigail frowned. How like him to be so awkward; they had said goodbye—not a very pleasant one, but still goodbye, and here he was again, just as she had schooled herself to be sensible about the whole wretched business.

'Please don't bother,' she told him, a little stiffly, and noticed as she said it how tired he looked. 'I was just on my way to get a taxi.'

He couldn't have been listening, for he took her by the arm and walked her back to where their mutual friend was sitting, calmly knitting as though she had the house to herself. The professor greeted her briefly and said smoothly, 'I was just telling Abigail that we must leave in five minutes.'

'Clever,' thought Abigail. 'Now he's got her on his side', but aloud she said, 'I'm most grateful, sir,' in the kind of voice she used on the wards when she addressed consultants. She saw him wince, which quite pleased her, and brightened still more when the idea that he might be going to pay her crossed her mind. She bade Mrs Macklin goodbye and followed him out on to the cobbles to the waiting car. The drive would take five minutes, perhaps a little longer, so there would be no need to talk—a view, apparently, not shared by her companion, however, for once he was behind the wheel he began testily:

'I find it impossible to talk to you, but there is something I must make clear. I have been deeply appreciative of your work for me—you are an excellent nurse, I can think of no one I would rather have to care for anyone I—loved. I should like you to remember that, Abigail.' He halted the car at the traffic lights. 'There is another thing I must say. My behaviour may have taken you by surprise—indeed, I am surprised at myself. I haven't been—sentimental for years. I intend to forget it and I hope that you will too.'

They had arrived at the Centrale Station. Before he could do anything, Abigail got out of the car, beckoned a porter, opened the car's door, hauled out her case, gave it to the man and then thrust her head through the window. She spoke in a voice thick with tears, and a little wildly.

'What a lot of fuss you make about nothing—nothing, do you understand?' and marched away without looking at him once.

London looked bleak and grey when she arrived the following morning. She got up early and went along to the restaurant and made an early breakfast; she wasn't hungry, but it was cheaper than having it on the train.

She took a bus from Liverpool Street to the agency and sat down thankfully in the waiting room. There weren't many other people there—the two girls who went in ahead of her came out looking so cheerful that she took it as a good omen when her own turn came. The stern woman hadn't changed in the least, unless it was to look rather more stern. She gave Abigail a sharp glance, said 'Good morning, Miss Trent,' and handed her a bill. 'I understand that after the case you accepted from us you worked independently in Amsterdam.'

Abigail, a little overcome by so much efficiency, said a polite good morning and that yes, she had, and took a look at the bill. It wasn't much, Mrs Morgan had only lasted three weeks, but seven pounds and fifty pence would just about take all the money she had. With commendable calm she asked, 'Is there a letter for me? Mrs Morgan—my patient—said she would forward my fare…but she forgot.'

The severe woman smiled thinly. 'Yes, I have a letter for you here.' She opened a drawer and handed Abigail an envelope and waited while she opened it. The cheque was inside. 'Perhaps you would like us to put it through the bank for you?' she enquired.

'Oh, please,' said Abigail thankfully. All at once the woman looked quite human. She paid the commission at once and stuffed what was over into her purse; it was amazing how much better she felt. She still had only enough to live on for a week, but a lot could happen in that time.

'Have you a case for me straight away?' she asked.

The woman shook her head. 'I'm not sure, but I think

not,' she got up and thumbed through the filing cabinet.
'There are several nurses wanted urgently for mental—
you're not trained for that?'

'No, only general.'

'A pity. It's most unusual for us not to have a number of cases waiting.' She resumed her seat and picked
up her pen. 'Come in again tomorrow morning, Miss
Trent,' she advised, 'there will probably be something.'
Her gaze swept over Abigail. 'You don't mind where
you go?'

Abigail thought of Bolly. 'London or somewhere not
too far away,' she said slowly, and added a polite good
morning as she went out.

She went to the Golden Egg again because her case
was heavy, and ordered a cup of coffee. She could of
course apply for a job in hospital—her own training
school would take her back, she supposed, but then
what about Bolly? It was impossible, after seeing his
happiness in Amsterdam, to condemn him to some back
room again; besides, if she went back into hospital she
wouldn't be paid for a month and how was she to manage in the meantime? She brooded over her coffee and
then went out into the street once more. She had to
find somewhere to sleep for the night—one night, she
told herself bravely, there would be a job for her in the
morning. She found a small hotel not too far away and
left her case in her room, then spent the rest of the day
looking in shop windows and eating as economically
as she could at Woolworth's cafeteria.

She was early the next morning and the first to go
in. She could hardly believe her luck when she was
asked if she would go to Virginia Water as a companion nurse to a widowed lady who was, most regrettably,

suffering from delirium tremens. It would involve some
night work, but there was daily help for the rough; the
pay was twelve pounds a week, all found. It sounded
ghastly, and Abigail had her mouth open to say an em-
phatic no when the woman behind the desk got in first
with the news that there was nothing else at present and
she was under the impression that Abigail wanted work
as soon as possible. 'You can always give it up after two
weeks,' she told Abigail. 'If you leave before that time,
I'm afraid we take you off our books.'

Abigail thought rapidly. It would certainly be an
awful job, and very underpaid, but it would be a roof
over her head. On the other hand, something much better might turn up in a day or two and she would miss it.

The woman at the desk tapped her fingers impatiently on the desk. She asked sharply: 'Well?'

Abigail started to get up. She ignored the other
woman's frown and began 'I...' but was interrupted
by the telephone.

She stood patiently while her companion lifted the
receiver and stated who she was. After a minute she
took the receiver from her ear. Her voice was frigid.
'This call is for you, Miss Trent. Most irregular, I cannot think what made you give this number.'

'But I haven't! I don't know who would want to...'
Bolly? the professor? Hardly. She took the receiver and
said worriedly, 'Hullo.'

The professor—and speaking as though they were
on the ward, together by a patient's bed while she listened to his instructions. 'Abigail? How fortunate that
you should be there. You have no case yet?'

She shook her head, just as though he were there to
see, and then said faintly: 'No.'

'Good. I want you for someone special—my niece, in Spain with her parents.'

'Your niece?'

'My niece—kindly don't interrupt me. Two weeks ago she swallowed three coins, pesetas. She was X-rayed and my sister was assured that nature would take its course. Unfortunately this has proved to have been too hopeful a view. She is now vomiting and dehydrated, and an operation is necessary. My sister refuses to have anyone touch Nina but myself. I intend going to Spain and bringing her back with me to hospital here. I should like you to come with me. You would be expected to remain in hospital with her until she is fit enough for her father to come and fetch her back. You will be paid expenses and your usual fees.'

The silence between them was profound until Abigail heard him explode with: 'My God, I haven't paid you!'

She said, 'No,' and waited, listening to the rush of her heartbeats; she was so happy at that moment that she would gladly have agreed to work for nothing.

His voice again; unhurried, concise. 'Abigail, you will go to Coutts' Bank,' he gave her the address, 'and ask for Mr Cross. Take your passport with you. He will pay your expenses for the journey and the salary which I owe you. It is Wednesday—there is a Swedish Lloyd ship sailing for Bilbao at six o'clock this evening from Southampton, you will have plenty of time to catch it. I will arrange to have your ticket ready for you. I will meet you when you dock in Spain. Is there anything else you wish to know?'

There was a great deal; she remembered that she hadn't agreed to go. Of course she would, but it would have been nice if he hadn't taken it for granted that she would come running.

'Abigail?'

'Yes, Professor.'

'Will you do this for me? Nina is very dear to me—she must have only the best—you remember what I said?'

High praise indeed and, she supposed, better than nothing.

'You have no other case?' he asked again.

'No—that is, I was just going to accept one, but I hadn't actually said that I would.' She looked across at the severe woman, silently fuming behind her desk, and watched her close the folder containing the widow with delirium tremens. She said, 'I'll be glad to help,' and heard him sigh.

His voice sounded very clearly. 'Abigail? I'm sorry—about your salary. I should have remembered—I was worried. Why didn't you ask me?'

She didn't answer but asked instead, 'Would you do something for me, please?' She heard his grunt and took it for yes. 'Tell Bollinger.'

'I have already done so—it was he who furnished me with the address of the agency. I will see you on Friday morning about seven o'clock.'

He rang off with a brief goodbye which she had no time to answer and she looked across at the severe woman, who looked positively grim. 'The idea,' said that lady, 'you have been on that telephone for more than five minutes! Heaven knows how many calls...'

'I'm sorry,' said Abigail, finding it impossible to feel anything else for the poor creature, condemned no doubt to spend the rest of her days at a dreary desk instead of going off to Spain to meet the only person in the world who really mattered. 'They'll ring again,' said Abigail kindly.

'I take it that you have accepted a post not connected with this agency?'

'Yes—I worked for a Professor van Wijkelen in Amsterdam—there is a case in Spain which he has asked me to take.'

The older woman stared at her. 'At least you're a sensible girl,' she offered. She meant plain, both she and Abigail knew it, but there was no point in being rude.

Abigail smiled, not minding in the least, and bade the woman good morning, then skipped out of the agency, still smiling. She went back to the hotel, told the desk clerk that she wouldn't want her room for another night and went upstairs to review her wardrobe. She had left her trunk at Bolly's lodgings, so presumably it was still there. She repacked her case; she would go and forage through her clothes, leave the pink dress in the trunk and then go to the bank. During the bus ride she occupied herself trying to guess what the professor would have done if she hadn't been at the agency when he had telephoned. Presumably he would have gone on telephoning at intervals throughout the day. She wondered, too, how long it would take him to go to wherever it was they were to meet in Spain. Bilbao was in the north, she knew that, he would drive through France and return that way. She hoped the little girl wasn't too ill, and became engrossed in trying to remember the treatment for such cases. As far as she knew they could be serious but not fatal; once the coins were removed the child should recover rapidly. She wondered why the mother didn't take the child to Amsterdam herself—after all, the professor was a busy man and it was quite a journey. She got off the bus pondering, and rang the bell of the shabby little house where Bollinger had lived.

Her trunk had been stored in a cupboard-like room, too small to take a bed. She sorted out what she wanted to take with her, packed the pink dress away in the trunk, gave the brown velvet to the daughter of the house, and left again. It was ten past twelve when she reached the bank, by now beset with the fear that no one there would know anything about her and what on earth was she to do if they didn't?

She was wrong—she had only to mention her name to the imposing messenger at the door to be whisked into an enormous room, occupied by a small, bewhiskered man who leaped to his feet as she was ushered in and offered her a chair.

He gave only a cursory glance at her passport and embarked at once upon the matter in hand. 'Professor van Wijkelen is an old and valued client of ours,' he said by way of opening, 'we are only too glad to oblige him in any way.' He rang a bell and a clerk slid in, laid a folder before him and slid out again.

'We have arranged for you to collect your ticket at the Southampton Docks office,' he began. 'Take a taxi from the station, Miss Trent, the driver will know where to take you. Here is your train ticket from Waterloo, and I have been asked by Professor van Wijkelen to remind you to take tea on the journey. Here also are the expenses for your journey and the salary due to you. If you would be so kind as to check the amount?'

Abigail, a little overawed by such smooth, effortless efficiency, did as he asked. There seemed to be much too much money. She said so and the bewhiskered gentleman smiled kindly at her. 'No, no, dear young lady—your salary, money in lieu of days off and spending money for your journey. There are bound to be a few comforts you will require on the journey.'

Champagne with my early morning tea, for instance, thought Abigail, feeling lightheaded. The professor must have extravagant girl-friends if that was the amount he found necessary for a two-day journey. She frowned, uneasy about the girl-friends. She put the money carefully into her handbag, promising herself to keep strict account of what she spent and to return the surplus when she met the professor, wished her new-found friend goodbye and was ushered out with grave courtesy.

She spent the next two hours shopping. Over a slightly extravagant lunch she made a list of things she needed and then made a beeline for Marks and Spencers. She had prudently left her case at Waterloo Station; now she wandered uncluttered from one counter to the next, making her choice. She settled finally for a pleated tweed skirt in a warm brown and oatmeal with a matching brown sweater and a gay little neck scarf. She bought a plain wool dress too, a soft blue, nicely cut and easily packed, as well as some undies. Lastly she bought an overnight bag with a wide zippered mouth so that she would be able to get at things easily while they travelled. She went back to Waterloo then, had a cup of tea, fetched her case and joined the queue for the train. It wasn't until she was handing her ticket to the collector at the barrier that she noticed it was for the first class.

It was pleasant to travel in such comfort and when the steward came along and asked her if she would like tea, mindful of the professor's instructions, she said yes. She had barely finished it when the train was at Southampton. It was in the taxi that she realised that she knew very little about the journey and still less about her destination. The professor hadn't bothered to tell her where they were going or how long they would stay, nor indeed, if her memory served her right, had he told her anything other than the bare bones of the case. But at the ticket office she found that she had underestimated him, for with her ticket was a long envelope addressed to herself. Abigail put it into her handbag and once inside her cabin, sat down on the bed to read it.

It was, naturally enough, typed and signed by Mr Cross and obviously made up from the professor's instructions. She was not to stint money upon her enjoyment during the short sea journey, it was stated. She would be met at Santurce at half past seven on Friday morning and she would be good enough to leave the ship at this hour, go through the Customs and contact the professor, who would be waiting for her. If by any chance he was not there, she was to go to the waiting room and remain there until he was. Their destination was his sister's house, situated some kilometres from Baquio, a small seaside resort half an hour's run from Bilbao. Probably they would stay the night there, but it might be necessary to leave before this; it depended on the child's condition. The return journey would take two days, if all went well. She was wished a pleasant journey.

She read the message through twice, then folded it neatly and returned it to her handbag. Presently, when she had unpacked, she would find a map and find out exactly where she was going. In the meantime she explored her cabin, a large and airy one on the promenade deck with its own tiny shower, and most adequately furnished. Even if she had been a fussy girl, which she was not, she would have had a job to find any fault in it. She put away her few things and went along to find out about table reservations, then wandered about the ship. It seemed half empty, which in mid-February was to be expected, but the restaurant, when she went along for dinner, seemed comfortably full. She shared a table with a young married couple and a man of about her own age, on his way out to Guernica where, he informed her, he had something to do with the tourist trade. And when she mentioned, almost apologetically, that she had never heard of that city, he spent the rest of the meal describing it to her, and a host of other, smaller towns besides, and when they adjourned to the bar for their coffee he obligingly found a map and explained exactly where she was going. It seemed natural enough to dance for a little while after that and they parted on excellent terms, with an agreement to meet before breakfast and walk the decks. All the same, it was of the professor Abigail thought as she got ready for bed.

The sun was shining the next morning and although the sea looked cold and the ship was rolling a little, the idea of exercise was inviting. Her companion of the evening before was waiting for her, and they walked briskly, arm-in-arm, pausing every now and then to view the vast, empty sea around them before going down to breakfast. They spent the rest of the morning lounging about on the comfortable promenade deck, reading and talking and playing the fruit machines. Abigail wasn't quite sure if she wasn't wasting the professor's money on them, although he had told her to have anything she wanted; when she won a minor jackpot, her relief was profound.

They went to the cinema after lunch and Abigail watched the film without seeing it because the professor's handsome, remote, ill-tempered face was printed indelibly beneath her eyelids. And the evening, although pleasant, went on for ever. She retired to her cabin as early as she decently could and hardly slept for excitement.

There were quite a number of people at breakfast, for some of the passengers were to spend the day ashore. She ate little, one eye on the clock, and presently, accompanied by the young man in the tourist trade, she walked along the deck for the last time, bade her companion goodbye and went down the gangway, paused briefly in the Customs shed and walked out of the door at its end, the porter with her cases hard on her heels. The professor appeared with such suddenness that she was strongly put in mind of a genie in a bottle. He said briefly, 'Good morning, Abigail,' tipped the porter, took her case, whisked her into the Rolls and got in beside her. 'You had a good journey, I hope?' His voice was cool and its chill swallowed up the warmth of her excitement at seeing him again.

She said pleasantly: 'Yes, thank you—I met some people...'

'I saw him as you left the ship,' his voice was dry. 'You must have been disappointed that the voyage didn't last longer.'

He was in a bad mood; probably he had been driving all night, or had slept badly, so she took care to make her voice sound reasonable.

'I don't wish that at all. He was a nice young man.

He's going to marry a Spanish girl in a few weeks, he told me all about her. I expect,' she went on in a matter-of-fact voice, 'it's my lack of looks that makes people confide in me—people always pick plain confidantes, you know.'

She was rewarded by a faint twitch of the corner of his mouth. 'Have you been driving all night?' she wanted to know.

'No, since about four o'clock this morning. We'll go if you're ready.'

An unfair remark. She had been sitting, composed and unfidgeting, for the length of their conversation. She stole a look at his profile; it looked stern and a little bad-tempered and although he was freshly shaved and as immaculate as he always was, his face was grey with fatigue. He had driven himself too hard. If he had a wife…she snapped off the thought before she became too immersed in it, and waited until they had left the quayside behind them and were on the road to Bilbao before she suggested that they should stop for coffee. 'It's twenty odd miles to Baquio, isn't it? Have we time to stop for a little while so that you could tell me a little more about your niece?'

He might have been tired, but he was driving superbly. The road was narrow and the traffic, even so early in the day, was dense. Abigail, gazing out of the window, could see that they were running through ship-yards and a muddled mass of factories, modern flats and tumbledown little houses. She was disappointed, but probably it would get better later on. The professor hadn't answered her. Only after he had negotiated a crossing jammed with traffic and sent the Rolls purring ahead once more did he remark, 'A good idea. We'll stop, there's a place in Bilbao which may be open.'

It was hard to see where Bilbao started and the ship-yards and factories ceased, but presently the blocks of flats grew larger and more affluent-looking and the shops, although small, looked more interesting. They passed a modern hospital and then a much older one and at last reached the centre of the city.

The main streets were broad and tree-lined with imposing buildings on either side and a good deal of traffic. The professor, who seemed to know his way about, turned the car into a side street and nodded ahead. 'Behind that store,' he said briefly. It looked like Selfridges on a small scale, with gaily dressed windows which she would dearly have loved to look at, but he drove round the block and parked the car at the back and led her to a row of shops on the opposite side. The café they entered was empty, indeed, only just open, but they were greeted with smiles and an unintelligible flow of words which the professor answered without apparent effort.

The coffee, when it came, was dark and rich and a little bitter, and Abigail was intrigued to find that the milk came in the form of a powder in decorative little sachets. She looked up, her face alight with interest and caught him looking at her with an expression which, although she couldn't decide what it meant, caused her to say quickly:

'About your niece, Professor...'

He went on staring at her. 'You understand why I asked you to come?' He spoke quickly, as though the subject was distasteful and he wanted to get it over with. 'I am sorry if I have interfered in any way with your plans, but I cannot take chances with Nina and I can trust you as a nurse.'

'And not as a woman?' Abigail hadn't meant to say that, and she was appalled at the frozen expression on his face.

'That is hardly a relevant question.' His tone implied rebuke. 'Nina is high-spirited and three years old. My sister is awaiting the birth of their second child, that is why I have made this journey; it was quite out of the question that she should travel that distance at such a time. Her husband is attached to the Netherlands Consulate in Bilbao. They have lived there for more than a year now, but Odilia remains very Dutch in her outlook. The idea of allowing Nina to go into any hospital other than the one in which I work is quite abhorrent to her, absurd though this may seem. I have no choice other than to come for Nina myself and bring a nurse with me.' He paused, his voice was suddenly curt. 'That is my only reason for asking you to return, Abigail.'

She said sensibly, 'Yes, of course, Professor, what other reason could there be?' and was pleased to hear that her voice sounded exactly as it always did, which was surprising, because she was engulfed in a wave of disappointment all the more bitter because she had been buoyed up by the false hope that there might be another reason. Despite his abrupt greeting when they had met, she had taken heart from his evident annoyance at seeing her with the tourist agent, but now it was apparent that his annoyance hadn't been for that reason at all, much more likely that he had considered she had been wasting precious minutes of his time while she said goodbye.

She drank the rest of her coffee in silence and said

rather defiantly that she was going to powder her nose. She had gone some steps from the table when she realised that she had no idea what to look for. She paused, trying to remember the Spanish for Ladies, but perhaps they didn't... She glanced over her shoulder at the professor, who said gently:

'You should look for flowers on the door, Abigail.'

She returned some five minutes later and he said at once, 'I see that you are big with information of some sort—am I to be told?'

'Well—there's no one else to tell,' began Abigail, 'but I'm not sure if it's quite...'

'My dear good girl, in this day and age? And you forget that I have a sister—a most outspoken woman, I might add. Further, I am completely unshockable.'

'Oh, it's nothing shocking,' said Abigail with endearing forthrightness. 'It's just that it was all so grand— like being on one of those Hollywood film sets.' She watched the corners of his mouth twitch. 'Powder blue velvet walls and little upholstered chairs and gilt wall lamps, and a carpet I got lost in, and I washed my hands in a gilded shell. I don't feel I shall ever get over it!'

The twitch came and went again. 'It sounds incredible and a little vulgar,' said the professor. He added gravely, 'I expect they do a roaring trade during the tourist season.'

Abigail laughed, her ordinary little face transformed, so that it wasn't ordinary at all, but very attractive. Then she became grave again. 'I'm sorry, I'm holding you up, Professor.'

They drove uphill out of Bilbao, and because it was now a bright, cloudless morning, she was able to see the mountains around them, with little green fields, each with its red-tiled house, shutters closed and rather shabby but delightfully picturesque with red peppers drying in colourful strings from the windows, and occasionally a man working in the fields and once a pair of oxen drawing a plough. She exclaimed at each new sight until she remembered that he had seen it all before and apologised for being tiresome. She turned in her seat and smiled at him, but he didn't reply, nor did he smile. It was as though he wished she weren't there beside him—but she was and, she reminded herself, at his invitation. Perhaps it was the Spanish air or the strength of the coffee which emboldened her to ask:

'Why do you sometimes call me Miss Trent and sometimes Abigail?'

They were approaching a town and he slowed the car's rush. 'I forget.'

She stared around her while she pondered this brief answer. It made no sense, for what had he to forget—but he gave her little time to think about it; they were approaching Munguia, he told her, where there was an interesting church of the Gothic period and the old tower of the Palacio de Abajo, and she obediently gazed in the directions to which he pointed as they passed through the small place, and then, because the silence was so heavy between them, she asked, 'Are we nearly there?'

'Yes. We go to Plenzia next and then take the coast road to Baquio. My sister lives a mile or so beyond the village.'

She sat quietly, not speaking until they reached Plenzia, and although she had promised herself that she wouldn't annoy him with any more comments, she exclaimed with delight as they entered the little town and turned on to the coast road, cut into the towering hills which ran down to the sea.

The road followed the hills bulging into the sea and began to descend. Baquio lay beyond and below them, and even the blocks of new flats along its sandy bay couldn't spoil its beauty. The Rolls tiptoed round a hair-pin bend and tore happily down the hill into the village, along its shore and then up the hill on its other side. The road curved presently so that the houses were hidden behind them and only the sweep of the rugged coast was before them. They slowed momentarily while an old man in the flat cap of the Basque country, and carrying a rolled umbrella, trudged past them, urging along a donkey almost hidden under a load of wood.

'He doesn't look strong enough,' said Abigail.

'They live long lives here—hard work and a good climate—they walk a great deal too.'

'I meant the donkey. I'm sorry for it, it should be free in one of those fields.' She sighed. 'I've heard that they aren't very kind...they eat horses and they like bullfights.'

'Are you showing me yet another side to your many-sided nature, Miss Trent? kind Miss Trent, gentle Miss Trent—the rescuer of kittens from gutters and old men from attics, the nurse who tends old ladies and grizzling babies.' He sounded so savage that she was struck to dumbness, and when she forced herself to look at him she could see that his mouth was curved in a sneer. He had made her sound a prig, a do-gooder, and she wasn't, just an ordinary girl, with her living to earn and doing a job she liked. She concentrated on hating him, but that didn't seem to help much, so she tried despising him instead, but her companion snapped, 'Up here,' and turned the car, with inches to spare, through an open gate on to a narrow, well surfaced road, leading, as far as Abigail's apprehensive eyes could see, straight up the side of the mountain, to lose itself in the trees which crowned its summit. She had decided that even the Rolls wouldn't be able to manage it when the professor swung the car round a right-angled bend and continued uphill, but now less steeply, but now she could see the sea again, only to lose it as they turned once more, this time into the trees, to emerge on to a wide sweep of tarmac before a modern and very large bungalow. They had arrived.

The front door stood open and even before they were out of the car a girl was coming towards them—the professor's sister, quite obviously, for she had his good looks, softened into beauty. She flung herself at him and he suffered her rather tearful embrace for a few moments with commendable calm and then spoke to her in Dutch, and she laughed a little as she turned to Abigail.

'Nurse Trent,' said the professor, 'my sister, Mevrouw de Graaff,' he turned back to her. 'Odilia, you do not need to worry any more, we will take Nina back with us and you will have no need to cry about her.' He patted her shoulder in a brotherly fashion and turned to greet a thickset, fair-haired man coming out of the house towards them.

'Dirk—I didn't expect to see you.' The two men shook hands and the professor went on, 'Nurse Trent, this is my brother-in-law, Dirk de Graaff.'

Abigail shook hands and stood quietly while the professor enquired after his niece. 'Nina? She's here? No worse?'

'She's in bed,' it was his sister who answered him.

'The nursemaid's with her for a minute or two, but she doesn't want anyone else but Dirk or me—it makes it difficult.' She glanced at Abigail. 'I hope she will like you, Nurse.'

Abigail murmured that she hoped so too and smiled reassuringly at Nina's mother because she looked so worried, as they followed her into the bungalow.

It was a roomy dwelling and most elegantly furnished. They crossed the wide hall and entered a room at one side of the bungalow with a wide window overlooking the sea and with a magnificent view of the coastline stretching away into the distance. The nursery, and a very nice one too, thought Abigail. There was a small white bed in one corner and the girl sitting beside it got up as they went in. She said something in Spanish and went away and the small creature in the bed cried 'Mama!' in a whining voice and began to grizzle. Her mother went to sit on the bed and spoke softly to the child, and presently said:

'She would like to know your name. She understands a little English—she speaks Dutch, of course, and Spanish too.'

Abigail looked with something like awe at this three-year-old who had already mastered more than her mother tongue and smiled at the pinched white face on the pillow. The child was ill, that was obvious, and despite her peevish greeting Abigail thought that when she was well again she would be a delightful small girl. She was blonde like her father, with enormous blue eyes. She had a distinct likeness to her uncle too; Abigail loved her on sight because of that.

'I only speak English, I'm afraid, and about a dozen words of Dutch. My name's Abigail.'

She smiled and Nina smiled faintly in return. 'Why?' she demanded.

Abigail thought it wise to ignore this question. Foreseeing language difficulties ahead, she said instead, 'I'm going to look after you for a day or two.'

The small mouth turned down ominously. 'Oom Dominic...'

'He'll be with us.' Abigail had the satisfaction of seeing the mouth right itself and marvelled anew that the child could understand her.

'Speak Dutch,' demanded the moppet, and added please because her mother told her to.

'Oom Dominic...' began Abigail slowly, not in the least sure what she was going to say.

'Is right behind you,' said the professor from the doorway, and passed her as he spoke to swoop down on his niece. It was obvious that they were devoted to each other, for the small face lighted up as Nina gabbled away to him, her two arms clutching him tightly round his neck.

Presently he disentangled himself and sat down on the side of her bed, still talking—explaining, Abigail thought, why he had come. When he had finished he listened patiently while Nina argued shrilly, and then said:

'Nina wants to leave now—this minute. I've told her we must wait until I have seen the doctor and studied the X-rays—it will give us the chance to pump some fluids into her before we go. Today, I think, from the look of her.'

He went on to give instructions and Abigail said, 'Yes, sir,' then he got up off the bed and went away, presumably to telephone the doctor. When the door had closed behind him, his sister asked, 'Do you always call Dominic sir?'

'Not always. Sometimes I call him Professor, although I suppose while Nina is with us I had better address him as Oom Dominic.'

Odilia smiled. 'And I suppose he calls you Nurse. I'm going to call you Abigail, if I may, and will you call me Odilia? What a pity you can't stay longer, but Dominic says he wants to get Nina to hospital as soon as he can, and he's bound to be right, he always is.' She sighed. 'I've been a dreadful nuisance, haven't I, but the baby will be here in another week and I simply will not let Nina go into a hospital here. Oh, they're very good, but I'm a dyed-in-the-wool Dutchwoman and if she's got to have something done then Dominic is the only one who must do it, and there was no other way; Dirk would have taken Nina to Amsterdam, but who could have gone with him to look after her? The nursemaid's a good girl, but she's not trained and she gets excited, and I'm no use either, I get so upset each time Nina's sick.'

The word had an unfortunate effect upon her small daughter. Abigail caught up a bowl and reached her just in time. She was sponging Nina's face and hands when the professor put his head round the door to speak to his sister and then in English, 'Oh, lord, at it again? No pesetas, I suppose?'

He strolled over to the bed and pulled a hideous face at his niece, who giggled weakly, but when he spoke to Abigail it was in his usual austere fashion. 'Glucose and water, Nurse—as much as you can get into her— getting a bit dehydrated, isn't she?'

He looked at Odilia enquiringly. 'Her things are packed? She had better travel in her nightie and dressing gown—we'll wrap her in blankets and she can sit on Nurse Trent's lap. We'll want several things with us,' he began to list them and Odilia interrupted him to say, 'I've got most of them. Abigail's going to sit with you?'

'Yes.' He stared across the room to where Abigail was sitting with her small patient, coaxing her to drink.

'I'll send Rosa in,' began Odilia, but he interrupted her. 'Nurse Trent will, I know, be glad to stay here and get to know Nina.' He took his sister's arm. 'Let's find those odds and ends and you can tell me how life's treating you—I must say you look prettier than ever.'

His sister smiled, she looked much happier now he had come. Abigail guessed that she had been in the habit of leaning on him whenever she wanted help.

They went out of the room together and Odilia said as she went:

'We'll have lunch together presently, all of us.'

'Thank you, that would be nice.' Abigail was still busy with the glucose drink and smarting under the professor's manner towards her. She would, she promised herself, say as little as possible to him on the journey back, and that would be of a professional nature.

The doctor came, held a consultation with Dominic and went again. Abigail had been present, because as it was pointed out to her, it would save time if she was told the results of their talk as they went along, so she sat between the two men, listening to the professor speaking Spanish with almost as much ease as he spoke English; it made her feel inferior until he said in English:

'How fortunate that you can't understand Spanish, for mine is so shockingly bad, I wonder Doctor Diaz can understand a word of it and I should be ashamed to speak it before you.'

She thought it was rather nice of him, but the idea of him being ashamed of anything he did was so amusing that she smiled and then straightened her face to gravity because she had discovered that whenever she smiled he seemed to dislike her more.

They were to leave at three o'clock, the professor informed her after Doctor Diaz had gone. They would spend the first night some two hundred and twenty miles away, midway between Biarritz and Limoges, and they would leave early on the following morning again, provided that Nina was well enough, and get as far as possible; if necessary he would drive on to Amsterdam, a matter of seven hundred miles, but only if it was advisable because of Nina. As it was he considered that they should be able to do the journey in two days. 'Indeed,' he went on, 'we must, for I have a number of engagements I cannot miss. I rely upon you, Nurse Trent, to take such good care of Nina that I shall be free to devote my attention entirely to driving, nor do I want any display of nerves, as I intend to drive fast when it is safe to do so.'

'I'm not given to nerves.' Abigail's voice was tart even while she wondered just how fast a Rolls-Royce went when pushed.

She lunched with Odilia and her husband and, of course, the professor, who when he did speak to her at all, engaged in the detached conversation of someone who had met her for the first time and didn't much care if he never saw her again. But Odilia was nice, Abigail liked her and she believed the liking was reciprocated. Abigail went back to her small charge after that and prepared her for the journey, and at the last minute Nina burst into loud sobs, shrieking her intention of staying

with her mama in the three languages at her command.
It was her uncle who picked her up out of her bed, whis-
pering something or other as he did so, causing the
shrieks to turn to an occasional snivel. Her mother, almost in tears herself, demanded, half laughing:

'Dominic, what are you saying—what are you promising, something wildly extravagant?'

'A bicycle—a Dutch bicycle, and I'll come down
in the summer and watch her ride it.' He smiled very
kindly at her. 'Don't worry, *lieveling,* everything will be
all right, she will be safe with us. Abigail is a splendid
nurse—I trust her, so can you. I didn't bring her all this
way without good reason, you know. I'll telephone you
this evening and again tomorrow and as soon as she's
well enough I'll have her home with me and Dirk can
come up to Amsterdam and fetch her back.'

Odilia smiled then and kissed him, then went over
to where Abigail was standing, holding blankets and
thermos flasks and all the impedimenta of a long journey. 'I'm so glad it's you,' she said, and kissed Abigail
too. 'We shall see each other again. Have a good trip.'

'We will, I'm sure, and I'll take care of Nina for you.
Good luck with the baby.'

The two girls smiled at each other and Abigail said
goodbye to Dirk, got into the car, and the professor arranged his niece on her lap. When he had tucked the
child around with a variety of wraps, he asked:

'Anything else?'

'The bowl and that packet of Kleenex tissues,' Abigail begged him, still practical even though he was so
close that his cheek brushed hers. She wasn't sure what
the journey was going to be like; perhaps Nina would
get worse, perhaps the professor would be bad-tempered

for the whole way, she didn't really mind; a thousand miles, or nearly that, her heart sang, as he got in beside her, even if he didn't speak more than a dozen words in those two days, he would be there, beside her. She smiled out of the window at Odilia and held Nina close as the professor waved too, then began a headlong dive down the road towards the gate and the road back.

Chapter 7

Abigail's vague fears about the road were justified; it looked a great deal worse too by reason of the angry black clouds racing towards them from the sea. It was barely three o'clock, but the day was already darkening, the road reeled from one bend to the next and the professor drove along it as though it were a motorway with no traffic in sight. Presently the road turned inland, following the river, with its wide, peaceful mouth ringed by a picturesque village before it changed to a turbulent stream tumbling between the rocks below them. 'Guernica,' said the professor briefly. 'We cross the bridge in the centre of the town and turn back to the coast.' A piece of news Abigail took with resignation; probably, she consoled herself, the coast road wasn't half as bad as the roads through the mountains crowding in on them as they approached the town—if there were any roads. They hadn't gone very far when the rain started, a fierce, heavy downpour which washed away any views there might have been. They passed through several villages, dismal in the wetness and with not a soul to be seen in their single streets, and streaked up towards the mountains Abigail sensed were in front of them.

'Lovely scenery here on a fine day,' observed her companion laconically. 'Is Nina all right?'

'Dozing,' said Abigail, 'worn out with excitement, I fancy. You know this road, Professor?'

'Yes—it's a good one—rather a lot of bends, but we're not likely to meet much traffic in this weather.'

He sent the Rolls swooping round a curve at the top of a small ravine running down to the sea on their left. 'We reach Lequeito shortly. There is a thirteenth-century basilica there—it is also famous for the tuna fishing championships each summer.'

He offered her these titbits of information rather impatiently, as though he found it a nuisance to say anything at all and her answer was a little cool in consequence.

'You have no need to talk if you don't wish to. I can read it up in a guide book when I get back,' and was disconcerted by his low laugh. He didn't bother to answer her, though.

He was driving very fast and, she suspected, in an ill-humour despite the laugh when, in response to Nina's urgent and plaintive whisper, Abigail asked him to stop. He shot her a baleful glance and she met it firmly.

'It is awkward, isn't it? but Nina's the one to consider, I imagine. Perhaps there's somewhere where we could pull in…?'

She said it with more hope than certainty, for it

wasn't that sort of a road; it snaked in breathtaking curves, mountains on one side, plunging ravines tumbling down to the sea on the other. Nevertheless the professor slid to a stop between one bend and the next. He got out, saying, 'Make it as quick as you can,' as he made for the side of the road in the pouring rain, adding as an afterthought, 'Do you need any help?'

'No, thank you. Give us three minutes.' She was already busy unwrapping Nina.

He gave them five, which, in view of the weather, was generous of him.

'You're very wet.' Abigail's soft voice sounded almost motherly as he got in beside her again. She went pink under the ferocity of his look.

'A singularly apt remark,' he commented. His voice had a bite in it, but as his glance fell upon Nina his face softened and Abigail felt a pang of envy that he would never look at her like that.

'She's all right?'

'Yes, she was a little sick as well, but she's had a drink. I'll cuddle her up and perhaps she'll go to sleep again.'

'Yes—you're all right until we can find somewhere where we can get tea?'

'Yes, thanks.' She spoke cheerfully and smiled at him, but all she got was a frowning glance as he started the car.

They came to an hotel on the side of the road, perched rather uneasily on the side of the cliffs above the sea, and although it looked deserted there was a light burning dimly from somewhere inside, despite its closed shutters.

'This will do,' said the professor, and drew up before its door. 'I'll carry Nina inside, you follow me in.'

She did so, pausing to catch a glimpse of the bay directly below them, fringed with rocks and the grey sea boiling past them to reach the sand. Inside she found herself in a small dark room, half café, half bar, rather smoky and smelling of the day's meal. But it was pleasant enough, with little tables scattered around, covered with red and white checked cloths. She sat down and took Nina into her arms while the professor went over to the bar. He came back after a minute.

'There's only coffee—do you mind?'

'Not a bit,' she answered readily, and longed for tea.

'What about Nina?'

'I've got milk and water for her. I brought the thermos with me.'

'Sensible girl!'

They drank their coffee in almost total silence; it was warm in the room and after a little while one didn't notice the smell of food.

Refreshed and warmed, they set off again; the road seemed even worse than before; now and again the clouds would lift just long enough for Abigail to glimpse the spectacular scenery on either side of them, but the rain still fell steadily, forcing the professor to slow his pace. He slowed even more as they went through Deva's narrow streets, with its harbour full of fishing boats and the sea breaking against the grim, grey cliffs. The road climbed out of the little town and wound its way towards San Sebastian, the sea still in view and the foothills of the Pyrenees ahead of them. Only in Zarauz did they leave the sea briefly as they passed through the town's main street, lined with a mixture of picturesque old houses, ornate villas and modern hotels. The professor hadn't spoken for a long time, and although Nina was awake she was content to lie quietly in Abigail's arms. She looked pale and listless, and Abigail, thinking of the long journey ahead of them, hoped that she would get no worse. She offered the child a drink, speaking in her clumsy Dutch, and Nina rewarded her with a weak giggle. 'Do you want me to stop?' The professor spoke without taking his eyes off the road, and when she answered that no, she thought she could manage, he didn't speak again, not until they reached San Sebastian, where, he told her, he would stop for a few minutes. 'For I don't intend to stop again until we reach Marmande,' he advised her, 'and that's just over a hundred miles away.'

It was a bare ten minutes before they were on their way again. As Abigail settled herself in the car once more and put out her arms to take Nina, the professor gave her a long searching glance, as though he had expected her to say something, and when she didn't he turned away and got into his own seat. As he started the car he said, 'There's chocolate in the pocket beside you—I imagine you must be getting hungry.'

'I'm perfectly all right, thank you, and so will Nina be until we reach Marmande,' her eyes searched around her and she nodded to herself, 'and if she's not, we've everything we need within reach. I rather think she'll go to sleep for a while, sir.'

He muttered a reply which she scarcely heard, but she did hear him when he said suddenly: 'Be good enough not to address me as sir at every other breath, Abigail,' and she spent the next five minutes or so wondering

what she should call him. All in all, Oom Dominic
seemed both suitable and blameless.

They crossed into France with hardly a pause, and
Abigail, who had been considering that they had been
travelling quite fast, discovered how wrong she was.
The road was a good one, and the Rolls, as though
aware that speed was essential, tore, silent and powerful, along it, with the professor, just as silent, at the
wheel. And when Nina piped up that she felt sick Abigail said at once, 'Don't slacken speed, we're perfectly
able to manage.' And manage she did.

They reached Marmande just after seven o'clock, to
Abigail's relief, for Nina had been awake for the last
hour of the journey, lying silent—too silent for a moppet
of three. The professor had barely opened his lips and
she, for her part, was heartily sick of her own thoughts,
for they had been far from happy. From the comfort of
the big car she had looked ahead into a future which, in
its very uncertainty, was unsatisfactory. It was a good
thing they had arrived, she told herself bracingly, for
now she would have something to do other than think.

The hotel wasn't a large one; it looked old and very
clean, though, and the foyer was comfortably furnished.
Abigail sat down once more and took Nina from the
professor and listened to him talking to the reception
clerk. Her French was quite good; the boarding school
had taken care of that. It amused her to hear the professor, in glacial, perfect French, refusing a double room
and explaining that she was the nurse, that the child
was his niece and that it was necessary for them to have
two rooms, each with a bathroom. The clerk smiled and
shrugged and beckoned the porter, apologising as he
did so. On their way upstairs, Abigail, just behind the

professor with Nina in his arms, said soberly, 'It would have been better if I had worn uniform, you know—I never thought...'

'You have a knowledge of French?'

'Quite a good one, as it happens.' She heard the tartness of her voice and was disconcerted by his chuckle.

The room she was shown into was well furnished and warm and the bathroom was more than adequate. She got Nina ready for bed, gave her a drink she didn't want, took her temperature, which was quite high, and tucked her up for the night. A few minutes later the professor tapped on the door to spend ten minutes with his small niece, studying her carefully as he laughed and joked with her. Presently, he asked Abigail: 'You're comfortable?'

'Yes, thank you. Perhaps I might have something here on a tray...'

'Certainly not. I have arranged for the chambermaid, a sensible woman, to sit with Nina while we have dinner. You will have it with me downstairs.'

'An invitation or an order?' she wanted to know quietly, and saw his unwilling smile.

'An invitation.'

'On the assumption that any company is better than none?'

The smile had gone; perhaps she had imagined it. 'If you wish, Nurse Trent.' He turned away. 'I'll be back to see Nina in half an hour, I will bring the maid with me.'

He was as good as his word. He walked in with a middle-aged woman with a kind, sensible face, and such was the strength of his niece's affection for him that she closed her eyes and promised to go to sleep at once when he bade her to do so.

They dined in an empty restaurant, which on a summer's evening must have been a very pleasant place. Abigail was hungry. She chose the soup, which the waiter assured her had been made in the hotel's kitchen—the asparagus tips and herbs, thickened with tapioca and piping hot, followed by cutlets with an orange sauce, and while the professor contented himself with cheese she allowed herself to be tempted by the little something the chef had whipped up for her; a delicious concoction of Chantilly cream, fruit, nuts and liqueur brandy, which, combined with the dry white wine the professor had chosen, had the effect of combining with the table lamps to give everything around her a rosy hue. Not that the professor made much effort to entertain her; he talked, it was true, at great length and with great attention to detail, of the local customs, and when he had exhausted those, he embarked on the customs of the Basque country. Abigail, listening politely, was strongly put in mind of her student days, when with rows of other nurses she had sat listening to lectures delivered by the various honoraries of the hospital. The professor's manner was exactly similar.

They had their coffee at the table and when they had finished she suggested that she should return upstairs and went scarlet in the face when he asked, 'Dear me, was I so dull?'

'Of course not,' she said hastily, 'I enjoyed it very much, but I don't like to leave Nina too long.' She frowned. 'She's…it will be a good thing when she's safely in hospital.'

His smile was mocking, and the scarlet, which had just faded, flamed anew. 'I didn't mean—that is…' She paused and added carefully, 'She's in safe hands with you, but we're an awful long way from home.'

'You think that she will get worse?'

'I don't know—it's just an idea, a feeling...' She looked at him helplessly. How could she explain the premonitions all nurses had from time to time? As it turned out there was no need for her to explain, for the waiter came hurrying over to their table to ask if they would go upstairs immediately.

Nina was being sick again. The maid had coped without worrying overmuch to begin with, but the child seemed unable to stop. The professor thanked her calmly, tipped her with discretion and sent her away, then went over to the bed where Abigail was doing all the necessary things which had to be done with a complete absence of fuss, and even though the child couldn't have understood the half of what she was saying, her gentle, placid talk and unhurried movements, which nevertheless got things done, calmed the child, so that she stopped crying and listened to what her uncle was telling her. He made it sound amusing; he fetched his case from his room, took off his jacket, and made preparations for putting up a saline infusion. He did it without haste, talking all the time, so that presently Nina laughed a little and laughed a little more when Abigail, swathed in a towel to protect her blue dress, joined in the conversation in her own halting Dutch, not minding at all when the little girl giggled at her comic way of pronouncing the words. The drip was up and running with a minimum of fuss, for the professor had shamelessly used all his powers of persuasion upon his small niece as well as promising her a bell to go on the bicycle and a little gold chain with a pearl on the end of

it for her birthday, as well as ice-cream every day as
soon as she could eat again. 'And heaven alone knows
what your mother will say to me when she's told,' he
observed in English.

'She won't care a fig,' Abigail assured him as she
cleared away his mess and tidied things away in his
case. 'She'll be so glad to have Nina well and home
again.' She shut the case on an unconscious sigh. 'How
fast is this to run in? There's to be a second vacolitre,
isn't there?'

He nodded. 'If she has a good night's sleep, I think
we had better press on tomorrow.' He handed her a bottle. 'Largactil syrup. Give her a dose, will you?'

Abigail did as she was bid, tidied the room, pulled
up a chair to the side of the bed and was on the point of
sitting in it when his hand hauled her to her feet again.

'No,' he said firmly, 'go and have your bath and get
into bed—use my room. I'll call you about three, have
a bath myself and an hour or two's sleep; that way we'll
both be rested. I'll get them to send breakfast up here
at eight o'clock and if everything's all right we'll get
away soon after. It rather depends on Nina.'

'But you've got to drive—I shall be quite comfortable here, truly—I can always doze in the car tomorrow.'

'Why do women argue?' he wanted to know pleasantly. 'Do as you're told, Nurse Trent.' He smiled suddenly. 'Please.'

There was no further use in argument. She collected
her night things and went away to the bathroom, then to
his room and got into bed; she was asleep immediately.

She wakened at once to the touch of his hand on her

shoulder, and sat up instantly. 'Nina's all right?' she wanted to know.

'Hasn't stirred,' was his reassuring answer. 'I've just changed the drip—it should be through by seven. Take it down if I'm not about.'

He went away leaving her to scramble into her dressing gown and slippers and pad back to her own room. A minute later he had wished her good night and disappeared.

The rest of the night passed uneventfully. Nina hardly moved, even when the drip had run through and Abigail took the needle out of the small thin arm and covered the tiny puncture with strapping, and when she opened her eyes, frowning a little, Abigail said:

'It's all right, darling, you're much better, aren't you?' and the moppet nodded and, obedient to Abigail's suggestion that she should go to sleep again, closed her eyes.

The professor came in a few minutes later, with his hair ruffled and an unshaven chin, but his eyes were as calm and untroubled as a child who had slept the night long. He nodded his satisfaction, patted Abigail on the shoulder, said 'Good girl' and then: 'How about some tea—I'm dying of thirst.'

Abigail rang the bell and waited to see what would happen. The maid who had looked after Nina came in answer to it, smiled a good morning and promised tea within five minutes.

The child slept peacefully while they drank it, sitting side by side on the other bed with the tray between them. Abigail poured second cups and enquired of the professor if he had slept well. 'You must have been tired,' she added.

His blue eyes swept lazily over her and she became aware that her hair was hanging in a mousy curtain around her shoulders, and her dressing gown, warm as it was, was hardly glamorous. To cover her discomfiture she asked, 'Do you intend to leave directly after breakfast, Professor?'

'Yes, as things are I think perhaps we should try and reach Amsterdam as quickly as possible. It's roughly six hundred and seventy miles.'

She thought. 'About fourteen hours' driving.'

He laughed. 'Less, with luck. There are some splendid stretches of road where I can give the car her head.'

'A hundred miles an hour?'

She wasn't looking at him, so she missed the engaging twinkle in his eyes.

'Probably more—are you nervous?'

'Not in the least.'

'Am I to take that as a compliment?'

'As you wish,' she forced her voice to casualness. 'Which of us shall dress first?'

'Would you like to? I imagine there isn't much to do for Nina, but if you will, perhaps you can do whatever needs doing before breakfast. She might have some tea—no milk.'

When Abigail got back to the bedroom, very neat as to hair and dress, and with her face nicely made up, it was to find the professor stretched out on the second bed with his eyes closed. She stood looking down at him, studying every line of his handsome face. He looked more approachable with a bristly chin, she considered, and lonely. He opened his eyes with a suddenness which took her completely by surprise and asked:

'Why do you look at me like that?'

'Like what?' She took a step backwards, and he got off the bed and stretched hugely, but all he said was: 'You have a very expressive face, Abigail, did you know?'

At least the rain had stopped. They got off to a good start soon after eight o'clock with a wide-awake Nina on Abigail's lap. For the time being at least she seemed a great deal better, a fact amply demonstrated by her chatter, which for the first hour at least was ceaseless. They stopped briefly at Limoges, having covered over a hundred and thirty miles in two hours. Refreshed by coffee and a glucose drink for Nina, they took to the road again, at first running through high country. But this didn't last long. Once more on level ground, the professor urged the Rolls forward, and they reached Châteauroux in time for a hasty lunch, more glucose for Nina, who had by now become silent and rather sleepy, and tore on towards Orleans and Paris.

South of Paris the professor broke the long silence to say, 'We'll stop for tea, and get through Paris before dark. What do you think about going straight on?'

She was surprised that he should ask her. He had seemed remote the entire morning; when he had spoken, he had been civil and that was all.

'It depends entirely on how tired you are. There's a great distance to go, isn't there? More than three hundred miles, and you've already driven more than that.'

'I'm thinking of Nina,' he reminded her coldly, and she saw that he wanted—probably intended—to drive through the night. She looked at the child on her lap, awake once more and looking decidedly sickly. 'Let's go on—you intended to anyway, didn't you?'

'Discerning of you—but you are the child's nurse—
I needed your opinion.'

They stopped shortly after that at a roadside hotel
and Abigail tried not to look as if she had understood
when the waiter referred to her as the professor's wife,
but her faint astonishment at his not denying it betrayed
her. He said shortly: 'If you have no objection, I'm sure
that I have not—it is a waste of time to correct such a
ridiculous mistake.'

Several telling replies to this piece of arrogance bub-
bled upon Abigail's lips. She longed to utter them, but
suppressed her feelings, outraged though they were,
sternly; now was not the time nor the place to have
words with the professor.

It took some time to get through Paris even though
the professor knew the way. It was obvious to her that
her companion was concentrating on his driving to the
exclusion of all else. She thanked heaven that Nina was
still quiet; the child was running a temperature again;
she could feel the heat of the little body through the
blankets and Nina's small face had become even paler.
They still had three hundred miles to drive, a long way
still, but there was a motorway into Belgium; presumably the professor would make good time once he got
on to it. She was perfectly right. He hadn't looked at
Nina for some time and she had said nothing to him, but
he seemed to sense that she was uneasy about her, for
he sent the car tearing along at a great speed, and yet,
thought Abigail, looking at him stealthily, he seemed
quite relaxed; his hands rested lightly on the wheel; he
wasn't frowning. Without looking at her, he said, 'Not
long now, Abigail.'

An hour and a half later, going through Bapaume, he asked her how Nina was.

'Dozing, but her pulse is up. She's got a temp. too.'

'Roughly two hundred miles to go—I'm going via Antwerp and on to Tilberg and Utrecht.'

A name which sounded reassuringly Dutch in Abigail's ears, it made home seem very near.

They had travelled quite some distance before he spoke again. 'Can you last out until we reach Amsterdam?'

'Easily.' Her voice was steady; even at the speed they were travelling at, the journey seemed endless and she was worried about Nina. Her relief when later, he said briefly, 'Holland,' was so great she could have cried.

'How is she?' he wanted to know.

'Asleep. I think when she wakes she'll probably be sick again.'

To her surprise he laughed, a normal, relaxed sound with no sound of tiredness in it. 'My dear Abigail, what a sensible girl you are! I should like to have you with me in a tight corner—although this one's tight enough—I can't think of any girl of my acquaintance who wouldn't have been in tears or hysterics long ago. Aren't you tired?'

'Yes,' said Abigail, smarting under his good opinion. Who wanted to be called sensible? That was twice in twenty-four hours! 'Aren't you?'

'Yes, but it's worth it.'

They lapsed into silence again until it was broken by the professor's forceful opinion of the rain which began to beat against the windscreen. After a little while he asked, 'Are you prepared for Nina; in case she's sick?'

'Yes.' Her answer was brief because she sensed that

he didn't want to talk. They were through Utrecht, on the motorway and only a few miles from Amsterdam, when Nina woke up and did exactly as they had expected, and in the ensuing minutes which followed, Abigail had no time to feel relief as they slid through Amsterdam's lighted streets and at last stopped before the hospital entrance. It was almost midnight.

The professor wasted no time but carried his small niece into the hospital and Abigail, left on her own, got out too, much more slowly because she was cramped and stiff, and now that they had arrived, deathly tired.

The entrance hall was empty, although she could see the night porter in his small office, but he had his back to her, telephoning; she decided to wait. She had no idea where she should be or what the professor wanted of her. Nina would go to the children's ward, but there would be a nurse on duty there.

It was quiet in the hall, the night sounds of hospital reached her ears faintly, but she was so familiar with them that she hardly heeded the far-off rustles and thumps and door shuttings and clanging of metal as some nurse cleared a trolley. Presently she peered through the porter's lodge window again; he had disappeared altogether now—there was a small inner room, so probably he had retired to eat his meal. She felt shy about disturbing him; besides, her tired brain felt unable to cope with asking questions in Dutch. The professor wouldn't be very long; he would have to go home and go to bed, he needed rest before he operated upon Nina, and the child needed a night's sleep in a proper bed too. Somewhere close by a clock chimed twelve and she went to the door and stood looking at the Rolls, still majestic despite its deplorably dusty condition. It was a pity her case was in the boot and that the boot was locked, otherwise she could have taken it and been in bed by now, although that wouldn't have been very polite, she supposed.

She shivered and went back inside and walked round once more. 'If ever I'm rich,' she said to herself as she walked, 'I shall give a bench—two benches, to this place. There must be a waiting room.' But she couldn't see one, only corridors, disappearing into gloom on either side. She hadn't been in this part of the hospital before, only to pass through it on her way in or out when she had been working there. She yawned widely and sat down on the floor, her back to the wall. It was a dark corner and she was almost hidden. She closed her eyes.

And opened them again almost immediately, because the professor was bellowing her name in a furious voice, which to her mind was far too loud for that time of night in a hospital, even though he was an important surgeon. She called hastily. 'I'm here, in this corner,' and before she could get up he was towering over her.

'Good God, girl, what in the hell are you lying there for?'

He was in a bad temper; he wasn't his usual cool, bland self at all, his voice was almost a snarl. He bent down and plucked her to her feet, keeping his hands on her shoulders, and she had a strong feeling that he would have liked to have shaken her. Before he could do so she spoke, her voice low and reasonable.

'I wasn't sure what you wanted me to do and I'm tired. If I could have my case I'll go over to the Home. How's Nina?'

The hands lost their ferocious grip and became gentle. 'Nina's asleep. Henk's with her, I'm too tired to be of much use. My poor girl, what a thoughtless brute you must think me!'

She looked up into his grey weary face. He looked every day of his age and a year or two besides, but she loved him a little more because of it. She would have liked to have told him what she did think of him, but that was something she would have to keep a secret, probably for ever and ever.

'No,' she said gently, 'I don't think anything of the sort. It's Nina who matters, and I'm perfectly all right. If I could just have my case—you could get home to bed.'

'Didn't I tell you? You're coming back to my house for the night. I shall want you on duty tomorrow morning at eight—you can move into the Home during the day.'

'But I can't—it's past midnight…'

'Don't tell me the conventions worry you,' he paused, 'although I daresay they do; you're that kind of girl.'

'No,' she snapped, very ruffled, 'I'm not in the least worried. Why should I be—even if you expected it? I was thinking of someone having to get a bed ready at this hour of night.'

'My dear good girl, Bollinger and Mevrouw Boot will have prepared a room. I told them I expected to be back at some ungodly hour.'

There seemed nothing more to say, he took her arm and they went out to the car again, and in five minutes had arrived outside his house on the *gracht*. Bollinger and Mevrouw Boot were still up. Bolly had the door open before the professor could get his key out and Abigail, quite forgetting him, flung herself at the old man.

'Oh, Bolly dear, how lovely to see you!' she cried, and hugged him fiercely before saying good evening to the housekeeper, who smiled and nodded and said a great deal, none of which made any sense to Abigail at all.

'A bath and bed, and Mevrouw Boot will bring up your supper,' ordered the professor, and when she would have protested, said:

'Please do as I say, Abigail. I want you on your toes tomorrow morning. We leave the house at a quarter to eight.'

Bolly had gone to get their cases, Mevrouw Boot was on the stairs, on her way to run a bath. Abigail said meekly: 'Very well. Good night. I hope you sleep well, you must be very tired.'

'Not so tired that I cannot find the time to thank you for your share in this whole business.' He stared at her from under frowning brows. 'You didn't complain once; you must have wanted to.'

A dimple appeared in her cheek. 'Oh, a dozen times.' She turned away as Bollinger reappeared with the cases, and started up the stairs after him. As her foot was on the first tread the professor said: 'Abigail,' and she turned round again. Bolly turned round too and watched from the top of the stairs. The professor had followed her across the hall; she turned round into his arms, and they held her with a gentleness she had never imagined as he bent to kiss her.

Abigail ran upstairs without a word or a backward glance and tried not to see Bollinger's delighted smirk. She refused to think about it while she undressed and had her bath and got her uniform ready for the morning, and then, warm in the little canopied bed, ate the delicious supper Mevrouw Boot brought her. She looked about her room as she ate. Not very large, but furnished with excellent taste with dainty Regency furniture as well as an ultra-comfortable easy chair and a soft carpet underfoot, it was exactly the kind of room she would have chosen for herself. She pushed the bedtable away and lay back on the pillows, drowsily contemplating the flower painting over the fireplace. The housekeeper would be back for the tray presently and she must stay awake and thank her. She closed her eyes and went to sleep even as she thought it.

She was called at seven and told that breakfast would be in exactly half an hour, and with five minutes to spare she went down the staircase, very trim and crisp in her uniform, her starched cap perched on her bun of hair, her packed case in her hand. Half way down the stairs she remembered that she had no idea where to go. There were several doors—she knew where the little sitting room was and she knew the great drawing room too, but there were other doors, all shut. One of these was flung open as she stood hesitating, and the professor said, 'In here, Nurse Trent. Good morning.'

He had already been at the table, with papers, letters and an open notebook before him. There was some coffee, half drunk, and a slice of toast half eaten. She sat down opposite him and gave him a wary greeting, and he lifted his eyes to hers briefly and asked her how she had slept.

He looked rested himself, she saw that at once, and as bland and cool as ever he had been. Abigail sighed and he said at once, 'Oh, would you rather have tea— I'll ring…'

'I like coffee, thank you.' She poured herself a cup and took a slice of toast. 'I see that you have slept well too, Professor,' and some small imp of mischief prompted her to add, 'Things that happened yesterday seem so different after a good night's rest, don't they?'

He put down the letter he was reading and stared at her with faint suspicion. 'And just what does that mean?' he wanted to know.

'Why, nothing—would you pass me the sugar? I expect you're one of those people who prefer not to talk at breakfast, I don't mind in the least if you want to go on with your letters.' She smiled kindly at him and helped herself to toast and marmalade, and although she knew that he was staring at her, she didn't look up; after a moment he picked up his letters again.

In the car, driving to the hospital, he told her:

'I telephoned Odilia last night—she asked me to thank you for taking such care of Nina. She sent her love too and hopes that she will see you again. She hopes too that you will find time to write to her.'

'Of course I will. She'll want to hear about Nina—all the little things, you know,' she explained, 'that mothers worry about.'

Nina was awake and quiet after a restful night—she had a little room to herself for the time being, but later, when she had recovered from the operation she was to have in an hour's time, she would be able to go into the ward with the other children. She kissed her uncle with childish fervour and kissed Abigail too, and presently the professor went away and Abigail busied herself getting the little girl ready for the theatre. She was to go with her, she had been told, and afterwards nurse her on day duty until she was fit to leave hospital. Zuster Ritsma had told her too that there was a room ready for her in the Nurses' Home, and would she mind taking her off-day each afternoon so that the day shift could cover her. Abigail, still thinking about the professor, said that she didn't mind in the least, and went off to X-ray with her little patient, so that her uncle could have a last-minute check of the three pesetas.

The operation was a complete success. The professor, with no difficulty at all, removed the coins through the smallest of incisions which would leave only the faintest of scars, and when the wound had been clipped, peered down his little niece's gullet with his gastroscope to make sure that nothing had been left behind, a state of affairs confirmed by the portable X-ray machine, trundled into the theatre before Nina was lifted on to the trolley ready to take her back to her bed. Abigail had stood by the anaesthetist during the operation, doing what was asked of her quickly and competently, her mind deliberately closed to any thought other than those connected with the job on hand, and back in the small hospital room once more, with Nina in bed, there was plenty for her to do and no time to think of her own affairs.

She had regulated the drip, taken Nina's pulse and charted it, inspected the tiny wound and written up the chart by the time the professor came in. He had Henk with him, and that young man, who had had no chance to speak to her that morning, said, 'Hullo, Abigail, nice to see you again. We must get together...' and Abigail murmured something, conscious of the professor's eyes upon her and wishing Henk wasn't quite so pleased to see her. But when the two men had gone she brightened a little, cheered by the thought that a little competition was supposed to be a good thing, and then chided herself for being a fanciful fool; the professor didn't care anything at all for her; she was a useful nurse, probably he knew how she felt about him and took advantage of it. It had been stupid of her to come running the moment he called...and as for his kisses, there were a dozen good reasons why a man kissed a girl, and none of them necessarily because he loved her.

She was kept busy for the rest of the morning, for Nina, once she was conscious, was rather cross and inclined to cry as well. Abigail, watching her drop off to sleep after she had given her an injection, was glad to go off duty for a few hours.

She had the same room in the Home as she had had previously. She unpacked her case, changed rapidly into her outdoor clothes and hurried through the well-remembered streets to Mrs Macklin's house. It would be nice to see that lady again; they would have time for a chat and a cup of tea before she was due back on duty. She stopped at the baker's shop and bought some cakes before turning into the peace and quiet of the Begijnhof.

Mrs Macklin received her with rapturous surprise. 'My dear,' she exclaimed as Abigail took off her coat, 'I knew you would be back, but I didn't expect you as soon as this—what has happened?'

Abigail told her while they had tea, toasting themselves round the little stove and drinking cup after cup of the strong brew Mrs Macklin liked.

'Dear Dominic,' she declared when Abigail had finished her tale, 'how like him to go tearing off for hundreds of miles to help someone. He adores Nina, of course, you'll have seen that for yourself, my dear, and he's devoted to Odilia—she's fifteen years younger than he is, you know, and they've always been very close. He missed her very much when Dirk was appointed to Bilbao—Dirk's a good man too, did you meet him?'

'Yes—I liked him too, and I thought Odilia was charming.'

'You say Dirk's coming up to fetch Nina?'

'Yes, I think so, though I think it all depends on the baby—when it arrives. Nina won't take long to get over this.'

'No. I suppose Dominic will take her back with him to his house when she can be moved, until her father can come for her. He'll need someone to look after her, though.' She gave Abigail a shrewd look and Abigail, aware of what her companion was thinking, said nothing. It wasn't very likely that the professor would ask her to go back to his house with Nina; a couple of weeks and she would be on her way back to England.

Nina was still sleeping when she got back and there was little to do but sit by the bed getting up from time to time to do the small tasks necessary for the little girl's treatment. The professor had come in again just after she had got back and gone again, well satisfied with his small relative's progress. He had hardly spoken to Abigail beyond leaving her fresh instructions and asking her to tell the night nurse that he would come again about ten o'clock. He scarcely looked at her as he bade her a quiet good night.

Nina recovered rapidly; long before she was able to eat them, she was demanding impossible and unsuitable meals of sausages and chips, pea soup and *pofferjes,* delicious, indigestible fried dough balls. Abigail, plying her with suitably milky foods, heaved a sigh of relief when ice-cream, often demanded, was allowed.

Nina was getting up each day now, sitting in a chair, swathed in blankets and wearing the new dressing-gown her uncle had bought her. It was pale pink and frilly and quilted and there were slippers to match. She was a pretty child and as beguiling as most small girls of that age, it was no wonder that he was fond of her. In a few more days she would be able to play with the children in the ward; the only reason she didn't do so now was because she might be tempted to eat the sweets and cakes their mothers brought in for them. And during these days, the professor came and went, saying little to Abigail that wasn't to do with her work until one evening when he walked in just before the children's bedtime, to find Abigail, with Nina and several other children from the ward.

Nina was curled up on Abigail's lap, the other children lay about her feet, rolled up or stretched out according to their several whims, each of them had a bulging cheek as they sucked on a bedtime sweet. Abigail was singing to them; she had a voice like a little girl's, rather high and breathy and sometimes off key. She was singing them nursery rhymes and children's songs which she had almost forgotten so that she had to sing da-de-da from time to time, but as none of them understood a word she was singing anyway, it really didn't matter. She was half way through 'Cry Baby Bunting' for the second time when Nina lifted her head from her shoulder and cried: 'Oom Dominic!'

Abigail stopped singing, as though the thread of her voice had been cut by the professor's scissors. He advanced into the centre of the small room, while the children, quite prepared to accept him as their uncle too, all began to talk at once. It was strange, thought Abigail, watching him, how they saw through his austere look and took no notice of his frown at all; he waved to them now and pulled a hideous face so that they roared with laughter as he came to a halt before her and bent to kiss his niece.

'I liked the one about the king in his counting house,' he remarked.

She had sung that one quite five minutes previously. 'Have you been here all that while?' she wanted to know. 'I would have stopped…'

'Yes, I thought you would have done.'

She said miserably, 'I wish you hadn't—I can't sing.'

'No, but it sounded charming, all the same.'

He picked Nina up and enquired of her how she was and left Abigail to meditate on sounding charming even when one sang habitually out of tune. Just then Zuster Ritsma came in and he went away with her to look at a sick child, leaving Abigail to shoo the children back into the ward and Nina into her bed.

It was two mornings later that he told Nina that she would be going home with him the next day. Abigail was making the bed, and Nina, sprawled on the floor, was playing with a doll, which she threw down to rush at her uncle and embrace his knees, shouting rapturously.

'Noisy little brat,' said her uncle fondly. 'You will accompany her, if you please, Abigail. Mevrouw Boot and Bollinger have enough to do without having this imp to look after—besides, they're a little elderly.'

Abigail folded a blanket with precise, neat movements. 'For how long, sir?'

'I can't tell you that. Why do you want to know? Have you another case?'

'No. I was just curious. Of course I'll come.'

'Odilia had a son last night, so as soon as she is up and about, Dirk will come and fetch Nina.'

Abigail smiled widely. 'Oh, I am glad, how lovely for them—Odilia is quite well?'

'Yes, she telephoned me an hour after he was born. Dirk is naturally delighted.'

'I can well imagine it. I suppose men want sons...' She could have bitten out her tongue when she saw the bleakness of his face. He turned away and when he spoke again his voice was without expression. 'I'll see the Directice about you leaving tomorrow, Nurse Trent—Zuster Ritsma will give you all the details.'

He walked away without another word.

She didn't pretend to herself that she hadn't hoped to go with Nina when the little girl left the hospital; she allowed herself to feel happy about it, but only in moderation, for the professor hadn't shown himself particularly pleased to have her. She supposed that she would stay ten days at the most, and then Nina would go back to Spain and she would be back in London again, looking for another case. Professor de Wit, when she had gone to see him one afternoon, had urged her to remain in Amsterdam. 'For,' he had said, 'Dominic must have any number of patients who require a nurse, you could be employed for months to come,' and she had taken heart from his words, hoping each time that she saw the professor that he might suggest this, but he never had done so. She packed her case with the few clothes she had with her and which she now heartily hated, and prepared to leave the hospital. There was another thing— she had received no salary, and because the professor had been so irritable when she had offered to pay back the surplus from her travelling expenses, she hesitated to say anything about it now. Perhaps he intended to pay her when she left Amsterdam. In the meantime, she was running low again, and Bolly had had nothing for some weeks.

They left after lunch the next day, with a jubilant Nina, her clips out, carried through the hospital in the professor's arms, and when he set her down in the entrance hall and she began to jig around with excitement, he exclaimed, laughing:

'No one would believe that I carved you open such a short time ago,' to which sally she screamed with laughter and asked to be told, for the hundredth time, how exactly he had done it.

He was called away on some urgent business or other soon after that, and they went home with Jan in a Mercedes she hadn't seen before, to be welcomed by Mevrouw Boot and Bollinger, but of the professor there was no sign for the rest of the afternoon.

Chapter 8

She was taken to the room she had had before and Nina had the room next to it; a room as charming as Abigail's and thoughtfully provided with a miniature chair to accommodate Nina's smallness, and a table to go with it. It took most of the afternoon to arrange her toys and dolls in exactly the positions she wished and by the time she had had her tea she was tired. Abigail carried her off to her room with the promise of a bedtime story if she was a good girl, then undressed the small creature and bathed her with a good deal of giggling and chatter, for they understood each other very well by now, even though they mostly spoke different languages. She was in bed, with a bowl of bread and milk, nicely flavoured with sugar and cinnamon, by way of supper, and Abigail sitting on the bed beside her, telling her, in English of course, all about the old

woman who lived in a shoe, by seven o'clock. The tale
took a long time to tell, because almost every word had
to be explained, which meant searching for it in Abigail's dictionary. They were hugging each other with
merriment over Abigail's peculiar way of pronouncing
even the simplest Dutch word, when the door opened
and the professor came in.

He said pleasantly enough, 'Good evening, Nurse
Trent, I see that you have settled in,' and went to bend
over his niece, to be hugged and kissed and chatted to
while Abigail got up and went to the pillow cupboard
against one wall and busied herself putting away Nina's
clothes.

It was to be a 'Nurse Trent' evening, she supposed a
little sourly. Come to that, it would probably be no evening at all; she hadn't the least idea if she was to take
her meals with him or have them served alone, or if she
was to have them with Bolly and Mevrouw Boot. She
decided not, remembering how annoyed he had been
when she had used the tradesmen's entrance. She shut
the cupboard door in time to hear him say:

'I dine at seven, Abigail. I hope you will keep me
company.'

She said thank you in a polite voice which hid her
pleasure, while she brooded over the difficulty of falling in with his moods. In the space of ten minutes she
had been both Miss Trent and Abigail; she found it a
little wearing on her nerves.

They were half way through their soup—hare soup
and home-made, as Bollinger informed her as he served
it, and they were alone in the elegant dining room. Bollinger had gone back to the kitchen to see about the next
course, and the professor, making polite conversation,

had fallen silent, and she, who had been turning over in her mind his insistence on calling her Miss Trent, found herself voicing her thoughts.

'I can't think why you will persist in calling me Miss Trent with one breath and Abigail with the next,' she remarked suddenly. She looked at him as she spoke and he was neither frowning nor smiling the faint sneering smile she so disliked.

He said simply, 'I told you once before. I forget.'

'Forget what?' she persisted.

'You may have restored my faith in women, Abigail, but it's been so long—I'm not quite used to it, perhaps I haven't quite learned to trust.' He paused and smiled at her across the table, and for fear that she would give herself away she said a little shortly, 'I haven't the least idea what you mean,' and wished that she had never started the conversation, while at the same time longing for him to go on. It was a pity that Bollinger came back just then with the *Boeuf Bourguignonne,* served, as it should be, in a brown glazed casserole; it smelled delicious and she was hungry, and so, she expected, was her host. Abigail ate with appetite and abandoned her questions for just sufficient polite conversation to make for good manners.

There was fruit tart next; an elaborate dish which not only contained fruit but cream and eggs and cream cheese. When the professor pressed her to a second helping, she hesitated. 'It was delicious…' she began.

'Then have some more—I don't think you've been eating enough, you've got thinner.'

He was right; she had been eating as sparingly as possible because she had had to pay for her meals in hospital and she was counting every cent now. She had told herself bracingly that it was a good thing, for she was far too plump, but she had sometimes been a little hungry. She passed her plate; in a week or two she would probably be on short commons again.

They had their coffee in the little room where she had had tea with Bollinger and when she had handed him the delicate Meissen cup and saucer he said blandly:

'We were talking about you.'

'No, not really.' She spoke too quickly, but it made no difference, for he went on just as though she hadn't spoken.

'You didn't understand what I meant, Abigail. Will it help if I call you Abigail all the time?'

'You mean you don't dislike me any more?'

She was unprepared for his explosive, 'Dislike you? My dear girl, I have never…'

She cut in ruthlessly, 'Oh yes, you have, from the very first time we met. I don't know why—perhaps you're one of those men who can't bear plain girls. I don't mind being plain—not any more, now I'm used to it, but you don't have to make it so obvious…'

He was looking at her gravely, his eyebrows arched, and she sensed that he was laughing silently, which irked her.

'Your eyes are lovely—you have a dimple, did you know? and the sweetest smile.'

'Which hardly adds up to good looks,' she answered him crisply. 'If you don't mind, we won't talk about me. How is your sister?'

He followed her lead without apparent regret and presently excused himself on the grounds of work to do. She sat on alone for another hour or two, staring into the fire, deep in thought. She had won his friendship; she was almost sure about that, and perhaps, just a little, his regard.

She saw him only briefly the following day; just long enough to be told his wishes concerning Nina. There was little enough nursing to do, for the little girl was almost well again and full of life and mischief—it was largely a question of keeping her amused and making sure that she didn't tire herself out. As he left the room, the professor said:

'I'll be away for a day or so, Abigail, so please feel free to go wherever you wish in my house. Bollinger will look after you. Nina will need more clothes, I imagine, take her to 't Kleuterhuis in P. C. Hooftstraat and get what you need and have the account sent to me— if she needs shoes, there's a good shop in the same street—Pennocks; they can send in their account too. Jan will take you if you wish it.'

They shopped two days later, with Jan driving them in the Mercedes, for the professor had taken the Rolls, spending the morning in the most agreeable fashion to them both, buying, without bothering too much about the prices, a new outfit for Nina and some red shoes which she had set her heart on. They went back to the house for lunch and afterwards Abigail tucked her small charge up for a nap, left Bollinger on guard, and went out for her hour or two's off-duty.

She went to Mrs Macklin's, and that lady was delighted to see her.

'Sit down,' she invited, 'and tell me all your news,' and Abigail took the chair opposite the old lady's in the small, overwarm room.

'Dominic told me that he intended asking you to remain with Nina until her father could come to fetch her, and I told him he was wise to do so, after all, what would he do with a three-year-old to look after and your Bollinger and Mevrouw Boot would spoil her hopelessly—besides,' she added dryly, 'his well-ordered household would have been chaos. He spends most of his days working, but that doesn't prevent him from expecting—and getting—a perfection of comfort which most of us only dream about. You like his house, my dear?'

'What I've seen of it—it's a great deal bigger than one would suppose from the outside, and the furnishings are beautiful.'

Mrs Macklin nodded agreement. 'It's been in the family for hundreds of years. Such a pity if Dominic doesn't marry again, because if he doesn't everything will go to a distant cousin of his, who farms his lands somewhere in Gelderland and dislikes city life, which means that the house here would be neglected, or worse, sold. No, Dominic needs a wife, Abigail, and children too.'

Abigail stirred in her chair, rocked by a brief, glorious daydream. She got up. 'I'll get tea, shall I?' she offered, anxious to have something to do, and as she went to the door: 'I expect he'll find a wife sooner or later. He has a lot of friends in Friesland, hasn't he?'

'Dozens. He's there now—I expect you know that.'

She hadn't known, and after all, there was no reason why he should have told her. She murmured something which meant nothing as she went through the door to the kitchen. Neither of them mentioned him again for the rest of her visit.

He came home that evening. Nina, tired out from trying on her new clothes, not once, but several times, had had her bath and was tucked up in bed, already half asleep. Abigail arranged the nightlight where the child could see it if she wakened, and prepared to go to her room. She left the door open as she always did so that she would hear if Nina called, and sat down in the easy chair by the window. She had meant to do her hair and her face and then count her money, something she had done several times in the last few days, as if by doing so she would increase the small sum left in her purse. Instead, she sat idle, thinking about the professor and wondering where he was and what he was doing.

He was on his way up his own staircase, having let himself into his house with surprising quietness, considering his size. She had heard nothing at all until he asked from the door, 'Is Nina asleep?' and then, when she turned round, 'Hullo, Abigail.'

He looked so pleased to see her that she forgot how untidy she was and that her face needed doing, and smiled warmly at him.

'Oh, nice to see you, Professor,' she spoke impulsively. 'Did you have a good time? Nina's been such a very good girl.'

He leaned against the wall, his hands in his pockets, smiling faintly.

'I'm glad to hear that. May I come in?'

'Of course—but don't you want to see her? She's not been in bed long, I daresay she's still awake. I put her to bed a little early because we went shopping this morning and she was excited and tired.'

He made himself comfortable on the side of the bed. 'What did you buy?'

'Oh, a zipper suit—a nylon one with ribbed cuffs and a high neck; she likes to play in the garden in the morning and she can't do that properly if she's wearing something she has to be careful of. And another dress—she only had two with her, you know, and a pair of red shoes and a little fur bonnet.' She paused, then added guiltily, 'I do hope I haven't been extravagant…you did say…'

He shrugged wide shoulders. 'I don't think we need worry about that. You're not out of pocket? You must let me know if you are.'

Here was a splendid opportunity to bring up the matter of her salary. She said, 'No…' but was interrupted by the entrance of Bollinger, who knocked on the open door and came in with a cheerful air. 'Nice to see you back, boss,' he remarked, 'I seen the car below and there's a Doctor Leesward on the phone for you. He says it's urgent.'

The professor, with a brief word of excuse, went out of the room and Bolly with him; Abigail was left to take off her cap and do her hair and her face, wondering the while if she would have the chance again that evening of bringing up the subject. No chance at all, as it turned out, for when she went downstairs for dinner, a few minutes early, it was to learn from Bollinger that the professor had gone to the hospital and was likely to be late home. She ate the meal as quickly as she could, trying not to feel lonely, then sat by the fire, knitting a pair of red mitts for Nina to match the new red shoes. She had been in bed for more than an hour when she heard the professor come in.

He had gone when she and Nina got down in the morning. They were eating their simple lunch together when he came in. He took his seat at the table to Nina's delight and after glancing at their plates, exclaimed:

'In heaven's name—fish, steamed fish and potato

purée!' He looked so horrified that Abigail burst out laughing.

'It's very good,' she said, 'and it's good for Nina's tummy. Besides, there's ice-cream for afters.'

'Good God, who perpetrated this menu?'

'Me,' said Abigail, paying no attention to her grammar. 'It's nourishing and easy to digest.'

'Are you eating it too?'

'Of course—it would be the height of extravagance to have something different—besides, think of Mevrouw Boot.'

'Very commendable. I hope you don't expect me to join you.' He spoke a little absentmindedly and with a muttered word of excuse, pulled some papers out of a pocket and became engrossed in them; Abigail could see that he had other more important things on his mind than his companions at table, so she urged Nina to eat up like a good girl, and went back to her own lunch.

Bollinger came in presently, bearing a magnificent steak, which the professor ate with the same absentminded air, while Abigail, who didn't care for steamed fish at all, tried to keep her nose from twitching at the appetising aroma from his side of the table. She ate the rest of her fish as a good example to Nina, and went on to the ice-cream, while the professor, with every sign of enjoyment, ate hugely of the apple pie and cream Bollinger had brought for him. The cream he shared with his small relative, who had asked, with a good deal of vehemence, if she might have some, but when he offered the dish to Abigail she refused with such promptness that he asked her if she didn't care for it—a singularly annoying question, for they had shared enough meals together by now for him to have noticed that she had never refused it before.

He caught her smouldering gaze and said coolly, 'Ah—I think I understand. I'm breaking my own rules, aren't I? I must say you look very ill-tempered about it.'

A remark calculated to stoke her ill humour, so that she said sharply:

'Yes, you are. You told me exactly what Nina was to eat and I've kept strictly to your wishes. She's clever enough to remember this the next time I give her rice pudding or egg custard. And I don't like steamed fish.'

He shook with laughter. 'My poor dear girl, how tiresome I have been! Excuse me while I explain to my niece.' Which he did, amidst a good deal of giggling from Nina and a bellow of laughter from himself, so rare a sound that Abigail stared.

'It's all right, Abigail, we're not laughing at you. Well, I must go back, I suppose. Would you walk round to Professor de Wit's for me this afternoon? There's a book I particularly want him to have.'

He smiled at her and her heart beat a little faster, and after he had gone she wondered if he could possibly be the same irritable, cold-seeming man she had first met. Probably Nina's company, she thought; he was so fond of the child, and she was indeed a dear little creature. Abigail was fond of her too; she would miss her when she returned home to Spain, and that would be very soon now.

The professor joined her for dinner that evening, and because she could see that he was tired, Abigail, beyond answering his brief enquiries as to the afternoon, made no attempt at conversation. They were eating Mevrouw

Boot's perfectly turned out chocolate soufflée when he said:

'Anyone else would have chattered—how did you know that I didn't want to talk?'

'Well,' said Abigail frankly, 'you looked a little forbidding, you know, and weary. I daresay you had something on your mind you wanted to think out quietly, and in that case you would hardly wish to make conversation, would you?'

'Do I usually make conversation with you, Abigail?'

She nodded her neat head at him. 'Oh, yes, but mostly you don't talk at all.' She smiled at him as she spoke, but he remained unsmiling, until:

'Do you find me a bad-tempered man, Abigail?'

She put down her fork and thought before she answered this. He was asking awkward questions again and if she gave the wrong answer he might change back into the same cold, irritable man she had always thought him. On the other hand it would be of no use to fib to him. She said finally:

'No, not bad-tempered—that is, not bad-tempered underneath, are you? otherwise the children would be afraid of you, and they're not, they're sold on you, aren't they? You have always been,' she hesitated, 'abrupt, as though…no, that's not quite right. I think you were annoyed at having to meet me; I had the strong impression that you disliked me, that you still do, but not always, and I can't understand that. Is it because I'm English? or perhaps because I'm nothing to look at, although you said it wasn't…'

'I'll say it again, if only to convince you. But you are right, I didn't want to meet you, I've had no interest in women—girls—for a long time, but after I had met you I found myself arranging for you to take over a case so that I could see you every day. Do you not find that strange?'

She shook her head, for it seemed no stranger than her own acceptance of his offer for the very same reason. She longed to tell him so, but something warned her not to say anything—not yet.

'Contradictory behaviour, was it not? And you know why?' His blue eyes searched hers, he looked suddenly grim. 'I was once married. It was a long time ago.' The bleakness of his voice hurt her.

'Yes, I know about that.'

He looked suddenly ferocious. 'Who told you? Not the servants—they know better.'

'No, it wasn't the servants, and it wasn't gossip either. It was the only way someone could answer a question I had asked.' She went on hurriedly, trying not to see the arrogantly arched brows, 'You see, I couldn't understand why you were sometimes…just as though you hated me…and others…' she became a trifle incoherent, remembering the other times. 'I got upset once or twice and—and angry, and to make me understand better, this—person told me about you—just that you had been married and had lost your wife. I didn't ask any questions, it wasn't my business.' She added with a little flare-up of feeling, 'It isn't my business now; you started telling me—I should never have dreamed of mentioning it.'

'It's something I don't talk about. I'm surprised that I'm talking about it now, but I wanted to tell you, Abigail—I had to tell you, before…' He paused as Bollinger came into the room to enquire where they would have their coffee.

'Oh, here,' said the professor impatiently. 'We'll ring when we're ready for you to clear, thank you, Bollinger.'

Bollinger was back very quickly, and a good thing too from Abigail's point of view, for in the deep silence in which they sat her thoughts were racing round and round inside her head, thoughts she hardly dared to think. If she had been a cool, poised girl, she would have used those few minutes to good purpose instead of allowing her brain to seethe with nonsense.

She poured the coffee when it came and handed him his cup across the table and met his eyes as she did so, her own troubled and bewildered.

He said thoughtfully, 'It's strange, Abigail, but in all these years I have never wanted to tell anyone—and I must admit to several—er—friendships in that time—about my marriage, but I want to tell you, because you're different; you know what it is to be unhappy and you're honest too and I think that you would keep a confidence. But you see, my dear, I have grown wary of women, and I found it difficult.'

'You're sure you want to tell me? You're not going to feel awful about it in the morning?'

He laughed a little and shook his head, then passed his cup for more coffee and she busied herself filling it, then put the cup down, forgetting to give it back to him, her eyes upon his as he began to speak.

'I married when I was twenty-five—fifteen years ago. Did you know that I am almost forty-one, Abigail? She was very pretty and gay too, she loved clothes and jewels and furs and fast cars and she was the kind of girl men like to be seen about with—I counted myself very fortunate when she agreed to marry me. It took me just six weeks to discover that she didn't love me, and another six

weeks for me to find out that I didn't love her. Perhaps
if I had loved her I could have forgiven her the affairs
she had. She was killed in a car crash, together with the
current boy-friend, five months after we were married.
I swore I would never love another woman again, for although I had no feeling for her, my pride suffered, and
although, as I said just now, I became—involved, shall
we say, from time to time, it meant nothing to me.' He
put out his hand for his coffee cup. 'Now you know why
I have never allowed anything—any woman, to interfere with my life.'

Abigail emptied the cooling coffee from his cup and
poured fresh with a steady hand, which was surprising, for inside she was trembling. It seemed to her that
she had been warned that, even though he liked her, he
had no intention of allowing his feelings to take over
from the life he had decided upon. What other reason
could he have had for telling her something he admitted he had never discussed with anyone? The only good
reason would be because he loved her, and he had had
plenty of opportunity of saying so; it could be dismissed
without a thought. He had felt the urge to talk; he was
used to her by now and presumably, as she was a suitable recipient of his confidences, he felt himself able
to talk to her. She summoned a smile.

'Thank you for telling me, Professor. It was a truly
awful thing to happen to you and I can well imagine
that it's made you wary of women. But it's a long time
ago. I'm sure you will find someone who will change
your views for you. Perhaps you don't get out enough
to meet people; you work so hard, don't you? There are
a great many nice girls in the world, you know.'

'You suggest that I should find one and marry her?'

'Yes, why not? Just because there's one rotten apple in the barrel doesn't mean that the whole barrelful is bad.' She made her voice as matter-of-fact as she could.

'But I enjoy working hard. If I took a wife she might try to change that.'

'But she wouldn't—not if she loved you, she would want to help you in every way she could.'

He looked amused. 'How?'

She was suddenly out of patience with him. 'How should I know? She's the one to answer that question.'

'I must remember to ask her when the time comes.' He spoke gravely, although there was a gleam in his eyes. 'And now, much as I have enjoyed this conversation, I have to go back to the hospital. There is a case...'

He told her about it and she listened with interest and asked questions too; it was another ten minutes before he got to his feet.

And as for Abigail, she rang the bell for poor patient Bollinger and went to sit by the fire, and when he came into the room, said how sorry she was that they had been so desultory over their dinner.

'That's OK, Miss Abby,' said Bollinger, busy with the table, 'I was right glad to see you having such a nice chat. The boss don't often talk. He must like you.'

Abigail swallowed from a throat thick with the tears she would have liked to shed. 'I do believe he does, Bolly,' she agreed sadly.

The professor was at breakfast when she and Nina went down the following morning. He lifted his niece into her chair, tied her bib, urged her to eat up her porridge and then turned his attention to Abigail, who had sat down silently after a quiet good morning. Unlike her, he seemed in the best of spirits.

'I'm going to Friesland tomorrow; Bollinger will be going with me, for he has to see about bulbs for the garden there. I think it would be nice if Nina were to accompany us—you too, naturally, Abigail.' He gave her a bright glance. 'I feel that Nina has deserved a treat, do you not agree?'

'Yes, she's been as good as gold, but are you sure you want me to come?' She coloured faintly and added hastily, 'She doesn't really need a nurse now.'

'No? Bollinger and I love her dearly, but I believe we should both be mentally deranged by the end of the day if there wasn't someone to take her off our hands for at least part of the time. I have business to attend to and Bollinger takes his bulbs seriously.'

Abigail couldn't help smiling at him. She had never seen him look so relaxed. 'Then I'll come, I should like to. What time do you want us to be ready?'

'Could you manage eight o'clock? We could make it later if you like—it's barely a hundred miles.'

'I'm sure we can be ready by then. Nina wakes early, you know.'

'Does she? She keeps very quiet about it.'

'Well, she gets into my bed and I tell her a story.'

'In English?' He was laughing again.

'A little of both. She understands quite a lot, don't you, poppet?' She turned to look at the small girl beside her, tucking into a boiled egg and fingers of bread and butter with remarkable energy. 'Yes,' said the poppet from a full mouth, adding rapidly, 'No—Mary, Mary, quite con…con…' a frown marred the small features, to be replaced by a rapturous smile. 'Little Boy Blue…' she began.

'Lovely, darling,' said Abigail fondly, 'you're a clever

girl, but eat up that nice egg and Oom Dominic will tell you something very exciting.'

The egg was forgotten. 'Oom Dominic,' she smiled eggily up at him, 'tell,' she commanded in an imperious pipe.

Her uncle told her and rather unfairly left a few minutes later, leaving Abigail to calm a very excited little girl. He didn't come back all day and Abigail ate her dinner alone, not sure whether to be relieved or not. She had spent a good part of the night and most of the day persuading herself that the only way possible to her was to forget most of what the professor had said and to remember that within a very short time she would be going away and would never see him again, and in the meantime to behave exactly as she always had done. Breakfast had been a test; she considered she had come out of it rather well. She talked to Bollinger as she ate, glad of the opportunity of explaining that she would be able to pay him some more money very soon—quite a lot of money, she pointed out; she hadn't been paid for three weeks, and there would be some money over, even after that, for she still had her fare intact. After her old friend had gone, she curled up by the fire. There would be enough left to buy some clothes; she occupied herself deciding what she would buy when she got back to London.

They were ready as she had promised by eight o'clock, with Nina in the fur bonnet and the red shoes to match the zipper suit. Abigail, standing beside her in the hall, wore the tweed coat, which she now loathed, her knitted beret and the scarf to match. She hated those almost as much; only the gloves Professor de Wit had given her gave her pleasure. Her boots still leaked, but

Bolly, bless him, had cleaned them beautifully and no one knew about the leak. But she felt shabby beside her small charge and she had an uneasy feeling that the professor shared her feelings as he came into the hall, for the look he gave her was a leisurely and searching one, starting at the pompom of her beret, and going slowly down to her feet. The little smile he gave her did nothing to mollify her ruffled feelings.

There had been some late snow during the night, just sufficient to turn the roads to slush and powder the bare trees, but once out of the city, the flat country on either side of the motorway was blanketed in white; only the road ahead of them gleamed blackly. Abigail, sitting comfortably in the warmth of the big car, with Nina cuddled close to her and Colossus beside her, felt sorry for the drivers of the slow-moving farm carts drawn by plodding horses, but Nina, untroubled by this aspect of the winter's morning, wanted to know about the horses; she wanted to know about the cows and the canals and the windmills and bridges too; Abigail's Dutch was strained to breaking point and the professor, helping her out from time to time with the right words laughed a good deal, and Bollinger glanced at him several times, surprise all over his wrinkled face.

They went by way of the sea dyke, over the Ijsselmeer, and there was nothing to see because the snow blotted out the view on either side and the road ahead was straight, fading into an unseen horizon. Abigail scarcely noticed when they reached the mainland and the professor told her that they were in Friesland. They went down the coast of the great inland water and then turned inland to Bolsward and on to Sneek, both of which small towns Abigail had but the briefest glimpse of, but what she saw enchanted her, for despite the snow and the grey sky and the lack of people about the streets, they were picturesque.

They turned off the main road presently, and then again, this time into a much narrower road, running between fields with no villages to be seen. They could, thought Abigail, be in the middle of a snow-covered desert, and had her thought answered by the professor, who remarked easily:

'A little bleak today, I'm afraid, but when it is clear weather, the country is charming.'

The road gave way to a still narrower one, made of bricks and uneven, with a signpost pointing to Eernewoude, but before they reached there the professor swung the car into a side lane lined with bare trees, and almost at once through an open gateway. The lane ended abruptly in a wide sweep of cobblestones and before them was the house.

It was an old house, with a multitude of gables, and built of rose bricks, and while not large, appeared roomy enough. Its windows were small and arched and its panelled door studded with nails. The door swung open as they got out of the car, Nina was whisked up into her uncle's arms, and with an invitation to follow him, Abigail went inside, with Bollinger behind.

It was similar to the house in Amsterdam, with the same square hall with its black and white flagged floor and its lovely linenfold panelling, but this hall extended back a good deal further and the staircase rose out of its centre and divided from a little landing half way up it. It smelled of wax polish and potpourri and was pleasantly warm. Abigail's coat was taken from her and she was invited to go into one of the rooms on the right of the entrance, but not before the professor had introduced the old woman who had opened the door. Joke, he called her, and it was apparent that he and she had known each other for a long time.

The room they went into was quite large and a little dark by reason of the weather outside and the small windows, but the lamps in their wall brackets gave it a cheerful air, as did the fire burning briskly in the old-fashioned cast-iron fireplace. It was furnished in much the same style as the small sitting room in Amsterdam; a happy blend of comfort and antiques.

The professor offered Abigail an easy chair by the fire and Nina immediately perched on her lap. Bollinger had disappeared. 'To see to those bulbs of his,' explained the professor. 'My gardener, the man Bollinger has replaced so well, is convalescing here, they will no doubt have a most interesting talk over their coffee.'

'However can they talk?' Abigail wanted to know, 'unless your gardener knows any English.'

'He does. He was in England during the war. Besides, they both know the Latin names of everything that grows, which makes it easy.'

The idea of Bollinger being so clever hadn't entered Abigail's head. She said in astonishment, 'How extraordinary, Bolly speaking Latin.'

'He's a clever old man when it comes to gardens,' replied the professor, and went to take the coffee tray from Joke.

Over coffee he said, 'I shall be busy for an hour or two. Can you amuse yourselves, do you think? The garden is quite large. It's stopped snowing again. I daresay if Nina's sufficiently wrapped up, she might like to make a snowman—there's just about enough for that.'

Abigail, thinking uneasily of her leaking boots, agreed because Nina wanted to go outside so badly, and moreover, the professor had finished his coffee and she sensed that he wanted to be gone. There was a wide stretch of lawn behind the house and plenty of snow to make the promised snowman. Between them they made a magnificent specimen and then snowballed each other and Colossus until they were warm and Nina was tired.

'Time to go indoors,' said Abigail firmly, and scooped up the little girl and bore her inside. Even after they had tidied themselves in the cloakroom surprisingly hidden in the hall panelling, there was still an hour till lunch. They went back to sit by the fire, and Nina, on Abigail's lap, recited her jumble of nursery rhymes. She was giving her own version of Baa Baa, Black Sheep when the professor joined them. He listened gravely to his niece's efforts, congratulated her with suitable enthusiasm and offered Abigail a drink before stretching himself out in the chair on the opposite side of the hearth. It was pleasant sitting there in the warm, delightfully furnished room. Abigail sipped her sherry, on the edge of a daydream, and was brought back to reality by his voice.

'Nina's going home in two days' time, Abigail. Dirk telephoned me. We shall miss her, shan't we?'

'Yes, very much.' She contrived to make her voice normal. 'Will she go by car?'

'Yes, Dirk will be here tomorrow evening and will spend the night, and they will leave the next morning. You will wish to return to England as soon as possible?'

She could only say yes to that and add: 'Is Bollinger to come with me?'

'Not unless you want him to, but it's entirely up to you—and him—to decide.'

Abigail looked relieved without knowing it. 'Oh, well, if he could stay—you see I shall have to find another job and—and somewhere to live, and if it's a case where I have to live in, I must find a room for Bolly. It would be nice if I could have it all settled before he goes back to England.'

'It would be nicer still,' said the professor, not looking at her at all but into his glass, 'if you would stay on for a while and work in the hospital.'

Her heart rocketed into her throat, she swallowed it back, staring at his downbent head. 'Oh, yes, it would, but is there a job for me there?'

'My dear good girl, we are as short of nurses here as they are in England. I can think of half a dozen vacancies…you don't mind where you work?'

'No—at least, I know Zuster Ritsma already and she speaks English, which makes it easier for me, and I prefer surgery.'

'Theatre?'

'Yes—I did six months.'

He nodded and put down his glass, half smiling. 'Good, that's settled then—how about having your room at Mrs Macklin's again?'

'Do you suppose she would let me? I should like that very much.'

'So will she.' He got up and lifted Nina into his arms. 'Shall we have lunch, and then while this young lady is having her nap, I'll show you round the house.'

Lunch was a gay meal and the food so good that Abigail felt constrained to mention it.

'Joke's daughter,' the professor told her. 'It's her husband who does the garden. Joke attends to the housekeeping although she has retired, but she's lived here all her life and it's home to her. She lives with Arie and her daughter in the little cottage behind the garage.'

They ate thick pea soup, followed by grilled sole and a salad; the sweet, as a concession to Nina's youthful appetite, was a pile of waffles and a great dish of whipped cream. They drank a dry white wine with it and the professor poured Nina's orangeade with the same care as he poured the wine. Abigail, watching the two of them, thought what a splendid father he would make, for he was surprisingly patient with children. Only with himself, she thought sadly, was he impatient.

When they had finished, he led the way upstairs to a small room on the first floor, where Joke was turning down the coverlet of a narrow bed with a carved headboard.

'Odilia used to sleep here when she was little,' the professor told Abigail. 'I've never changed it, it seemed so right for a little girl. It hasn't been used for a long time...' He frowned a little and Abigail busied herself with Nina because she could guess why he was frowning—there might have been a small daughter of his own in that room. Out on the landing after tucking Nina up under the pink eiderdown she asked, 'Have you really got the time to take me round? I shall be quite happy on my own if there's something else you want to do.'

'There's nothing else I want to do,' he spoke briskly. 'Let's go downstairs first, shall we?'

There were two other rooms besides the sitting room

and the darkly splendid dining room; one a vast drawing room, hung with silk panels in a faded strawberry
pink, with an Aubusson carpet on its floor and dark
green curtains of velvet. Its walls were lined with cabinets displaying china and silver and glass and on either side of its vast fireplace were velvet-covered sofas
flanked by rosewood sofa tables. Here too the chairs
were a happy mixture of modern comfort and antiques
and what paintings there were were light flower studies or pastoral scenes.

The other room was the library, its walls crowded
with books, and from the look of it, frequently used.
The furniture was heavy and smelled faintly of tobacco
and leather, and Abigail wrinkled her nose. 'Nice,' she
commented. 'What a marvellous collection of books. I
suppose most of them are in Dutch.'

'Some—there are quite a number in English, though,
and German and a few in French.' He gave her a sidelong glance and smiled. 'I have to keep up with my
studies, you know.'

She agreed gravely, 'Yes, of course, but I expect you
write too, don't you?'

'Only when I have something worthwhile to say.'

He led her back into the hall and up the staircase
to the bedrooms, more numerous than she would have
supposed, each with its narrow windows and each too,
with its own colour scheme, pale vague blues and pinks
and greens which acted as magnificent foils to the beautiful old furniture, and was echoed again in the thick
carpeting.

Abigail sighed gently as they went downstairs again.
'It's a beautiful house, as beautiful as your house in

Amsterdam—have your family lived here for a long time?'

They were back in the sitting room, facing each other across the fireplace with Colossus between them. The professor eased himself into his chair and answered her in a leisurely fashion.

'Yes, three hundred years or so. My family are Friesian, you know, with strong ties with Amsterdam. While I was married we came here very seldom. My—wife disliked it, it is so quiet, you see. Only the country around us and a handful of small houses, but I find it delightful.'

Abigail nodded. 'And Amsterdam—surely you love your house there?'

'Yes, equally, I suppose—but here I can escape, you see.'

She saw very well. Away from the bustle of the hospital and his eternal round of patients and still more patients, this old house would be like a quiet heaven. She said so and was rewarded by his smile. 'You see how you have changed me,' he said quietly. 'Before I came to know you I should have suspected you of saying that merely to please me.'

'Isn't that a little conceited of you?'

'Yes—but perhaps you don't know that for a number of years I have been regarded in the light of a good— what is the word?—catch, I believe. I have come to regard any girl who agreed too readily with me or said something obviously meant to attract my attention or win my approval as highly suspect.'

'So that's why you accused me of toadying. But they may have meant it—they might have been charming...'

'Just as my wife was charming?' He gave her a bit-

ter little smile. 'Do you not say in your own language:
Once bitten, twice shy? I am very shy, Abigail.'

She eyed him warily. He looked irritable again and
all set to say something ill-tempered. Perhaps it would
be a good idea to talk about something else.

'You have a lovely garden,' she told him brightly.
'Do roses do well here?'

The look of bitterness left his face; he looked as
though he was going to laugh. 'Excellently—there is
a large bed in the centre of the lawn at the back of the
house, and there's a rose walk besides, at one side.'

'I should have loved to have seen it,' said Abigail re-
gretfully. 'We had a rose garden, when we lived in the
country. Bolly was very good with them and my mother
had great bowls of them around the house.'

He said deliberately, 'Tell me about your parents,
Abigail.'

'I don't think I want to…'

'Yes, you do, only you have buried them deep down,
haven't you? You shouldn't, you know. Happy times
are for remembering. When did you move to London?'

She found herself telling him about her childhood
and her parents, and Bolly and the pleasant house they
had lived in, and he scarcely interrupted her, sitting
in his chair, smoking a pipe and staring at the ceiling
and not at her at all. When she had finished she felt as
though she had talked all the sadness away for ever and
left only happy memories. She sat up straight, aware
that she had been talking for a long time. 'I'm sorry,' she
said shyly, 'I didn't mean… I must have bored you…'

He got up and pulled her to her feet and stood in
front of her, her hands still in his. 'No, never that. You
deserve a happier future, Abigail.'

She reddened. 'I don't pity myself in the least; I'm very fortunate to have a job—and there's Bolly...'

'Don't you have other friends?'

She answered reluctantly. 'Yes—quite a number, but one doesn't burden friends, they have their own lives.' She fidgeted under his steady gaze. 'Shall I go and fetch Nina down?'

'By all means. I have to work for half an hour or so.'

He sounded aloof, even annoyed, perhaps because she had refused to talk about herself; indeed, thinking about it she thought that perhaps she had snubbed him although she hadn't meant to do so. She went slowly from the room and up the lovely staircase to where Nina was waiting impatiently to be got up.

They went back after tea, and Abigail, half hoping that the professor might suggest that she and Nina should sit beside him, was disappointed. The two men talked about gardens and gardening for the whole of the journey. Nina had dropped off to sleep, curled up like a kitten in her lap, Colossus slept too, and Abigail was left with her thoughts again, and they weren't very happy.

She dined alone, for the professor, Bollinger informed her, had gone out. 'Some big do or other,' he confided. 'All got up, he is, and very handsome too. Must give the ladies a treat. I hear you're to work in the hospital for a while, Miss Abby, and very nice too, if I may say so. You'll be living with that nice Mrs Macklin again?'

'Yes, Bolly, though I don't know for how long. I'm so glad for you—you're happy here, aren't you?'

'Not half! Lovely bit of garden in that house where we went today, and no one breathing down your neck— I missed me garden, Miss Abby.'

'Oh, Bolly dear, I know, and I'll never be able to repay you for giving it all up when Father died. What should we have done without you? You've been a real friend. I hope I stay for ages, just to make you happy.'

'Won't you be happy too, Miss Abby?' He sounded wistful and full of curiosity all at once.

'Yes, I shall, actually, Bolly.' She didn't look at him. 'I think I'll go to bed early, I'm almost as tired as Nina.' She gave him a sweet smile and presently wandered through the quiet house and up to her room.

She didn't hurry over her bath and it was an hour or more before she was ready for bed, and when she went into Nina's room as she always did at bedtime, it was to find the child awake. It took only a few minutes for her to discover that Nina wasn't ill, only excited. She had slept and wakened and remembered that she was to go home in a day's time and she wanted to talk about it. Abigail fetched her some warm milk from the kitchen and then curled up beside her on the bed while she sipped it, very slowly and with pauses for excited chatter. But presently she had said it all and the milk was nearly finished. She edged nearer Abigail. 'Not pretty,' she informed her, fingering Abigail's dressing gown, a serviceable one she had received from her aunt and uncle at Christmas. Nina was right, it wasn't in the least pretty; a dim red, thick and woolly, it made Abigail's plumpness assume enormous proportions and the colour merely emphasized the mediocrity of her features.

'Hideous,' she agreed, and Nina cheerfully echoed her. 'But it's warm,' Abigail went on, just as though Nina could understand every word she said, 'and it covers me up. I hate it.'

'What do you hate with such vehemence?' asked the

professor from the door, and Abigail jumped and said crossly, 'Don't you know that you shouldn't creep up on people. It's most upsetting.'

He advanced into the room, looking twice his usual size in his tails. Definitely a reception, thought Abigail, eyeing his snowy waistcoat and white tie. He bowed his head in mock humility. 'My apologies, Abigail. I had no intention of frightening you, only to make sure that my niece was sleeping.'

He looked at her enquiringly as he spoke and she made haste to explain.

'She's had some milk, and now we've had a little talk, she'll go back to sleep. I'll stay with her until she does.'

He said nothing to this, merely bent to kiss Nina and be hugged before going to sit in a rocking chair in a corner of the room, blandly ignoring Abigail's look of enquiry in her turn.

'Baa, baa, black sheep,' demanded Nina sleepily, and Abigail obediently repeated the verses; she did so several times until she saw that the child was asleep again, and got up quietly to leave the room. On the way to the door she paused. 'Good night, Professor,' she whispered to the silent man sitting so still, and was shocked into a gasp, for he was beside her, going through the door almost before the words were out of her mouth.

The landing was dim and warm, through the half open door of her room she could see the cheerful glow of the bedside lamp. Somewhere downstairs Bollinger was tramping about, closing windows and shutting doors. For a moment she had the illusion that she lived in a safe, secure world which she shared with the professor, a world where she was cherished and loved and even, absurdly, admired. She tightened her mouth to prevent her lips quivering with the sudden horrid threat of tears, and with a nod in the general direction of the professor, who was behind her, started towards her room. But he wasn't behind her, he was beside her, in front of her. His arms were round her and all so quickly that she had no means of eluding him, and anyway, she didn't want to. He asked: 'What were you hating?'

The question was a surprise, all the same she answered it truthfully.

'My dressing gown—it's hideous.'

He held her away from him and surveyed her slowly. 'Indeed it is—not your own choosing, surely?'

'No.'

'Then go out and buy yourself the most glamorous garment you can find,' he advised her.

Perhaps not quite the right moment to mention her salary, but probably as good as any; at least they were alone and uninterrupted. She opened her mouth and began: 'I wonder...'

'Don't talk,' said the professor with a touch of his old imperious manner, and kissed her. He kissed her several times, and with a fine disregard for good sense, she kissed him back.

It was only when, five minutes later, she was in her room again, that she remembered that he had said nothing at all and she, to her chagrin, had. Not much, but enough. It had, at the time, seemed quite natural to address him as Dominic darling.

Chapter 9

She went down to breakfast the next morning, with Nina holding her hand; she looked as calm as was her habit and her neat appearance gave no indication of the sleepless night she had passed. Most of it she had spent reassuring herself. The professor might not have heard her, she had told herself over and over again, and even if he had, it didn't really matter, but these brave thoughts were reduced to meaningless nonsense by the certain knowledge that although she hadn't spoken loudly, she had certainly repeated herself several times—there was nothing wrong with the professor's hearing either. Her pale cheeks reddened painfully as she entered the dining room with the gaily chattering Nina dancing beside her, a prey to a variety of expectations, all of them unthinkable.

None of them materialised. The professor was sitting on the side of the table, with a cup of coffee in one hand and the telephone in the other. He lifted his eyes from the thoughtful contemplation of his elegantly shod feet, met Abigail's look with a vague one of his own, said 'Morning,' and broke into a lengthy monologue in Dutch. When he had finished he listened for a moment, frowned, said something loud and rather violent, which she was glad she couldn't understand, gulped his coffee and said:

'I must go, Abigail—something's turned up. Tell Dirk to come to the hospital as soon as he arrives.'

He dropped a hand on to Nina's small head and ruffled her hair, nodded to Abigail and left the room, and very shortly afterwards, the house, banging the house door after him quite unnecessarily.

Abigail drank coffee while Nina munched her way through her breakfast. She felt a little let down, just as one would feel when, having screwed up courage to go to the dentist to have a tooth pulled, one was told that there was no need. The professor couldn't have heard her. Perhaps he was a little drunk; after all, he had been to a banquet or something similar. It was a pity that this comforting theory was quite shattered by her complete certainty that he wasn't the sort of man to get drunk, not even slightly. All that remained was that he had heard her, and—mortifying thought—had dismissed the incident as so trivial as to be beneath his notice.

Dirk arrived a couple of hours later, had coffee with them, an enraptured Nina on his knee, gave Abigail a brief account of his wife and son's health, and departed for the hospital. She saw neither him nor the professor until dinner that evening, when the conversation was of Spain, Odilia, the new baby and his journey back the following morning.

The professor had talked to her, from time to time, with his usual faint aloofness; he certainly hadn't bothered to look at her overmuch. She retired to her room early, pleading packing for Nina, wishing the two gentlemen a cool goodnight as she went.

She was getting ready for bed when she remembered that although she was to go to the hospital on the following day, no one had told her how or when she was to go and the professor would either be gone or on the point of going by the time she and Nina got down in the morning; she decided to pack her own case too, so that, if necessary, she could leave at a moment's notice—she went down the back stairs too, and explained to Bollinger. She then returned to her room, slightly out of temper, to sleep fitfully and be awakened much too early by a joyful Nina wanting to get up and dress and go with her papa on the instant.

They were early for breakfast, only to find that the professor had left the house at six o'clock that morning to undertake an emergency operation. There was still no sign of him by the time Dirk and his small daughter were ready to leave in the former's Mercedes-Benz 350 SL; they were making their final farewells when the telephone rang and Abigail answered it. The professor's voice sounded quietly in her ear. 'Abigail? Ask Dirk to come to the telephone, will you? And Nina.'

It was a short conversation; Nina gave Abigail a last hug, Dirk wrung her hand and they had gone. She went back into the house with Bollinger and Mevrouw Boot, wondering what she was supposed to do. At the end of an hour she decided to go to the hospital. She couldn't stay in the house without a patient and she had a job to go to anyway—besides, she still had to find out if Mrs Macklin would have her again. She put on her outdoor clothes, fetched her case downstairs, said a temporary goodbye to Bollinger and went to the front door. The professor opened it as she put her hand on its massive brass knob.

He said instantly, 'Running away?'

The unfairness of this remark stung her to snap, 'Don't be ridiculous! I'm on my way to the hospital. You asked me to work there, if you remember, and there's no reason for me to remain here any longer.'

He answered this logical remark by shutting the door firmly behind him and leading her by the arm across the hall to his study. He shut this door too before taking off his coat and tossing it untidily over a chair, then he caught hold of her arm again and propelled her across the room, so that she was standing by a window with the cold, unkind March light on her face.

'Did you sleep?' The question was unexpected and she was taken off her guard. She faltered: 'Well, not...' she looked up at him, aware that her face wasn't at its best in the harsh grey morning. He didn't look tired, nor did he look aloof, and the little irritable frown had gone completely, and his eyes, which had looked at her so coldly on so many occasions, were warm and twinkling. She began again: 'Not very...' to be interrupted:

'I heard you, dear Abigail, did you think that I did not?' He put a hand lightly on her shoulder. 'You and I, we have to talk, but not now. Zuster Ritsma wants you on duty at midday; it seemed quicker to come and fetch you than telephoning.' A smile touched the corners of his mouth. 'That's not true, I wanted to see you—that's why I came. I didn't know that you would be packed and ready, but as you are, we had better go. Will you come with me?'

Abigail smiled at him; she felt happy and excited and intensely curious as to what they would talk about. 'I'm quite ready,' she told him, in a voice which shook very slightly with these feelings. He took his hand from her shoulder and ushered her out into the hall. Bollinger was there, standing by her case. He carried it out to the car for her, his face alight with smiles. He shut the car door on her, wished her goodbye, admonished her not to work too hard and then stood on the steps to watch them go. Abigail turned to wave as they reached the corner of the *gracht*.

They were almost at the hospital when the professor spoke.

'I have a great deal of work which must be done,' he sighed, 'and this evening I have to go to Brussels for two days. When I return, there are things to tell you, Abigail, dear girl.'

She turned her head to look at him and for a fleeting moment his eyes met hers and he smiled. Two days seemed a very long time, but if that was what he wanted, she would wait. She said rather breathlessly, 'Very well, Professor,' and when he said on a laugh, 'Did you not call me Dominic?' she repeated obediently, 'Dominic.'

They parted in the front hall of the hospital and she didn't see him to speak to alone after that. True, he did a round in the children's ward where she had been sent to work, but beyond asking her one or two questions about the baby she was bottle-feeding, he said nothing. He hardly looked at her—indeed, she had the strong impression that he was deliberately avoiding her eye.

Only as he came to a halt at the ward door did he turn round to look back at her, a look, brief though it was, to destroy the ridiculous doubts which had edged into her mind during the day.

The two days were endless, even though they had been busy ones on the ward, and her off-duty had been fully occupied settling in again with a delighted Mrs Macklin. She had visited Professor de Wit too, who seemed to take it for granted that she would remain permanently in Amsterdam and invited her for tea the following week. The day the professor was to return was a renewal of winter. Abigail walked to work through the bleak coldness of the city streets, sure that, despite the fact that it was the first week of March, it would snow before nightfall—not that she minded, for Dominic was coming. Within a few hours she would see him again, and the world, despite a regrettable shortage of money and her still leaking boots, seemed a lovely place.

She looked at the clock as she went to feed the first of the babies. Even now he might be getting on the plane although it was early enough—too early perhaps, but some time that day…beyond that delightful thought she was careful not to think; there was a good deal of work to get through, and she would need all her wits about her to get done. She dismissed the delights of the future and picked up an urgently crying baby.

It was a tiresome morning; Zuster Ritsma was off duty, the other two nurses spoke only the most basic of English, and it was a relief when Henk strolled on to the ward and after doing a round stopped for a chat. They were standing with their backs to the door and he was telling her in his inaccurate unidiomatic English about his latest girl-friend—a lady, it seemed, of many charms but a good deal older than he. He asked anxiously of Abigail: 'Too old, you think?'

Abigail laughed at him. 'Of course it's too old,' she spoke gaily. 'A gap of how many? fifteen years, isn't it? It's absurd—but of course it's not serious—just a passing fancy and a chance to have a good time.'

He rolled his eyes at her and said dramatically, 'My *lieveling*...' and Abigail, trying not to laugh at him said, 'No, no—your darling,' and laughed then because he looked so funny and she was so happy she could have laughed at anything. The slight sound behind her caused her to turn her head. The professor was standing behind them, in the doorway, only a foot or so away, staring at her; her smile faded before the iciness of his eyes.

He said with a cool blandness which hurt her, 'Good morning, Nurse Trent. Henk, I want you in the theatre in ten minutes.' As he turned away he added in a voice like a razor's edge, 'I'm sorry to interrupt your—er—conversation.'

He didn't wait for Henk, who, preparing to follow him, exclaimed, 'And what's he in a rage for? And he's back hours earlier than he said. Perhaps he missed his dollybird in Brussels.' He saw the stricken look on Abigail's face as he said it and added hurriedly, 'I joke, Abigail—he has no dollybird. *Dag*.'

He hurried away after his chief and Abigail, left alone, went to see why the baby in the first cubicle was crying. She had no idea what had come over the professor; he hadn't looked like that for a long time now and she had been quite unprepared for it. She tended the baby with gentle, competent hands, telling herself that something must have happened in Brussels to have upset him, trying to ignore the fact that he wasn't a man who was easily upset.

He did a round in the afternoon, surrounded by students, with his senior registrar and Henk flanking his every movement. He was delightful with the children and curt with everyone else. Abigail, trailing along behind Zuster Ritsma, felt sorry for the students, who, unless they came up with the right answers to the professor's barked questions, were subjected to a withering fire from his tongue and a look of such irritation that the most stouthearted of them were quailed. From the safety of Zuster Ritsma's rear, she watched him; not only did he look ill-tempered, he looked weary too. Perhaps when they were alone together he would tell her what the matter was. He glanced round and she caught his eye and gave him a small loving smile which stiffened on her face as he looked through her. She felt her cheeks pale and for the rest of the round didn't look at him at all. Only after he had gone, and it was time for her to go off duty, she made her way down to the porter's lodge and asked where he was and if she could see him. The porter looked surprised, but he went to the switchboard and after a few minutes he shook his head. 'Professor van Wijkelen is *weg*,' he told her.

She walked slowly back to the changing room. Why had he gone without leaving a message? She stopped in the middle of the corridor. Surely she hadn't imagined all that he had said to her—worse still, mistaken his meaning?

She had cheered up a little by the time she reached Mrs Macklin's house, having persuaded herself that Dominic would come that evening. She stayed in the little sitting room, her ears strained for his footsteps, and when Mrs Macklin wanted to know if he was back, explained in a colourless voice that yes, he was but that he seemed to be busy.

'Not too busy to see you,' stated Mrs Macklin decidedly, and when Abigail gave her an enquiring look, 'He's a different man since he met you, my dear. It's amazing what love will do.'

'Love?' faltered Abigail.

'You love him, don't you? He needs someone to love him and to love. He has become so embittered over the years that I was beginning to think that he would never allow himself to love another woman, but I think you have changed that. I wonder why he doesn't come.'

Abigail looked up from the contemplation of her nails. 'I don't know. When he went away, he said—he said there was no time to talk then, but when he came back…he came back this morning, but he's…something's happened. He's not coming.' She was sure of that now. 'Perhaps tomorrow.' She looked appealingly at her companion. 'I expect he's tired.'

The old lady eyed her thoughtfully. 'You're tired too, Abigail. Go to bed, my dear. Things are always better in the morning.'

Abigail did as she was told for the simple reason that she didn't much care what she did and bed was as good as anywhere else; contrary to her expectations, she slept all night.

She was off duty at four-thirty the next day too. The morning passed quickly enough; there were two cases for theatre and she went with both of them; tiny babies with pyloric stenosis and the professor operating. If he saw her in the theatre he gave no sign, but she hadn't expected him to. She stayed by the anaesthetist, performing the small duties he required of her throughout the two operations. When she got back from her dinner it was to discover from Zuster Ritsma that the professor had been to see his patients and since he would be operating for the rest of the afternoon, the chance of seeing him was slight. She went off duty a little late, spinning out the minutes in case he should come; she even went a long way round to the hospital entrance in the hope of seeing him, despising herself for doing so—she had never thought much of girls who chased men, and here she was doing just that. There was no sign of him, so she went back to the Begijnhof and after tea went for a long walk. Let him telephone and find her out, she told herself bracingly, it would serve him right if she wasn't there at his beck and call. Only he didn't telephone. She went to bed early and cried herself to sleep.

She was on at one o'clock the next day and would work until nine in the evening. Zuster Ritsma was on too and a couple of student nurses, and because the ward was full and some of the children and babies were very ill, they were kept busy. It was well after three o'clock when Abigail went to the office to pour the tea for Zuster Ritsma and herself. They had barely sat down to drink it when the professor walked in.

Zuster Ritsma looked at him with resignation. She had been on her feet for a long time and now here he was, wanting to do a round, she supposed. Before she could speak he said, 'No, no round.'

'A cup of tea?' she smiled her relief.

'Thank you, no.' He hadn't looked at Abigail, but he gave her the briefest of glances now, a look of cool enquiry which prompted her to ask:

'You would like me to go, sir?'

'Since it concerns you, Nurse Trent, I see no need for that.' He smiled thinly. 'We are now fully staffed, or nearly so; it only remains for me to thank you for the help you have given us and tell you that there is now no further need of your services. I am sure that we are all most grateful to you for the way in which you helped out, but I am sure you will be glad to be free to arrange your own future.'

Abigail listened to this speech with absolute amazement; she wasn't even sure if half of it were true to begin with, but she could hardly challenge him on that score. She was a freelance nurse, under no obligation to give or receive a month's notice, so presumably the hospital could terminate her job when they wished. She found her voice and filled the awkward pause with an over-hearty, 'Oh, splendid, I shall be able to go back…' Her voice petered away, because unless someone paid her, she couldn't go back to England; she hadn't got her fare any more, for she had paid Mrs Macklin for her room, and she had been paying for her meals in hospital too. She could borrow from Bolly, but that was something she wasn't prepared to do; she had leaned on Bolly enough in the last few years.

Neither Zuster Ritsma nor the professor appeared to notice her hesitancy.

'We shall miss you, Nurse Trent,' said Zuster Ritsma kindly. 'You are good with the children, is that not so, Professor?'

'Very good.' He spoke shortly and turned to go, his face blandly polite, no more. 'You will leave tonight, Nurse Trent.'

It was a command, no less, and she seethed, but she didn't bother to answer him, nor did she look up as he went. He could at least have wished her goodbye. She blinked back tears and said shakily, 'I'll make a fresh pot of tea, shall I? This lot's cold.'

And Zuster Ritsma, after one look at her face, sat down at her desk, instantly absorbed in the papers on it, so that Abigail had time to compose herself and subdue the searing misery and bewilderment and rage which worked so strongly beneath her starched apron.

It was a good thing that the rest of the day proved to be so busy she had no time to think at all, and when at length it was nine o'clock and she was free to go, she made her farewells as quickly as possible before hurrying through the hospital which had suddenly become alien ground. She couldn't get away faster, she told herself.

She had told Zuster Ritsma about her delayed pay and that kind soul had been sympathetic but quite unable to do much about it. She had sent Abigail down to the hospital office where they dealt with such things and she had been met with blank looks and shrugged shoulders. As far as she could understand from the clerk she wasn't on the hospital pay roll at all; Professor van Wijkelen had engaged her to work for him and had made himself responsible for her salary, and beyond suggesting that she should find him and ask for herself, the clerk had no advice to give.

She went past the porter's lodge without hearing the man on duty wishing her good night and plunged outside into the dark. The desultory snow had ceased again, the pavements were wet under her feet and she shivered as she ran across the forecourt. She was totally unprepared for Jan's voice calling, 'Miss, miss!' from the car which slid silently alongside her. He smiled and opened the door, saying in his heavily accented English, 'I am to take you home, so please to get in.'

Abigail shook her head. 'Thank you, Jan, but there must be some mistake—Does the professor know that you've come to fetch me? And anyway I don't want to.'

Jan looked at his most fatherly. 'I am just this minute told by the professor to take you home, miss,' he contrived to look worried. 'He will be angry if I return and say that you would not go with me.'

She got in beside him, answering his polite remarks absentmindedly while her mind ran on and on, trying to decide what she would do. To remain in Amsterdam was unthinkable, to go back to England was impossible for the moment. She would have to get a job until she had enough money. When they arrived at the Begijnhof she thanked Jan and asked if he would take a message for her. 'To Bollinger,' she explained. 'Just tell him that I've gone away for a few days and he's not to worry, Mrs Macklin will let him know more about it later.' It sounded harmless enough like that, by the time Bollinger got worried enough to ask Mrs Macklin, she would certainly have another job, and she could always think of something to tell him when the time came. It was all a little vague, but it would have to do. She wished Jan goodbye and reminded him not to tell anyone else but Bollinger what she had said, and he agreed cheerfully, wishing her *Tot ziens* as he went back to the car, a hopeful form of farewell to which she was unable to subscribe. She wished him goodbye and went soberly indoors.

Mrs Macklin was in the kitchen making their bedtime drinks. She turned and smiled as Abigail walked in, saying, 'There you are, child—how nice and early. You must have been walking fast.'

'Jan brought me in the car.'

'Dear Dominic, what care he takes of you.' Mrs Macklin spoke with a satisfied pride which sparked off Abigail's held-down feelings.

'He does nothing of the kind,' she declared hotly. 'He doesn't care a brass farthing for anyone but himself! He's cold and heartless and I detest him. He's given me the sack, today—this very afternoon—just like that— he said...' she choked. 'He owes me weeks of salary too...' She burst into tears.

The whole story came out; in fragments which didn't make sense at first, but Mrs Macklin had patience. Slowly she sorted out the facts from the fiery condemnation of the professor's character, the bewilderment as to why it had happened and determination, repeated many times, never, never to see him again. 'And I would rather die,' declared Abigail in far too loud a voice, 'than take a penny from the man!' She turned a tear-blotched face to her listener. 'I love him so,' she said miserably.

'There is, of course, a mistake somewhere,' said Mrs Macklin with kind firmness. 'Someone or something has caused him to behave like this.'

Abigail took a drink of cooling cocoa which she didn't want. 'But why didn't he at least tell me? I thought he trusted me, I even thought that he was beginning to love me a little—that's absurd, of course. Look at me, no one ever looks at me more than once—no man, that is.' Which wasn't quite true, but she was in the mood to exaggerate. 'And Dominic least of all.' She put down her cup. 'I'm going away, Mrs Macklin.'

'Yes, dear. Where to? England?'

'I can't—I haven't any money, at least, not enough.'

'I will gladly lend…'

'You're a dear, Mrs Macklin, but no, thank you, I won't borrow unless I'm quite desperate. If I could get a job somewhere away from Amsterdam, just long enough to save my fare. I must get away.'

'You're sure that's the right thing to do, Abigail?'

Abigail got up and took the cups and saucers over to the tray on the table. 'Yes, I'm sure. I couldn't stay, you see, I might see him. I haven't known him long, I should be able to forget him.'

Both ladies knew that this was a silly remark, but neither of them said so. Mrs Macklin nodded her head and offered:

'In that case, I believe I can help you. I have a friend, a Mevrouw Hagesma. She lives in Friesland, in a tiny village north of Leeuwarden. She's had a stroke and although she can get about, she finds it difficult on her own. Her daughter is going home to be with her, but not for a week or so. I think she would be delighted if you would go and stay with her and help her. The only thing is, she's very poor.'

Abigail said quickly, 'She need not pay me; as long as I could have a room and some food, it would give me a chance to decide what to do—there must be some work I can do, I don't care what. Even if it's only a few gulden a week—I don't need much to make up the money for my fare.'

'I still think you should borrow from me, my dear.'

Abigail crossed the little room and planted a kiss on the smooth, elderly cheek. 'What a kind person you are, Mrs Macklin, but I won't. I'll go to your friend if she'll have me, at least I'll be out of the way.' She gulped, determined to put a bright face on things. 'I'll go back to England just as soon as I can and get a job and then Bolly can come back.'

'He's very happy at Dominic's house,' Mrs Macklin reminded her.

'You think he'd like to stay? If—if Dominic would keep him and he'd be happy, then that would be wonderful. He deserves better than I can offer him.' She sighed. 'Could I write to your friend tomorrow and ask...?'

'She sits up till all hours,' Mrs Macklin interrupted her to say. 'I'll telephone her now.'

Ten minutes later Abigail said wonderingly, 'Well, I can hardly believe it—all fixed up so quickly. I'll pack tonight and leave on that early train—you're sure it runs?'

'Yes, my dear,' Mrs Macklin smiled at her. 'I shall miss you. What am I to say if—when Dominic calls?'

'He won't. He's—he's finished with me, I think. Perhaps he remembered his wife and thinks I should get like her—he must be mad,' Abigail's voice rose a little, 'if he thinks that. His wife was lovely, wasn't she? with lots of men-friends. I couldn't be more different—perhaps that's why. I mean, I'd be such a safe, unexciting sort of wife, wouldn't I, because he would never need to be jealous of me.'

Mrs Macklin quite rightly took no notice of this diatribe. 'What shall I tell him?' she repeated.

'That I've gone to another job; he'll not want to know more than that, if he asks. And please don't tell him where I am or about the money.'

Her companion gave her an understanding look. 'No, dear. Now go to bed, you have to be up early in the morning. What about Bollinger?'

Abigail explained about him. 'I don't think he'll worry, not for a little while, and if he comes to see you, if you'll just tell him that I'm working—another case—and that I'll write.'

She said goodnight and went away to pack and then to go to bed and lie awake until it was time for her to get up. The night had been very long. She dressed with relief, had a sketchy breakfast, took Mrs Macklin a cup of tea, wished her goodbye and left the house.

The train journey to Leeuwarden was uneventful. Abigail, watching the flat, wintry fields as they flashed along, saw nothing. Because of her sleepless night she was quite unable to think; wisps of conversation flitted in and out of her tired mind, snatches of things she had said and done in the last few weeks since she had met Dominic, came and went, tangling themselves into a frenzied, half-remembered muddle which did nothing to improve a rapidly worsening headache. She got out at Leeuwarden and a kindly ticket collector sent her to the station café to have a cup of coffee while she waited for the bus, which wasn't due for an hour. There was a map on the café wall, and she studied it, glad to discover that the village she was going to was a long way away from Dominic's home. As far as she could make out, it was on a side road, half way between Leeuwarden and Holwerd on the coast. The side road, according to the map, ended at Molenum, which was the place she was going to. For the first time since she had accepted the job, she wondered what sort of a house she was going to, and what kind of a village it was in.

Molenum, when she reached it, was small; one shop, a post office in the front room of a small house in its main street and a very large church. The landscape was rolling and wide and there weren't many trees. There was a chill, damp wind blowing in from the sea, some miles away, and absolutely no one to be seen. She watched the bus lumber away and went into the shop.

The woman behind the counter was tall and gaunt and middle-aged, dressed severely in black. She stared at Abigail in a disconcerting way which she found a little daunting as she said: *'Dag, mevrouw,'* and then, 'Mevrouw Hagesma?'

The stare melted into a nice smile. The village was so small, probably everyone in it knew she was coming; she smiled back as the woman came from behind the counter and pointed up the narrow cobbled road, past a row of dollshouse-sized cottages, to a house standing alone; it was just as small as the others, but it had a garden all round it. Abigail said *'Dank U'* and picked up her case and started towards it, aware that, as she passed, the spotless white curtains at the little front windows were stirred by invisible fingers. She opened the gate and walked up the narrow brick path and knocked on the old-fashioned wooden door; it had a small square shutter in it which opened to allow an eye to examine her before the door was opened.

Mevrouw Hagesma was tall and gaunt too, and quite old, but her face was kind and her eyes were as bright and blue as a little girl's. It was then that Abigail realised that she would have to speak Dutch, something she hadn't thought about before. She embarked on a few muddled phrases to which the old lady listened with grave courtesy, and then said slowly, her speech thickened by her stroke, 'A friend of Mrs Macklin's is a friend of mine,' and led the way into the living room.

She walked with a stick and very slowly and one arm hung, not quite uselessly, at her side.

The room was comfortably furnished and tidy, but the pristine cleanliness Abigail knew was a Dutch-woman's pride was absent. The old lady waved an arm clumsily around her and shrugged her shoulders, and Abigail understood the gesture to be one of apology be-cause not everything was exactly in its place, nor was it quite spotless.

It was surprising how, after those first few minutes, they managed to understand each other. Abigail had a room like a cupboard at the top of the ladder-like stairs—she unpacked her few things and went down again to find Mevrouw Hagesma making coffee. While they drank it, and with the aid of the little dictionary Abigail always carried with her, she found out all she needed to know about the old lady as well as telling her as much as she thought necessary about herself. Mev-rouw Hagesma nodded and smiled her slightly lopsided smile when Abigail had finished. 'We shall be friends,' she told her, and although she spoke in Dutch, Abigail understood her very well.

Abigail had expected the days to drag, but surpris-ingly they didn't. There was so much to do in the little house, and once Mevrouw Hagesma saw that she was a good housewife, able to sweep and dust and polish and not grumble about it, she was content to leave a great deal to her. Not that Abigail allowed the old lady to be idle. She had her exercises to do each day, and her reading, and Abigail was helping her to write once more with her still partly paralysed hand. Mrs Mack-lin had telephoned several times too and Abigail had longed to ask about Dominic but didn't, and Mrs Macklin didn't mention him.

Each morning, just before dinner time, Abigail took Mevrouw Hagesma for a walk, a very short one, down to the village shop, where she rested for a little while and then back home again. It was a slow clumsy business, but the old lady looked forward to a gossip with Mevrouw Beeksma in the shop and most mornings there were customers there too so that the gossip became half an hour's chat, something which the old lady enjoyed very much although Abigail found the elderly, soberly clad ladies unexciting. They spoke Fries, which made it impossible for her to understand them, and when they spoke to her in careful, slow Dutch, she still had difficulty in understanding them. She got into the habit of wandering round the little shop, examining the crowded shelves, looking at the tins and packets, learning their prices for the sake of something to do, and when she found that Mevrouw Hagesma enjoyed correcting her wild attempts to speak Dutch, she suggested that they should spend a little time each evening struggling with that language and improving her deplorable accent. It passed the long hours before bedtime and the old lady, now that she had something to occupy her mind, began to improve rapidly.

Abigail had been there ten days when Mevrouw Beeksma told her that her daughter had been taken ill and had been taken to hospital in Leeuwarden. Abigail, wrestling with the shopkeeper's pantomime of screwed-up face, hands clasped to back and urgent bendings, tried to guess what complaint the poor girl had. Renal colic, perhaps, or even a slipped disc—she made a sympathetic murmur and listened to Mevrouw Beeksma bemoaning the fact that she wouldn't be able to go and see her each afternoon, because there was no one to mind the shop. If only there was someone to take the place over for an hour or so each afternoon, said poor Mevrouw Beeksma, looking gaunter than ever.

'I will,' said Abigail, not stopping to think.

'Wel, neen,' declared Mevrouw Beeksma, and then: *'Waarom niet?'*

Why not indeed, thought Abigail, she had been wanting a job—here it was. For the first week it hadn't mattered too much because deep down inside her she had hoped that Dominic would come thundering after her. But of course he hadn't, and now it was urgent that she should earn some money; she would have to go when Mevrouw Hagesma's daughter came, it would be splendid if she could earn enough money to go straight back to England before that time.

'Three hours each afternoon,' said Mevrouw Beeksma, 'and I pay two gulden an hour.'

Abigail did sums—six gulden a day for six days, that would be thirty-six gulden. She needed more than that, but perhaps she could sell something.

'Yes,' said Abigail.

She was slow that first day. The ladies of the village who came for their groceries had to help her with their change and point out just what they wanted, but Abigail, who considered the job as a gift from heaven, didn't make the same mistake twice. By the fourth afternoon she was managing very well and Mevrouw Beeksma pronounced herself satisfied. 'Another week,' she told Abigail, 'and my daughter will be home.' She smiled and nodded and strode out into the windy street to catch the bus.

It was cold again, just like winter, as indeed it still was. A few snowflakes, blown by the sea wind, settled on the window ledges of the shop. Abigail watched the bus disappear into the empty countryside beyond the village and went back into the shop. She had been working hard all the morning, turning the little house upside down for the weekly clean Mevrouw Hagesma considered absolutely necessary, and today, for the first time, the old lady had helped a little and talked cheerfully about her future, so that Abigail felt heartened by her progress. There had been a letter from Mrs Macklin too, full of messages from Bollinger, who was a little puzzled but quite content to take Mrs Macklin's word for it that Abigail was happy. She took the letter out of her pocket now and read it through as though she might have missed something in it—something, some news of Dominic, but he wasn't mentioned.

She put the letter away with a little sigh, put on the white apron, much too large, which was Mevrouw Beeksma's concession to hygiene in her shop, and got out the stepladder. The apron got terribly in the way and Abigail muttered rudely; it wasn't as though it was necessary—the shop was cleaner than anything she had ever seen in her life, there couldn't be a germ in the place; still, as her employer wished her to dress up in it, she supposed she should. She hitched it up round her pretty legs and climbed the steps.

She had been up there perhaps ten minutes, dusting bottles of pickles and gherkins and onions, when the door opened, allowing a draught of cold air, a few persistent snowflakes and the professor to enter.

Abigail put the pot of gherkins she was holding carefully back on the shelf, for her hands felt strangely incapable of holding anything. Her heart had leapt, stopped and then begun to hammer at her ribs in a most unnerving fashion. She had no breath; all she could do was to sit and stare down at the top of his head, until he looked up and saw her. They stared at each other for a timeless age before she asked idiotically, 'Is there something you want?' just as though he was a housewife come to buy tea or coffee or a few slices of cheese.

'You,' he said in a rough voice, and went on staring. 'Come down, Abigail.'

Somewhere at some time she remembered she had read that one should always begin as one meant to go on, especially when it concerned matters of the heart. It seemed to her a sound idea. She stayed where she was.

After a silence which she found unendurable the professor said in quite a different voice, 'Please come down, Abby, I want to talk to you,' and when she still didn't move because truth to tell she found herself incapable of doing so, he began again, but this time in a loud rough voice.

'I can no longer sleep because of you, nor can I eat— presently I shall be unable to do my work. It is intolerable that a small mouse of a girl like you can reduce me to this miserable state. Each time that I have sent you away I have racked my brains for an excuse to get you back; I thought at first that I could hold out against you, but I find that there is nothing to hold out against, only gentleness and kindness and honesty and a smile to twist my heart, my dearest darling.'

'You have behaved abominably,' said Abigail severely, 'and I will not be your dearest darling until I know why you did.' She watched the rueful smile touch his mouth.

'I came back from Brussels hell for leather, longing to see you again. I found you with Henk, laughing
up at him—you are so pretty when you laugh, my darling—I listened to you talking and it seemed to me that
it was I whom you were discussing. I wanted to hurt
you then as I was hurt.' He sighed, he went on humbly,
'It has taken me all this while to swallow my pride, for
I have to know…'

He was interrupted by the opening of the door. Old
Mevrouw Henninga from one of the houses across the
street shook the snow off her cap, bade them good day
and asked for tea. Abigail had to descend her steps then.
She found the tea, served her customer, gave her, for
once, the right change and wished her a polite good day,
while the professor, not to be outdone when it came to
manners, opened the door and closed it after her.

When he spoke he forgot to be humble. 'And why in
the name of heaven are you serving behind a counter?'
His voice a snarl.

Abigail prudently climbed her ladder again; there
was a distinct advantage in being a little above him.
'I'm earning my living,' she explained haughtily.

He glared at her under lowered brows. 'Why here in
this back-of-beyond place? Why aren't you in England?
I went after you and you weren't there.'

Abigail's heart began to beat its own happy little
tune, spreading a tingle of excitement over her.

'I'll tell you why I wasn't there,' she said, and struggled to keep her voice cool and calm and slow. But it
came out in an excited babble. 'I had no money—no
money to go back to England, and do you know why?
Because you haven't paid me—not for weeks,' her voice
rose a little. 'You sent me away without references and

didn't even bother to ask if I had somewhere to go, just like a Victorian servant girl; for all you cared I might have gone on the streets!'

'On the streets?' he looked thunderstruck. 'My dear little love, what a brute I have been! Can you ever forgive me? You see I could think of nothing else but you and Henk, laughing together—and you are so young...' he was leaning on the counter now, looking up at her. 'For years now I believed that I had built myself a new life, a nice safe life in which women didn't matter, in which I could work without getting involved with anyone—any girl. And then I saw you and lost my heart, my lovely girl, but not without a fight. I told myself that you were clever and scheming with your quiet voice and your friendliness and kindness. I fought very hard, my darling, but then I discovered that I didn't want to fight any more. I have used you very ill, haven't I?'

Abigail smiled. 'Indeed you have.' She paused. 'We weren't talking about you at all, only about Henk's latest girl-friend.' She went on primly, 'Listeners never hear any good of themselves.' She frowned quite fiercely at the professor. 'There is something else. I am considered quite old for my age.'

'Abby...' The door opened once more and a small boy sidled in and demanded *bischuiten*. The professor, curbing impatience with a visible effort, handed him a packet from the counter, took his money and put it in the till.

'He wants three cents change,' advised Abigail from her observation post, and watched while the professor rang up the till to the manner born and proffered the coins.

'Give him a sweetie,' and when the boy had gone, his

cheek bulging with a toffee, she explained, 'It's good business to give the children sweeties when they come on an errand.'

She didn't say any more because the professor was looking at her with such tenderness and love that her breath deserted her. He said now, very firmly, 'Abigail, I have never proposed to a girl on top of a stepladder before, but that's what I intend doing unless you come down.'

He held out his arms and she jumped straight into them; they held her so tightly that she could feel his heart beating under her cheek. Her voice a whisper, muffled by the thickness of his jacket, she said:

'Only Mrs Macklin knew where I was, and I asked her not to tell.'

'And she kept her word. Bollinger and I put our heads together when I got back from England and I went to see her, but all she would tell me was that an old friend of hers needed help until her daughter could go to her.'

She felt his kiss on her hair. 'Abby, my darling girl, if you wish to tell me off I promise you that I will be very meek.'

'Don't be ridiculous!' She looked up into his face, smiling, and he bent his head to kiss her.

'Will you marry me, Abby?'

'Yes, dear Dominic, of course I will.' She would have said more, but the professor's hold tightened so that she had no breath, or almost none, and when she at last essayed to speak, he kissed her silent. It was an enjoyable silence which at length Abigail broke.

'Dominic—wait a minute, there's something important—what about Bolly?'

The professor loosened his grasp very slightly so that

he could see her face. 'A useful addition to our household, wouldn't you think, my darling? He's terrific with animals and gardens and, I've no doubt, children too.'

'Oh, he will be pleased—he's splendid with them.'

'Then we must do our utmost to give him every opportunity to be splendid, mustn't we?'

She smiled, and the dimple came and went. 'A bad-tempered little boy just like his father,' she murmured.

'And an adorable mousy little girl just like her beautiful mother.'

They stared at each other happily, contemplating a blissful future, and for good measure the professor kissed her again.

'What shall we do?' asked Abigail, feeling that one of them at least should be practical, but it seemed that Dominic had everything arranged.

'You're coming back with me to Amsterdam, my love. Arie's sister is on her way over to take your place with Mevrouw Hagesma—Jan's fetching her, I'm sure she'll understand when we explain.'

'About Amsterdam,' said Abigail. 'Where…?'

'Bollinger and Mevrouw Boot will have everything ready for you—and before you protest, Mrs Macklin is already at my house. You will stay there until I can arrange our wedding, my dearest—in the church in the Begijnhof, don't you agree?'

Abigail nodded, savouring the delight of being loved, indeed her ordinary face had become quite transformed by it so that the professor exclaimed,

'How very pretty you are, Abby,' and since it was obvious that he really believed it she smiled at him with delight and lifted her face for his kiss.

Presently: 'How long do we have to play at shop?' Dominic wanted to know.

'Until the bus gets in at half past four—and it's not playing at shop. I get paid—two gulden an hour.'

The horrified incredulity on the professor's face would have satisfied any girl who might have considered herself to have been badly treated, but Abigail wasn't any girl; she loved him. Looking into his stricken face she remembered that she hadn't yet told him this indisputable fact, and did so there and then, and the professor, holding her with powerful gentleness, kissed her at great length until she reminded him that she should get behind the counter, 'Just in case someone should come, dear Dominic.'

He glanced over her head at the snowflakes whirling past the shop window in a last wintry onslaught before spring made nonsense of them. 'Anyone coming out on a day like this would be mad,' he declared, 'and if they do I will serve them for you, my dearest heart.'

'Well,' conceded Abigail, 'you managed to sell the *bischuiten* very nicely. All the same I just can't stand here...'

'Oh, yes, you can,' said Dominic in a voice which sounded so certain of this that she found no point in arguing with him about it, and it was, after all, quite delightful with her head on his shoulder and his arms around her.

'If you say so, dear Dominic,' she said meekly, and kissed him.

* * * * *

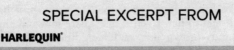
*Can Chase McCabe help Mitzy Martin with matters
of business when the beautiful single mother has him
thinking of matters of the heart?*

Read on for a sneak preview of
The Texas Cowboy's Quadruplets,
the third book in Cathy Gillen Thacker's heartfelt series
Texas Legends: The McCabes.

"So, the boot is finally on the other foot."

Mitzy Martin stared at the indomitable CEO standing on
the other side of her front door, looking more rancher than
businessman in nice-fitting jeans, boots and a tan Western
shirt. Ignoring the skittering of her heart, she heaved a sigh
to convey just how unwelcome he was. "What's your point,
cowboy?"

Mischief gleaming in his smoky-blue eyes, Chase looked
her up and down in a way that made her insides flutter. "Just
that you've been a social worker in Laramie County for
what…ten years now?"

Electricity sparked between them with all the danger of
a downed power line. "Eleven," Mitzy corrected. And it had
been slightly longer than that. Since she'd abruptly ended
their engagement…

"My guess is, very few people are happy to see you
coming up their front walk. Now you seem to be feeling
that," he continued with an ornery grin, "seeing *me* at your
door."

Mitzy drew a breath, ignoring the considerable physical
awareness that never failed to materialize between them.

She gave him a long, level look to show him he was *not* going to get to her. Even if his square jaw and chiseled features, sandy-brown hair and incredibly buff physique were permanently imprinted on her brain. She smiled sweetly. "Well, when people get to know me and realize I'm there to help, they usually become quite warm and friendly."

He surveyed her pleasantly. "That's exactly what I hope will happen between you and me. Now that we're older and wiser, that is."

Mitzy glared. She and Chase had crashed and burned once—spectacularly. There was no way she was doing it again.

He stepped closer, inundating her with his wildly intoxicating scent. "Mitzy, come on. You've been ducking my calls for weeks now."

So what? "I know it's hard for a carefree bachelor like you to understand, but I've been 'a little busy' since giving birth to quadruplets."

He shrugged. "Word around town is you've had *plenty* of volunteer help. Plus the high-end nannies your mother sent from Dallas."

Mitzy groaned and clapped a hand across her forehead.

"Didn't work out?"

"No," she bit out. "Just like this lobbying effort on your part won't work, either."

"Look, I know you'd rather not do business with me," he said, even more gently. "But at least hear me out."

Don't miss
The Texas Cowboy's Quadruplets
by Cathy Gillen Thacker.

Available October 2018 wherever
Harlequin® Special Edition books and ebooks are sold.

www.Harlequin.com

HARLEQUIN®

SPECIAL EDITION

Life, Love and Family

Save **$1.00**
on the purchase of ANY
Harlequin® Special Edition book.

Available wherever books are sold,
including most bookstores, supermarkets,
drugstores and discount stores.

Save **$1.00**

on the purchase of any Harlequin® Special Edition book.

Coupon valid until December 31, 2018.
Redeemable at participating outlets in the U.S. and Canada only.
Limit one coupon per customer.

52615971

5 65373 00076 2 (8100)0 12386

Looking for more satisfying love stories
with community and family at their core?

**Check out Harlequin® Special Edition
and Love Inspired® books!**

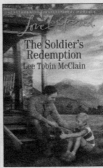

New books available every month!

CONNECT WITH US AT:

Facebook.com/groups/HarlequinConnection

 Facebook.com/HarlequinBooks

 Twitter.com/HarlequinBooks

 Instagram.com/HarlequinBooks

 Pinterest.com/HarlequinBooks

ReaderService.com

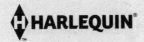

**ROMANCE WHEN
YOU NEED IT**

HFGENRE2018

Love Harlequin romance?

DISCOVER.

Be the first to find out about promotions, news and exclusive content!

Facebook.com/HarlequinBooks

Twitter.com/HarlequinBooks

Instagram.com/HarlequinBooks

Pinterest.com/HarlequinBooks

ReaderService.com

EXPLORE.

Sign up for the Harlequin e-newsletter and download a free book from any series at **TryHarlequin.com.**

CONNECT.

Join our Harlequin community to share your thoughts and connect with other romance readers!
Facebook.com/groups/HarlequinConnection

**ROMANCE WHEN
YOU NEED IT**

HSOCIAL2018